In the Face of Jinn

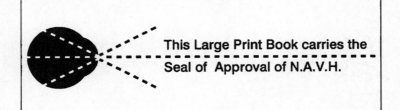

In the Face of Jinn

Cheryl Howard Crew

WHEELER PUBLISHING

Map by Mark Stein Studios

Published in 2005 by arrangement with St. Martin's Press, LLC.

Wheeler Large Print Compass.

The text of this Large Print edition is unabridged.
Other aspects of the book may vary from the original edition.

Set in 16 pt. Plantin by Liana M. Walker.

Printed in the United States on permanent paper.

Library of Congress Cataloging-in-Publication Data

Crew, Cheryl Howard.
    In the face of Jinn / by Cheryl Howard Crew.
       p. cm. — (Wheeler Publishing large print compass)
    ISBN 1-59722-033-7 (lg. print : hc : alk. paper)
    1. Americans — Islamic countries — Fiction. 2. Women
— Islamic countries — Fiction. 3. Islamic countries —
Fiction. 4. Missing persons — Fiction. 5. Sisters —
Fiction. 6. Large type books. I. Title. II. Wheeler large
print compass series.
PS3603.R49I5 2005b
                                    2005009662

To my mother,
who loved people,
and
my father,
who loved life

National Association for Visually Handicapped
-------------------------- *serving the partially seeing*

As the Founder/CEO of NAVH, the only national health agency solely devoted to those who, although not totally blind, have an eye disease which could lead to serious visual impairment, I am pleased to recognize Thorndike Press* as one of the leading publishers in the large print field.

Founded in 1954 in San Francisco to prepare large print textbooks for partially seeing children, NAVH became the pioneer and standard setting agency in the preparation of large type.

Today, those publishers who meet our standards carry the prestigious "Seal of Approval" indicating high quality large print. We are delighted that Thorndike Press is one of the publishers whose titles meet these standards. We are also pleased to recognize the significant contribution Thorndike Press is making in this important and growing field.

Lorraine H. Marchi, L.H.D.
Founder/CEO
NAVH

* Thorndike Press encompasses the following imprints: Thorndike, Wheeler, Walker and Large Print Press.

Acknowledgments

I would first like to thank Diane Higgins, my editor at St. Martin's Press, whose grace and deftness as a coach and a senior editor has truly been a pleasure. I am deeply indebted.

Nichole Argyres, thank you for your support and the endless e-mails it took to break in this very green writer.

Donald J. Davidson — my copy editor — your breadth of knowledge and your resolute pursuit of style and detail took me to a new height.

And Steven Snider, your jacket artwork, haunting and relevant, awed me.

What a pleasure and an honor it has been to work with the erudite St. Martin's Press team. As always, incredibly fearless in their picks, I thank them all.

My dear father-in-law, Rance Howard, my earliest inspiration, taught me story with such honor and discipline. Thank you, Rance. My mother-in-law, Jean, whom I sorely miss, taught me priorities, strength, and patience. Juggling a passion and a family — no one did it better than Jean.

Jennifer McLean, from grammar to content, played a big part in this writer's evolution.

I'd like to extend a special acknowledgment to Terry and Judine Brooks, as well as the Maui Writers Conference, for their invaluable counseling to new writers. Terry, your notes and words inspired me at a most crucial juncture. I thank you.

Jayne Pliner, how do I thank you for your dogged support, your cogent notes, and your unflinching intent to help me find an agent and publisher? It worked, Jayne. It worked.

Dear Mary Evans, what an extraordinary lady and agent you are. How many drafts did you slog through? Intelligent and lion-hearted, you're a being who lives in the mode of goodness. Your expertise with story and your understanding of people and business continues to amaze me.

To Matthew Snyder, and the formidable, but civilized troupe of professionals at CAA, I thank you for supporting me through the years.

As for the inimitable David Brown, his years of encouragement and invaluable assistance to this fledgling artist, I will never be able to express the impact you have had on my dream. Thank you, David.

I would like to especially thank Bob Dolman, who read my earliest fiction, smiled and endured every digression, and never hesitated to share and comfort me as a friend and as a writer.

Martha Sugrue, Janet Schur, Linda Shaio, May Rawls, and Kathryn Conover . . . my "sisters," my *behins*. The hours you gave me — fierce notes and unflagging support — literally got me through the years of writing this book.

Stacey Winkler, my original *behin,* who has read everything of mine, has always been there with her intelligence, her humor, and her fine eye. What the worlds of finance, literature, marketing, showbiz, and probably politics have regrettably not had access to, I, and fortunate others, have. Thank you, my dearest friend.

Mr. William Goldman, your e-mails, your sage thoughts, and your delightful wit and candor kept me hopeful and kept me moving. I appreciate it.

And I must thank my good friends Owen Lock and Sheila Phelan. Owen, your tutelage, and vast knowledge, of well . . . just about everything, kept me thinking and kept me laughing. And Sheila, thank you for helping me find my way in a world that seemed as foreign and daunting as the Northwest frontier.

Matthew; Diane; Sally; Mr. Black, with his penchant for choice words, God bless him; dearest Louisa; my children, especially my daughter Jocey who gave me some of my best notes; Sondra, Floyce, and Mike, all of whom have braved their way through the years of my obsession, and my many drafts — I can't thank you enough.

Nazim Ali and Nancy, don't know where to begin. My time with you, Ali, your family in Pakistan, and your willingness to share your wisdom and your goodness will forever impact my life.

Milt Bearden, Robert De Niro, Brig. General Raza, and Major Moheen, I could not have gotten through the NWFP without your assistance. No rhetoric here, literally would not have made it, I'm afraid. Thank you for helping me to see Pakistan in a way that few are privileged to experience.

To the good people of Pakistan, Afghanistan, and India, the gracious friends and

10

neighbors of Lala Musa, and to the many Muslims, Hindus, Christians, and Jews who like myself just want to share, coexist, and enjoy one another's differences, you continue to illuminate.

And then there's the man, my man, my mainstay, and my mentor for life. No secret weapon here, everyone knows — thank you, Ronny.

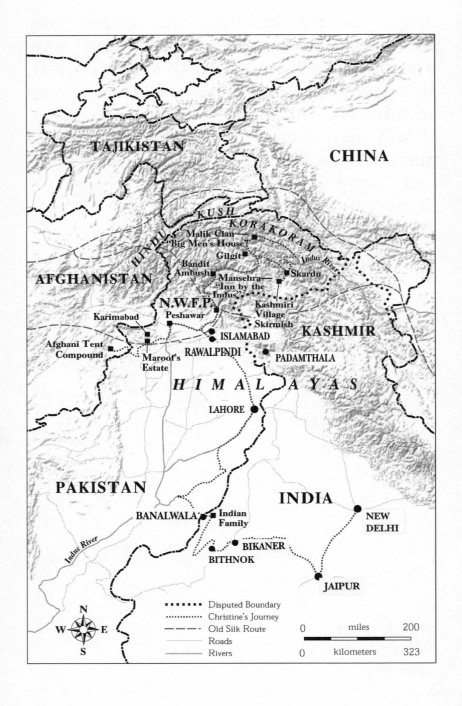

TAJIKISTAN

CHINA

KUSH

KORAKORAM

Malik Clan
"Big Men's House"

Gilgit

Bandit
Ambush

Indus River

Skardu

Mansehra—
"Inn by the
Indus"

AFGHANISTAN

N.W.F.P.

Kashmiri
Village
Skirmish

Karimabad

Peshawar

KASHMIR

Afghani Tent
Compound

ISLAMABAD

Maroof's
Estate

RAWALPINDI

PADAMTHALA

H I M A L A Y A S

LAHORE

PAKISTAN

INDIA

BANALWALA

Indian
Family

NEW
DELHI

BIKANER

Indus River

BITHNOK

JAIPUR

••••••• Disputed Boundary

········· Christine's Journey

— — — Old Silk Route

——— Roads

——— Rivers

N
W E
S

0   miles   200

0   kilometers   323

Prologue

It was a massacre, a slaughter, not a battle as the media sympathetic to the rebels would soon claim.

As the first volley of automatic fire reverberated through the market, merchants desperately pulled at tin shutters to protect their wares, but their efforts were futile. Rebels fired indiscriminately, then looted and torched the stalls. Wild-eyed children stood watching, their mothers darting in to scoop them up, only to be cut down. Old women, their mouths agape, wailed as their slain families lay scattered and broken.

The rebels defiled and tormented their captives until their leader called out. They were the victors, but it was time to depart. There was a staccato burst of automatic rifle fire. Then, sparing the lives of a few children and one or two mortally wounded, the rebels continued down the road through a landscape nearly devoid of life. As they walked off in a ragged line, rain began to fall. Soon the sewage ditches would overflow and obscure the dirt road and soak the tangle of bodies.

For the region and time, the bloodbath was not unusual. But some of the debris seemed out of place. There was paraphernalia from somewhere else, perhaps another world, a torn backpack bearing a decal with the tiny silhouette of a skier; an expensive camera, lens cracked and body ripped open, a bright-yellow windbreaker and a baseball hat that bore a patch with the letters "UCLA." There were other things, too, body parts, not dark-skinned like the rebels' or even like those of the impoverished children, but white and seemingly untouched.

Chapter
1

"Dabboo —"

Red lacquered talons flashed through the air as the skinny Indian woman, clad in purple polyester, lunged at the Muslim merchant.

"Dabboo, stop!" Christine yelled, and grabbed at her guide, nearly tripping over a pile of silk and wool carpets.

"Did you hear her?" Dabboo screamed. "She called me a goat in heat, a goat who soils itself for cash. Bloody cow!"

"She can hear you," Christine hissed, trying to hold her close.

"Nonsense!" the Indian cried. "The Muslim doesn't even know English. She's illiterate!"

Christine dared to look at the woman who sat atop her own pile of extraordinary rugs. Wearing a chador, the traditional headscarf of Islam, the woman stared past them at the opposite wall of her small mud hut, refusing to acknowledge them. In Delhi, Dabboo, with her oversized European hats and shiny pantsuits, was well known and liked. But by the 1990s especially in the northern areas of Kashmir, the Muslim merchants had become wary of the Western importers and their Indian agents, who seemed to expect they could buy the finest products for paltry sums. Christine's sister and business partner, Elizabeth Shepherd, had already agreed that they would need to pay more this year, but the merchant had balked at every offer.

Dabboo continued to complain, and despite Christine's warnings, she was as loud as ever. The woman obviously didn't know English, but her eyes were fixed, and her lips were thin and unyielding. Whatever had been said between them, and Christine had only caught a few words, it was clear that the negotiation had stalled.

"Chris," a voice called from outside.

Liz had heard the commotion and was coming through the goat-skin entrance into the hut. There were ornate screens and carved walnut doors that cut in and around the piles of carpets. Tables and small teak and ebony furnishings were stacked precariously to one side, and brass and copper pots, wood boxes, and lac toys were stacked on the other. With all the merchandise, a portly Muslim woman, and an enraged Hindu, the space was already tight enough, but they had to talk.

Christine had carelessly thrown a headscarf on, but Liz loved her Indian saris, and that day she had insisted on wearing one that was neon green and tight fitting.

"She shouldn't be dressed like that in here," Dabboo reminded her.

Dabboo was wearing a ridiculous sun hat, a shiny purple pantsuit, and nearly a hundred bracelets, but at least she was covered.

"I know. C'mon." Christine sighed, and Dabboo followed.

"Are you blaming me, Chris? Because I tell you, the woman is incorrigible, just incorrigible."

Christine could only nod as they made their way through the maze of handicrafts and over the Kashmiri carpets to where Liz was waiting.

"I heard screaming," Liz began, her eye already caught by the colorful batik wall hangings that lined the mud-and-grass dwelling.

"She called me a goat!"

Christine rolled her eyes. "She told the woman her daughters looked like donkeys —"

"I said no such thing!"

"I heard you!"

Liz's hand shot up to silence them. "This is not working."

"No," Christine agreed.

"I only —"

Liz's hand went up again. Glaring, Dabboo jerked at the wide rim of her hat, pulling it in so the merchant couldn't see her. "I only said," she hissed, "that she was lucky her daughters didn't resemble donkeys. It happens. These people sleep with their own, you know."

"Oh, Dabboo . . ." Liz groaned.

Christine turned and flashed a quick smile at the merchant, for whatever good it might do. Then she turned back. "They hate each other."

Liz looked to Dabboo for an explanation. The petite Indian cocked her head. "What can I say? The woman is a pig. But this is all part of the haggle — a bit of the show. You understand?"

"But we go home tomorrow," Liz said.

"Yes, yes . . . of course. You Americans worry too much. Kashmiris, Pakistanis, Tamils, Bengalis . . . I handle them all. I

18

will fix. You will see."

The Indian flashed a huge smile. Liz seemed confident, but Christine wasn't so sure.

"Call me if you need me," Liz said to Christine.

"We won't need you," Dabboo assured her, and turned once again to face the merchant. Liz patted Christine on the arm, when, suddenly, the merchant snarled something behind them. Whatever it was she said, Dabboo nearly leaped across the rugs to get at the Muslim. The age-old hatred of these two people who two generations before had all been one people under the British still surprised Christine. Dabboo strained against them, screeching at the merchant.

"*Maf kijiye*," Christine called out, trying to apologize to the woman, but the merchant wasn't taking any chances. Tilted forward on her rug, she had pulled a thick-handled knife from beneath her headscarf.

"Dabboo, out!" Christine shouted, pulling Dabboo toward the exit. Dabboo started to object, but Christine wasn't listening. She glanced up just to make sure the woman hadn't come after them. She hadn't, yet. But Christine also wasn't taking any chances, and managed to ma-

19

neuver both Liz and Dabboo through the goat-skinned flap and out of the hut.

Once alone, Christine spun around. But there was no sign of a knife, only the woman eating from a plate of some kind of meat bones.

Moving cautiously, Christine stepped over the uneven floor of piled merchandise, ready to bolt, should the knife appear. But the knife was nowhere to be seen. And now Christine wondered if Dabboo was right and it all was "a bit of the show."

As Christine neared the merchant, her eyes darted about, looking for her backpack. Fortunately, she hadn't listened to Liz, and had packed a gun that Ullas, Dabboo's husband, had given her for the trip. This was her third trip to Kashmir, Liz's fifth, but still Christine thought her sister was a bit gullible when it came to people. She was anxious to retrieve the backpack, just in case.

Circling wide, Christine nearly stumbled over a buckled rug as she swept up her backpack. The woman didn't react, didn't look, only gnawed at the bones. With Dabboo out of the hut, the woman seemed to have calmed. Christine came back around, watching as the woman licked at her fingers. She tried to remember where

Dabboo had left off in the negotiation, and only hoped that her smattering of Hindi would be enough.

"*Namastay* — I mean, *Salaam alekum*," Christine uttered, awkwardly clasping her hands in greeting.

The woman looked up, eyeing the American buyer. Her mouth began to move as if she was about to speak. Instead, she raised her greasy chin, and spat long. Christine followed the spittle as it sailed past her, just hitting the top carpet of a pile that she and her sister had spent days selecting. Still, spit was better than a knife at the throat. Christine went on to say what an honor it was to see so many beautiful carpets. The woman spat again.

Christine ignored the gesture, and mentioned how much her own mother loved Kashmiri carpets and how many of them they had bought through the years.

The woman's mouth twisted. Christine closed her eyes. She could hear the shot of saliva hit their pile and strained to hold a smile.

Christine was befuddled. Was it her Hindi, or was the merchant just no longer interested in selling? She thought about getting Liz to help, but to a Muslim a woman dressed in a neon green sari with her shoulders, neck, and arms exposed, and wearing designer sunglasses, and a full head of brown hair that a scarf could barely contain, probably would not be appreciated. Then Christine remembered a neighbor in Los Angeles, a Muslim, who — The words were barely formed when the old merchant jerked her head to the side and spat once more.

Christine stopped talking. That last shot was a particularly offensive projectile, and the woman's aim was precise, hitting the center of the carpet. Christine dreaded telling Liz about the soiled carpet and had to restrain herself from spitting out that Dabboo was right. *There was an uncanny resemblance between the old woman's daughters and her livestock!*

Desperate to make this acquisition work, and remembering that the woman was armed, Christine went over and downed the cup of tea offered her earlier by one of the daughters, a tea that was sure to have her running back and forth from window seat to toilet on their flight back home. She reminded herself that they had spent three days dealing with this woman, a vendor who represented more than six villages. It had taken two-thirds of their trip just to sort through the merchandise. They had to buy.

"Dari sundar ke sab Kashmir, ke sab Kashmir!" Christine cried out, telling the old woman that her carpets were the prettiest in all of Kashmir, *in all of Kashmir!*

The woman wasn't speaking, but she wasn't spitting either. Still, Christine didn't trust her and held her backpack close.

Christine had opened her mouth to speak when the old woman waved at her to stop. She had heard enough.

"You will pay cash. You understand?" she rasped. "U.S. dollars, no rupees, no checks, no credit cards. And now I will hear what you are prepared to offer?"

Like her aim, the old woman's English was perfect.

By the time Christine emerged from the hut, Dabboo was frantically puffing away at a hand-rolled *bidi*.

"You are finished already?" Dabboo called out. "How much did you give her? Not too much — Promise me you didn't give that silly cow more than eight hundred!"

"She kept spitting, Dabboo."

"So she spat! How much did you promise her?"

Christine shrugged. "Twenty-two hun-dred."

"U.S.?"

Christine nodded.

"You Ameri-cains!" Dabboo hollered, taking another drag of her bidi. She in-haled so deeply, Christine thought she might suck in the entire cigarette, burn her fingers, and choke. Instead, she barked at her husband. "Ullas!"

Liz and Christine had also hired Ullas as their driver, but they could only watch help-lessly as Ullas, all two hundred and sixty pounds of him, caught the door of the van and held it open. Muttering to herself, Dabboo, her bracelets clanking, took Ullas's large hand as he lifted her into the passen-ger's seat. He checked to make sure that her seat was fully elevated and that her silk cushion was in place. And still the crown of Dabboo's sun hat never reached the ceiling.

That night they stayed in a rest house in Kangra, just south of Kashmir. Christine and Liz took the deluxe room furnished with two cots, a cupboard, lots of plastic flowers, a stone figure of Lord Ganesh from Orissa, enamelware from Jaipur, and several miniature paintings of the Hindu god Vishnu.

Elizabeth and Christine Shepherd had been buying exotic merchandise for over ten years. It was now March of '98, and despite personal scandal and political upheaval, President Clinton and his team of Democrats had managed to bring down the deficit and the American economy was booming. What had started as a San Fernando Valley import outlet grew into Shores, Inc., with seven prime locations in Los Angeles and San Francisco. Still, as Christine examined the cheap Indian statue, she had to admit that the golden days of buying village crafts for next to nothing had probably passed.

"I should've let Dabboo do it," Christine groaned, setting down the elephant idol.

"Yeah, well, Kashmiris are tough," said Liz.

"I swear to you, she wouldn't say a word," Christine said, throwing a hand-dyed cover off her bed. "She just spat."

Christine watched as Liz carelessly pulled back the cover and crawled easily onto the flimsy cot.

"You're not going to check for bugs, or snakes . . . or something?"

Liz pulled a mirror from beneath her cot. She seemed more concerned with the shape of her eyebrows. "Time to wax, I think," she said.

Christine got up on one elbow and watched her sister pick at her face. The only chest of drawers in the room was covered with Liz's cosmetics, and as Liz reached down beneath her cot into an oversized piece of French tapestry luggage, Christine thought of her dad and how he would enjoy seeing Liz teeter on a cot in the middle of Kashmir, trying to extract an overstuffed, black-satin toiletry bag. Christine had brought a backpack and a cheap duffel that had been a promotional giveaway. It was enough. Except for her interchange with the rug merchant that day, Dabboo usually dealt with sales. Christine and Liz took care of everything else.

"Dad was here, wasn't he?" Liz remembered.

Christine smiled. She and her sister were so different, but they often shared thoughts. "Wasn't Kashmir. Delhi and Varanasi, I think. With Cloid."

"I forgot about that." Liz dabbed her face with cream. "Cloid must've been on assignment . . . That was nice of him. Big highlight for Dad, I bet."

It was a big highlight, Christine realized. When her dad had returned home, he talked for weeks of temples and beggars and sacred cows, but he mentioned little of Cloid. He couldn't. His friend was here on business, federal business, and Cloid couldn't share much. Her dad and Cloid *had* come to India, but Cloid, his best friend, and twenty years his senior, was a special agent for the FBI, and her dad was a chemical engineer who had a family to support. Christine had known Cloid since she was a toddler, but Cloid Dale's life had always been shrouded in mystery, and Christine knew her father had envied him.

"If that idiot hadn't plowed into him," Liz added, "I bet he would've helped us with the company."

Their dad had been killed in a car accident, and although he had been dead for years, Christine still hurt. She tried not to be bothered that all her sister thought about these days was the company. "I don't think carpets were his thing," Christine reminded her.

"It's not just carpets. It's textiles, and furniture, and jewelry and" — Liz leaned across her cot to Christine and whispered — "and dark men with knotted calves."

"Knotted calves . . . Oh, that would've put him over." Christine rolled her eyes, but had to smile. She liked broad backs herself. She was only twenty-nine, Liz, five years older. Neither was married, but already they had covered most of Europe, and now they were working their way through Asia. She had the feeling Liz could keep traveling, never go home, whereas Christine counted the days of each buying trip. Still, she enjoyed her sister's company, hedonist that she was, and knew her dad would've approved of the business they had started and succeeded with, if only for the adventure.

Liz finished her face, creamed her hands, then stuck out her leg to use up the excess, when suddenly she froze. There was something beneath Christine's cot.

"What is it?" Christine gasped, thinking snake. Cautiously, she bent over the edge of her cot. All she could see was her dirty nylon backpack. She had left it open and something was sticking up out of it. Not a snake, but worse, the unmistakable handgrip of a gun, a .40-caliber pistol to be exact.

"Shi—" Christine muttered under her breath and snatched at the bag before Liz could swing her legs off her cot.

"Chrissy, give it to me."

Christine tried to ignore her, stuffing the gun back down into the bag.

28

"Give it to me. I mean it. Before someone gets hurt."

"I need it," Christine insisted, clutching the bag to her.

"For what?"

"She had a knife."

"So."

"Sooo, she had a knife!"

"It was just a ploy," Liz said, taking the bag from her. "I swear. Cloid has turned you into such a reactionary. Please tell me you didn't bring this over on the plane."

"I wouldn't do that. Ullas gave it to me, and for good reason. If that woman had charged —"

"What would you have done? Shot her?"

"No . . . It's just that Ullas thinks a gun might not be such a bad idea when we're dealing with Muslims."

"I think it's that wife of his he should worry about," Liz said as she checked the gun's safety. "It's going back."

Christine groaned loudly and fell back against the thin pad of the cot as Liz buried the gun deep between the many layers of clothing in her suitcase.

"People do get killed, Liz."

"Those kids were killed by fanatics, not by some villager trying to make a living. Anyway that was months ago, south of here — way south."

Having locked the suitcase, Liz slipped the key inside her toothpaste holder.

"It was Gujarat Province," snapped Christine. "I know exactly where they were."

"And we're not anywhere near there," Liz snapped back, throwing the bag, minus the gun, back to her sister. By now, Christine was muttering to herself.

"Please, don't mutter. I hate it when you mutter."

"I was just saying that Cloid would want me to carry a gun."

"Cloid's an ex-Fed. He'd have you carrying a gun to the toilet if he had his way." Liz crawled back onto her cot. "C'mon, Chrissy, don't get weird on me. We're almost home."

"These people scare me."

"What are you talking about? You loved taking that old hag on," Liz scoffed. "You loved it!"

"I lost us money."

"I didn't say you were good at it, just that you loved it. You probably even loved the way that disgusting woman spat."

"It was an effective tactic."

"Now you do sound like Cloid."

Christine wasn't particularly comfortable leaving her sister alone with Ullas, but Liz was emphatic. They had four crates of merchandise waiting in Delhi to be inventoried. Dabboo could help with customs, but Liz was right; this was India, and Christine would need at least a day to make everything ready for transport.

Except for the merchant with a knife and another who tried to sell them carpets that had somehow been urinated on by a water buffalo, it had been a good trip. One last village remained on the itinerary and Liz wasn't going to skip it. It was decided that Ullas would stay with Liz while Christine and Dabboo went on ahead to New Delhi.

Liz kept the van, and Dabboo managed to find another vehicle, a used truck that she picked up "cheap, very cheap," from a local farmer.

By local standards, the trip had been quite uneventful. After five hours with Dabboo driving on broken and dusty roads, they had killed only one dog, sent tumbling two men who had been riding the same bicycle, and accidentally grazed the hindquarters of a camel. In the third world, Dabboo assured her, that hardly counted.

Christine squinted her eyes trying to see into the brown smog that nearly obscured

New Delhi. The Hilton Hotel was just ahead.

"Once we finish with your shipments, you might want to visit Old Delhi," suggested Dabboo.

The Indian woman not only assisted them on their buying trips, she also owned her own two-person travel agency. "Of course, I have someone who can take you around, if you'd like — Nehru Museum, Khan Market, Humayun's Tomb —"

Dabboo clucked her tongue. They had pulled into the hotel, but there was no one to greet them. "These people are useless," she harped, sticking her head out the window. "Bellman!"

At the sound of her shriek, a bellman appeared. Christine climbed out as the bellman helped Dabboo come down off her silk cushion. She snapped at him in rapid Hindi, and the young man ran around the back of the truck and began unloading boxes. Christine went to help, but Dabboo waved her over as she lit up another bidi cigarette.

"I would've mentioned some of the great silk houses we have here in Delhi," Dabboo started, taking a long, deep pull from her cigarette. "But I think you and Elizabeth are very different. Yes?"

32

In contrast to Liz's elegant saris, Christine was wearing her usual traveling garb, blue jeans and a mail-order cotton shirt. Liz had made her change the sweatshirt.

"Uh . . . yeah. Guess I'm not much of a shopper."

"How tragic," Dabboo said, shaking her head. "Will you need me for anything else?"

"I could use another pair of sandals."

Dabboo glanced down at Christine's ragged footwear. "Yes, lots of cowshit here."

Slipping the bidi between red lips, Dabboo reached high to Christine's shoulders and steered her toward the main street. "See that building, two hundred meters . . . the one with the red flags?"

Christine nodded.

"Across the road, there is a market. They have everything, cheap, very cheap, but only with lots of haggling. Of course, haggling is your thing now. Am I right?"

Christine didn't have time to comment. Dabboo had already turned away. She was climbing back onto her silk cushion.

"If you need anything," Dabboo said, grabbing the wheel while flicking her bidi over Christine's head, "call me on my mobile. Otherwise, I shall be back tomorrow

33

to take you and your sister to the airport."

"They'll be back in time?" Christine asked, closing the car door after her.

"You worry too much. She's with my Ullas." The Indian woman turned the ignition, waved once more, and was gone.

That night Christine called her mother in Los Angeles to let her know what time the plane would arrive and asked her to bring the Suburban to pick them up. Christine wanted to take the crafts that were breakable with them on the plane; Dabboo could ship the rest. Her mother's two dachshunds were barking in the background, making every word an effort until they were finally relegated to their "playroom," Liz's old room, complete with chenille cushions and a playpen full of their favorite stuffed toys. Christine could picture her mother shuffling back in and around the old kitchen banquette with a terry-cloth robe and slippers that she had worn for over a decade. And overhead there were window curtains parading tiny puppies and yellow beach balls that matched the yellow of her kitchen. Between her church work, her husband's monthly pension check, and only two small canines to be responsible for, Marsha

Shepherd had very little to worry about. Life was good, quite a departure from twelve years earlier, when she had lost her husband of thirty years.

Christine gave a quick rundown of the trip to her mother, omitting the part about the spitting merchant. Then she asked her about her blind cat, her own mutt, and some videos she had forgotten to return. The animals were fine, and her mother had remembered to return the tapes weeks ago. Little else was said. Marsha and her girls had been well indoctrinated by her stoic husband. In all matters, the less said the better. Except for the minor infraction of a mother inquiring after her daughters' health, the call ended quickly.

Cloid, or "Cloidhopper," as he was known on AOL, Yahoo!, the Net, and Hotmail, was not on his computer. A retired FBI agent, and a family friend, Cloid Dale occasionally contracted out, doing most of his investigative work via the Internet. But it was early morning in Los Angeles and Cloid was probably already out on the firing line, getting his usual morning practice in before the rifle range opened to the public. Christine would try calling him later, but for now she'd have to settle for e-mail.

Unlike the call to her mother, Christine began her e-mail with the story about the Kashmiri rug merchant, her knife, and her immeasurable store of spittle. She went into great detail estimating the velocity of each round, the angle of fire, and the distance to the top carpet. She and Cloid had spent so many years on the firing line together that she knew the old man would cross-check her figures with his own calculations. She had gone over her own numbers several times. She knew she would get an earful when she got home if she made a single mistake. Not only was the merchant skilled (Christine noted that the spittle stains fell into a remarkably tight group), but also, as she had told her sister, the old woman's use of her unusual skill as a tactic for negotiation was very effective. Either way, Cloid would agree, the merchant had prevailed. Christine had overpaid.

A nice spring day in New Delhi meant that the temperature would not exceed one hundred degrees. It was now barely noon, and already one hundred and four. Christine was sure that the market would be packed with tourists and feel even hotter.

A flurry of brightly colored saris and bicycles carrying whole families swerved around her as she checked the time. She wanted to pick up her sandals before Liz returned. Tickets were bought, the merchandise catalogued and ready to go, but she still had to check out of the hotel.

She had called her sister on her mobile phone that morning. As always, the connection was lousy, but from what Christine could make out, Liz and Ullas had arrived at the village early that morning, had purchased, and were headed back to Delhi. Except Liz had hinted at another village that Ullas had heard about. It was so like her sister to buy right up to departure. Still Liz had ended the call, promising that they would make the flight and not to worry.

As bicycles sped by, something clipped the back of her heel. Christine gasped and hobbled across the bustling intersection to a crowd of grinning Indians and their vehicles, eager to take her anywhere.

"Lady!"

"Hey, Madame, wanna ride?"

"Very cheap, very cheap."

Christine managed a glance at her heel, chafed but not bleeding. A man stepped up, pulling a rickshaw.

"You Ameri-cain? Yes, good price for Ameri-cain. You see, come. Come!"

"Na, na," Christine muttered as she limped through the men. She looked and saw that she would have to cross another busy street to get to the market. She spotted three children running across and caught up with them. An old beggar with no legs and glazed eye sockets teetered in the middle of traffic. Small, bronzed fingers clutched at her jeans as she jumped onto the opposite curb.

As the horns of the trucks warbled around her, Christine was sure her nerves would fray by the time Liz arrived. She was already regretting her decision to leave Liz with Ullas. He was a good enough man, but Ullas didn't have the savvy that Dabboo had, and Christine worried that her sister trusted too easily.

"Madame, paisa, paisa, paisa," pleaded a skinny, knobby child who looked about four years of age. He reached up with his left hand for money. He had to; his right hand was missing.

Christine groaned, and reached for her wallet. She had been in Delhi long enough to know she wasn't doing the child any favors. Parents would often maim their children for money. Still, the beggars, especially the children, had their intended effect, and Christine acquiesced. She handed him ten rupees and walked quickly ahead.

The moment she turned off the boulevard onto the narrow street of stalls and lean-tos, Christine felt herself sway with the horde that flooded the Delhi market.

Liz was right; she was paranoid. It was the height of the season in India, and even though the street was jammed with gullible tourists, Christine felt the hawkers had singled her out.

Jewelry, candy, and cheap leather purses were pushed into her face as Christine made her way over to a stall of footwear. She grabbed a pair of sandals, fending off the vendors in stalls nearby.

"How much?" Christine asked a grizzled Hindu.

"Seven dollars."

Christine thought about bargaining, but paid the man at once. She needed to get back to the hotel. Liz would be waiting.

As she pushed her way back through the market she caught a glimmer of bright color. An Indian in long orange robes was pointing to the sky while flashing a stained and tattered sheet with a horoscope printed on it. The couple he was trying to con wasn't interested, but even before they turned away, the Indian had spotted her.

His gaze was unnerving, and at first she thought he had just caught her staring. So she stepped over to another stall, but saw that the Indian had started toward her. She was in no mood to be harassed. She cut across the market, through a throng of people. Careful to avoid the piles of cow dung and trash, Christine walked along the back of the stalls until she came to the market's entrance. Crossing, she watched for bicycles, and saw the man in orange emerge from the crowd. He had followed her.

Christine rose up on her toes, cringing from the pain in her heel. She could see the Delhi Hilton down the boulevard. It wasn't far, but the stranger was actually pursuing her. She'd have to go for a taxi.

When she came to the intersection where the glut of drivers loitered, she paused. She had never seen so much traffic, but when she felt a hand on her shoulder, she almost leaped off the curb.

"Jago!" a teen yelled, his arms waving. The motorized scooter swerved and Christine jumped back, the vehicle just missing her.

"Missus?"

The air was hot and it smelled and her heel hurt, but most of all she was worried about her sister.

"Missus, please."

She had run into these fakirs before, these fortune-tellers who would reveal your future for a hundred rupees. What was her problem? Why didn't she just turn and tell the man she wasn't interested. She had a nagging feeling that the con wanted more.

"I'm sorry for this," he began.

Christine spun around to face him and caught a whiff of something different from the dirt and diesel fuel she was used to. "No, thank you," she snapped. "I'm not interested."

The fortune-teller looked startled, even frightened. At first, Christine thought he was reacting to someone behind her, someone threatening. She looked around, but there was no one.

Christine left him, walking back along the road, intent on finding an opening in the traffic. The man stayed with her.

"Please, Missus . . . I am sure now. It is you."

Christine gave up and returned to the corner. She waved across the road to the taxi drivers. The one at the front of the line jumped into his car and joined the crush of traffic, signaling that he would have to go around the block.

She would have to wait, and while she waited the man in orange stood patiently beside her. He uttered something and she looked down at the pavement, trying to ignore him. She saw that he was missing two toes on his left foot.

"I saw you in my dream," the three-toed man said.

Christine looked up and she caught another scent of something sweet. His teeth were stained and his orange robes were threadbare, but the man smelled like flowers.

"Please, I have to catch a plane. I don't have time —"

"You are correct, missus. You are already too late."

"Too late for what?"

The smell was stronger now. "All right, how much —" she said, reaching into her bag.

"No," he said, clasping his hands in respect while he mumbled a few words of Hindi. He was perspiring and she realized *he* was afraid. A wave of intuition came over her, and she felt compelled to talk to him.

The taxi pulled up beside her.

"Wait, okay?" she told the fortune-teller.

Christine bent down to the driver to pay

him for his trouble, but the man in orange didn't wait. She called out after him, but he didn't stop. By the time she caught up to him, the sidewalk was teeming with tourists.

"Excuse me," she called out, pulling money out of her purse. "I'll pay you," but the fortune-teller only quickened his pace. The man was moving out of reach and her heel was throbbing. She had to act. So she lunged, pushing people aside to get to him.

A pair of Germans started yelling at her, probably cursing. It didn't matter, because she couldn't understand them anyway. All she cared about was that the three-toed man in orange had stopped. He had no choice. Christine had grabbed onto his sleeve.

"Here," Christine said, handing him a fistful of rupees.

"No! No money," he waved at her, almost knocking the money out of her hand.

"I'm sorry," she apologized. "I just wanted to hear your dream, or fortune, or whatever it is you want."

"There is no more to say. You have karma that follows you. Now please go and do not pursue me."

He clasped his hands once more and whispered something under his breath. She couldn't catch his words; she wasn't supposed to. His prayer was not for her.

Chapter
2

Christine was hyperventilating and had to stop. It had taken weeks to get a meeting with General Raghavan, and his secretary was waiting.

"Do you need a paper bag?" her mother asked.

"No, no, I'm okay."

But she wasn't, and Christine squeezed her eyes tighter. She needed a moment, just a single moment, to blot out the noises of villagers crying, people running in terror, and the images of what she imagined could be the final moments of her sister's life.

Liz was missing and with her any sign of what had happened to her. Christine had already heard all the excuses of inclement weather, of villagers who, after a massacre, would scurry about picking up the remains of loved ones. And, of course, there were the scavengers. . . .

"Damn," Christine muttered under her breath. Cloid had warned her to keep her emotions in check. She had already harassed countless government officials, both Indian and American, had even been thrown out of the offices of the Ministry of Defense, and as Cloid told her, the chief investigator of India's FBI counterpart, the Central Bureau of Intelligence, was their last option.

Still, Christine couldn't catch her breath. Now she was visualizing dogs snarling, snatching at the body parts, the evidence, the evidence that the authorities said they needed.

"Miss Shepherd, if you'd like, I can tell the general —"

"No, no. I'm all right. Really."

"Here, take this," Dabboo insisted.

Her mother steadied her as Dabboo pushed two grainy-looking green balls into her palm.

Christine stared at Dabboo, whose eyes were as bloodshot as her own, then took a swig from her water bottle and downed the nasty-tasting herbs.

It had been three weeks since the disappearance of Liz and Ullas. After Christine had gotten back to her hotel that day, the

45

day she and Liz were to return home, she found Dabboo crumpled outside her door, nearly in hysterics. She was clutching her mobile phone, redialing Ullas's number over and over. Another village had been attacked less than five kilometers from where Liz and Ullas were supposed to be traveling and Dabboo couldn't reach her husband. It took nearly twenty minutes to calm her down. They turned on the television and called the police, the embassy, anyone they could think of to get information. That night the two women even tried to drive to the village, Padamthala, but security forces had erected roadblocks. Dabboo ended up staying with Christine for three days and nights until Christine's mother could fly in from the United States.

Since then there had been little communication between them. There didn't need to be. Christine knew what her friend was going through. Ullas had been Dabboo's life.

As the three women followed Raghavan's secretary down the corridor, Christine recalled Dabboo, a bidi in her hand, her long red polished nails bitten to the quick. The benches at the Indian police station had been cold and hard, and neither of them

46

had slept. It seemed as if they had talked all day to police, but as they waited with others to give yet another detailed description of their loved ones, Dabboo told Christine that she didn't know why Ullas had stayed with her all these years. Her family had offered him no dowry when they married. Like him, she was poor. But she was smart. He liked it that she was smart. He liked her shiny suits and her big hats, and loved to drive for her. He didn't even mind that she couldn't gain weight. The boys in school had always teased her by saying she was more boy than girl. So, when she couldn't have children —

"Mrs. Shepherd," General Raghavan called out, breaking her reverie. "Miss Shepherd, Mrs. Ravini, please have a seat."

The chief of the central bureau of Indian intelligence was tall, handsome, and articulate. He was everything you could imagine the head of any government body could be. Yet his office was small and drab. Mangled blinds that needed cleaning could barely block out the hot rays of the sun, and the general's shirt collar was stained with perspiration. He apologized for the sparse furnishings of his office, setting up a couple of folding chairs. Cloid Dale, who had flown in the day before, was already in the room, seated next to Lieutenant Joseph Riccardi, an officer of the State Department.

"I assume you know Mr. Dale and Lieutenant Riccardi."

Christine nodded at Joe. She hadn't expected to see him, but she wasn't surprised. Her friend Cloid, a former special agent, had no official standing; Riccardi would have to be included. He offered his hand to Marsha Shepherd.

"We haven't had a chance to meet. I'm Joe Riccardi from the State Department. Your daughter Christine and I have been working together through the embassy."

Her mother took the political officer's hand and nodded, the same way she had been nodding for weeks. Christine wished her mother had taken a dose of Dabboo's herbs. She looked at Cloid, hoping to see some shred of hope. As always, the old Fed couldn't be read.

As the general droned through the usual courtesies Christine could feel her mother's body tense, bracing for the worst. Dabboo was hunched over her bidi, taking short puffs, and Christine waited. She wondered if Raghavan was aware of how each sigh, each movement on his part, only prolonged the agony. He explained how urgently his government was working to find the perpetrators of this crime. He talked of witnesses, of people who had sold Liz merchandise, of a boy who remembered her van as it pulled into Padamthala. He recited dates, findings, impressions, and theories. It didn't take long to realize that the chief of Indian Intelligence wasn't telling them anything they hadn't heard for weeks.

What was strange, however, was the way Raghavan never once addressed Dabboo or mentioned Ullas.

Except for the day that Liz and Ullas disappeared, Dabboo had shown little emotion. But tears were forming in her eyes. It had to be humiliating the way Raghavan ignored her. Dabboo's cheap sari and dusty sandals probably marked her as a person of lower caste. Suddenly, Christine had had it with the rhetoric.

"You don't know anything, do you?" she blurted out.

Christine expected to feel her mother's hand upon her knee. It was a signal she had grown accustomed to. But this time, her mother didn't try to stop her. Christine stood to leave, and then saw that Raghavan had finally acknowledged Dabboo. He had leaned in close to her, his words low and comforting. He was saying something that made the frail Indian woman pause. She had stopped puffing, had stopped moving.

"What's he saying to her?"

Cloid stepped up next to her. "Let's give them a minute, okay?"

Christine looked at her mother, both sensing the worst.

"It's all right," Riccardi assured her. But he was whispering, and Dabboo's large, dark eyes were welling.

"It's not all right," she said, and stepped toward Dabboo.

"Chrissy, don't," Cloid urged, but Raghavan was already up, meeting her as she approached.

"I've done this badly," he said. "I'm sorry. I didn't mean to startle you."

The general was actually blocking Christine from Dabboo, who was now almost completely tucked into herself. Her cigarette hung limply from her fingers.

"I was just telling Mrs. Ravini about her husband. I'm afraid it's been confirmed that he was killed in the attack."

"Ullas is dead?"

"Liz," Marsha breathed. "Oh my God, Liz is dead."

"We don't know that," Cloid said.

"Believe me, Mrs. Shepherd. There's

50

nothing to suggest that your daughter was even there."

"But they were together," Christine said.

The American officer named Riccardi was suddenly behind her. "We're checking everything, the area, the surrounding villages. Maybe someone saw her after —"

"But Liz and Ullas were together!"

"Excuse me. Excuse me!" Dabboo cried out as tears streaked the hollows of her face. The room hushed as the Indian wrapped a scarf around her head. Her face barely showed. Now truly the outcast, she turned to Raghavan. "You are done with me then?"

The general nodded. He said something to Dabboo in Hindi, his tone respectful. Christine thought she picked up the words "murderers" and "revenge," but Dabboo hardly seemed consoled.

"Right," she barked, and rose to her feet.

The two women faced each other, not knowing what to say. "I'll call you tonight," Christine said finally.

Dabboo had to choke back a sob. She wiped a small brown hand across her nose, cocked her head, and left the room.

"These are terrible times for my people," Raghavan said.

Christine turned to him. "I can't believe you can't find Liz."

"There are thirty-seven reported missing, including your sister. I wish I had an answer for you, but it takes time. Between the —"

"Weather and animals . . . I know."

Cloid squeezed her shoulder. "Take it easy, Chris. Everyone's doing what they can."

"Your sister was aware of the travel advisory in that area. Am I correct?" Raghavan asked.

Christine had already been asked that question a hundred times. The Indian knew that. She wasn't about to answer.

"I asked that because maybe there's another explanation. Maybe Miss Shepherd decided to visit Rajasthan or southern India. We have many beautiful areas that are popular with the tourists."

"She is not a tourist," Christine said.

Raghavan turned away from her, focusing on her mother.

"Mrs. Shepherd. You had two daughters traveling alone in a highly volatile area. I was wondering what your husband thinks of such practices?"

"My husband passed away years ago."

Christine felt Cloid's grip tighten on her

shoulder. It was clear what the chief of Indian intelligence was implying, even to her mother.

"I'm sorry. I should've realized. A woman alone makes it very difficult, I'm sure. Then I should ask. Is it possible that your daughter just decided to extend her vacation and neglected to contact you?"

"Nope," Cloid cut in, stepping in front of the women. "No, sir. Not possible. I've known these girls all their lives."

The back of Cloid's neck was dark red. He was older, but taller and wider than the general. Still, he offered his hand, his arm as rigid as the sound of his voice. "But thanks for your help."

"I hope you don't think I was —"

"We'll call if we have any questions."

"Of course," Raghavan replied, and took his hand.

"Appreciate it." Cloid gave the Indian's hand one tight jerk.

Any evidence of what had happened, now almost a month old, would be in a clinic in Delhi, or still on site in Padamthala. It would be a while before Cloid and Riccardi could gain access to the clinic, but after their meeting, Raghavan seemed eager to offer them a visit to Padamthala.

When they reached the site of the massacre, Christine had little time to look through the rubble for signs of the colorful things Liz might have worn. She was told that Padamthala had been a thriving village of forty-five inhabitants, all Hindu, mostly women and children. Six had survived, one of them an old man who still occupied a charred space that had once been his home. At his feet were a bowl of water and a few pieces of bruised mango. He was alone, and seemed anxious to socialize. But he couldn't focus on a picture of Liz, nor could he stop talking long enough to hear Christine's questions about a white woman with brown hair and green eyes. He could only talk of his wife, mumbling incoherently, speaking to no one in particular.

When they got back to the hotel, Christine found her mother sleeping. It was three in the afternoon, and Marsha Shepherd woke up groggy. Marsha thought the heat was getting to her, but the room was well air-conditioned. Sadly, Christine realized it wasn't the heat. It was probably depression, and it was time to encourage her mother to go home.

The next night after she had managed to

get her mother and Cloid on their flights, her mother to Los Angeles and Cloid to Washington, where he would continue to push for Liz's search and rescue, Christine had ventured out on her own. She picked a place where the food was supposed to be safe, but as it was, she had very little appetite and ate only a little buttered *nan* and *paneer.*

When she stepped out of the restaurant, there was still light, but already strings of lights had been hung everywhere as vendors continued to hawk their wares. She could hear the incessant honking of traffic in the distance. In the marketplace, however, she only had to worry about dodging cows and bicycles . . . and children. No matter how late it was, there were always children, begging, pulling at her shirttail to give them pennies. She thought about ignoring them, but then remembered how Liz enjoyed the children, not seeing the runny eyes or the distended bellies. Dabboo would often raise her bony arms in exasperation. After all, they had a schedule to keep, and Dabboo would finally have to yell at the kids, scattering them like a flock of pigeons.

"Hey, lady," a particularly dark-faced boy called out. "You Ameri-cain?"

"Yes," Christine said. "I'm an American. Are you Indian?"

The children laughed as if she had said something funny, and she moved on. Still, she was gathering a crowd as she made her way to the hotel. It had taken a while to get used to the way the street people would stare. She learned long ago never to take her video camera. Otherwise, dark faces would press in upon her as she walked, anxious to catch a glimpse of themselves on the camera's LCD screen.

Even without the camera, they stayed with her. But by the time she entered the hotel lobby she was oblivious to them. Christine stepped into the elevator, thinking she might visit the Ministry of Foreign Affairs again, or maybe she would call Joe Riccardi and see if he could get her another trip out to Padamthala.

The room key turned easily in the lock, so the idea that someone could've broken in never entered her mind. With the last of the day's light streaming through the drapes, she almost missed the man sitting in the chair by the television. Her impulse was to scream, but the man leaned forward, his hands up.

"Please don't be loud."

Christine remembered she had given

Ullas's gun back to Dabboo, but there was a lamp behind her that she reached back and clutched.

"You are Miss Shepherd. Is that correct?"

The room was dim, and against the light the Indian looked even darker than he was, but Christine could see him now. He looked familiar.

"Nikhil Sahgal. Remember? The Ministry of Defense?"

Christine did remember. After waiting for two hours for someone credible to talk to, she had lost her temper. It had been a miserable day, saved only by the security guard who had escorted her out of the building, an older, gracious gentleman who had shared with Christine that he had also lost a family member, a niece who had been murdered.

Still, when Nikhil Sahgal shifted in his seat, Christine grabbed at the lamp.

"No, wait! I've come about your sister."

Christine hesitated. "They found Liz?"

"I've been told she's been taken for the trade. I'm sorry."

Christine just stared at the man who called himself Sahgal and wondered if she had heard him right.

"Someone's trying to sell my sister?"

57

Nikhil nodded. "It's hardly uncommon, you know."

"Why should I believe you?" She was still holding the lamp.

"You have no reason, except that it's been a month since Padamthala was attacked. Our labs are slow, even backward, but a month? That's a long time and not a word. Haven't you thought about that?"

Her hold on the lamp eased. Christine *had* thought of that. So had Cloid. Kidnapping had come up, but there had never been a ransom note.

The security guard she had met at the Ministry of Defense went on to tell her that he had friends, not only people he knew in the government, but also people who worked on the streets, who cleaned offices. In particular, General Raghavan's office. The information wasn't difficult to uncover; the files were clearly marked. For weeks, the Indian Bureau had suspected that Liz had been kidnapped. But the Shepherds had never been told.

The hotel room had grown dark. Christine reached back again for the lamp, but this time she flicked its switch. Its light cast eerie shadows on the stranger.

"Why are you doing this?" she asked.

"Because I know how it feels to lose a

loved one . . . and I am also doing it for money. If I help you, then you will need lots of money. Money for me, because I could lose my job — I could be jailed for what I'm telling you. And money for your sister, to buy her freedom."

"How do you know I have money?"

Nikhil cocked his head. "You have many stores, Miss Shepherd. Good karma."

His friends had been thorough, Christine thought.

"Talk to your embassy, talk to CBI if you need to, but don't mention my name or you'll never see me again. I'm taking a great risk in telling you this."

"Where would we meet these people?"

"In the desert. . . . Part of the trip would be by camel."

Christine was already shaking her head. Nikhil stood.

"Maybe you're not interested in saving your sister. Forgive me."

He started past her, and she stopped him. "Why can't you just call them, offer them money?"

"This is not ransom, Miss Shepherd. Nor will your sister be wasted on the sex trade here in India. This is a very different business. You will be competing with buyers from Africa and the Middle East.

And because she is an American, they will need to move her quickly. No. We will have to go there, and soon."

Christine felt a rush of hope, the first concrete sense that her sister was alive. No equivocation. Just hope.

Except who was this man? Who was Nikhil Sahgal? He wanted money, and he wanted her to go with him, alone. He made it clear that he couldn't risk his friends, friends who knew people who sold humans. As a special agent for the FBI, Cloid had talked of contacts. She imagined he had used informants, had needed them, and had even protected them. If what she had heard was true, then she also needed Nikhil.

Or, she thought, she could go to the police, the CBI, her embassy, even the press. They would arrest Nikhil and they would go after his friends. It would take months. If all went well, they might even make a bust. But Liz would be lost.

By the time they had agreed on a price, light was beginning to reappear behind the drapes. Christine was grateful that Nikhil spoke English. She was so nervous, and excited, at the prospect of finding Liz that her Hindi probably would've confused everything. Nikhil's price was twenty thousand dollars at the start of the trip and twenty thousand once he got her to the right people. Once she found Liz, she agreed to wait a week before appearing before any media. Her story would be short and vague. Neither she nor Liz would be able to identify anyone. And only because Liz's captors had had a change of heart was Christine finally contacted and told where Liz could be retrieved.

Nikhil pulled out a map. They would be driving west into Rajasthan, into the Thar Desert. The plan was to leave that night, stay in Jaipur, then leave before sunrise. Between Bikaner and Jaisalmer they would leave the road and go by camel. It was only a day's ride, but Nikhil told Christine that she would need to wire money, lots of money, to a bank in Jaisalmer before they left Delhi. He told her it could easily be in the tens of thousands, maybe more, but once a deal had been struck, the slave traders would want their money within hours.

After Nikhil left, Christine walked about the room in distress. She wanted to call Cloid, then remembered that he was still traveling to Washington, and would be for another day.

Fractured images of Liz as a child

flashed through her mind, running through the sprinklers, fighting over a piece of cake, playing Monopoly after bedtime in their closet with a flashlight poised above the game board in the bedroom they had shared . . .

She would call Raghavan and Lieutenant Riccardi to check out Nikhil's story as best she could, and she would call Dabboo. She needed to borrow back Ullas's pistol. Any other time, she would have tried for a background check on Nikhil. Cloid would've done it for her. But there was no time. She was only vaguely aware of the sex trade in India, mostly migrants from Bangladesh and Nepal. She had never heard of trafficking Americans. Of course, Nikhil had made it clear they were anxious to move her out of India. Liz was special. No brothels, but there could be some sheikh who wanted to add her to his harem or maybe some particularly prosperous chieftain in Outer Mongolia for all she knew. Whatever their plan, Nikhil was right. She needed to get to her while she was still accessible. Once they moved her out of Central Asia, there'd be almost no chance of finding her.

It wasn't until after lunch that she heard from General Raghavan. The phone rang and Christine stumbled out of the shower. Dripping wet, she asked Raghavan to meet her that day. He couldn't. So she asked him about Liz, about kidnapping, and about the sex trade.

It took the general a moment to respond.

"Are you still there?" Christine asked.

"Yes, Miss Shepherd. I'm just wondering where you could've heard such a ludicrous story. We have no 'sex trade' as you call it, and kidnapping . . . Well, it just doesn't exist."

He was lying, and he wasn't even good at it.

"I know how frustrating this must be," he continued. "But really, you must be patient. As I mentioned to your mother, I'm sure there has been some misunderstanding and we will find your sister in some remote location, just needing a little time to herself."

Christine could barely restrain herself. "You can't believe that."

"I remain optimistic, but I can assure you to talk about kidnapping or any kind of illegal trade can only make matters worse. I trust you will keep these thoughts to yourself?"

When Christine didn't answer immediately, the general asked about her visa, its expiration. She told him she had another month. It was probably a lie. It no longer mattered, because as soon as she hung up she called the embassy. The receptionist told her that Riccardi was on another line and would call back. It didn't take long, and as she suspected, Riccardi had already heard from Raghavan. His voice was strained. The State Department officer sounded a little desperate. He wanted to meet soon, within the hour if possible. Christine told him she had a massage appointment, but that she would call back when she had a better idea of her schedule. There was no point in continuing; she didn't trust either of them. After she hung up, she looked at her watch. Cloid would land in about twelve hours. By then she and Nikhil would already be on the road, traveling by car into Rajasthan. She didn't know how Cloid would feel about this, but it was clear that the governments would be of no assistance. Christine would have to try to find Liz on her own.

Within two hours, Nikhil arrived at her hotel with a touring car packed with bottled water and a crate of fresh bananas and oranges. There would be places along the way, but Nikhil didn't need a sick American on his hands and hoped she would stick to the fruit until they had secured her sister. She told him she would. Christine didn't tell Nikhil of the calls or of her fear that Riccardi or some Indian operative would show up at her door before Nikhil could arrive. But Nikhil did arrive, and on time, as planned.

It didn't take long to get out of the city, but after a night of nervous anticipation, Christine was ready for a few hours of peace. Nikhil must've felt the same. Once he turned onto the highway going toward Jaipur, he fell silent. Christine sat behind him, content to stare out her window at the monotony of the desert. But there was no peace. Images of Liz as a captive began to edge into her reverie. Christine tried not to think of Liz in the hands of some sheikh, or bound and gagged and transported with others like animals. She closed her eyes and thought of Jaipur, where in centuries past moguls rode their elephants, bejeweled and massive, through turbaned masses and bright pink structures. She loved the city, the history of it. Liz, as she recalled, could care less about the history. In saris almost too bright to look at, she ran from shop to shop, trying to pick from hundreds of displays of twenty-two-carat jewelry, many studded with semiprecious stones. That first buying trip had been an especially costly one, Christine recalled, but they had managed to resell all of their purchases. The memories of her sister bangled and haggling made her smile, and time went quickly.

Nikhil pulled into a rest house on the outskirts of Jaipur. No pink, just a dirty yellow structure that was virtually vacant. The plan was to pay cash and leave early the next morning. This was fine with her, except she was anxious to reach Cloid, and her mobile phone battery was down.

"Telifon hai?" she asked the clerk.

The Indian gave a quick nod toward a dusty black phone behind the counter. The cord on the phone was short; she would have to make her call there. As Nikhil paid the man, she pulled out her calling card and dialed the operator. When the innkeeper gave Nikhil the two room keys, Christine reached for one.

"Go ahead. This may take a while."

Nikhil held the key. "I'll wait."

The international operator came on asking for what seemed like too many numbers. Christine could barely respond; the men were watching her. She gave the numbers, but when Cloid's familiar ring

66

sounded in her ear, once, twice . . . It was enough. She hung up.

"It's busy," she lied. "My uncle. He's been sick and I —"

"You can try in the morning," Nikhil replied tersely and gave her her key.

Christine woke before sunrise. The large antiquated adapter for the battery charger was hot to the touch, so much so that Christine had to use a towel to disconnect it from her phone. Still, her phone had charged, and she eagerly dialed Cloid's number. When Cloid picked up, there was no greeting, no inquiry as to who it was, just the words, "Have they found her?"

Christine told him she thought they had, but it was not the Indian Bureau, or the police, or any of the agencies, it was someone else. And she told him about the security guard, his name, where he worked, and what he knew. She was confident Cloid wouldn't expose her informant, even if he was frightened for her. And he was, until she told him she had a pistol. That helped.

And then Christine talked about her call to Joe and the general. At first, Cloid was quiet. The politics were hardly new to him, but they had both liked Riccardi. In the end, however, "a frivolous business-woman," "an errant daughter," even "a missing thrill seeker," would better serve the governments than "an American kidnapped and sold to the highest bidder."

Cloid then made some offhand comment about the friction between India and Pakistan, and the State Department probably believing they had more important things to worry about than some woman who had disappeared while buying rugs.

He apologized and admitted that slave traders were a little out of his realm, but the idea of her rushing out into the desert with a stranger to meet people who wouldn't hesitate to seize her scared the hell out of him.

There was a knock on the door that made her jump. "Let's go, Mrs. Shepherd," Nikhil cried.

There were sounds of traffic outside her window and the sun was up. It was time to go. With the frame of mind Cloid had dropped into, they could spin potential disasters for hours. Christine ached for the old man. Other than advice to keep her gun close and her mobile phone charged, there was nothing else he could do for her. Mimicking Nikhil, she reminded him that she was a rich woman with "many stores and good karma," that she had dealt with merchants before, and that in less than forty-eight hours it would be all over. It would all come down to money.

Cloid hoped so.

While Nikhil turned the knob on the car radio to find a clearer station, cards with pictures of the Hindu gods Brahma, the creator, Shiva, the god of destruction, and Vishnu, the preserver of the universe, hung and twirled beneath the rearview mirror. Indian music with its twanging sitars and shrill female vocalists blared out at her as Christine resisted an urge to cover her ears. She had been subjected to the tinny sound for almost three hours, ever since they left Bikaner.

"How much longer to Bithnok?" she asked.

"Soon," Nikhil said, and turned down the volume.

They had been driving all day, and Christine felt anxious. Bithnok was a small village, barely more than a tea stop, just a few kilometers off the main road, south of Bikaner. From there, Nikhil said, there was little traffic and it shouldn't take long to find a cinder-block stand with more bottled water, Kit Kat candy bars, and camels to rent. They would have to ride at night, but by morning they would arrive. There would be no livestock, no fields, just an isolated mud dwelling in the desert. There was nothing on the map Christine could identify, only open wasteland, but Nikhil swore to her they were out there, his friends and the people who would guide her to Liz.

Staring at the landscape, Christine took a sip from a water bottle and leaned back. It was a wide expanse of brown marred only by red dots, the red turbans worn by shepherds tending their sheep and goats. Patches of green mustard plants and home gardens surrounded by sandstone to keep out animals reminded Christine of other animals, scavengers, carrying off the human remains, and Christine gasped at the image.

"Did you say something?" Nikhil asked.

Christine looked up at the Indian's reflection in the rearview mirror.

"No, I was just . . ."

She didn't finish, but her response was enough, and Nikhil turned his attention back to the road.

From the backseat she could see a colorful sticker pasted to the dash of the car. It was also of the Hindu god Shiva, except this figure had a third eye in the middle of his forehead with tiger skins barely covering his loins. There were serpents coiling around his body, and the god carried what looked like a human skull. It was very unlike the twirling card of Shiva, who had the form of a dancer with four hands poised and surrounded by a ring, which, Christine knew, represented Earth. There were so many different versions of their gods, Christine couldn't keep up with them. The Shiva with the tiger skins and skull unsettled Christine, and she looked away, back out the window, as the road passed beneath them.

When she glanced up at the side mirror of the car, she saw Nikhil, and the same kind face she remembered that day at the ministry. A shock of white hair made him look older than he was. He had told her he was fifty-four, and she tried not to look surprised. Nikhil also told her that he had a wife and four children and that he had at one time been a full colonel in the Indian army.

"Christine, look," Nikhil called to her, pointing in the distance.

At first glance, Christine saw only barren desert, but as she watched, there was the slightest ripple of movement, and suddenly a flock of antelope, delicate, and graceful, emerged from the dust and loped out of sight.

Three weeks earlier, an Indian clinician had apparently stopped at a small roadside Hindu shrine not more than a half mile from Padamthala. His own temple was miles away and he wanted a momentary respite before starting the day. He worked for a clinic in Delhi that had been contracted to examine any remains found in the destroyed village. When he had finished appealing to his gods, he opened his eyes and saw what looked like a piece of rotten meat protruding from a pile of trash at the base of the shrine. The Hindu waved away the flies and studied the lump, which appeared slightly charred, like most of the remains he had seen. The clinician went back to his truck and brought back a box from which he pulled a plastic baggie, gloves, and a magnifying glass to inspect the meat.

Green threads, what appeared to be garment silk, were pressed into the flesh. He guessed it was part of a hand, even a palm. What intrigued the clinician most was not that the evidence had been so far from the village, animals absconding with human remains had always been a problem, or that he could still recover identifiable tissue four days after the attack. It was the color and the texture of the piece that was curious. The clinician doubted that the tissue came from anyone in the village, or even from an Asian. The Indian went back to his car, retrieved a small ice chest, and carefully placed the specimen inside it.

It would be weeks before the specimen would be pulled for examination at the clinic, and days after that before Joe Riccardi would be called. General Raghavan had hesitated, but after Christine Shepherd's disturbing call, he had no choice but to call the American embassy.

By the time Raghavan reached Joe Riccardi, Nikhil and Christine had made it to Bithnok, and they had made it to the camel station. Nikhil was correct. It hadn't taken long. While Christine and Nikhil loaded the camels and prepared for their trip into the desert, Joe left the embassy and met with his superior at his *haveli* in eastern Delhi. While standing in the lattice-carved entry of the old Indian residence, Joe told him of Raghavan's call, and of Christine's call a couple days before. He hadn't taken it seriously at the time; he had seen it before with others whose

73

family members had mysteriously disappeared. Christine had become desperate, ready to believe anything, even something as far-fetched as women being sold into slavery.

Joe and his boss immediately fired off a cable to Washington, not to anyone in the State Department, but to the Office of Operations of the CIA. Joe Riccardi was not a political officer, as he had told Cloid, Christine, and Raghavan, he was an intelligence officer working undercover for the CIA.

It didn't take long to get his instructions from the senior agent; it was crucial that he contact Christine, get her to assist with verification, and put to rest any notion of an active flesh trade before it made its way into the press.

Calling Cloid Dale, a former special agent for the FBI, was not something Agent Riccardi was eager to do, but Christine had checked out of her hotel two days before. So Joe called Cloid in Los Angeles, first telling him of the evidence found at the Hindu shrine. The line went silent, and Joe wondered if the old man was not fully awake. But Cloid was awake, and although he wasn't surprised that there would eventually be proof of Liz's demise, he had begun to hope she was alive. Still, Cloid agreed with Riccardi that the United States needed to send its own DNA experts to verify Liz's remains. Joe asked for Christine's phone number. Cloid complied, giving him a home and work number in Los Angeles.

The CIA agent thought about telling Cloid about Christine's phone call, the former Fed thought the same, but there was no mention of the idea that Liz might've been picked up for the slave trade, or of Nikhil Sahgal. Besides, Cloid had other concerns. So did Joe. Neither of them was completely sure where Christine was at that moment, and, retired or not, Cloid was as hesitant to divulge information as Joe was.

Of course, Cloid had an advantage. He had Christine's mobile number, but by the time he dialed it to tell her of the specimen that was found at the shrine and their suspicion that it was Liz's, she was deep in the desert and out of range.

Chapter
3

Eyes closed, Christine could almost visualize her disk player as it re-created the sound that had always lulled her into slumber, the comforting hiss of millions of granules of sand gently stirring over one another. Even in her sleep she anticipated the next selection, "The Rain Forest," watery drops full and resonant, frogs croaking, and the wings of birds beating rhythmically at the wet foliage.

But there was no sound of raindrops, just the thin whistle of wind. She felt the dryness and yearned for the moisture of the forest. The wind blew and sand whipped about her, and there was no comfort. The rain forest was a memory. Then Christine heard him above her. She bolted up from her half sleep, hitting him hard in the chest, and tried to open her eyes, but grit flew into them.

"Nikhil?" Christine breathed. "You scared me." She lay back down, and feeling a tug at her blanket, she thought first of a snake, a "viper," Nikhil called them.

"What is it?" she asked squinting, barely able to make out his form above her. She started to rise slowly, but he fell on top of her and forced her flat.

"Iss . . . all righ'," he panted as he held her down with one hand, using his other to pull away the blanket.

"What are you doing?" she asked, alarmed. As the first whiff of his breath hit her, she knew. He was drunk.

Christine reached under her bedroll for her bag, for her pistol. But Nikhil had not been so drunk that he hadn't anticipated she might go for her gun, and he pinned her before she could react.

"You're hurting me. Let go!"

"I don't wanna hurt you," he mumbled and rubbed his hand over her. She had learned to tolerate the odor of camel, but when the Indian turned his head, his tongue and lips pressing against her throat, she thought the stench of alcohol and sweat would overwhelm her. She struggled against him, but he held her fast.

"Nikhil, listen to me! You're drunk."

She heard the snap of his buckle, then his zipper.

"Shuddup."

"My sister — you have to help me find my sister."

"Forget your sister! Forget her! Now they'll kill me because of you."

Christine gulped air and clenched her fists. She vaguely remembered Nikhil on his phone before they had turned in for the night. Her mobile wouldn't work, but he had brought a satellite phone. After muttering something to her about family business, he walked a little way from camp, yelling into it. They had ridden for hours before setting up camp, and even when Nikhil returned, and started drinking, she barely noticed. She was tired and sore.

"Nikhil, stop. Please. Just tell me what happened?"

"Don't figh' me!" His hand was between her legs, trying to rip through her jeans, but the denim was too strong. He moved his hand up, popped the button, and jerked at the zipper.

Without thinking, Christine bit out blindly, tasting grit and sweat as her teeth sank into the flesh of his cheek. The Indian howled, rearing back, and she pulled free of his grip.

"You stupi' bitch!" he yelled, grabbing at his face.

Her arm came from underneath her and she managed to snap her wrist back and stiffen her hand. She lunged, punching into blackness, hoping to catch his nose and stun him. Instead, she caught the hollow of his shoulder. She had missed, but her dread was pitifully brief as he drove his forehead downward into her face.

The blow to her nose was startling. For an instant, her consciousness faltered, but when he yanked down at her underwear, she felt the pubic hair tear from her body and cried out.

Nikhil paused, his mouth working its way up her neck to her ear. "C'mon, Christina . . . It will be okay . . . righ'?"

"It's not," her voice broke. "It's not okay, you bastard."

He wasn't listening. He was already at her breast. She tried to heave him off, and for her trouble a broad, wet tongue wiped across her breast. Christine grimaced, squeezing her eyes shut. As he sucked and gnawed at her, tears ran down her cheek.

"Be still, Miss Shepherd," he whispered. He pulled at himself and suddenly she felt him between her legs. The sand displaced beneath her as her bedroll caved from their weight. He would move over her, pause, then move again. He was muddled, she realized, unsure of how to keep her down and still take her. But she was losing circulation fast, her legs already numb.

Christine thought of her gun, his gun now, and her stomach knotted.

"Is it more money? I'll pay you more, but you have to stop."

Nikhil didn't answer, just forced two dry fingers into her.

Christine winced, stifling a cry. "Nikhil, please . . . I don't understand."

But she understood enough. Something had changed, and now Nikhil Sahgal would keep her money, rape her, and then kill her.

Nikhil tried to kiss her, and Christine pleaded with him again. It was futile. He wasn't listening, and so she yelled, and threatened, until finally the Indian uttered something vulgar, pulled his fingers out of her, and pushed himself inside.

Her skin burned raw and her face was swelling from where he had struck her. He had wrapped around her once again, and when the acrid odor of her own blood swamped her senses, she could only blink against the pain. She looked up at the star-mottled sky. Tears and sand had covered her cheeks, leaving a thin film of sticky grit.

"I love American women . . . They're so . . ." — his lips pushed into her ear — "so simple."

Christine loathed him. She envisioned swinging her arms from underneath her and going for his eyes. They would be open and she would dig deep, gouging, knowing even as she imagined it that if she was going to stop him this way, she couldn't hesitate or shudder, as she, in fact, shuddered now.

"No. . . . no . . . stop . . . it hurts," she whimpered, the gruesome fantasy passed over.

Mucus ran over the top of her lip, and she could taste blood. Her nose had to be broken. There was nothing out here, she realized. No medical person, no one to . . .

Her thoughts skipped to her gun, anticipating the coldness of its muzzle pressed into the back of her skull. Nikhil was breathing faster, and Christine tried to forget the gun. She had to think, had to free herself . . . but she needed her body.

Christine struggled beneath his weight, feeling nothing. Still, she must've inadvertently moved against him because the Indian rose ever so slightly. And suddenly she knew what to do.

She pushed, almost grunting at the effort needed to lift the dead weight of her hips to meet his. When she finally managed it, he moaned. And his grip eased.

Again she pressed against him, gently, carefully. . . . A whiff of stale air, alcohol, and he lifted, too, hovering for just a moment . . . waiting for her. Her body bristled with a new sensation. Her limbs were tingling and she had to restrain herself. She was desperate to bolt. Instead, she raised her hips.

The darkened shape of his head hung above her as Christine continued to move with him, coaxing him higher, waiting, withholding, so he wouldn't come, until the pins and needles subsided and she could take her body back. His breath quickened and Christine flexed her fists and worked her feet, moaning with him. The feeling was back in her arms, and she reached blindly for hardened leather. Her boots were tucked underneath her bedroll, just where Nikhil had instructed her to put them, "where vipers can't crawl into them during the night."

He started to come, and Christine moaned. The Indian moaned back . . . lost.

She waited . . . and waited, her body alive, blood rushing, her face hot, staring, concentrating. Then her mouth opened and the moment came. She screamed, startling him, startling herself, as she swung the heavy boot through the darkness into the black hole that was his head. He tilted to the side, then fell backward as Christine twisted and scrambled from beneath him.

In the light from the last embers of their fire, Christine could just make Nikhil out, his pants bunched around his knees and the frantic movement above them. He stared in her direction, his mouth moving in sharp angry angles as he cursed at her.

Frantically, Christine slipped on her boots, almost falling on weakened limbs. She held her breath, tugging at her jeans, cringing as she pulled at the zipper and hobbled toward the other side of camp. Christine strained to make out the camels, but couldn't tell if she was approaching one of the animals or a small dune until her fingers sank into coarse fur. She felt her way to the beast's huge, misshapen head while the camel's long bottom jaw cranked lazily as it chewed. She jerked at the reins and the beast let out a tired, gurgling sigh as she tried to climb onto its hump. The camel litter, a seat used for transport, had been removed. She quickly glanced around, but couldn't make out anything. She jumped up behind the camel's hump and held on with both hands.

Taking a deep breath, she slapped the camel and braced for the inevitable lurch that would probably throw her off. But there was no lurch; the camel just bawled loudly as if she had offended him in some way.

"C'mon!" she yelled. Christine slapped the animal again and whooped the way she had when she had ridden horseback back home. Nothing. She snapped her head around. She heard something and noticed only a flicker of smoldering wood left. Christine couldn't see him, but she knew he was listening. The camel squalled again. Her body jerked involuntarily, then stilled.

Her breath held, she heard him. He was muttering to himself . . . and he was biting, chewing, his teeth breaking into the hard stick candy she had seen street people in Delhi gnaw on.

The light appeared, its beam narrow, almost blinding her.

"Are you finished, Christina?"

The sound of his movement through the sand caused her to hit the camel again.

"You're hurtin' him, Miss Shepherd."

Christine forced her eyes to stay open in the glare and soon the form of something behind it started to emerge. She threw her leg over to the other side and jumped. One of her boots fell off, and she hustled to put it back on. She looked behind her, and there was only blackness. She wondered why Nikhil had turned off the flashlight. He had to be as blind as she.

"I've got to move," she said to herself. Her boots weren't laced, and it was hard to push through the sand.

"Christina," he called. "Where you goin'?"

Even though it was cool, beads of sweat broke out on her skin. She plodded forward. There was so little light. Eventually, her eyes had to adjust.

A bush of some kind bristled beneath her, and she came down on a rock. Her knee throbbed. The Indian's voice wafted eerily to her across the hundred or so yards that separated them. She decided to chance tying her boots. If he ran directly at her, she should have time to get moving.

Then her laces were done, and Christine was running.

Chapter
4

"Check your targets," the range master shouted over the horn.

Chrissy couldn't move fast enough. "Bull's-eyes! Bull's-eyes . . . all bull's-eyes" kept tumbling through her young mind as Christine Shepherd, barely nine years of age, sprinted over the cracked ground. Dry sage scraped at her leg, and she tripped, falling sideways. Her shoulder smacked the dirt and a ripple of pain moved through her. She suppressed a feeble whine trying to sit up, holding her shoulder, thinking of her target, and not catching the motion next to her.

It wasn't as if she hadn't fallen before, but there were shouts from the firing line behind her. Chrissy squinted into the hot summer sun to see what the commotion was about. Suddenly the glare vanished and she was shadowed by the giantlike *figures of Cloid and her dad. Her dad had Cloid's old six-shooter and was pointing at something next to her.*

Then she heard it. A hiss, like the sound of the brush she had stepped through a thousand times.

"Get outta there!" her dad yelled. Cloid's thick fingers gripped her arm, bruising her, as the shot rang out.

The snake was half sprung, its headless body still poised to strike, hovering, as if someone had caught it in a photo. Chrissy eyed the sizable rattle, and a cry caught in her throat. Then the reptile fell back onto itself. Chrissy cried out, rolling away from it. Her dad cursed, and she immediately felt stupid and cowardly. She was one of them, a marksman. She was supposed to be tough.

"Sorry, Dad," she started to say, but suddenly he was beside her rubbing his hand over her legs.

"Did he get you, honey?"

Chrissy didn't understand the question, but when he turned her leg, the girl saw the two holes in her calf. Her dad had warned her about rattlers. People died from their venom and now she had been bitten. Panic started to take hold of her, but when she spoke her voice sounded calm . . . tough.

"It's okay, Dad . . . It doesn't hurt . . . You gonna suck it?"

And suddenly all the men down the line, even Doug, the line officer, were walking alongside her as her dad carried her to the range house where Cloid lived. He had a snakebite kit and an ambulance was already on the way. She had never seen her dad so scared. Yet she recognized the glint of pride in his eyes as she joked with his friends and the ambulance driver. And when they got her to the hospital and she was stuck with more needles than she could ever imagine, she never cried once. Not once. It was one of the best days of her life.

Christine tried to hold onto the memory of that feeling, but gusts of sand in the middle of the Thar Desert were whipping against her body and Christine didn't feel brave. She leaned awkwardly into the sand dune, feeling blindly for puncture wounds. If she had been bitten, she knew, she would be dead within the hour, if not in minutes.

She ran her hand over her leg. There seemed to be no small sticky craters in her skin. Squinting against the spray of grit, she looked out across an endless stretch of dark obstacles. Her eyes had adjusted, but the change was unsettling.

There were forty-three species of reptile in Rajasthan, the arid region of western India, and she suddenly wondered if all snakes hissed, or was it just rattlesnakes? Some silent viper might have bitten her already and there could be pinpricks somewhere on her body that she wasn't even aware of.

Would she even feel the venom? Or would she merely pause, tingling with a new sensation as her heart locked in her chest and her lungs collapsed? By then, she imagined, her brain activity would already be skipping, missing with each signal. Then Christine could picture herself on a vast carpet of sand, yielding to her body's distress, rigid with shock as the white marbles of her eyes receded into her head.

Christine fell back against the slope of sand. The burning in her face had abated to a dull throb. She felt heavily congested and concluded that her nasal passage was packed with dried blood. At least she could breath.

She looked up into a canopy of stars. There was the expanse of the Milky Way, with Polaris, the North Star, and the Big Dipper, and she could see most of Cassiopeia. She thought about the North

Star and how the universe seemed to revolve around it. It was fixed and would be there tomorrow, hardly seen, but there nonetheless. For the time being, her universe definitely revolved around it. Without it, she would be lost. She had watched the constellations cross over her and knew that night was nearing its end. Rajasthan was just about the same latitude as Los Angeles, and she thought about the times she had stared up at the night sky at home. The city made too much light to see the stars well. So her dad used to set up his telescope at the rifle range in the Angeles Forest just outside the glare of the city. There God's universe waited for them.

The wind had eased and Christine barely noticed the shelf of sand that had risen around her while the stars moved overhead. She was thinking of Cloid and his old range house that she had known as a child. The last time she had visited Cloid, the living room, the room that looked out on the firing lines of the range, had seemed dim and empty, with only cardboard boxes and trash bags piled in the corner. The furniture was threadbare, and the room smelled of mildew and menthol. There were stacks of magazines, political and foreign, along with Cloid's gun catalogs and his newspaper articles, dog-eared and meticulously organized . . . For what? Cloid Dale had been retired for years. She had heard him complain about the kids who were frequenting the range nowadays, and he hated what was happening at the Bureau, the reorganizations, the changing personnel rules, the new people . . . And the worst of it was his friends were dying off.

Christine tried to be sympathetic. Neither she nor Liz were going into the Bureau as Cloid had hoped. Liz had always wanted to sell imports, travel, and see the world, but not as a special agent. And outside the life at the rifle range, Christine didn't consider herself Bureau material. Still, she had fond memories of Saturdays at Cloid's range house. Her mother came a few times, but she got tired of serving the men as they droned on about guns and international politics. So the moment Liz was old enough to take instruction, she would bribe the ten-year-old with a copy of *McCall's* to occupy herself while her sister shot at targets and tin cans. Christine's earliest memory was of herself propped over a huge rusty toilet bowl while Liz watched over her. Outside the door of Cloid's bathroom, her dad and Cloid would host the oddest collection of white starched shirts, fatigues, tie-dyes, and plaid shorts. Except for her mother, Liz, and Christine, the house was filled with men. After a morning on the firing line, they'd come down, gathering in Cloid's cramped, dingy kitchen. Some had capped, perfect teeth, others had hardly any teeth at all. Most of them had nothing in common, except that they loved to discuss bolt-actions, big-bore ammo, and stock engravings. And they had their stories, so many stories.

"There's spies in there," Liz would whisper, and the girls would peek out of the bathroom at Cloid's friends, ominous creatures from a world barely imaginable. Christine loved watching the men and hearing their stories, but Liz only wanted to go home and play dress-up.

A multilingual babble, thickened with liquor, the English bits oddly accented, floated over the desert.

Careful not to touch her nose, Christine brought her arm over her eyes. She was thirsty and tired. She just wanted to sleep and forget about the man following her.

For four hours Nikhil had tried to explain himself, sometimes shouting through the whirr of wind that often descended on

92

the region. He apologized for "touching" her, for trying to make her feel good. He told her he "came to her" only because he felt bad. The call earlier had been from his friends. The deal had been called off. He had been duped. The slave traders had duped them all, and his life was ruined.

The woman the slave traders were willing to sell was not Elizabeth Shepherd, not even an American. She was a Tajik, a "stinkin' Tajik," Nikhil groaned, a creature who probably wouldn't even sell.

Nikhil apologized for the mix-up. He said he should have known better than to trust slave merchants and even said he wanted to bargain with her. But Christine didn't rise to the bait, and the Indian didn't insist. He was as trapped as she was. He couldn't trust her, and she couldn't trust him. There was no Liz, no final payment. His only recourse was to offer her to the merchants. She could pretend to haggle, to give him whatever amount he would ask for in exchange for her freedom, and promise not to go to the police. But in the end she knew he couldn't let her go.

"Christinaaa," he called out, taunting her when she wouldn't respond. He started making sucking sounds that made her shudder, but there was still a fair distance between them. Not a lot, but in the dark she had at least been spared his company for over an hour. Once she thought she had even lost him. However, sounds carry in the desert and when Christine tripped over a clump of dry scrub, she cried out and the Indian tried to home in on her.

She stared up at the sky, and guessed that it was around four in the morning. She figured that Nikhil had raped her just after midnight and tried to move past the memory of the violence and the feeling of torn flesh between her legs. She didn't have time to dwell on what had happened to her. All she cared about just then were her feet and legs losing strength. She had been stumbling on the desert sands for hours.

Christine closed her eyes, pushing the small of her back into the sand and carefully stifling a groan. She wondered about the chance that Nikhil would pass her in the darkness if she stayed quiet.

Then Nikhil's camel bawled woefully and Christine stood. Her boots sank and her breath started coming in audible gasps. Christine bit down into her bottom lip. It was already numbing. "Shit," she muttered to herself.

Christine lifted her foot and stepped

ahead, concentrating on the sound of the sand as she slogged through it. She'd move and hoped the exertion would be enough to hold off a panic attack.

Their destination had been due west, just north of Jaisalmer. She forced herself to breathe slowly and tried to ignore Nikhil's drunken gibberish behind her. If she could get to Jaisalmer, there might be someone . . .

Once it's light, her mind whispered, *he'll kill you.*

Christine wiped at her mouth and found it was wet. There were tears streaming down her face. She felt so disoriented. When had she started to cry?

Her supplies, her medicine — everything that could help her — was on that damn animal. She hated camels. They stank and the air stank, and then she was sobbing.

Christine loathed the irrational fears these attacks provoked. She could hear Nikhil behind her and she stumbled again. Polaris skewed as she fell. Cool sand seemed to envelope her body, and she felt herself submitting to the hysteria.

"I can't do this — I can't! Lizzie, I'm sorry," she whispered, sputtering through the wetness. She tried to recall the last time she had seen Liz. She was sitting on the bumper of the van, trying on bangles, a thirty-five-year-old woman playing dress-up.

Christine could barely catch her breath. The realization that her sister was dead seized her, and she couldn't shake it. All she could think of was that she had failed. *The woman was not Liz, but a Tajik . . . someone else.*

A scream tore through the dead air, and Christine jumped, her breathing fast, her face and lips numb. She *was* hyperventilating, but she couldn't rest. She strained to see behind her and noticed that the wind had died down. The descent of silence seemed otherworldly, and she wrapped her arms around herself, trying to ease the shaking of her body.

"Scare you, Christina?" His voice was disconcertingly calm. "Did I get you?"

Nikhil chuckled and Christine crawled out of her spot in the sand and clambered up the dune. As she slid down the other side she glanced up into a rash of stars and thought about Jaisalmer, the last city in India, the end of the line.

Christine checked again for the North Star. She was still heading west as she had intended, as she recalled Nikhil had intended.

She heard Nikhil grumble some instruction to the camel. He was closer, but it was still too dark to see.

Yet he had to know that she was just ahead of him.

Nikhil would continue west as they had planned, as he had planned, but even in the darkness he seemed to sense that she wouldn't veer from the plan. She could've lost him long ago . . . anytime, but she hadn't. And then it came to her. The realization was so upsetting that her thoughts skipped past it. She tried to rationalize that she had no food, no water, that the desert was vast — but they were all excuses.

As Nikhil continued to taunt her from behind, her eyes welled up at the humiliation. He was male, an *Indian* male. There were fewer choices in this part of the world for women, and he was counting on her fear of not daring to lose him.

"*I'm* not Indian!" she insisted, her gasps for breath deepening, doubting that any Indian woman would have had the nerve to escape.

But, her mind turned, *even an illiterate villager had enough sense not to venture out into the desert alone. Much less with a man she didn't know.*

Nikhil had said American women were simple, and she felt just that. Her body was trembling, and she tried to convince herself that if he came upon her, she could handle him. Her father had taught her some judo, and she knew guns. She was not simple, not just some female . . . and then something in her gave way.

Her feet stopped, and she could no longer feel her own arms around her. Her senses had dulled and her teeth were chattering.

Christine was terrified, and the feeling of being so utterly alone closed in around her. She tried to remind herself that Liz needed her, that she was Glen Shepherd's daughter. But in the end she was only a female, and a coward.

The authorities had paid little attention to her plight. Her value was limited and, American or not, she had come to the third world, and now she was succumbing. She felt like a battered woman who had accepted her fate, and she called out.

"Nikhil?"

Moments passed. For an instant Christine thought she had lost him, and panic filled her. "Nikhil, where are you?"

There was only the lonesome whoosh of sand and wind. She started to breathe hard again, looking for some sign of movement. Then, finally, she heard him.

"Here. I'm right here."

The maleness of his voice seemed to linger. She couldn't see him, but she guessed he wasn't far. *He had taken his time. He knew she would finally surrender.*

Christine stood up and started walking toward the sound of his voice, no longer conscious of the ache in her legs.

Somewhere deep inside she felt she was just a woman and couldn't go on. Then the sucking and kissing sounds charged the air and Christine let the weight of the sand hold her. She felt dizzy and sick. She had to force herself to remember that he could bury her in a dune where her body might never be discovered. Or he could take her to that mud house, the one where his friends waited. She had been raped, her nose broken, and still she might be worth more than a Tajik.

There were more kissing sounds, more distinct. He wasn't far away.

Her ankle gave out as she stumbled into a small sinkhole, the strain hardly felt. It wasn't that she wasn't afraid of what he might do, but the fear of dying alone was worse and her feet moved toward the sound of his voice.

The kissing sounds stopped, and Christine was so tempted to tell him that she'd pay him the other twenty thousand, fifty if he wanted it. The Tajik, the traders, even the rape . . . What had happened between them wasn't his fault; it was a mistake. She wouldn't have to go to the police, she told herself. She could say that, could mean it. Then maybe he wouldn't kill her —

There was the sharp sound of a match striking, and Christine froze. She watched as a light, a soft flickering glow raised in the darkness as Nikhil brought the match up to a half-burnt cigarette. His head was angled away from her as he cupped the match against the breeze.

He wasn't more than fifty yards away. The Indian looked like something from the dark streets of Delhi, and she could make out dirt and clotted blood where she had almost bitten off part of his cheek. She craved the feel of her .257 Roberts, but her stomach turned. Even if she had a chance to kill him she would be left alone.

Unaware of her, Nikhil shook out the match, leaving only a hint of orange in the darkness. The cigarette's fiery tip burnt brightly as he inhaled deeply, then the pinpoint of fire drew downward, held, and rose again. The cigarette's movement was languid and deliberate. The wind squealed around her and still she thought she could hear him sigh.

"C'mon, Chrissy. I'm tired."

The sound of her childhood name surprised her, sobered her. She thought back to the range and how, one night, the black sky over the firing line was so perforated with starlight that it seemed it could rupture above her. She had been caught by the spectacle, and Cloid had chastised her. She wasn't paying attention. Her old mentor didn't care about stars. He was interested only in the array of firearms that he had laid out before her. That day Christine had come in first in yet another national rifle competition; two weeks later she would meet Jeremy; and within a year her dad would be killed in the car accident.

But on that starry night she could only think of Cloid's collection of Chinese and Russian and German steel. Cloid had feigned indifference to her victory, but she knew he was as excited as she was, and he waited patiently as she picked through the hardware. A Colt, a Browning, two Remingtons, and an old Smith & Wesson that Cloid had won in a cockfight from some guy in Spain were carefully set in with the rest of the artillery. As Cloid broke in and out of stories of cold-war derring-do, the girl held up an M-14 and

101

dreamed of being a hero, an adventurer, like Cloid, like her dad.

But the girl who had won national competitions, who had imagined herself a champion, had ended up behind a desk in San Fernando Valley. She would be thirty in another year, had never gone to college, was ten pounds overweight, had one blind cat, and four overdue-book notices. And Jeremy, her first love, had married a girl from Fresno. She wondered when she had become so average, so pathetically . . . *simple*.

Christine heard the Indian sigh again somewhere beyond her. The glow of the cigarette had vanished.

"All right, Miss Shepherd," Nikhil said. "Just stay where you are. I'll come to you."

But Christine didn't stay. She had remembered how the M-14 had felt light in her grasp, and she also remembered that her sister needed her. To her surprise, her legs responded. Her movements were mechanical and rigid, but this time she was moving away from him. Christine looked up at Polaris, instinctively marking the position of the Big Dipper with Cassiopeia directly across from it.

She tried to recall the maps she had studied. To the south there was more desert, too much desert. And east . . . She couldn't remember. But to the north there was something . . . Lines, and symbols. Christine only hoped it meant civilization. Still she had to lose him, even if it meant losing herself.

"Chrissy . . . Where are you? Christina . . ." More kisses. "C'mon, sweetheart."

Christine couldn't hear him. She was walking, thinking about the sky. Just before sunrise Cassiopeia would be lost beneath the horizon. Christine lamented the loss of her favorite constellation, but by that time she would be free. At fifteen degrees per hour, with the stars rotating counterclockwise, it would be sunrise in less than two hours. That gave her plenty of time.

She could hear the motion of the camel as it plodded through the sand. She couldn't see Nikhil or his cigarette, but she could hear him. Between kisses, he would mumble to himself.

Her lips cracked and bled as she squeezed them tight. She didn't trust herself. There could be no noise from her as he passed by. There was feeling, though; her lips stung. The numbness had subsided and she knew the anxiety would quickly follow.

Let him go west, Christine resolved. She

would head north.

Nikhil only paused once near her. She stood rigid, not even a breath. Only the rapid thump in her chest sounded in her ears, reminding her that she was still alive. Christine could hear him bluster as he moved away from her, confident that she was just ahead of him.

Once he was a safe distance away, she dared to smile, when something hissed beneath her. She froze. She stood in the noisy scrub, willing herself to move. With each step, the brush railed against her. Sweat was catching at her brow. Still, Christine dared a viper to appear. Finally she stepped onto a gentle bank of sand and a last breath of nervous tension escaped her lips. She grinned full out, and the injuries to her face flared with new pain. It didn't matter. She was determined to survive.

Nikhil had no way of knowing all the nights she had spent tracking the stars with her dad. Christine knew her chances for survival were slim, but her life would not end so easily, so simply.

The sky was full of stars, surreal in their numbers and luminosity, and she was suddenly awestruck. Here she was in the Thar Desert, in India, in a place so foreign. It was unlike anything she had ever experienced, and for a moment she thought she could feel her dad. The sense that he was watching, guiding her, was overwhelming, and Christine felt cocooned in the gentle eddies of sand that whirled about her.

"Dad?" she whispered.

And as the voice of her tormentor diminished in the distance, the triumph of that day on the rifle range twenty-five years earlier returned. She managed a smile at the thought of being a marksman again, and headed north.

Chapter
5

Two battered jeeps and a Toyota van, their
windshields cracked and caked with dust,
were parked in front of a teashop, taking up
almost the entire width of the rough mountain road.

Goatskins stretched between rough-
hewn lengths of poplar shaded a motley
group of Pakistani men. Reclining on one
of many string cots set up at the mountainside truck stop, a man sipped from a
stained teacup while his lieutenant, turbaned in a sweeping knot of almost unnatural white, spoke quickly to him. Many of
the men were lingering over their tea, some
dozing. The Muslims were clad in the
comfortable tunic and trousers typical of
Pakistani men, but their leader Farrukh,
distinguished himself in fatigues. A loose
pile of tattered red cloth encircled his
head.

As the rebels rested, the Indus River crashed angrily through a boulder-strewn ravine on the other side of the road. That the road and the teahouse were still accessible attested to its being early spring, but the monsoon was on its way.

A truck pulled up and four strangers crawled out. They wore black turbans, their leader in all-black *hijab*, the predominant color of Shiite Muslims. His Islamic outfit was heavily layered in scarves, making him seem even wider and more formidable. Unlike the three who followed, each of whom had a Kalashnikov slung carelessly over his shoulder, the visiting leader carried no weapon and wore a ring with a black *yakoub*-marble set in a thick band of 22-karat gold. It was the same type of stone worn by Imam Ali, the martyred cousin and son-in-law of the prophet Muhammad who had founded the religion of Islam in the early seventh century. According to Shiite Islam, Ali not only was the legitimate successor to Muhammad, but he also held a unique spiritual position that enabled him to intercede for humans within the spirit world.

Other Muslims did not agree that Imam Ali was Muhammad's successor, and shortly afterward he was murdered. His death triggered a schism between Muhammad's followers, the sect called Sunni, and the other claimants, the Shiite Muslims. The enmity between the two has endured for almost thirteen centuries. Still, the lieutenant with the white turban needed no prompting. He approached the Shiite leader, embracing him as one Muslim to another. The lieutenant gestured toward his own leader, but Farrukh sipping his tea made no effort to acknowledge the visitors. Nor did his men. They suspected the visitors *were* Shiite, and could barely tolerate their presence.

The Shiite leader smirked to cover his discomfort as he uttered a dispirited greeting.

Evidently too tired to respond, the red-turbaned Farrukh barely budged. His lieutenant made no apology, only directed a young boy to bring two cups of tea. The boy bowed, backing away as one of the black-garbed visitors shifted his hand to his Russian automatic. Their identity confirmed, guns appeared, shots were fired, and with what seemed sleight-of-hand, the lieutenant struck, leaving the handle of a knife protruding from the chest of the Shiite leader.

The impaled body stayed upright momentarily, the man's eyes opened wide in disbelief. The lieutenant tugged at the knife to retrieve it, then wiped the blade clean against the stranger's tunic before the body collapsed.

The remaining two Shiites dropped their weapons as Farrukh sat up on his cot. He craned his neck and slowly approached the group to examine the bodies of his countrymen, one a simple villager, the other a rebel leader like himself. A rivulet of blood reached the toe of his boot. Aware that his followers were watching, he ignored it.

He turned to face the two survivors and sighed. He saw no reaction in their eyes, only the droop of their shoulders and a look of resignation in their faces.

Raising his hand, he cuffed one of the men, then scolded them both like children as they dropped to their knees before him. Their heads bobbing, the men begged to be spared. Farrukh signaled to the boy, who quickly ran over with two more cups of tea. He handed a cup to each, then sent them on their way. Their vehicles left behind, the two Shiites started down the road. Neither of them dared to look back. Allah had been merciful.

A bearded man with a square face and a Hunza hat rolled at its edges appeared from behind the tea stall and signaled to his son. The boy had already cleared the broken pieces of porcelain and bullet casings from around the bodies and was ready to grab the legs of the larger Shiite as his father pulled at his shoulders. By the time the Sunni band of men and their rebel leader had returned to their cots, the bodies of the Shiites had been dragged to the back of the teahouse and out of sight.

Chapter
6

The sun was high. Christine had torn her undershirt to wrap it around her head, but the remnant kept blowing off, and finally she let it go.

At times Christine would pause, recomputing her position, trying to remember which way was north. She guessed it was early afternoon, and as she moved she occasionally scrunched her lips, reminding herself that she had to stay focused and not let herself babble. The heat and the monotony of the terrain made withdrawal seductive.

It wasn't long before Christine couldn't stand straight. So she leaned, intent on keeping her forward momentum, her arms heavy and limp at her side. The familiar hiss of the scrub was no longer heeded. She was only aware of the movement of sand as her boots trudged through it. She didn't know what propelled them to move, and sometimes she looked down and winced at the sight of her own feet, not recognizing them.

Her lids were almost swollen shut, which, given the glare of the sun, was almost a blessing. Christine frequently had to stop and blink to moisten them. The contours of the desert were disappearing and what color remained seemed to be fading.

What finally caught her eye amid the blur of brown was the carcass of a jackal. She stood over the remains, and hot tears streaked down cheeks caked with dirt. Christine had suspected that she was going in circles, but until she came upon the stinking bones a second time, she wasn't sure. There was very little flesh on the jackal's skeleton, and Christine recalled wanting to believe it was a dog so she could hope that humans might be nearby. But the carcass wasn't a dog. Her knees gave out and she sank into the sand.

She lay back against the slope above the bones, and the sun bored into her body. The sand against her back was no longer cool and she didn't have the energy to burrow deeper.

She thought of the animal next to her

and wondered how it had died. Its form was intact, so a predator couldn't have killed it. Maybe it had got lost and died of thirst. Was that possible? Could animals of the desert really get so disoriented that they would collapse and yield to the sand as she was doing?

Christine felt the breath in her body deepen as a deathlike calm began to take her.

Get your ass up, a voice commanded from within.

Christine tried to lick her lips, but her tongue felt too large; it filled her mouth. The small voice grew insistent. The heaviness in her chest was building, and she thought she might suffocate. Then her tongue pushed through to the dry air. Even her scabby lips felt oversize as she lamely probed them. The voice continued to harp at her, but she was too exhausted to heed it. Christine's eyes closed, and she waited for the inevitable stinging, but there was none; her tear ducts had gone dry.

The searing heat, the ache in her body, and the dryness in her mouth seemed to subside as Christine pulled away. And there was music. It wasn't the same music she had heard on the radio, but it had an eastern lilt, a strumming of strings that was pleasing. In that moment, she realized that she had come to India for a reason. It was to die. She wasn't scared.

The sound of the strings resonated within her, and Christine felt herself losing the sensations of the heat and pain. The music was distant at first, and then it became louder, closer. She wondered if she chose to open her eyes, would she be moving upward, lifting through the clouds to what? The heavens?

Her eyes did open, but all she could see was the dark underside of the arm that shielded her face from the glare. Then the glare vanished and Christine felt the heat recede. The music stopped as something cried out above her.

Christine's reflexes were sluggish, and it took every effort to bring her arm down. She groaned as a painful awareness of the sand, the heat, and the carcass beside her returned. Something shadowed her. She heard her breath blowing in short gasps as she propped herself up, barely managing to raise her head.

All she made out was a creature with what appeared to be the sun poised upon its head. Christine remembered a Hindu temple she had visited in Delhi and wondered if she might be meeting a god. She

114

tried to speak, but didn't have the strength.

The creature bowed, palms together in the traditional Hindu greeting, and said, *"Namastay."*

Christine didn't respond. She couldn't take her eyes off the sun over its head. And there was something beside it, something small and bony, and just as Christine thought it might also be some kind of carcass, it brayed. Then the sun started to descend upon her as a tall, lanky man knelt beside her. Black, bushy eyebrows that fell into a hard V shape in the middle of a furrowed brow reminded her of Nikhil Sahgal.

Her world tilted. Her mind was swirling. All she could see were those eyes that stared at her from beneath a bulbous saffron turban.

"No, no, no . . . Go away!" The cry came out as a half sob, and her chest heaved as she tried to get her breath.

"Maf kijiye! Maf kijiye!" the man yammered, clasping his hands while his head bobbed up and down before her.

Christine managed to stay up as she swung at him. She couldn't get Nikhil out of her mind. She flailed at the stranger, and the donkey brayed again.

"Apko dard hai? Maf kijiye — apko dard hai?"

Her arms still raised, she hesitated. She had heard the concern in his voice, even understood a few of his words. Then she saw that he had a stringed instrument slung over one shoulder.

It's not Nikhil, the voice in her mind began.

Christine dropped her arms, giving in to the weight of her head. It tipped back and her eyes closed. Again she felt the heat recede as the man bent over her. She managed to squint into his dark, leathery face. The man's eyes were yellowish, not yellow like his turban, but a morbid color.

"Kya ye sirias'hai?" the skinny man whispered, asking how sick she was.

"What?"

He tried again, but appeared to be pulling away. Christine abruptly realized that he wasn't pulling away; she was falling backward.

Lying against the sand, Christine briefly stared up into craggy brows, and her lids were so heavy she couldn't keep them open. As she eased into unconsciousness, her body lifted and seemed to float while a scent of spice wafted over her.

Christine's mind wandered, but the spice

remained. There was also the smell of animal as the stranger shouldered Christine onto the donkey's back. The animal protested loudly then sank beneath her as the stranger whipped it. In seconds, the donkey was moving steadily along and she was barely conscious of the dreamlike world she was moving through.

It seemed as if she had just been placed on the donkey when something gripped her from behind. As she slid off the animal, her face skidded over a bony haunch and her upper lip split. Christine didn't feel the wound, only the warmth of the blood seeping between her lips.

She was carried out of the brightness into a cool, dark place. Amid memories of home, Christine heard whispering. She managed to crack one eye open, catching a glimpse of dark faces. They seemed to be everywhere, and hands were all over her as she was laid flat, covered, then pushed up again. Her head lolled forward and she groaned.

"Qui' it," she said. But the hands were insistent, holding her head up as a cup was brought to her mouth. A bitter liquid trickled between her sore lips.

"No . . . Taste bad . . . ba' . . . ," she whined.

Her stomach moved to her throat. Her eyes sprang open in surprise, and a sea of swarthy faces stared at her as vomit filled her mouth and nose. The acids from her stomach burned her throat and lips, and she gasped for breath. Hands turned her head and she threw up, spasmodically gulping between heaves. She was on her side and her ear was wet where vomit had streamed into it. The voices were muffled, but she could hear someone crying . . . and screaming. She couldn't understand the words, but at moments she was conscious of her own lips moving. *She was the one screaming.*

Then she was running, and falling, rising and falling again. Nikhil was behind her and the donkey brayed. The mesh of sounds and rush of glimpses merged until blackness descended.

A blur of yellow and pink came into focus, revealing splotches of broken sandstone mottled and flaking above her. There also appeared to be a long brown snake streaking across the ceiling to the corner and down the wall to a huge brown socket.

"Wi . . . re . . . ," Christine heard herself utter. She moaned. Her neck was stiff.

A spicy scent mixed with the rank odor

of vomit lingered in the air as she managed to turn her head. Indian women and children, with barely a swath of cloth to cover them, were sitting on top of embroidered pillows and woven cotton durries that covered the floor. A fuzzy blanket had been drawn over her. It reminded her of the Mexican blankets her friend Marina had given her when she slept at her house as a girl. Marina's brother used the synthetic fur to line the dash of his car. This blanket, however, reeked of camel and tickled Christine's nose. She rubbed it. Pain radiated through her face and she gasped.

A match was struck, a candle put before her. An arm ringed with ivory bracelets extended toward her as a woman with a birthmark that showed reddish against an almost black complexion whispered something to her.

"What?" Christine said quietly, taken aback by the huge ring in the woman's nose.

The woman stepped closer, still whispering. The flame showed her eyes, large white orbs that stared at Christine in astonishment. There were several strands of silver jewelry laced over her forehead with a flowered veil flowing down over her shoulders. Others around the room were also adorned in jewelry and layers of embroidered cloth, but they were hesitant to approach. Finally, the matron of the group appeared. She wore little jewelry and no veil, and an ill-fitting sari barely covered the woman's ample presence. There was a red *bindi* between her eyebrows, but her skin was dry and heavily wrinkled and the religious spot was hardly discernible. Mumbling something under her breath, she laid her hands on Christine to feel her temperature. Whatever it was she felt, it must've been acceptable, because the woman grinned, exposing a few decayed chips of enamel. Before Christine could respond, she was pushed up and given another drink. Remembering the bitter liquid of her dream, she recoiled.

"*Chai . . . chai . . . ,*" the matron said, urging her to take the cup.

Christine finally acquiesced, grateful. It was sweet, milky tea.

"Thank you," she croaked. "*Dan . . . yivad.*"

All the women in the room reacted, smiling and nodding.

"Where . . . where . . . ?" Christine couldn't finish. She ached everywhere.

The matron frowned, not understanding.

Others behind her shook their heads until the woman with the birthmark and the nose ring lifted a youngster onto Christine's cot. The little girl couldn't have been more than seven years of age.

"Yes, madame?" said the girl.

"Speak English?" Christine asked.

"Yes," said the girl.

Christine took a breath and braced to make the effort to talk. "Can you . . . tell me where I am?"

"Yes," the girl repeated.

Fighting off a wave of sleepiness, Christine waited. The little girl looked blankly at her, and Christine realized she had reached a dead end. She felt exhausted, and for the moment, the little Hindi she knew eluded her.

Taking down the child, the matron scolded the younger woman and hobbled out the door. Christine glanced around the room and saw that she occupied the only cot in the room. The others had slept on the durries.

A very sleepy young woman whose hair was full and shiny came through the door. Unlike the other younger women she wore no veil, just some simple silver earrings with a brilliant green *bindi* that shone in the early morning light.

"You speak the English?" she asked Christine as she stepped beside her.

"Yes."

"Good," the girl said, and smiled. "I speak also the English. *Mara nom Shweta* —" The girl raised a delicate hand with henna-colored nails to her lips. "Oh. I very sorry. My name Shweta."

"Christine," Christine offered.

"Kharizheen," the matron said in a manly voice while the women around her giggled, parroting the old woman's pronunciation.

Shweta faced Christine, her face flushed. "Welcome in my home."

"You can call me Chris,"

The girl nodded. "Kharis."

"Is this Jaisalmer?"

"No, no Jaisalmer. There is only my home."

Christine thought of nomads, but the room seemed permanent. "And the man who wore that yellow . . . ?"

Christine swirled her finger over her head and there were more giggles. The girl first told the matron what it was their guest was saying, and then nodded. "You speak of my uncle."

The dark woman with the birthmark and the dangling ring in her nose smiled proudly. Christine guessed she was the man's daughter.

"You very sick and there is too many wounds," Shweta said. "We want to fix you, but —"

"*Danyivad.*"

"You welcome," said the girl. "Excuse me," she added tentatively. "How the wounds come?"

"An animal," Christine began, already spinning what she would say next, when the uncle came in with the matron.

Shweta greeted her uncle while helping Christine to sit up on her cot. It seemed all the women were anxious to slip pillows behind her and Christine got the feeling that the skinny Indian who had rescued her was the head of the family.

"*Namastay,*" Christine said.

The greeting was nasal, but generally clear, and she was surprised how little her face hurt. Christine gently fingered a mound of poultice over her nose, and smiled at the uncle whose yellow turban was much darker than the sun she had thought it to be.

The women in the room smiled back, but the man's eyes darted, avoiding her glance.

Christine tried to thank him in her minimal Hindi. The children in the room snickered as she muddled on, until the Indian finally bowed. Leaving Christine in midsentence, he left abruptly.

"Did I say something wrong?" Christine said.

Shweta blushed as she translated. The matron laughed the loudest while the other women chattered between more giggles. Christine wondered what she had said that was so funny.

"Forgive me," Shweta said. She gestured toward the dark woman with her birthmark, her bracelets, and her nose ring. She wasn't much older than Shweta. "This is a new wife of my uncle."

Christine nodded to the woman she had mistaken for his daughter. Then Shweta turned to the matron and another old woman, who seemed to have a few good teeth.

"Number-one wife and number-two wife for my uncle."

"The skinny man with the turban?" Christine asked.

Shweta translated, and the two older women howled. The young wife slapped them both, smirking and saying something that sounded snide. It must've been funny as well, because the old women could barely stand. Christine asked Shweta to translate, but the girl was too red and Christine suddenly understood.

"My uncle very —" started Shweta. "How do you say old . . . old times?"

"Old-fashioned?"

Shweta nodded eagerly. "Yes. Very old-fashioned."

"One wife, too modern . . . *Ji?*" joked Christine.

"*Ji,* too modern."

Shweta translated, and the women seem to agree, reeling off into conversation.

Later the women left to feed the men while Shweta tended to Christine's wounds. Christine liked the girl, who couldn't have been more than fifteen. She seemed eager to talk of her family, her five brothers, her two sisters, and her parents, who worked in a factory that cut semiprecious stones in Jaipur. When Christine asked where she had learned to speak English, Shweta said that she and three other women took English in a nearby village. She wanted to learn as much as she could before she married.

"You're getting married?" Christine asked.

Shweta glanced down nervously. "Yes. I very fortunate to make much-important match. I to marry a brick maker from Bikaner."

Shweta's smile was tight and Christine thought she chose her words a little too carefully.

"Does . . . he . . . have other wives?"

Shweta didn't understand.

"Old-fashioned? Is he . . ."

The girl laughed, but Christine sensed it took effort.

"No, he is no old. Modern, I think."

"Is he handsome, your betrothed?" Christine asked.

The girl shrugged, keeping her eyes down.

Christine realized Shweta had probably never seen the man she was destined to spend her life with. But before Christine could inquire further, Shweta asked how Christine came to be in the desert alone. It was Christine's turn to be vague. She stammered something about a sandstorm and getting separated from her guide. Shweta clearly knew she was lying, but didn't push.

"I very sorry, but I must uncover you now."

The girl waited for Christine to nod, then lifted the blanket and the indigo sari the women had slipped on her after the uncle had brought her in. Shweta hardly hesitated to part Christine's legs. It seemed it was the uncovering of her body that was more difficult for her.

"You not hurt so much?" Shweta asked as she salved the wounds where Nikhil had inadvertently ripped away a patch of pubic hair.

"Not so much."

For several moments, they didn't talk as Shweta nursed her with the unconscious ease of a family member.

"You say animal did this?"

For a moment Christine considered telling her the truth. But then the girl's expression turned fearful, and Christine couldn't.

"Yes, *ji*. It was an animal. A bad animal."

Shweta nodded, lowering her eyes. "I very sorry, Kharis." She inhaled sharply and creases etched her forehead as she fought to contain herself. Christine was glad she hadn't spoken of Nikhil and wondered if the girl was thinking about the stranger in Bikaner.

The next day, Christine insisted on walking to the toilet. The rags the women had placed beneath her in bed were chafing her backside and she needed to get up.

Shweta helped Christine across a small courtyard occupied by various family members, including a one-hundred-and-two-year-old matriarch who sat cross-legged while smoking a giant pipe. The family's home was a low stone structure that housed twenty-two people. Sparsely furnished with a few blocked ethnic prints adorning the yellow sandstone walls, there were four sleeping areas separated by lacquered screens made of camel skin, with tie-and-dye and hand-blocked bedding, and a few string cots. Figurines of Hindu gods were mounted and placed about, while bent rabbit ears crisscrossed atop the only television. Between puffs the old woman and her grandchildren laughed at a seventies-style rock-'n'-roll host who prattled on in Hindi.

"Hellah, lady. How'd you?" cried three boys who suddenly darted into view.

"I'm fine. And you?"

There was no more conversation. Just a loud *whoop!* and the boys scattered while women Christine assumed to be their mothers stood by, content to watch. In her travels, she had noticed that Indian women might stand idle for hours, infants and toddlers affixed to their bodies. Just then it was between meals and the day was hot.

Except for observing the foreigner, a curious but apparently popular diversion, there wouldn't be much physical activity until dinner.

As they headed to the back of the dwelling, Christine heard a snort and felt a spray of mucus before Shweta could warn her of the chained water buffalo. Christine jumped back from the panting beast, sliding into a patch of muddy sludge.

"I sorry, Kharis," cried Shweta, steadying her. "She just birth and Uncle sell baby. She not happy, I think."

"No," Christine agreed, wiping the slime off her arms.

Two teenage girls were crouched behind the irate buffalo, scooping up the fetid dung and applying rows of buffalo patties to the rear wall of the dwelling. The primitive fuel would dry and later be used to cook their meals. The air was black with flies and the ground sodden with urine and fresh manure, and Christine almost slipped again. She forced a smile, and the girls grinned back as they pressed dung between their palms. Beside them was a ramshackle wooden box, the size of a large telephone booth. It reeked horribly.

"Hella, lady!"

Christine gasped at the chorus of voices

behind her. Carefully, she planted her feet and turned. The three boys were back, with other boys and girls of all sizes, and all, it seemed, eager to practice their English.

As Christine studied the herd of beaming faces, a brave few shrieked what might have been another greeting. She wasn't sure and wondered if that was how she sounded to them.

Trying not to retch at the odor, she carefully said, "Hel-lo." The kids squealed with laughter, the boys punching at one another, the little girls tittering and hiding their faces. They said "hel-lo," over and over again.

How could they stand it, Christine wondered? The heat, the dung, the stench — just the general monotony of their lives offended her. She fixed a smile and tried not to judge them, but their existence was so foreign to her that she decided that they couldn't know better, when she heard someone yelling.

"Kharizheen! Kharizheen!"

Christine looked out into the desert and saw the three wives. The younger two each carried a large painted jug on her head; the matron balanced a monstrous bundle of brush with only a glimmer of teeth showing beneath. Even with their unwieldy cargos the women kept upright and managed to wave vigorously at their guest.

Christine waved back. "Where are they going?"

"The village," Shweta said simply.

"Is it far?"

Shweta cocked her head side to side. Christine recognized the gesture from Delhi. This time she knew it meant "Not really, no big deal."

She looked out in the direction the women were headed. It was flat and desolate except for dry scrub and the occasional banyan tree. It might be hours before they reached the village. Christine watched the wives grow smaller, their bright saris billowing with the breeze as they chatted among themselves. Bangled and made-up (even the matron), they walked as if carrying their burdens was no chore at all.

The scrawny uncle and his women . . . all three, Christine mused. Yet they seemed to manage. Christine would have bet that the old woman's pipe held a fair amount of opium. All during her musing, small children scampered up and down off her cot, the visits short but continuous. And twice Christine saw Shweta's brother, Rahul,

131

bend so the old woman could run twiglike fingers through his tufts of dark hair, all the while grinning.

In Delhi, city life seemed more vibrant. In spite of the clouds of dust that rose from the congested roads, the colors were dazzling. There were designs and patterns, wherever one looked. Lavishly adorned vehicles, even huge Bedford trucks bore six-foot portraits of veiled beauties that teased and intrigued. Truck horns trilled and honked constantly as children dashed across their paths while, here and there, a sacred cow lingered uninhibited amid the chaos. But children were everywhere, some crippled by their own mothers to make them more poignant beggars. And forgotten old widows scavenged among strangers in mounds of trash that lay unattended. Even on streets teeming with bodies, people were alone.

Out here, at the uncle's, the wilderness had its own civility. The old woman spending her last years, sucking on a pipe with her progeny crowded around her, seemed content. And now Christine could hear the faint laughter from the wives whose red and fuchsia saris dotted the landscape. There were few luxuries, but even fewer frustrations.

Shweta had asked about the United States and said she actually knew a girl who lived in San Francisco. They corresponded regularly and Shweta seemed eager to leave the desert and her family.

Christine couldn't blame her, but thought of the duplex in which she had lived alone for years, not knowing her neighbors, and hardly dating. Her mother complained that she didn't visit enough, and she didn't. If it wasn't for the company, she'd never see Liz. She was too busy, her friends lived too far away, and it seemed like there was never enough time to socialize. Christine was grateful that there wasn't some stranger in the next city she would have to marry, but she had struggled with her own feelings of isolation, and suddenly Christine wasn't so sure who knew better.

"Kharis, do you need help?" Shweta asked, waiting for her to make a move toward the box.

Christine brought herself back to the here and now, dodged the mud, the dung, and entered the box. She stared at a filthy ceramic slab set in the ground, and held her nose, grateful that Shweta couldn't see her.

The next morning, Christine kept her

eyes closed, feigning sleep. She heard the women rustling about, but needed time to think before engaging in Hindu protocol. She appreciated their hospitality, but wasn't used to the constant attention. She had been with them for three days and still had no plan.

The uncle had offered to take her by donkey to the next village, where his brother-in-law was the prosperous owner of three camels. They could use the creatures to transfer her to Bikaner. It was hardly a metropolis, but there would be a phone. She could call Cloid. Without a passport or money, she felt helpless.

And then Christine heard his voice. Images and options charged confusingly through her mind as Shweta greeted Nikhil Sahgal at the door. By the time Christine opened her eyes, he was already peering down at her.

"Hello, Christine."

There was no surprise on his face; Nikhil knew he would find her. Shweta stepped up beside him.

"You awake. Look!" she exclaimed happily. "Your husband come to you."

"He's not my husband," Christine snapped.

Shweta looked perplexed. Nikhil said

134

something to the girl in Hindi. He was talking too fast, but when he turned back to her, the way he looked at her with almost a sneer, she knew she was in trouble. Christine lunged at him, but Nikhil caught her hand. He said something to Shweta as he pulled her up off the cot and steered her toward the door.

"Shweta," Christine pleaded. "Don't listen to him!"

He jerked her back against him, keeping her arm bent behind her. "Knock it off," he hissed while smiling at members of the family who had gathered in the doorway. Nikhil gave her arm a twist, but Shweta's brother saw it and started yelling. She felt Nikhil brace himself for a fight. She could see the uncle, his lanky frame rigid and his jaw clenched, was clearly holding himself back. Nikhil repeated the warning, and this time Christine picked up *"mara patni,"* "my wife."

"Na mara patni! Na!" Christine shouted and he twisted her arm once more, pushing her toward the door. The uncle and his nephews glared at him as he passed, but they didn't intervene.

"Please," Christine cried, "he raped me."

Shweta looked frantic. She didn't understand.

Christine tried again. "He's the animal! He hurt me . . . Nikhil's the animal!"

"Shut up!" he shouted, taking her to the camels.

The old woman watched from her cot in the courtyard as he moved past her. Christine tried to twist away, but couldn't. Her body throbbed with new pain.

"Wait, please!" Shweta called out.

"My wife and I are in a hurry."

Shweta caught up and stood facing Christine, forcing Nikhil to pause.

Christine was crying so hard, she could barely speak. "I'm not his wife. He'll kill me. Please believe me."

Tears came to Shweta's eyes, but Christine could see that she was scared. She started to speak, but the old woman snapped angrily at the girl, her voice surprisingly strong. Shweta took off her scarf and draped it over Christine's head.

"Shweta —"

The young woman shook her head in warning as tears streamed down her cheek. "No, Kharis. You too sick. Your husband take care of you."

Nikhil pushed Christine along, nudging Shweta aside. It wasn't much, but enough to provoke Rahul. Her brother moved toward Nikhil, but the uncle grabbed him and a quarrel broke out as Nikhil forced her onto the kneeling camel. Pain flared between her legs and she stifled a cry. Christine braced herself as the beast rocked to its feet and, for a moment, she considered letting the movement throw her off. Her neck might break, but at least her suffering would be over.

Behind her, Rahul and his younger brother, who didn't trust the stranger any more than Rahul, argued with the uncle. Even the young wife with the many bracelets and the birthmark tried to intervene, but when the uncle began to yell, waving his arms wildly over their heads, the family's entreaties ceased.

Christine tried to catch the young wife's eye, but the woman wouldn't look her way. When Christine turned away, and the uncle averted his eyes, the woman signaled to her stepson.

As Nikhil took the reins of her camel, Christine saw that the children were also silent. The old woman leaned against the doorway, her thin lips working as she gummed something. Her expression held no sympathy for Christine. She had survived the time of *sati*, when wives were expected to mount the pyre with the bodies of their deceased husband. To her, Christine's dilemma hardly warranted notice.

Atop his camel Nikhil led Christine's mount around the back, bypassing the fenced garden where the family cow chewed at shoots of mustard. The back of the building was covered with neat rows of buffalo patties; the girls had finished. Christine tried not to cry.

Once they had passed into the desert, she looked back. The low sandstone dwelling with its few livestock and its small garden seemed insignificant in the vast wasteland.

Just as she was about to turn away, she saw Rahul and his brother scoot around the back on two bony donkeys. They hollered as they switched the animals into a frenzy to catch up. The boys were nearly young men, so they had to bend their knees to keep their legs from dragging on the ground. Christine almost cheered when she saw them trotting to her rescue. But they lurched to a stop while still a hundred feet behind her.

Nikhil looked back and shouted angrily. Rahul quickly retorted. Grumbling under his breath, Nikhil jerked at the reins.

The boys moved forward as Nikhil pulled her behind him. Shweta's brothers seemed intent on following them. For how long, Christine didn't know.

They had ridden into territory dotted with scrub brush and bumper crops of sugar cane and wheat. But somehow Nikhil had managed to steer clear of any villages. The former security guard had said little to her but looked around frequently to see if the boys were still behind them. And they were. They followed until the sun dipped low in the sky. Then she saw that they were dropping back, until finally they were gone.

It would be dark soon, and without the boys as witnesses, Nikhil would hurt her, or worse. Her eyes darted about the camel litter she sat in, hoping to find something she could use to defend herself, when she heard a faint sound off to her right. Her eye caught movement; there were people in the distance.

Cringing at the pain in her groin, she sat up on the camel. It was greener in the distance. More fields, she thought. She counted seven people working in the fields, and behind them she saw buildings. Not just a few mud cubicles, but actual buildings. It had to be a village.

She could scream, but what good would it do? The sun was descending. Christine figured she had twenty or thirty minutes of light left. Her heart beat wildly as she considered jumping off and running, but she was still too far from them.

A couple of the workers waved to them.

Christine looked over at Nilhil. He had also seen the people, and for a moment she thought he had planned to take her to the village. Then her camel bawled as its reins were jerked hard to the left, away from the villagers.

Christine's breath came fast and hard as she tried to decide whether to jump. The sun was going down. She had to move. As she drew a breath, Nikhil looked back at her. That dead-eyed stare was all it took. She swung her leg around, jumped, hit the ground, and stumbled facedown.

Dirt dug into one side of her face, like sandpaper. She couldn't believe she remained conscious. As Nikhil screamed at her, the small voice in her head blurted, *Go Go!* and she was up and moving.

The people seemed to be running toward her. She was desperate to believe they would help her while behind her Nikhil was cursing and whipping at the camels.

"Bachao!" she yelled, pleading for help. *"Bachao!"*

Christine looked back, veering sharply

away just as a hairy, sinewy haunch knocked her sideways to the ground. She was gasping through a mouthful of dirt, but had only grazed her cheek. She heard the camel kicking, turning back toward her. She tried to move, but she was too slow, and in an instant the beast was over her.

Sand and brush thrashed about her. Something nicked her left forearm and she cried out. Then it was gone and she rolled over, stunned, her stomach churning. Blinking away the sand, Christine managed to sit up, holding her arm. There was a deep V-shaped cut where the camel had clipped her. She threw up while Nikhil and the camel, puffing from the exertion, circled her.

"See what you did," Nikhil said. "You have to ride with me now."

"Fuck you," she groaned.

Christine pressed her hand against the oozing wound and rose to her feet. Nikhil laughed, said something, but Christine wasn't listening. Her legs were pumping beneath her and all she could think of were the sprints she had run in high school. She hadn't been very good. Now, as her legs carried her toward help, she realized she had missed her calling — marathon runner. A strained laugh escaped from her. She wanted to stop, but already the camel was huffing along in a phlegmy pant directly behind her. She tried to step aside, but Nikhil seized the back of her sari. Dazed, Christine hardly reacted as he dragged her alongside the camel. Finally, she planted her feet, stopped, twisted around, and bit down deeply into his forearm. With a scream, he dropped her. Now the people were shouting, and Christine strained to lift her head. She saw that the villagers had stopped running toward them. She raised up her arm. Blood streamed between her fingers, and a wave of nausea swept over her.

"Had enough?" Nikhil said, smiling down at her from his camel.

Her chapped lips had cracked opened, and her own blood tasted sour. Christine nodded weakly.

"Good," he said.

Nikhil extended a hand and she feebly climbed to her feet. The Indian's face reflected the bright orange of the sun, and Christine thought he looked appropriately demonic. She turned to see that the people were still not moving, but they were waving and trying to call to them. She was close enough to make out their dark complexions. No surprise there, except their clothing was different. They wore long tunics over baggy pants and some of them had thick coils of white cloth spun around their heads while others wore small colorful caps.

"Who?" was all she had the strength to ask.

"Savages."

Christine saw that Nikhil was scowling at the field workers. He hated them, she realized. Their mouths worked feverishly while their arms flailed about and the thought that they might hurt her scared her. Still she couldn't imagine anyone worse than Nikhil. She stepped forward.

The ground beneath her had become rough, uneven. Christine wondered if it had been worked at one time but now lay fallow. She slowed, dodging a hole, then another hole, and her ankle turned and she almost tripped. Panting, Christine stopped and looked behind her. The sun was sinking toward the horizon as Nikhil and the camels loomed before her, blocking the last bit of flame from the sky. Then she saw Nikhil reach into his saddlebag and pull out her gun, Ullas's gun.

The semiautomatic seemed dull and lifeless as he leveled it at her. Christine was tired of running, until she saw something round and dun-colored protruding from the ground. It was just ahead of Nikhil's camel and to its right, and she turned away, her feet dragging beneath her. Nikhil shot. It was close, but Christine did not flinch. She only moved to her right, and Nikhil followed.

The villagers were still waving madly, not far really, but Christine knew they would be her last sight.

When the blast came, it was much louder and hotter than she had expected. There was an instant of force, and then she was on the ground. She tried to get up, but couldn't rise. Her legs felt warm and moist, and in the twilight she could see that they were drenched in blood. Numbly, she looked up.

The blast had spun her about, and she landed facing west. The sun had vanished, leaving only a lit sky to aid her. She could barely make out the pieces of camel and supplies that littered the ground before her. The camel she had ridden was down on its belly, frothing huge bubbles of blood that swelled, popped, then swelled again from its nostrils. Beneath the animal lay what looked like a sizable portion of torso and hip,

144

patched with blood-soaked khakis.

Before her mind could grasp that Nikhil was really dead, the cries from the villagers unexpectedly returned as if someone had just turned up the volume. She managed to turn her face and stared at them, clumped together before her a hundred yards away. Their arms were thrashing about, frantic, intent on . . .

They're signaling a mine field . . . I'm in a mine field.

Chapter
7

It was three-thirty in the morning and Cloid had been asleep for less than an hour when the phone rang. He snatched at it.

"Cloid Dale here."

"Cloid?"

It was Marsha, Christine's mom. Her voice was thick with emotion and Cloid felt that flutter in his chest, his body already anticipating the worst.

"I'm here."

"Cloid . . ." Her voice broke. "It's Chris. She's — she's been in an accident . . . a land mine. My god, a land mine."

"Is she —"

"They don't know. It must've just happened."

Cloid finally caught a breath. In India nothing "just happened."

Communications dribbled in over days or weeks, not hours. If they weren't calling to inform next of kin, then there was still hope. Cloid took down the names of the people who called. State and the Bureau would be easy; the CIA would be a pain in the ass. An investigator from CBI? Cloid didn't recognize the name, had to be one of Raghavan's underlings. Whatever the response, Cloid knew it wouldn't be swift.

It took days filled with circuitous rounds of phone tag, testy secretaries, and the unceasing drone of recorded messages to determine that there had indeed been an accident and that Nikhil Saghal was dead. The information had been slow in coming, but Cloid finally got his background on Nikhil Sahgal. Fifty-four years of age, the Indian Christine had been traveling with was six-foot-one, and two hundred and ten pounds. Sahgal was of Chinese and Mongolian descent, a former colonel in the Indian army, and had a wife and four children. It appeared that early in his career there had been some kind of gross dereliction of duty, although the file on that was uncharacteristically vague. But later, it became clear that Sahgal had committed a number of infractions over the years, one of which was a complaint filed against him by another government employee, a woman. Cloid guessed it was not an offense to which the Indian government was likely to assign any importance. The report was incomplete, and there was no follow-up of the incident in the files.

The thought that Christine might have perished in a land mine explosion that spewed pieces of the ex-colonel for almost a hundred yards was traumatic enough. But it was India and its sluggish bureaucracy that frustrated Cloid most. It took another three weeks just to verify that Christine's body had not been found at the site of the accident. With news of Liz still pending, Cloid was ready to get back on the plane.

Remnants of Christine's clothing, her passport, and a few old packets of antibiotics were all that the Indians were willing to admit they had found. Finally, an old Vietnam buddy who had married the daughter of a former Indian minister of Parliament, called in with some interesting data. There was a goat herder who thought he saw a woman on the desert, a kid at a teahouse who might've served Sahgal and Christine, and finally a man at a camel station who after a hundred-rupee bribe admitted that he had rented Sahgal and an American woman two camels.

It wasn't much to go on, but after a

meeting at the Bureau with Special Agent Thomas Rogers, Cloid learned that an Indian family had claimed to nurse a woman who fit Christine's description. She had been separated from her husband in the desert and was in pretty bad shape when they found her.

Traveling the hinterlands of India as husband and wife was not a bad idea, given the locals' religious views, but Cloid wondered why she would ever strike out into the desert alone. That didn't make sense.

"How'd they get separated?" Cloid asked.

Rogers shrugged. "The family didn't say."

"And she was hurt?"

"Not hurt exactly. Fried's more like it. They found her wandering in the desert, although they did say something about animals getting at her." The agent grimaced. "I don't know what the deal was with that. Guess she was pretty lucky they found her?"

"Who'd you talk to in India?"

"Mostly bureaucrats. You know how that can be."

"I'll need some names."

Rogers shook his head with an almost inaudible cluck of his tongue. He leaned back in his chair, looking far too comfortable and far too sharp. Hugo Boss suit and moussed bangs would never have made the grade in Cloid's squad, when hair was crew cut or short and out of the way and a black suit and white shirt were the uniform. The agents he had worked with tried to be inconspicuous; Rogers looked like he was posing for a magazine.

"All right." Cloid sighed. "You got anything else for me before I look up some old friends in Delhi?"

The agent tensed, shifting in his chair. "I don't know if you should do that."

Cloid smiled. "Of course, I should. It would stir things up a bit, and I doubt the Bureau would want the Indians ruffled over this anymore than they already are. But if you can't tell me —"

"Look," Rogers said. "There's not much. The family's mostly illiterate and I was told we couldn't really count them as a reliable source."

"Why not?"

"You know, they're . . . those untouchables, nomads. 'Scheduled Castes,' I guess they're called."

Rogers was sitting upright, no longer comfortable, and Cloid liked that. Rogers had even taken an unconscious swipe at his hair.

"So," Cloid exhaled, "Sahgal came . . . and he and the woman left. That's it?"

Rogers hesitated. His wheels were spinning, a little stiff, still too new, but spinning nonetheless. "There was . . . some conflict," he admitted. "If you choose to believe those people."

"I do."

Now it was the knuckles. Rogers was working them. Cloid waited until the young agent finally extracted a dull crack. "Maybe I'd better talk to someone first. This is getting a little —"

"A little risky?" Cloid broke in. "Might say something you shouldn't?" *You little shit,* Cloid thought to himself. *The Bureau must be hard up these days. Or maybe they just don't give a damn what happened out there.*

Cloid leaned forward, breathing what he knew to be very stale breath into the rookie's face.

"Kevin —"

"Tom," the agent gently amended.

"Check with Johnson if you want. It's a waste of the SAC's goddamn time, and mine. But go ahead, and when he hears that I didn't get what I needed, he'll understand why I had no choice but to —"

"No choice but to do what?"

Cloid stood and Rogers almost jumped out of his seat.

"I'm — I'm sorry," he almost stammered. "I just don't know if I can."

"You can. I'm giving you permission. Sit down and quit fucking around."

Tom Rogers sat, his bottom barely grazing the seat. He was popping all his knuckles now. Cloid also sat, his eyes piercing the agent.

"So there was a screwup," Cloid concluded. "Was it the embassy?"

"No . . . I . . . I don't know what you mean?"

"Yes, you do. You said there was a conflict and you didn't know if you were allowed to divulge information to me, even though I sat where you are not so long ago? Shit! I helped invent the Counterterrorism Task Force!"

"It wasn't really the embassy. It's just that with the Kashmir situation and the nuclear flare-up between India and Pakistan, relations are a little strained. We're trying to let things settle a bit, not . . . not, ah . . ."

"Make noise!"

Rogers nodded nervously.

"Well, tough. There are two Americans not accounted for, and if I don't start getting some answers, I'm going to make a helluva lot of noise. Might even write a goddamn book!"

Rogers could barely disguise his panic. "No, don't do that. Certainly I can tell you what happened. You should know, Mr. Dale, that the Bureau is doing everything possible to locate Miss Shepherd."

"Just tell me what you've got."

"Yes . . . okay. Ah . . . there's not much except that the woman was still in bad shape and Nikhil Sahgal just snatched her. The family didn't like it. Got a little rough, it sounds like. If you want to —"

"Believe those people. I know," Cloid finished. "Who's your source?"

The agent sighed, stalling. Cloid gave him a moment, and then exhaled loudly gripping the arms of the chair to rise again.

"Aamir Bechara," Tom relented.

"One of the embassy attachés?"

Rogers nodded. "The family didn't want to let her go, but they couldn't do much. Sahgal was the man, you know. Claimed to be the husband. The Indian consul doesn't have a record of any marriage, but the guy was Hindu. Could've had five wives as far as they know."

"So he forced her to leave?"

"No, I asked that. I guess there's no such thing as 'force' between husbands and wives in India." He smiled. "My wife's from Chicago. Can you imagine? She'd beat the hell outta me if I tried to force her to do anything."

Cloid looked up. Rogers wore a stupid grin. Cloid tried to recall whether he himself had been so obviously stupid when he started at the Bureau. He hoped not.

"Yeah. Well, maybe you'll get lucky and they'll send you over there."

Not catching the sarcasm, the agent seemed pleased. When Cloid stood, Rogers quickly jumped up to shake his hand. Cloid took his hand.

"Thanks for your help, Kevin. Appreciate it."

Tom Rogers started to correct him, but thought better of it. "If there's anything else, please call me. I hope you got what you needed. It's just that they don't, uh . . ."

"Want anyone to stir it up," Cloid added impatiently. "Probably not."

Cloid mumbled something under his breath, and before Special Agent Rogers could say good-bye, the older man was out the door and gone.

That night Cloid heard from Raghavan in the Central Bureau of Intelligence in Delhi. They had finally gotten confirmation that Farrukh Ahmed, a Muslim separatist, a terrorist, had been responsible for the destruction of Padamthala. Raghavan assured Cloid that Ahmed was just another extremist, more of a nuisance domestically than internationally, hardly an Abu Nidal, and that they should have him in custody anytime. Ahmed had razed villages, had even killed other Muslims, anyone who dealt with Westerners, especially Americans. But kidnapping, Raghavan emphasized, was not included in the government's profile of Farrukh Ahmed.

What General Raghavan didn't say, but Cloid knew, was that both governments were already spinning scenarios that had nothing to do with terrorists, or foul play, or anything other than a young woman's whim for exotic travel. Raghavan told Cloid that the tissue that had been found by the Hindu shrine would be released soon so that a DNA test could be performed in an American lab. He didn't go beyond that, and had nothing to say about Christine.

For a couple of weeks after the land mine explosion there had been a flurry of activity. Two officials from the Indian consulate in Los Angeles and two minders from the State Department had visited Cloid and Marsha. For days they were bombarded with questions.

It became clear that Nikhil Sahgal, a low-level government employee, had signed out on medical leave. His wife was predictably oblivious, unaware that her husband had trekked across the Thar Desert in the company of another woman. But in May, just after India exploded its first nukes, Pakistan did five of its own. Any questions that the bankrupt Muslim state was not nuclear capable had been answered, and Cloid had a feeling that Sahgal's proximity to Pakistan at the time of his death was more of a concern than another land mine accident.

Cloid confronted Raghavan. It took a couple of calls, but the general finally admitted to his call with Christine, but when asked about a flesh trade, the Indian was emphatic that such a practice within their borders was impossible.

Ultimately, it was the confirmation of Sahgal's death that gave the Indian government license to ease its own investigation.

Land mines that were intended to eliminate Muslim extremists, Kashmiri rebels, and Pakistani spies might have also eliminated a traitor. Everyone it seemed, the United States included, was anxious to draw the distasteful mishap to a swift conclusion.

Back at the range house, Cloid's hands flew over the yellowed keyboard. His Everex computer was six years old, obsolete by anyone's measure, but like its operator it still had plenty of life in it, and Cloid was determined to utilize it to its end, or his. Whichever came first.

An Internet search for the name Farrukh Ahmed revealed that the man Raghavan described as a mere nuisance had already killed two hundred and sixteen people, seven of whom were Americans. With eight attacks in six years, Mr. Ahmed had made the top five of India's most wanted. The fact that India and Pakistan had been at war for fifty years was old news, but the Kashmiri conflict had already claimed twenty thousand Indian lives since 1971, and the list of dissidents was growing.

Cloid's fingers paused on the keys and he leaned back in his chair, unconsciously rubbing his chest as he tried to piece together what had happened to Christine. He took a breath to ease the tightness and reached for the phone. Even at this late hour he knew Marsha would be up. He thought of her friends at her church initiating a series of prayer chains and wanted to have faith; he was desperate to believe that both girls were alive. After Glen Shepherd's death it had been easy to slide into that role of surrogate father, a role that Cloid, a Bureau pensioner and an old bachelor, had coveted but never found time for. For both girls to die in such bizarre circumstances would be a cruel irony, a freakish twist of fate that he refused to accept. However, he was seventy-two years old and he had seen many strange things.

He sat, staring at the computer screen, and rubbed at his chest. Through the weeks the pressure he felt there had worsened and the idea that he might be having heart trouble had occurred to him. He knew he couldn't go on much longer without checking in with his cardiologist, but anything was better than the remorse he was fighting. Marsha had been right; he never should have left Christine.

Trying to ease the tightness in his chest, Cloid burped. The open window beside him was black. The night was overcast and no star was visible. He felt tired and depressed. His eyes closed. The phone rang, startling him into wakefulness.

"Damn it!" His glance shifted to the illuminated clock — 11:58 p.m. It would be late afternoon in India. The Pacific Time clock hardly existed for him anymore. He picked up the phone, anticipating some more questions from the Indian government.

"What?" he barked.

There was static.

"Cloid? Cloid? Can you hear me?"

Christine's voice was distant, muddied by cross talk on the line. But Cloid could hear her. He swallowed, trying to quell the rush of emotion that threatened to overwhelm him. He managed to sit upright, leaning his shoulder against the desk for support. He took a breath and yelled into the phone.

"Chrissy . . . sweet Jesus. You're alive! Where the hell are you?"

"Pakistan —"

Strange voices, more distinct, foreign, broke in on the line.

"Chris? Chris!" His cool façade, carefully cultivated during almost three decades on the bricks with the Bureau, disappeared. He gripped his chest, almost panicked.

Christine's voice abruptly emerged from a rush of gibberish. "Cloid, what? What is it?"

He tried to regain control of his breathing. His chest was pounding. There was another burst of static on the line.

"Who the hell was that?" he managed.

"They're friends. They saved my life."

"You're in Pakistan?"

"Yes, but —"

"Where? And when are you coming home?" Cloid barked.

"I can't talk to you about it now. These lines aren't great. I'll lose you."

More static.

"Yes, you will talk," he shouted.

"Please, Cloid, I don't have much time. I need you to wire funds to Islamabad, and then have someone I can trust meet me in Peshawar."

The line had cleared and Cloid could hear her, but the place she mentioned caught in his mind. Peshawar was a city near the Afghanistan border, and it scared him. The place was filled with drugs, and arms, and terrorists. The local fundamentalists had even tried to burn down a U.S. consulate there once, with the bureaucrats still in it.

"Christine . . ." He tried to sound calm.

"You're scaring me. I don't know if —"

"I know. I just can't explain now."

Cloid turned away from the phone, grimacing against the cramping of the muscle in his chest. He was hurting, but his imagination was burning with images of guns and knives with exotic steel blades, possibly at Christine's throat, and suddenly Cloid was sure she had been taken for ransom, or worse, as an American hostage.

He had to keep his head; he had to help her. "What do you need?"

The voices behind her erupted and Christine responded, apparently in the same language . . . slowly, awkwardly. Cloid strained to detect any note of fear in what she said, but it sounded like . . . *Were they giggling?*

Cloid couldn't tell who was talking, but there was no mistaking the voices. They were women, and now he could hear them clearly. Christine was speaking in gibberish, and yes, it was giggling.

"Chris, are you really okay?"

"I'm sorry, Cloid," she said, returning to him. "Yes, I'm fine. Just a little banged up."

"The land mine?"

"Yeah, but can you write this down? I'm

161

afraid of these lines."

"Hold on, I need a pen." Cloid gasped as another spasm took his body. He laid the phone aside and jerked open a drawer, grabbing at a bottle of aspirin. He twisted at the cap.

Christine started talking to him, but he couldn't respond. The contraction in his chest was almost more than he could stand.

"Hang on," he puffed. Finally he bit at the cap, wrenching it off, and ate what was left in the bottle. He buckled over on the desk, holding until he could tolerate the pain. He still felt like he was dying, but at least he could function. He took the phone.

"You're in Peshawar?" he roared, disoriented.

"Not yet. What's wrong?"

"Just tell me what you need," he snapped gruffly, grabbing at a pen.

Christine hesitated, then said, "I need someone with military experience to meet me at the Pearl Continental Hotel in Peshawar in three days."

She needed a contact. Why? And then Cloid thought about Farrukh Ahmed. Did she know? And if she did, what in the hell was she thinking?

"Can't you just come home?"

"No."

"She's gone, honey."

There was a long pause.

"You saw her?" Christine's voice was barely audible.

He sighed. "No, but they're running a DNA test on something they found."

For several seconds she didn't answer. Even the voices behind her had quieted.

"You don't have to help me if you don't want to," she insisted, her voice wavering. "But I need someone who knows his way around."

Cloid didn't know what to think. Was she in trouble or was she still intent on going after Liz? More static intervened when something hot and unbearable shot into his shoulder. He cried out, then quickly uttered, "Goddamn cheap lines."

Christine was silent. The line had cleared, but neither of them spoke. The distance and their situations rendered them both powerless, so Cloid just reassured her that he would find someone "with experience." Finally, the blessed static and distant voices of party-line babble began to fill the void.

Big tears came down beside his nose. Christine wanted to go to Peshawar, a place that was probably out of Cloid's reach. The old man was desperate to tell her to stop whatever silliness she was planning and to come home. But what if she couldn't.

"I miss you," she muttered.

"Me, too, kiddo."

He gripped the phone, holding on until he could hear the click of her phone when the line finally disengaged.

Cloid let out a long, painful sigh. He felt relief that she was alive, and terror that her ordeal was not over. He had to remember that she *was* her father's daughter and had virtually been raised on the rifle range. She had been exposed to a mind-set Cloid wasn't particularly proud of, but it might save her . . . or get her killed.

Then Cloid was reminded of his own dilemma, and gave in to the throb in his chest. He doubled over, fingered the lever to get a dial tone, and called his neighbor, who wasted no time in getting him to the hospital.

Chapter
8

The sun had been up for nearly two hours by the time Cloid Alder Dale was wheeled into the intensive care unit. The space was stark white, sterile, and serene, except for the high-pitched sound of the hospital bed as the attendant adjusted it. The old man didn't stir.

The nurse came in moments later. She connected him to several monitors, aligned the tubes from the various drips, and took readings for his chest. He tried to speak.

"Yes, Mr. Dale?" the nurse replied. "I couldn't hear you."

She bent close, but his lips had stopped moving. Accustomed to the vagaries of medicated patients, the nurse stood erect, smoothed her white uniform, and finished taking notes. Before she left, she pulled at the blinds to prevent the patient from getting overheated in the strong morning sunlight, and took a try at adjusting Cloid's bed. The bed squealed. She stopped, concluding that Mr. Dale would let her know later if he was uncomfortable. After an additional check of Cloid's IVs, the nurse left the room, gently closing the door behind her.

Half a world away and due east, Christine was mounting concrete stairs to a space that was not so sterile or bright, even during the day, where only a single, shuttered window provided light. The accommodation resembled a bunker and at night the concrete room was damp. The glare of a fluorescent tab of bug repellent protruded from the peeling walls and filled the room with an eerie glow. Lying on a thin pad atop an iron-and-string cot, Christine grabbed at the scratchy blanket, pulling it up over her head. The green glow bled through the loose weave of camel and sheep hair and she closed her eyes. She thought about Cloid, her call to him the day before, and the sound of his voice. He didn't sound well. And when she had told her new friends that evening at dinner of her plan to go to Peshawar, they also seemed distressed.

The people who had cared for Christine

since Nikhil's death had worked tirelessly to make her time with them agreeable. She was their guest, and they did what they could to please her. And she thought of that, just that, as she turned over on the cot, cupping her ears, desperate to block out the sounds of an argument from the room above her. She had grown used to the faint illumination of the mosquito light, but the angry voices kept her awake.

Ruhee was crying, and Nazeem, her young husband, was yelling. Christine had tried to learn Urdu, Pakistan's national language, but she could still barely hold a simple conversation. Her ignorance, however, did not keep her from knowing what Ruhee and her husband were fighting about. She felt the grinding ache in her stomach that usually meant the local food had gotten to her, but this time the cause wasn't parasites, or the recollection of Nikhil's messy death, or even the rape.

For the first six weeks of her stay with the Javid family, they had continuously watched over her in a hospital in Lahore. Each took a turn, including Samina, who had spent her twelfth birthday sitting cross-legged on top of the narrow cot. Sometimes the men would be near, but they never approached, never spoke, only watched until one of the women of their family was free to replace them. Then when the poor villagers' money ran out, and the doctors rejected their offers of poultry and goats, they took her back to their village, Banalwala. The Pakistanis had clothed her, housed her, fed her, and prayed for her. Through her bit of Urdu and the family's attempt at English, Christine began to understand the tremendous value Muslims attributed to their guests.

The villagers had no education; they were farmers and laborers, simple in their desires and committed to Allah. Submission to their God and going to the mosque to pray five times a day were an integral part of their religion, part of Islam. And Islam was their life.

Christine recalled the hate in Nikhil Sahgal's voice when they had first seen the Javid men toiling in the fields along the border between India and Pakistan. He had called them savages. Yet it was the savages who risked their lives to save her after Nikhil's camel triggered the land mine.

Nazeem was one of the men who had crawled over treacherous ground to reach her, and Ruhee sat for hours by Christine's bedside after the explosion. A large iron grate, set in the center of the second-floor concrete to communicate through, made it difficult not to eavesdrop. And now as Christine listened to the two young newlyweds argue, she tried to rationalize her reasons for deceiving them earlier. She had lied to the family, saying that she had needed their help in finding her husband. But there was no husband. She had used their faith and their goodness to pursue another Muslim, a man she believed had kidnapped her sister.

Something knocked on the ceiling and Christine sat up, staring up into the expanse of concrete that separated the floors. Ruhee and Nazeem's words ran together as they quarreled.

"Please," Christine whispered, but there were no footsteps on the stairwell, no guttural commands from Arshad, the head of the household, no solace from Amagee, the revered grandmother, no intervention from the pregnant Zubeda, Arshad's wife, or any of the Javid family. Ruhee, the newest Javid daughter-in-law would have to deal with Nazeem herself.

Christine heard the girl pleading with him. *Why did she go on?* Even Christine knew that her efforts were futile.

The voices above Christine had gotten louder. She couldn't see them, but she could feel it, could hear it in their voices. "Ruhee . . . please," she whispered and walked to the spot where she knew they were directly above her.

He's going to hit her.

Christine closed her eyes, but the sudden intuition, the certainty, that he would hit her wouldn't leave.

When Nazeem struck his wife, Christine almost recoiled from the impact. She forced herself to breathe. Her dad had always claimed she had had an overactive imagination, but her mother had known better. Marsha Shepherd had had her own sights and sounds, wild imaginings that had plagued her through the years.

The day Liz was expected to return to Delhi, she had been talking to her mother, who was in Los Angeles and more concerned than usual about Liz's decision to split off from Christine. She had had a dream, didn't want to talk about it — angry, in fact, that she had even mentioned it. Liz would be fine. There had been other dreams, images that she believed were products of stress or too much sugar. "Or maybe," Marsha quipped, "it was just a mother's fate to be eternally haunted by imaginary threats to her young." But on that particular morning Christine's mother had already decided that, this time, she would blame her deranged state of mind on the ravages of menopause. Except her mother wasn't deranged, and now Liz was missing, or kidnapped, or murdered.

Christine's knees gave way against the iron frame of the cot. She crawled up onto the thin pad, tugging at the blanket and pulling it back over her head. She shuddered. "Women's intuition," "sympathy pains," even "karma," a concept of spiritual justice she had picked up in India, flickered through her mind. Christine was frantic to rationalize what she had felt. But it was all too strange to her, and she was tired, tired of waking up to the relentless whine of prayer over a loudspeaker each morning, tired of sleeping for days in the same outfit, tired of trying to eat while flies swarmed over her food, tired of the filth, the poverty.

Ruhee's sobs broke above her and Christine tried to ignore the sounds and remember that she had to find Liz. Cloid had told her that the Indians had found something. She didn't ask what, because in her heart she knew it couldn't be Liz, just as she knew Nazeem had hit his young bride.

Christine stared through the dim green

of her room at the opposite wall, her eye catching a cheap wall plaque of a wide-eyed child holding flowers with the words "Love" and "Knowledge" written on two oversized flower petals. Beneath the plaque was a metal and reed-woven chair where Christine laid her *dupatta,* a headscarf that had to be worn with guests, or any time she left the house. A bright pink pair of slippers stitched in gold thread, a gift from the family, lay at the foot of the chair. Embroidered wall hangings with lines and lines of verse taken from their holy book, the Koran, hung on two walls. In between one set of wall hangings was a picture of Nawaz Sharif, Pakistan's prime minister. In between the other set, Muhammad Ali Jinnah, the father of Pakistan. Fifty years before, Jinnah had led the Muslims in a bloody migration, dividing India to create the new Muslim state.

But the Indians and the Pakistanis were still fighting, and sometimes Christine awoke in the night, feeling that she couldn't breathe. There were too many rules to follow. She was a Christian, an un-believer, but the Javids were tolerant, even gracious. She was their guest.

As custom dictated, she was not allowed to assist in her care; it would be considered an insult to the men of the family. Five times a day the Javid women would kneel on threadbare floral carpets, their heads covered, and rub at their prayer beads while the men of the village collected at the local mosque. Some days Christine would be allowed to join the women, her face nearly covered by her scarf, while they shopped in the bazaar, careful not to look at men or shake someone's hand. Then, when they returned, she would go to the roof with Samina and any number of neighbor children (the number changed daily), taking their places between unfinished pylons of concrete, with steel rebars protruding, and fly fighting kites with glass-woven string that cut at each other until a winner was called — a lone kite still flying.

But most of her time was spent with the Javid women, visiting with neighbors or each other. As the women cooked and cleaned they would call to one another through the iron grate, keeping each other company throughout the day.

The Javids had no phone, no air-conditioning, no heating, except a stone hearth on which they cooked their food. But they did have an antenna, and Christine sat for hours with the family crowded in beside her, watching one of two stations on their black-and-white television.

One day there had been a news bulletin. The report was in Urdu, but Christine hadn't needed a translation. She had been out of the hospital for only a week and her tears soaked the gauze beneath her eyes as she took in the aftermath of another merciless attack. By that time, Farrukh Ahmed had claimed responsibility for Padamthala, the village where her sister had disappeared. And now it seemed that Farrukh had killed again. Like Padamthala, the Indian village was mostly Hindu. Christine had not told the Javids of Liz. They were Sunni Muslims, like the madman who had probably taken her sister, but most of the Javid women were crying. Arshad, the head of the clan, who was always gruff and intimidating, watched with downcast eyes as grass huts burned to the ground.

The Javid family hated the Hindus and their many false gods, but they didn't believe as Farrukh did that, except for Muslims, everyone was evil. The Javids were Rajputs, an old clan descended from ancient warriors. The men were burly, and a little frightening. Still, they had cared for her, an American, an infidel, and for that, Muslim or not, Sunni or not, she knew

174

Farrukh would kill them just as quickly.

Then that morning, weeks after the Hindu village had been destroyed, and three months after Liz's disappearance, there had been a dark, grainy photo of Farrukh Ahmed in the village paper. The terrorist and his group had been spotted in the North-West Frontier Province, moving west, toward Afghanistan.

She had resisted calling her mother or Cloid. She had been traveling illegally with an Indian government employee who had been killed in a minefield. And now she was residing with a Pakistani family. There would be too many questions, and Christine wasn't ready. She needed time to heal and think. But now she had been a guest of the Javids for six weeks. It was time to move on.

The day she had seen Farrukh's picture, she made her plan. She called Cloid from the headmaster's house, a pious educator who had moved from Karachi to Banalwala with his daughter and her husband's family. He possessed the only mobile phone in the village and was happy to extend the privilege. That night the headmaster came to dinner, as did one of the Javids' neighbors and four of her eight children. The woman had lost her husband the

175

year before when one of the iron grates between their floors had accidentally been left open, and he had fallen through. The headmaster had lost his wife two years earlier in a car accident. Zubeda, Arshad's wife, who was already large with their fourth child, confided to Christine she thought they would make a good match. Any other time, Christine would've enjoyed watching Zubeda as she skillfully brokered the couple . . . but not tonight.

At dinner, between plates of crispy lamb, *machli ka salan*, a fish curry that had become her favorite, spicy lentils fried in *ghee*, and milk confections that the women had picked up from one of the stalls at the bazaar, Christine lied to the family. She told them that now she was feeling better she needed to find her husband. At first the women blushed and whispered among themselves, explaining to the neighbor about Christine's call that afternoon. They had all been with her when she spoke to Cloid, and had assumed that he was her husband. Abagee, the eighty-year-old patriarch (his name meant "father" in Urdu), even averted his gaze from his precious TV.

Remembering their faces, their guileless expressions as they prodded her to tell them more, all the while piling more food onto her plate, Christine felt her skin ripple with the shame of what she had said to them. *It all fell into place so easily, too easily.*

The women, Christine recalled, including young Samina and the neighbor woman with all the kids, were desperate to hear of the mysterious man at the other end of the phone line. Christine had wanted to sigh at the universal condition of female sentiment; instead, she had dropped her eyes and tried to blush. It must've worked, because Ruhee giggled and Zubeda said something that seemed funny to the others. Abagee, however, seemed unimpressed and returned his gaze to the TV. Ruhee could barely contain herself. Tortured by sheer anticipation, she kept turning to her young husband and gripping his sleeve. Nazeem gave her a perfunctory smile, then also turned back to the TV, which was broadcasting yet another assembly meeting with their prime minister.

The men mostly conversed among themselves. They tore at their lamb, waving their hands in brusque gestures, oblivious to what the women were going on about. As generous as the men had been to her, she still had to be on her guard around them. And because she was a woman, they expected her to be. However, at the mention of Peshawar and the need for an escort, Zubeda's flawless teeth disappeared and Christine thought she could detect the slightest shift in Arshad's composure.

"Your husband is in Peshawar? It may no be good," Zubeda had commented. "Peshawar no a good place."

The large Pakistani woman had waited. It was barely a moment, but Christine knew that she was hoping that their guest would take back her request. When Christine didn't, Zubeda had no choice but to translate her wish. Abagee, her father-in-law, his spindly legs tucked beneath him on the taut twine cot, barely grunted while toothless gums worked the lamb. A woman's need to be with her husband was no revelation and hardly warranted a response.

The headmaster listened quietly as the neighbor woman asked again in Urdu for them to repeat what the American woman had asked of them. Zubeda repeated Christine's request.

Behind them, Amagee, the grandmother, raised her thin leg into the sink to wash her feet. She was preparing for prayer, and the old woman's lips were already moving over scripture. Still, when Amagee caught Christine looking at her, she managed such a sweet smile that Christine thought she might not be able to go through with the deception.

Even the young granddaughter, Samina, whose own mother had married at seventeen and moved farther south, had suddenly become serious. She glanced nervously at Arshad, her *mamu,* her favorite uncle. She knew little of the danger that Christine was asking the men to chance, but she sensed her aunts' upset. Soon the twelve-year-old would be betrothed and her husband would be a Rajput like herself. But for now she watched her aunts, waiting for some kind of signal. And she got it. The nod from Zubeda was barely discernible. Samina gathered the children who darted around them and took them outside.

Ruhee's face was ashen and drawn. She looked sick and made no pretense at hiding her dread. When she started to whimper an objection, Nazeem snapped at her under his breath, startling Christine. Nazeem had given no indication that he had even heard her request, but he had, and his wife went quiet. The men did not interrupt their conversation, and only Zubeda spoke.

"*Chai,* Kharis?" she had offered.

Zubeda hadn't called her by her formal name in weeks. It had always been *behin* or *behinji,* which meant "little sister." Still, Zubeda was married to the head of the clan. *It wouldn't do to distress a guest.* The Muslim woman had risen stiffly, almost formally, to prepare tea.

The noises from upstairs had stopped, and Christine tried to figure how long it had been quiet. Only the buzz of the mosquitoes flying around the poison green tab disturbed her reverie.

Zubeda had told her that on a Muslim girl's wedding night her mother-in-law would help her create a ball of scented bread dough, and when the young groom entered their bridal room and lay on the bed beside her, the girl was supposed to use the dough, gently rolling it over her husband's body, to ease them into the awkward union.

And then she heard a whimper, drawn out, and then words of comfort as Nazeem tried to console his wife. The argument was over. Christine knew the girl would acquiesce; her husband would go, would

180

keep his promise to their guest, no matter how dangerous the journey. The strangers the women had married became their new life, but Ruhee and Zubeda were fortunate; the Javid men were good Muslims.

Christine felt her breath quicken, despite her attempt to rationalize her actions. She hadn't had a panic attack in a while, and thought she was probably due. She picked up a bag that had held candy that Arshad had brought home as a gift. She and Zubeda had finished it off quickly, but she could still smell the cardamom and sesame as she held the bag to her face. As she breathed deeply, Christine allowed her eyes to drift along the gentle curves of Arabic characters painted above the door, holy verse of the kind that was written on anything that would take pen or paint — homes, buildings, even rocks and cars. It wasn't vandalism; it was Allah's wish.

Christine tried not to be rattled by thoughts of wrathful gods — Christian, Muslim, Hindu, or otherwise. Weeks of village lore had begun to get to her, tales of the familiar stench of evil that rose from the graves of transgressors, of maggots wriggling, sometimes multiplying, in the orifices of dying murderers. And then there were the toads. It seemed there was always some particularly corrupt and slanderous Pakistani politician who was spewing toads somewhere. And what about the beliefs she had grown up with, not the least of which were the Ten Commandments?

Christine looked up. She thought she had heard something, but there hadn't been any sounds between the lovers for hours. Until that night, Christine had never heard Nazeem speak above a whisper to his young bride.

There was the hiss, however, the steady buzz that assured her the mosquitoes were on the other side of the room and not near her. In the spring and summer, even the poorest of families chose to live with the dizzying green aura. She imagined it was preferable to malaria, but that night she couldn't take it. Rolling off her cot, she decided to take her chances with the pests and yanked at the mosquito insert. The mossy glow went to black, and for a moment Christine felt disoriented. Suddenly she was sure she did hear something.

Muslim lore had it that those who were good and spoke the truth would breathe out the fragrance of flowers. Christine had already reconciled herself to bad breath. Still, she hoped good intentions were enough to avoid anything cold and slippery moving up her throat.

But she had heard something? Christine set down the bag and rose from the cot. She felt her way over to the wall facing the street. The shutters were closed, as they should be at that hour.

"Damn it," she muttered. She wanted to open them, but she was scared. Taking a breath, she gripped the latch, turned, and pulled the shutters wide.

The cool air sobered her. Even in the sliver of moonlight, the minaret of the mosque stood out like a beacon in the void. She shuddered and was irked that she was starting to believe in their superstitions. She glanced around the star-blotched sky expecting . . . expecting what? *Jinn, maybe?*

Zubeda had warned her not to wear perfume or sing at night, otherwise the creatures that cruised the airways between heaven and earth might be tempted to descend and take her. Christine was suddenly tired of their stories. She looked up into the sky and lamented that she didn't have any perfume with which to entice the amorous spirits who could take the form of birds, or animals, or even tall, lanky Pakistanis with pointed teeth and ears.

Christine could tell from the stars that it was late and remembered that the time Jinn were said to occupy the mosques were between the hours of midnight and two. She checked her estimate against an inexpensive plastic wristwatch that one of the many visitors had given her as a gift and saw that it was a little after one in the morning.

Zubeda had said that they like to take pigeons, especially dogs, possess them, and . . .

She had already heard all the tales of confused old men and errant fakirs who had stumbled into the mosque during the forbidden hours only to be confronted by something — something with eyes of fire. Even with the intervention of an imam or a village healer, the old men would burn with fever for days, then die.

Since toads and maggots and body odors weren't enough, Christine decided she might as well confront the spirits, too, and she glared hard at the mosque, hoping to see a shadow, a pigeon, anything. It was the time of the Jinn, and all she wanted was just one sign that the people in this part of the world weren't crazy.

"Where are you, you horned . . ." The words died in her throat. The stillness was daunting and she shivered.

I'm tired, she decided. Since the land mine explosion, sleep had frequently eluded her, and now, of all things to keep her awake, she was worrying about phantoms.

With heavy lids Christine picked over the dark blocks of crude dwellings. She stared down into a moonlit maze of narrow pathways. During the day the paths were a crush of bicycles and animals and children. But now there wasn't a single human soul. Her gaze returned to the mosque. She tried not to be afraid of its foreignness, its Arabic scripture, its words of wisdom and doom. Women were not allowed to pray there. It was the men during the day and the Jinn at night.

She couldn't imagine what it would be like to go to the mosque. If the superstitions were true — and the Muslims believed fervently they were — she would die. Still, if God had wanted her dead, she would not have survived the land mine. Getting this far had to mean something.

Christine felt a breeze at the window and became aware that her cheeks were wet. She was crying.

At dinner, the men's tunics and trousers had been dusty from the fields. Their bodies were probably sore. Now they would lose five days in the fields transporting their guest, and Zubeda was pregnant. Nonetheless, they had not complained. Their country was bankrupt and overwhelmed by political and economic problems, and they talked of factories closing and the corruption that kept the people in poverty. But the men had heard Christine's request. Though they probably shared their women's trepidation, there had been no discussion of whether they would help, only how they would get her to Peshawar.

After dinner the men had gone to the mosque. They had prayed to Allah and had prayed to their own spiritual teacher, who had been dead for over a decade. And when they slept they would dream, and it was in their dreams, they believed, their teacher would appear to show them the way.

And if not, they would still go. But Arshad and Nazeem were farmers, not soldiers, and Christine wondered when had she become so driven that she was willing to endanger innocents?

She stared at the minaret where, in just a few hours, the muezzin would call over the loudspeakers for morning prayer. She no longer felt like challenging the spirits.

She closed the shutters.

There *was* something above her. There was no sound, no bodies shifting, but she could feel it. Nazeem was asleep, but his new wife of four months was awake and suffering alone. Except Ruhee wasn't alone. The concrete between the women was not enough to separate them, and Christine suffered with her.

Chapter
9

Cloid reached up to scratch his head, and pain slashed through his leg where they'd opened it to take the veins needed to repair his heart. And now his leg hurt, his chest felt violated, and the IV needles in the back of his hands made him feel like a track-riddled addict desperate for a fix.

Gritting his teeth, Cloid braced himself and pressed the button. The bed moved unwillingly beneath him, screeching defiance. Then the beeping on his heart monitor ceased, and Cloid sighed. It wasn't the first time. So he waited, counting off the seconds. He started to perspire, trying not to overreact to the glitch when the monitor suddenly kicked in just as he was about to buzz the nurse. He glanced at his blood-pressure reading. It was up. He wanted to cuss, but he needed all his energy to concentrate on Chris. The kid was alive, damn it! While he had been combing the western and northern regions of India looking for her, she was in Pakistan!

Cloid felt a slight pull in his chest and groaned at the thought that he would have to pace himself. Still, he had managed the twenty-five-thousand-dollar wire transfer to Islamabad. Chris's mother had helped him draw from the daughters' line of credit from their company. Then he had to find a reliable banking institution in Islamabad. It had taken half a day, but Chris would get her money in time.

So far, there had been no more news of the DNA tests. Liz had been missing too long for Cloid even to be curious; the tests were only a formality. Cloid knew that, and so did Joe Riccardi, but Christine wouldn't let go so easily.

Cloid had been out of ICU only two days before the nurses on his floor were complaining that he needed his own phone line and a fax machine. Faxes had been coming into the hospital even before he arrived by ambulance. The thought that he might not survive the operation was not an option, and Cloid had been on his cell phone, making arrangements, even as they strapped him to the gurney.

At the time Liz disappeared, Cloid

couldn't get anything out of India. For decades, Central Asia had been virtually ignored by the international community. Even Joe Riccardi, a political officer, was having trouble getting through his own bureaucratic duties. The Indians were preoccupied with Kashmir, and the Americans with everywhere else. The Balkans, Iraq, China, and North Korea were taking up all the press, until the Indians decided to disclose their nukes. It didn't take long for Pakistan to respond, and suddenly Central Asia became the new hot spot. For Cloid, the timing couldn't have been better. Within days, he received over a dozen faxes.

Then Chris called. That short, nearly fatal crossing over the minefield put her into an entirely different world, a world he knew very little about.

Cloid picked up the faxed background report on a retired Australian SAS trooper who would be meeting Chris in less than thirty-six hours. Cloid hoped the man could be trusted.

He read again that Reginald Duke had been stationed in Vietnam, Papua, New Guinea, Malaysia, "picked up a wife in Thailand, another in Turkey."

Cloid rolled his eyes, then read that after

Duke's retirement he fought for the Chechens, the Algerians, "had been loaned to the CIA for some work in Tehran just after the Shah was booted . . . was later commissioned by the mujahideen against the Russians —"

Cloid liked that, but skimmed to the end of the narrative. His leg was in agony.

"Reginald Duke received good marks for tradecraft and accomplishment throughout his career with the very demanding SAS . . . is presently unemployed, residing with family . . ." *With both wives?* Cloid wondered. ". . . along with five goats, two water buffalo, and a satellite dish in a village in Thailand."

The agent Cloid had talked with assured him that even though Mr. Duke was retired, he seemed anxious to take another assignment.

With two wives, Cloid had no doubt that he was anxious. He reached for another fax, and his leg spasmed. Spitting curses, he waited for the pain to subside, then moved slowly, carefully, toward the document.

Two other good men were available, but they were younger than Duke, greener. Cloid worried that they might be inclined to take Chris up on whatever scheme she

191

was set on. Cloid just wanted her picked up, forcibly if necessary, and escorted home.

Cloid thought his agency contact had picked well. He had been under the knife when someone had to be found to meet Chris in time. He hoped Reginald Duke could get the kid home in one piece. He sighed. There wasn't much in the way of dependable manpower out that way. That would soon change with the press already in a frenzy over the nuclear issues between India and Pakistan. But for now, the Aussie was his best bet. He was tough, and the guy seemed to know his "ragheads." Cloid had no intention of letting Chris go farther. She was coming home.

An aide brought in Cloid's lunch and set it down on a table by the bed. It was just past noon, still too early to call his man in India, so he started jotting down notes. He wondered if Chris was aware of the nukes. He was sure that atomic warfare between India and Pakistan was not a contingency she had considered. He hoped the possibility would scare the hell out of her.

The old man had to force himself to relax. It had all happened too fast, first Liz, then the land mine. Now that shy youngster who had spent nearly her entire childhood with her father's cronies was on her way to a center of terrorist activity. For a moment he felt that familiar rush, and an almost perverse appreciation for the difficulty of her situation. He envied her the experience. Then, as if on cue, an image of Chris, beaten and raped, flashed into his consciousness, and a wave of apprehension rolled over him. He missed the days when he'd been so calculating, that issues affecting people and their lives hardly concerned him. *I used to be one cold bastard*, he thought. And Cloid yearned for that again. He was old and soft, and it was a shame that he cared so much. If he wasn't careful, softness might get Chris killed.

He picked up a fax from a Lebanese friend who had spent three years wholesaling rugs from the Afghan camps along the Pakistan-Afghan border. The man had worked most of the Middle East, the Philippines, and even Russia. He was experienced in wholesaling and the black market, and still thought the Pashtuns and the tribes were tough characters. The area Chris was heading into was off-limits to foreigners, meaning Westerners — especially Americans. The tribes thought of themselves as merchants. Living a somewhat loose interpretation of Muslim dogma, they were tradesmen of drugs, guns, and, sometimes, humans. The average price for a captive was $35,000; journalist or tourist, it didn't matter. The merchants had their price and expected a short negotiation and a swift payoff. They had more important matters to attend to, like their guns.

Despite his reticence, Cloid was already running the numbers for ransom in his head while he admired some color photos of a few tribal copies of M-16s, Degtyarevs, Tokarevs, swivel guns, AK-47s, Uzis, Lugers, Glocks, Lee-Enfields, even a M-3 burp gun, a small .45-caliber submachine gun designed for tankers that he found particularly endearing. One had been his constant companion in Vietnam. He thought it was probably better suited to the dry interior of Afghanistan than Vietnam. It had been difficult to keep it functional in Vietnam. But it was small, and its fat, slow-moving, .45-caliber bullet was a good man-stopper.

Of course, the Kalashnikovs were in the majority. The tribes had picked up thousands alongside dead bodies in the eighties during the Russian-Afghan conflict and had probably replicated many thousands more since then. Not to mention the huge quantities available on the black market from the overstocked arsenals of the former Soviet republics bordering Afghanistan and Pakistan. The Russian automatic was easy to use, easy to load, light, effective, cheap to make, and very difficult to break. The Pashtuns and the Afghans were superb craftsmen, and their arm and drug bazaars were the largest in Central Asia. Their sidearms and rifles were their glory, and the prints he leafed through were just a sampling. He couldn't wait to see what they had in rockets, mines, and explosives. If only he were a decade younger . . .

One advertisement showed a woman covered from head to toe, training on a new Chinese automatic called a Short. She had to be from one of those breakaway Soviet republics, or Iran, or even Iraq, where women were expected to fight alongside the men. It would be different on the Pakistan frontier, where women were cloistered in family compounds and kept in purdah, which meant "for men's eyes only." Those were women who could only be seen by the males of their immediate family. Cloid remembered seeing some television special on the women, clad in burqas, a colored sheet with only a cloth mesh to look through, a ghost with a peephole.

Suddenly Nikhil Sahgal came to mind. Cloid wondered again what had happened out there in the desert. He had a feeling that the explosion was the very least of it. The Indian family all but admitted that Chris had been forced to go with Sahgal. Cloid tried to breathe. His chest hurt. He hurt all over.

He had to stop. Chris was out there, and if she didn't have some maniac at her throat, then she was probably still intent on going after Liz, which meant Farrukh. He admired her guts, but she was going to Peshawar where males ruled. Just minutes from there were the tribal areas in which the government of Pakistan had no jurisdiction. And then there was the border with Afghanistan. And beyond that, being a female was hazardous. The Taliban, a horde of thugs, orphans left over from the Soviet-Afghan conflict, and their spiritual leaders, the mullahs, were rapidly taking control of Afghanistan. They imposed sharia, a strict, fundamentalist form of Islam, on the people, and except in Pakistan, where the people, like the Taliban, were mostly Sunni Muslims, there was little support for the fledgling government. Nonetheless, the Taliban were notorious for their inhumane treatment of women, and Cloid hoped Chris would have enough sense to steer clear.

He looked around at the tubes and IVs hanging over him. His real lifeline, his computer, was at home. Cloid would be out of the hospital in three days. By then, he hoped Chris would be on her way home. He was still bothered by the female voices he had heard speaking in the background during Chris's call, the ones who seemed to be teasing her. That Chris was being held for ransom, or as a hostage, might still have to be considered, and the procedure he'd learned in the Bureau dictated that he cover all options. He just wasn't ready to explore that issue yet. Kidnapping might not be a part of Farrukh's profile, but there were plenty of others out there who would not hesitate to take her — for anything — ransom, political advantage, slavery, or sex.

Cloid couldn't predict where he would be in a few days. If he had to spend another night in this goddamn hospital room, he thought he might croak. But for the moment, he was still kicking. So was Chris. And that was enough.

It was time to call New Delhi.

Chapter
10

"Are we . . . this is it . . . Yes? *Ji?*"

Nazeem cocked his head, which didn't tell her much. Either he didn't understand or he didn't care, or yes they had arrived and it wasn't a big deal.

They had already dropped off the two hitchhikers that they had picked up along the way. A nod, Allah's blessing, *"Khuda haviz,"* and off they went. The hitchhikers had taken no notice of Christine, who had ridden with them for the last four hours. She didn't even know their names; she wasn't supposed to. With the hitchhikers out of the van, Nazeem slid to the opposite corner. He seemed grateful for the space to pitch back and forth without fear of touching Christine.

As they came up beside a rickshaw driver, Arshad said something to Nazeem in Urdu and the driver Arshad had hired for thirty rupees slammed on his brakes. Nazeem asked for help. The man had no chin or brow; he seemed to be wasting away. Still, he pointed back and forth, his gestures animated and his voice strong. Nazeem listened to the man, cocking his head with an occasional *"Tika,"* in between, acknowledging he understood.

It had been a while since Arshad and Nazeem had seen their cousins in Rawalpindi, the old capital of Pakistan, and it was clear they weren't sure of where they were going. The Pakistanis didn't seem to believe in maps, but unlike their American counterparts, the men weren't shy about asking for help. They had already talked to a family of cyclists, a fakir, and a beggar, that last bit of advice costing them two rupees.

Finally Arshad pointed furiously, directing the stubbly, towheaded driver onto a narrow street. Except for bicycles and a horse-drawn tonga, there were no other vehicles. Tall tenements flanked each side. The van turned, then almost slammed into a line of concrete fragments that stuck up from the ground, blocking nearly half the passage. That didn't deter the driver, who spit phlegm out the window and turned the wheel. Even the screech of metal didn't

faze him. The road ended in piles of garbage and more concrete. A large pig and
two stray dogs picked through the refuse
while children in dirty RC Cola T-shirts
played alongside them. Faded laundry
hung on lines that zigzagged across the
stained and cracked concrete facades. Afternoon prayer sounded in the distance
and Christine was surprised to see so many
men still on the street. By contrast,
Banalwala, the Javids' village, seemed to
drain of its males when prayer time came.

With a loud crunch, they hit something,
and the odor of gasoline filled the van.
Women and children came out onto their
balconies to investigate. As the engine
roared, they watched curiously to see if the
driver could power his way out of the rut.
Christine gripped the doorjamb with one
hand and her nose with the other. Nazeem
muttered something to Arshad. Christine
couldn't hear Arshad's reply. She looked
outside. The neighborhood seemed bleak,
not just poor like Banalwala, but depressed. She looked at Nazeem, who had
been silent for most of the ride. He seemed
nervous, and maybe just a little afraid. He
must have sensed her studying him, because his eyes turned to her. It was the first
time he had looked at her during the trip.

That morning a steady stream of tears had run down his wife's face as she helped him load the van. She had made no attempt to hide the bruise on her jaw where Nazeem had struck her. She made no fuss, and no one asked how she'd come by the bruise.

Setting off beyond the village to visit family was usually met with celebration, and half the village turning out to see the neighbors off. But not this time. With little comment, Samina and Amagee helped pack the van. Even the children seemed to sense that this trip was different. Only Zubeda, heavy with child, packed whatever medicine they had left for Christine, gave her some guavas, and assured her that everything would be fine, *Inshallah,* God willing.

The van's engine roared, and Christine was jolted back from her memory of the tearful departure. Nazeem was still looking at her and she almost cringed under his gaze. But then he smiled, almost sheepishly. Suddenly, Christine realized that it was Nazeem who was ashamed; his wife had acted inappropriately.

Up front, a deep guttural sound came from Arshad. The driver reciprocated with his own grunt, then switched off the engine. Apparently they would work their way out of the rut later.

When the smoke cleared, a mob of ragged children stood at the opening to one of the buildings. The kids in Banalwala would've been on them already, grinning and eager to see new faces, but these kids hung back. Two Pakistani men walked past, dressed in collared shirt and pants, their arms draped casually around each other. Their eyes were large, the whites showing bright against their dark brown complexions. They looked at the van and its occupants suspiciously. The jagged Arabic scrawls painted on the buildings reminded Christine more of gangland graffiti than of the gentle swirls of religious verse common in Banalwala.

Arshad turned in his seat, and Christine held still so he could check that she was properly covered. After three days of wearing the dark purple *shalwar qamiz* given to her by the Javids, it was nice to have a change. It was the beginning of June and hot, and even the light pink gossamer blouse and pants that covered her completely felt cooler. Arshad said nothing and turned back around. She had obviously passed inspection. In Islamabad, the capital of Pakistan, where they had stopped to retrieve her money, Arshad wouldn't allow her to talk with the bank representative, a woman in Western dress, until Christine's *dupatta* hid any sign of an errant auburn lock.

The kids in the doorway watched cautiously, stepping aside when the strangers approached the doorway.

"*Salaam alekum*," Christine smiled.

"*Walekum salaam*," a couple of the older ones muttered. Arshad and Nazeem paused, glancing inside the building.

"How pretty," Christine commented. She touched a piece of yellow garland sticking up from the hair of one of the little ones, repeating the compliment in Urdu. The little girl stared up at the white-faced foreigner as if paralyzed, her mouth agape.

"*Valid sahib kither hai?*" Arshad barked, demanding an audience with the girl's father.

An older boy started to respond when a man yelled from inside. The kids scattered, and a Pakistani in his thirties, unshaven but ruggedly handsome, came out with his arms outstretched. The men embraced, exchanging greetings. The man yelled back through the doorway then snapped something at one of the smaller kids, a five-year-old who didn't move quickly enough. After a moment, a second man with a pinched chin and a single gold tooth came out of the house and embraced them. Christine waited until Arshad turned to her. He started to give her instruction when the first cousin stepped around him, taking her hand.

"Welcome to my home, Lady Shepherd."

Christine was startled by the man's touch. She glanced at Arshad and Nazeem, checking to see if her hesitancy was misplaced. It wasn't. Arshad spoke tersely. The cousin smiled, withdrawing his hand.

"So sorry, lady. You are American, but my cousin doesn't like American hello. Taking hand is USA, is it right? I see it on TV?"

"Yes, it's right . . . sometimes."

"Sometimes?" the Pakistani laughed loudly. "Oh, I see, maybe I watch wrong show, *hai!*"

"Maybe," Christine responded, not smiling.

"This is Khraz," Arshad declared stiffly. Then to Christine, "This been Uncle . . . Janoor."

Janoor laughed as if Arshad had said the funniest thing. Janoor corrected Arshad in a fast, choppy dialect that Christine couldn't follow.

"You must forgive Arshad," the Pakistani grinned. "His English is not so good as mine. I am Janoor, Arshad's cousin."

"I think Arshad's English is very good. *Bohat acha*," she threw in for emphasis.

"*Bohat acha!* Very good, Lady Shepherd. You watch Pakistani TV, I think," he said mockingly.

Unlike his cousins, who wore the traditional garb of Islam, a long cotton shirt that came down past their knees and a pajama-style pant, Janoor sported a silk shirt with pleated slacks, something (if Christine didn't know better) that looked like it had just been picked off the rack at a local Gap outlet. Arshad uttered something, and Janoor's cocky grin disappeared. The cousins eyed one another, then, grunting under his breath, Janoor introduced the thin, gold-toothed man next to him.

"This is my brother, Setin. His English is only small. I sorry."

"*Salaam alekum*," Christine said.

Setin mumbled under his breath. Janoor looked exasperated, then bumped Setin, who blurted out another greeting.

"Hal-lo, main name Setin." He wore a short-sleeve shirt like his brother, making no effort to hide the blue and black streaks on his arms.

"Hello, Setin, my name is Christine."

It took her some effort to avert her eyes from the needle marks. Not that Setin would've noticed, his eyes were on his feet.

"My Urdu is not so good," she continued. *"Maf kejiye."* The shy Pakistani finally glanced up at her and grinned. He was about to say something when Janoor butted in.

"That's all right, Lady Shepherd. I teach you. Here. I take your bag." And with that Janoor stepped in front of Arshad, close to Christine. Before she could object, he was lifting the backpack from her shoulders. He leaned in, pressing up against her. Christine didn't dare look back at Arshad. If she reacted, Arshad would be obliged to defend her.

She felt like the maiden who had been rescued by a prince who had unwittingly committed himself to a lifetime of service. Fortunately for Arshad, Christine wouldn't need him for a lifetime, just until Peshawar.

Janoor moved back to the doorway and bent at the waist. With a sweeping motion of his hand, he gestured Christine inside. His position made it impossible to pass without touching him. He was playing with her, and she could almost feel Arshad's angry breath behind her.

It was obvious that the cousins didn't get along, but Janoor knew Peshawar. Until she could meet Cloid's contact, she would need them both.

Before Arshad could lash out, Christine drew her *dupatta* tight across her face and glared at the Pakistani. It was enough. Janoor stepped back. Christine didn't look back, didn't need to. She knew her poor prince would follow.

The time to go to mosque came and went. Arshad and Nazeem missed prayer, which bothered Christine. In Banalwala there hadn't been a single day that Arshad had ignored the muezzin's entreaty. She didn't know whether it was the custom not to go if the host didn't, or whether Arshad just didn't want to leave her alone. Christine thought it was the latter.

Janoor's wife, Ashmay, Setin's wife, and his two sisters were in the kitchen fixing dinner. Unlike the Javids, Janoor and his family were city people. They had a stove and a refrigerator, and Janoor boasted that they even had a Western toilet. But it was so filthy that Christine actually missed the hole she had been accustomed to in the village. As with the Javids, she was a guest and expected to eat with the men while the women of the household served them. The mood in the room was tense, and Ashmay stayed especially close to her husband, trying to anticipate his needs.

Ashmay wore the draped blouse and pants of Muslim women, but unlike the Javid women, her *shalwar qamiz* was drab and threadbare. Wisps of her hair were already white, and her nails were heavily ridged and yellowed. Christine thought she looked sick. When she caught Ashmay's eye, she smiled. Ashmay didn't react at first. It was almost as if she were confused by the attention. Janoor muttered under his breath, and Ashmay averted her eyes, pouring his tea. Then her eyes flicked up, and Christine smiled again. This time, Ashmay's mouth turned up at the corners, her face reddening. Christine started to speak to her, but Setin's wife scowled at her. Christine's first thought was that her hair was showing, and her hand went to her head to make sure the scarf was secure. It was, but her gesture didn't seem to mollify the wife. The woman's scowl only deepened.

The eyes of the dog were cobalt blue, and fear washed over Christine when she tried to step back. Too late. The icy grip of the possessed dog's eyes, the Jinn's eyes, was already paralyzing her limbs. Christine tried to shout for help, but no sound came from her throat. She stared silently, frantically, in horror, conscious of the mosque and its colored glass inserts that suddenly appeared black and hollow. For an instant, Christine remembered the shadowed hollows of her own father's eyes after he had died, and she cried out his name. Except no one could hear her because she was dreaming. But only a fragment of Christine's consciousness was aware of this, and the nightmare continued.

It was black outside, the middle of the night, the forbidden time. Christine had left her room, and now she would die. The Jinn who had taken the form of a dog would certainly take her.

She moaned and her head dropped in despair. Beneath her, gossamer swirled in and around tiny feet that were decorated with semiprecious stones. Her own feet were large and hardly as delicate as the adorned insteps that seemed to extend from her. Christine reached down to touch them, then noticed that her fingers were ringed in gold. Her nails were brilliant red and her hands were painted in intricate designs of henna. She heard the low growl before her and remembered the beast. She looked up. The dog's eyes were still on her. She tried to move. It stepped toward her, and when she opened her mouth to scream, it was Liz's voice that cried out instead.

Christine turned away from the Jinn and spotted Liz across a wide river. Beside her, kneeling at the water's edge was Zubeda, whose own feet were tiny and jeweled, tucked beneath the folds of her flowing *shalwar qamiz*. Liz watched sorrowfully while Zubeda, her hands also delicately hennaed, threw brightly colored flowers into the river.

The dog and mosque vanished, and Christine called out to Liz and Zubeda. Liz glanced up, meeting her eyes for only an instant, then returned her gaze up the river. Beneath her, Zubeda continued to throw flowers into the water. Christine called again, but neither of the women reacted as if they had heard. Zubeda's face was drawn. She was crying, and Christine saw that the same drifts of gossamer that had entranced her moments before hung limp on the Muslim woman's wraithlike form. The ripe, protruding belly that Christine had always associated with her friend was gone. Even in her dream the suggestion that Zubeda's baby had died was clear, and Christine awoke.

Still in the grip of the nightmare, Christine stared wide-eyed around her, where darkened forms snaked along the far wall. She heard crying.

"Shhh . . . shhh," Christine rasped. "The Jinn'll hear." The crying got louder, and there was a scuffle behind her. She whipped her head around and saw that the sliding glass door leading onto the balcony was open slightly. Just inside, it appeared that the shadowed forms had shifted. Christine thought that the Jinn must've entered the room while she was asleep.

She swung her legs around, then ran to the open door. Children scrambled from beneath their bedding, flattening themselves against the wall, staring in terror at the mad woman. Christine turned. By then the oldest girl had scooped up a three-year-old boy, who was still in the blankets, crying.

The toddler pressed tightly against his sister, crying even harder, and Christine went to him. She knelt before the cluster of children, and her body swayed. She was disoriented, and her eyes darted around the room at every sound. Moonlight shone glaringly through the glass and Christine got up to pull on the curtain, but the single panel could block only some of the light. She would have to put up with the brightness.

"Stop. Shhh," Christine snapped at the children. The girl held her brother's mouth, trying to muffle his blubbering. But the boy was hysterical, and Christine had to stave off her own panic.

While the children cowered in front of her, Christine was remembering Amagee's story of the confused old men who had been attacked by spirits in the mosque. She noticed that she was shivering, and she felt her forehead for sign of a fever. Christine was certain she had been caught by the Jinn, and that it was real, and not a dream.

But her skin was clammy, even cool. She rolled her head forward and saw the children in front of her. They were whimpering and her breath caught. Then, slowly, Christine started to focus and saw the room, the mounds of bedding, the light that came through the glass door that was not nearly as bright or menacing as she had feared.

"I'm so sorry," she started. *"Maf kejiye, maf kejiye."*

When she bent toward them, the older girl shrieked, begging the American woman not to hurt them. Christine caught the word, *"Shaitan,"* the Pakistani's word for Satan, and tried to think back into the fog, moments before. They thought she was possessed. Christine closed her eyes, wondering if she was.

It was a dream, another nightmare. And Zubeda . . . she was by the river . . . thin . . . barren, just as in the dream the night before.

Except tonight there was Liz.

Then Christine remembered she was at the cousin's house. She was in Rawalpindi, on her way to Peshawar, to find the terrorist . . . to find Liz.

It had taken her weeks in the Javid household not to wake with a start each morning. But the dreams were beginning to fill her thoughts, and Christine couldn't help but wonder if they meant something. The Pakistanis certainly believed they did, but she was an American, a Christian.

Christine heard voices. The commotion was coming from the hallway. She went to her door, cracked it open. Nazeem and the cousins were standing in the corridor, bunched up outside Arshad's room. When Arshad exited his room, he was carrying a

213

bundle of belongings. He was leaving.

Still wearing her *shalwar qamiz* from that day, Christine snatched her *dupatta* off the bed and threw it over her head. As she headed back toward the door, she almost fell over the children, who scampered away. Christine tried to calm them, but Arshad's voice sounded almost frantic.

Out in the hallway, two of the smaller children ran to their mothers while the rest ran down the stairwell. Christine tried to explain, but Arshad's face was pale. He was shooting off what sounded like instructions to Nazeem. When Christine approached, he could barely meet her eyes.

"Kiya howa hai?" she asked.

"Zubeda . . . *bebe,*" he uttered.

Even before he opened his mouth she knew it was about Zubeda and the baby. She nodded, and tried to accept that he had to go. But something else was wrong. Arshad was packed to leave, but Setin's wife started yelling at him. Once she looked at Christine and pointed at her, her eyes boring into Arshad as he tried to ignore her. She was reminding him of his duty. When Nazeem and Janoor tried to intervene, she would snap at them, and they would cock their heads and look away. It took a few moments, but finally Chris-

214

tine understood. Zubeda was having her baby, but Arshad was still expected to fulfill his promise to his guest, and he would.

"*Mujhe chorain!*" Christine snapped at Setin's wife. She fell silent. Christine told Arshad he had to go, and that Nazeem could take her. Although the cock of his head was barely perceptible, he acquiesced and started down the stairs. The sister started to object, but Christine ignored her, following Arshad down to the first landing. When she got to him, his hands were nervously twisting at the cloth neck of his bundle.

"Is she . . . hurt?" Christine asked.

He nodded. "How is said . . . Doctor cut all right . . . Cut . . ."

"Caesarean?"

"*Ji.*"

"Have they already cut her?"

Arshad stared at her, not quite understanding. Frustrated, he explained to Janoor, who translated for him from the second-floor landing.

"They no cut yet," Janoor yelled down to her. "She's going to Lahore . . . two, three hours. It's not good when they cut our women. Infection, you know?"

Arshad and Christine were partially hidden in the crook of the stairwell, but it didn't keep Janoor from leaning over the balcony to overhear their conversation. Christine tried to whisper, but Arshad had other things on his mind.

"Khraz," he said quietly. "I sorry."

He flicked his eyes toward Janoor, upstairs, and she realized that he was worried about her. He dropped his eyes, and she looked at him. She had to resist an impulse to throw her arms around him, a man whose importance and bearing had scared her for nearly two months.

Instead, she did the unspeakable and took his hand, pulling him back up the stairs. She thought of Zubeda and the baby. With no money, there was little chance of good care. Zubeda was just another poor farmer's wife. Arshad's hand felt cold in her grasp and she thought again of the Jinn in her dream. She felt cursed.

Christine inadvertently squeezed Arshad's hand as she pulled at him. Arshad stopped. He couldn't tolerate her touch any longer and he quickly muttered an apology as he drew his hand away. In the dim stairwell light, she saw that his eyes were red-rimmed. She had never seen him look so helpless. Christine looked up. Setin's sister and wife were looking down at them.

Christine immediately regretted her impulsiveness in touching him. She should've known better, but she was desperate to give him money in private. Still, there would be no coaxing him up into her room.

"Please, Arshad, wait," she whispered.

Christine ran back up to find that Janoor had moved over to the open door of her room. She ignored him and ran past to take money out of her backpack. She kept her back to him, but she could feel his eyes on her. She tried to clench the wad in her fist, hiding it, but when she turned, Janoor made no attempt to avert his eyes. Christine got a glimpse of Ashmay behind him and saw the concern on her face. Clearly, his wife didn't trust him. Christine tried not to react as she maneuvered past the Pakistani and back down the stairwell.

Arshad didn't seem surprised when she gave him the handful of rupees. She could feel the shame well up in him, but he didn't recoil.

"*Meharbani karain,*" she pleaded. "*Su . . . ye . . . ,*" she said, stumbling. Then she begged him to let her help "her sister." "*Mein nain apni behin ki, madad karai hai.*"

His eyes were welling up, and she repeated the phrase, saying it faster, clearer, the second time.

Arshad choked back a sob, but held her gaze. "I be back," he rasped.

Christine cocked her head, *"Inshallah."*

He looked at her and smiled weakly. *"Inshallah, bahin. Inshallah."*

Then he left.

They were just above her. Christine felt their eyes, but she needed a moment before she could face Janoor and his family. The cool concrete of the wall felt good against her back.

Except for Nazeem, Christine was once again with strangers. This time, with people she didn't trust. Keeping her head down, she started up the concrete steps. Grime and mold caked the cracks of the stairwell all the way up. There were no pictures of Pakistani leaders, or holy men, or even pictures of children holding flowers. The walls were bare.

She glanced at her watch. It was just after one. She only had to get through the night, then a few hours on the road. When she stepped onto the landing, Nazeem was the first to meet her.

"Sorry, Khraz," he said. She realized he was talking about their commitment to her, not Zubeda. He was the only one who could watch out for her now, and he was ashamed. *Another prince,* she thought, and she realized that his cousins were as unsettling to him as they were to her.

"*Inshallah,*" she whispered. She tried to smile. He smiled back, but it was a tired smile. Then he stepped aside, almost knocking Setin over. The nervous addict quickly dropped back, mumbling something to his wife and sister. The group dispersed. The children went with their mothers as Christine returned to her room. Janoor, however, was still at her door, leering, as she approached.

"*Chai?*" Ashmay asked.

As always, Ashmay was at Janoor's side. Christine shook her head, but thanked her.

Ashmay could barely respond; her husband's eyes were fixed on Christine. Again, Christine waited for Janoor to move. He reached for her. In spite of herself, she flinched. Janoor's lips stretched into a wicked grin. He patted her shoulder.

"Don't worry, little *behin.* Janoor will protect you."

"Khraz, go to bed," Nazeem called out from his door. "We go in morning."

Christine nodded and tried to slip past, but Janoor wasn't moving. From down the hall, Setin's wife called out to Janoor.

Janoor cut her off with a single barking gesture and Christine realized that Janoor's deference to the sisters earlier had only been for Arshad's benefit. In the meantime, his eyes never left Christine.

"Yes, Khraz," Janoor mocked. "We leave too early. Don't make Janoor pull you out of such a pretty sleep."

She smelled fresh perspiration as Nazeem stepped in front of her. His fists were clenched, and he was poised to fight. Janoor didn't dare move back into her room, but he didn't move aside either. And Christine didn't move, so the three of them, sandwiched together, remained in the doorway.

Christine braced herself. She was ready to defend herself if she had to, or to help Nazeem if it came to that. She looked around for something she could use as a weapon, when Janoor finally emitted what sounded like a strained chortle. Then the Pakistani shouted something terse, and he and his family returned to their rooms. Nazeem stayed planted in front of her until the corridor emptied. He turned and faced her. His face was ashen and he looked terrified.

"Khraz," he started apologetically, but she didn't let him finish.

"We pray for Zubeda, *ji?*"

He nodded. Christine gave him a smile, then stepped past him and closed her door. It was several moments before she heard him start back to his room. She checked the door: no locks, and the door handle was loose. She sighed. A pang of homesickness washed over her, and suddenly she hated it there. She thought of Pakistan and India's recent parade of nuclear might and decided both countries with their Farrukhs and Janoors and Nikhils could blow each other to glowing embers and she wouldn't care.

Please God, give me enough time to find Liz first.

Then she heard movement from Nazeem's side of the wall. He paced . . . sat . . . stood, then paced some more.

His loyalty tore at her heart, and she clutched her scarf to hold in her sobs. Liz and Farrukh and Peshawar receded from her mind as she worried about Zubeda and the baby. The baby would die and, probably, so would Zubeda. And there was Nazeem, poor Nazeem, who was in over his head. He would guard her with his life, but, in the end, he was a farmer, not a man of violence.

Nazeem was rising from his cot again.

He kept pacing. He couldn't settle down.

She sat on her cot and stared out into the moonlight. Arshad was out there, trying to get to his wife. The roads were impossible. It would take an entire day to reach Lahore, and she already knew from her dreams that he would arrive too late.

Chapter

11

The steady pressure in her bladder had become a torment as a bus, its horn squawking, kicked up a torrent of dust. Road bits cracked at the glass in front of her and Christine closed her eyes. Her eardrums vibrated with the screech of another horn, this one even louder. Then someone shouted, bicycle bells whirred, a kid squealed, and Christine's eyes sprang open. There were no dead bodies, just two boys on a rickety bicycle with a pack of smaller kids behind them, darting across the road, playing Russian roulette with the traffic.

"The Grand Trunk is one crazy road, huh, Lady Shepherd?"

Christine barely acknowledged Janoor, who sat up front with his own driver. By simply keeping quiet, she had managed to avoid responding to most of his comments since they left Rawalpindi, but now her bladder *was* bursting. She'd have to say something. She turned to Nazeem.

"Nazeem," she whispered. "I need to —"

Setin, who sat on the other side of Nazeem, was staring at her again. His eyes were huge as he absently rubbed at the needle tracks on his arm. Out of the corner of her eye, she saw a swelling down low on his tunic. She looked away. Nazeem hissed something at the addict — again.

"Maf kijiye . . . ghusalkhana," she whispered, asking for a bathroom. Nazeem flushed and averted his eyes. Up front, Janoor shifted in his seat. He had heard her.

"There is nowhere. I am so sorry," he shouted.

She had mentioned the unmentionable, and Christine could feel the pressure in her bladder give just a bit as she wet herself. She was stupid to have waited so long. A row of lean-tos filled with dirty wares came up on their right. There had to be a hole back there somewhere, she thought. She started to ask Nazeem again, but he had turned away. Talk of a bathroom was taboo; she'd have to engage Janoor.

"What about those shops?" she shouted over the engine. "There has to be —"

Janoor twisted in his seat and almost

growled. "No, Lady Shepherd! It's no American TV here — no pit stop. You will wait, *hai?*"

The cousin had no objection to pulling over an hour before when the men left the van to pee out in bare bush, she thought.

She looked at her watch. "How long before we're there?" she asked, trying not to sound bothered.

"No long, Lady Shepherd. You wait."

Janoor faced forward. There would be no more discussion. Christine curled up into the corner of the seat, expecting that her bladder wouldn't hold much longer.

More warbling and another bus accelerated past them. Pakistani hitchhikers were hanging from its exterior. Christine resisted the urge to cover her eyes as the bus narrowly missed a gas truck. Torsos and legs swung out from the elaborately painted vehicle. The bus swerved and the Pakistanis somehow held on. Then a motorized rickshaw overtook their van on the left, nearly colliding with a bullock cart.

Their driver spat out the window, leaned on the horn, and followed the rickshaw. Christine held on as they overtook the bus on its left. The passengers were laughing and grinning as the bus swayed beneath them. *Why wouldn't they grin? Should they spill, the journey would be a shortcut to Allah and paradise.* Nazeem looked over at her and Christine realized she was scowling. She turned away just in time to catch a glimpse of a massive Bedford truck approaching from the opposite direction. The painted face of a veiled woman took up the entire side of the truck. It seemed to peer at her from between the hanging bodies. *Get used to it, Ameri-cain.*

And then the beguiling countenance was gone, followed by another shower of dirt and rocks.

Christine thought about the pain in her bladder, thought about simply letting go, then Janoor glanced back. He smirked and said something to the driver in Urdu.

Nazeem tensed next to her. His head was down and he exhaled miserably. The young Rajput knew she was suffering, but he couldn't help, and suddenly she realized it wasn't about her, or her discomfort. Nazeem was embarrassed. They were all expecting her to let go, and if she did, Nazeem and Arshad would be dishonored. Janoor turned up the Indian music, probably to rattle her.

She thought of Arshad, who was probably hanging from some bus, dirty from the road, his scalp dripping. He had always been sensitive about his appearance. Still, prince to the end, he had left them the van. Hitching would be the cheapest way to get to Zubeda, and he would need every rupee for his wife's care. Suddenly the frenetic beat of the music helped her concentrate. Christine forced herself to forget about gas stops and think of Peshawar instead, and the ache in her belly eased.

The nap had been short. Still, sometime during her twenty-minute respite, they had left the lush green fields of the Punjab Province and had entered the barren plains and rocky hillocks of the North-West Frontier Province of Pakistan.

The Grand Trunk, the main artery to Peshawar, traveled across a long bridge over the Indus River and the last bit of green she would see for a while. As the van rocked and tilted over the uneven boards of the old bridge, Janoor regaled them with gruesome stories of vehicles and people who had plunged to their deaths in the thrashing waters below. The van took a final lurch off the bridge and Christine managed to stifle a gasp. She knew Janoor was listening, waiting for her to cry out.

They hadn't driven very far before she saw a sign for the Peshawar Development Authority.

"Cover the face, lady," Janoor warned as they approached a military post. Christine already had her scarf pulled tight across her mouth. The border guard hardly glanced in, just took the hundred rupees of routine graft from Janoor, and they passed through.

"You safe now," Janoor said, looking back. "I just don't want no problem. They shoot you here if you cause problem. You understand?"

Her *dupatta* drawn, Christine remained poised. She was glad he couldn't see her smile. When Janoor didn't get a chance to humiliate his cousins, he fell into a foul mood. She didn't pee as he had hoped, and now he couldn't even scare her. Janoor jerked his head around in a pout, and even Nazeem had to smile.

Another sign for Peshawar flew by. They stopped, and Christine looked out the window. Except for two piles of stones on each side of the van and a skinny pole blocking traffic, with an equally skinny Pakistani raising and lowering the barrier, there wasn't much. A withered, almost ebony hand reached through a crack in

Janoor's window and seized a crumpled bit of currency. More graft. The guard slapped a lever, the slender barrier shot up, and they drove through.

"Is this it? asked Christine. "Is this Peshawar? Are we in?"

"Yes, Lady Shepherd. You in."

Janoor's tone was ominous. He and the driver no longer joked. Soon the dust-laden air around them was churning with Pashtun tribesmen. Their elaborate turbans trailed fabric that billowed behind them as they strode, guns slung over their shoulders, leathery hands resting on the hilts of knives or swords. Rickshaws pulled by scorched old men, and clutches of women hauling monstrous grass bags, wove between and around the fearsome looking men. Some women's heads were covered by scarves the size of small table-cloths, other women were clad in burqas that covered them entirely. The women moved like spirits intent on remaining invisible.

As they drove out of the old city, they went through the Afghan district, where impoverished refugees lived in lean-tos. Christine was reminded of the slums in the United States, but commerce bustled all around. There were so many shops that some stalls pushed out into the street, forcing vehicles to drive around them. Moneychangers crouched before their establishments and waved rupees as they hollered into the crush. Rooms were offered at a hundred rupees, three U.S. dollars a night, but one was expected to haggle and huff, and usually one had a gun. Everyone had a gun; it was Peshawar.

Hawkers, motorcycles, *chai* carts, mule drivers, mosques . . . and more mosques. A Mercedes darted in front of them, and its driver spat out the window. A glob of green mucus flew back against the van's windshield. Their driver cursed under his breath. At one moment they would be squeezing through a labyrinth of primitive pathways, and then the street would widen and the city seemed almost progressive.

Christine glanced at Nazeem, expecting him to be as curious as she. Even Setin was looking out the window. But Nazeem's eyes were stretched wide with panic. Christine's scarf had slipped, and suddenly she felt naked. Wild-looking men were striding past the van, and she couldn't get the scarf up to her face fast enough. Nazeem gave her a hard look and she held the scarf in place until they arrived at the Pearl Continental Hotel.

"G'day. You Christine?" the stranger asked, approaching her the moment Christine entered the lobby.

Christine just stared at the Australian, wondering who he was while trying not to be distracted by a black, misshapen mole just over his right eyebrow. There was a second and even larger one buried into one of his sideburns. They were large sideburns, shaped like a T-bone steak, a style that had gone out of fashion in the U.S. decades earlier. But it was the man's skin that concerned her. He had obviously burned and peeled so many times that his face had finally discolored into a permanent patchwork. As a redhead, she knew the look, just never to that extent.

Before Christine could respond, the Aussie shoved his cigarette between his teeth and took her hand, shaking it, while his other hand, the left hand, "the dirty hand," the hand used only for the toilet, rested on her shoulder. Christine glanced nervously at Nazeem and his cousins, who were waiting for her just outside the entrance. However, the doors were glass and Nazeem wasn't pleased. Fortunately, the man released her.

"Reggie Duke," the man began, eyeing the American dressed in *hijab*. "Dale's girl, right?"

Christine nodded.

"Nice outfit."

Christine knew that Reggie Duke was being sarcastic, but all she could think about were those ugly melanomas and the cigarettes, and she wondered which cancer, skin or lung, would get him first.

"Yeah, you, too," she said and tried to smile. She still couldn't believe Cloid would send her someone who was so conspicuous. The man was wearing worn fatigues. His Aussie hat was stained, and a well-used rucksack hung from one shoulder. A belt with three pouches crossed his chest and another circled his waist. What looked like a huge Bowie knife in a flaking scabbard hung from his waist belt with two smaller knives tucked in beside it.

Christine needed a moment to think. "I need to check in first."

"Help yourself," Reggie said, taking another drag on his cigarette.

Christine left the Aussie and headed over to the registration desk. The lobby of Pearl Continental was clean and strangely

Western in its décor. In Peshawar, it was the best hotel in town at 300 rupees a night, about ten U.S. dollars. It seemed quite civilized, though a sign requested all visitors to check their arms at the desk. Maybe Bowie knives didn't count.

"Can I help you, ma'am?" the clerk asked in heavily accented English.

The brand of "Ameri-cain" must glow from her forehead, Christine decided. The man was in a suit. So, she took a chance and dropped her scarf. When he didn't react, she told him she was checking in.

"Your name?" he asked.

Christine hesitated. The clerk waited patiently as if her reluctance to tell him her real name was not unusual.

The Aussie appeared behind her. "Just give him cash."

"I can handle this."

"Bloody hell, woman, you're in a Pakistani border town. Just give him cash."

Christine paid the clerk, took the room key, and walked toward the elevator. She waved to the cousins. They were all waiting for her — Janoor, for his money, Setin, a fix, and poor Nazeem, who just wanted to go home. She was in Peshawar. Nazeem had gotten her there, had dutifully fulfilled her request. She had met Cloid's man, and now she was supposed to cut him loose. Which was fine with her, except there was something about Reggie Duke she didn't trust.

Then she saw the Australian glance at a man in the lobby, a Caucasian, sitting on a couch, nursing a cup of *chai*. The man was casually dressed, minding his business, but Christine knew better. She had seen too many of them through the years. Her bet was that he was CIA.

She stopped, just short of the elevator.

"Forget something?" Reggie asked.

They have a problem, Christine realized, *and I'm it.* She didn't know what it was precisely, but she knew that they couldn't just force her to go with them. They were in a city where the Pakistan government had little jurisdiction, and the United States had none. At least the man on the couch was good enough not to look up. The Australian, on the other hand, looked like he had been caught with his hand somewhere it shouldn't be.

"Is he with you?" she asked.

Reggie waited for a guest to pass, out of earshot. "We can talk about it in your room," he whispered.

"I was told you would help me find my sister."

"We'll talk in your room, I said."

"You going to help me or not?"

The Aussie glared at her, but was suddenly perplexed. Cloid Dale had told him of the woman's sister, had warned him that Christine might try to resist, but there was no mention of *Pakis* or *spooks*. He needed to talk to Dale, and he needed to up his fee.

"I've got to make a call first. Head on up." Reggie didn't wait for her to reply, just pulled out his mobile phone and stepped outside the lobby through a side door.

Christine noticed that the man who looked like a CIA operative had left the couch and was looking through some tribal trinkets in a small gift stall near the front entrance, where Janoor and Setin waited patiently outside. Nazeem, however, had entered the lobby. He looked poised to do what? Run? Fight? Something. He must have sensed something was wrong. His shirt was soaked with sweat, and he was rooted to the floor, almost paralyzed by his own resolve to watch over her. She smiled at him, trying to reassure him, but he wouldn't relax.

Christine didn't know what to do when suddenly she realized she needed to pee . . . and a chance to think.

By the time Christine had exited the ladies' room, where there were freshly painted stalls, marble countertops, American Standard toilets, and real toilet paper, Reggie was waiting. He flicked his cigarette down on the lobby floor, mashing the butt with his toe. There were others on the floor, an international array of butts, in fact.

Christine saw that the cousins had joined Nazeem inside, but the three of them had stayed near the entrance. The CIA operative, however, had vanished.

"Your friend left," she said.

Reggie ignored her, facing her squarely so the Pakistanis at the door couldn't see their faces. "Is the bunch at the door staying?"

"Maybe —"

"Maybe," he demanded, "you'll say your good-byes and we'll try to figure this out."

Christine didn't argue, but as she approached Nazeem she knew that he wouldn't leave her. Even Janoor seemed genuinely concerned for her welfare, now referring to her as his "little sister." Nazeem had told Janoor of her "husband," and when Christine admitted that Reggie was not a relation, but merely someone who was supposed to help, Janoor perked up.

"I have friend who knows a top-notch businessman. He knows all very important persons in the Frontier Province. I take you, yes?"

"Who is this businessman?"

"Only top-notch, a Pashtun who sells lots of things, maybe furniture, maybe rugs, maybe —"

"Maybe guns?" she asked.

Janoor only shrugged, which meant, yes, which meant that there was a good chance that he had either sold to Farrukh or at least knew something about him.

"Maybe knows husband, too. I don't know," Janoor announced. "We go and ask, okay? Then get back by dark. My cousin young and too nervous, I think. No good for him here, *hai?*"

Janoor whispered something to Nazeem about "the crazy Frontier" and how they had become men of courage. There "the wives," their village Banalwala, and Janoor brought up Ruhee's name at least twice. Christine didn't pick up all of it, but Nazeem smiled, enjoying whatever it was Janoor was teasing him about. For a moment Christine thought she might be able to trust Janoor . . . for a price.

Negotiation was short. Janoor's fee would be three hundred dollars, his friend, one hundred dollars, while the top-notch businessman would be extra, and from the extreme cock of Janoor's head at her inquiry, a lot extra. But Janoor was adamant; taking Reggie Duke with them was not an option. He reminded her that they would be on "tribal land," where foreigners, especially Westerners, were not allowed. Smuggling in a woman was dangerous enough without bringing in a six-foot-tall, blond Australian.

While Janoor made arrangements, Reggie followed Christine up to her room. He admitted that he had been hired to take her home, but now his job was also to make sure she didn't get herself killed. As for the spook in the lobby? He swore to her that he didn't have a clue who the bloke was; nor did Cloid. Obviously, someone had got wind of her arrival.

Christine just listened. She thought about calling Cloid, but it was past midnight in Los Angeles. She looked at the red-faced Aussie and decided she believed him. Anyway, she couldn't imagine Cloid aligning himself with the Agency; he hated those guys.

Reggie did his job and argued, but as he

suspected, any woman who traveled with Pakis wasn't likely to listen to reason. Christine was determined to go. And she didn't seem to care what the authorities thought, or that Farrukh Ahmed's profile claimed that he wasn't into abduction, or that she would be traveling into an area that was off-limits to foreigners. Her sister was missing, and Christine wasn't going to stop searching until they had proof that Liz was dead, or until she found Farrukh.

When Christine told Reggie of Janoor's proposal and that he had to stay behind, the Aussie cursed again, cursed once more, then made it clear that he had no intention of letting her out of his sight. He knew the area and the clans. His plan, whether she agreed or not, was to hire a truck, pack it with Afghans, and follow her. He'd be disguised and ready to go within the hour; Janoor would never be the wiser. Christine was skeptical and asked about his disguise and the truck he would drive, and about the Afghans he would hire. Reggie glared at her, and she thought he was going to curse again. She asked too many questions. All she had to know was that he would be behind her, and available, in case there was trouble.

Chapter
12

As their van roared and bounced over the bare-rock countryside, Christine thought of Mars. The North-West Frontier Province was like another planet, and she couldn't imagine anyone residing in such harsh conditions.

Just after they set off, Janoor admitted that the "top-notch" businessman also dealt in heavy artillery and wanted to know if she had any interest in his wares. She knew how Cloid would respond, and toyed with picking up an RPG and a supply of grenades. She assured Janoor she was. The Pakistani grinned. If she was really serious about finding Farrukh, she'd need guns. The Aussie had brought his own hardware, "traveling shit," he called it, but she wanted her own, especially in an area where even ten-year-old boys were well armed.

She glanced behind her at a car packed with a family of Pakistanis. Behind them was a Bedford truck hauling water buffalo, and behind the Bedford truck was Reggie. Between the vehicles, the clouds of dust, and the tent-sized burqa that covered her with only a cloth mesh to look through, she could barely make out his pickup truck. She turned back around and kept watch by glancing periodically in the rear-view mirror. While Janoor jabbered on about warlords and hundred-year feuds between tribesmen, Christine watched as the family of Pakistanis turned off the road. When the Bedford cattle truck began overtaking them on the left, she got a clear view of Reggie's pickup. Even through the grid of her burqa she could see the two swarthy individuals sitting in the cab up front. Like the others, Reggie was wearing a turban with a shawl wrapped over his head to cover his hairy sideburns. It was over a hundred degrees, but the tribesmen liked their air-conditioned cabs and their shawls. Tips of automatic rifles and RPG launchers stuck up above the cab and out from the sides of the truck. Christine had never seen so much firepower in her life, but Reggie wasn't taking any chances. A flatbed of armed Afghans sat poised behind him, moving easily over every rut in the road.

In the meantime, Janoor entertained her with stories of the notorious drug lords who owned luxurious estates just outside Peshawar. But from what Christine could see, the North-West Frontier was dry and barren, with little vegetation and even fewer trees, hardly the sprawling castled estates that Christine had been used to in Europe. Janoor assured her that there were estates, nonetheless. Instead of expansive lawns and intricate mazes, the fiefdoms created in this region were stone and mud fortresses enclosed by high, thick walls and brown, rocky landscapes. In the Punjab Province there had been green fields of new mustard, and golden crops of wheat, and home gardens. And there were the women, scarved and covered, wandering back to their homes from the village bazaars to prepare the evening meal. But since they had left Peshawar, Christine had not seen any women. Just as she was about to ask about them, Janoor told her to crouch low and stay quiet. It was another checkpoint, manned by Pakistani militia. Once Janoor had paid the bribe, they drove through. Christine started again to ask about the women, but Janoor had conveniently occupied himself in conversation with the driver. She took that opportunity to check on Reggie. She looked into the mirror, catching Reggie's pickup just as it came to a stop at the checkpoint. She watched as Reggie's driver paid off the guard and continued through without incident. Then the quiet in the van registered, and Christine realized that Janoor had stopped talking. She could feel his eyes as she shifted her gaze away from the mirror.

"Do these, ah . . . 'lords' live here year round?" she asked.

He had said something, but she had cut him off in time, careful to pick up from where he had left off.

"Only one is not here. I tell you the truth." Janoor sighed, turning around in his seat. "Very sad, Lady Shepherd. Raza Sherazi has very good power here. He helped many people. Ten percent, I think, of all Peshawar just work for Raza. Many people. Very sad, very good man. But I think your country keep poor Raza for a long time. Yes . . . for long time."

Janoor sighed again, shaking his head. Their driver, Chacha, mumbled something to him. "Chacha" meant "the father's brother," or "uncle," but Christine doubted that the guy was any relation. It was Chacha who actually knew the "top-notch" businessman.

"Chacha right," Janoor said. "We hear Ameri-cain jails nice place to stay."

Chacha smiled at this.

"Is this true, Lady Shepherd? Many killers in U.S. have free place to stay for long time, *hai?*"

Janoor twisted around to look at Christine, but she was looking out her window. The sun was lowering in the sky, and she was remembering Nikhil just before the land mine explosion.

"Maybe Raza no want to return to Peshawar. In Pakistan we have no nice jails. If you too bad in Peshawar, we kill very fast. No jails here. Pakistanis no have big money like U.S. Jails a waste here, I think. You understand?"

This time Christine met his eyes. Even through the grid of the burqa she could tell that the Pakistani was desperate for a reaction. Then Setin whispered something to Nazeem. Janoor laughed, but Nazeem remained quiet. He was staring out at the strange shadows of rugged terrain and massive strongholds, and she knew he felt as foreign there as she did.

Christine thought of her dream about Zubeda's baby, her belief that it was a bad

244

omen and that Zubeda's baby would die, and she felt stupid. Janoor had picked up a portable phone in Peshawar and they had called the hospital in Lahore before they left. Zubeda had survived the operation, and Arshad had made it to her in one piece, and baby and mother were well.

Just as the light left the sky Christine heard gunshots, one close by. She flinched, and Nazeem jumped in his seat.

The men roared. "It is a whole lot of wild after dark, you know," Janoor yelled. "Lots of bang-bang. And those Pashtuns. They such good businessmen. They don't waste that poppy. You help them out, Setin. Okay? So they don't waste that good poppy? Maybe they share?"

Setin was rubbing his arm furiously, and he barked out a strained laugh.

Christine caught a glimpse of something in the mirror and whipped her head around. The burqa tightened around her as she twisted in her seat. Two trucks, both packed with men and guns, were overtaking Reggie's pickup.

The men in the van, except for Nazeem who was also turned in his seat, had stopped talking.

"What's happening? What are they doing

to that truck?" Christine tried not to sound panicked.

Janoor glanced back, cocked his head, and muttered, "Make some money, I think. Those tribesmen good businessmen. Your husband, good businessman?"

Christine and Nazeem watched helplessly as the pickup was forced to a stop. More dust obscured her view, but Christine could see that even with his Afghans, Reggie was outnumbered.

As Chacha turned at the next curve Reggie's pickup disappeared from sight.

"Just like Ameri-cain TV. Lots of guns. Good fun, *hai*, Lady Shepherd?"

Christine couldn't see him, but Janoor was grinning again. She could hear it. And suddenly she was sure that the Pakistani was responsible for the ambush. She turned towards her window, trying not to seem bothered. Her burqa was so twisted she couldn't see anything. It didn't matter; options were running through her head. If she only had a gun. But she didn't. She had no choice but to go on.

There were more gunshots, closer, but Christine managed to remain still. She felt a ripple of reaction in Nazeem, but he also resisted the impulse to jump. Janoor stopped grinning and said something to

246

Chacha. The driver responded, black tobacco juice dribbling from the corner of his mouth. He spat out the window just as they approached a massive wooden gate with marble inlay. It was hardly dusk and still two floodlights flashed on as the van lurched to a stop, dust billowing around them.

"Too much dirt, I think. We wait, yes?" Janoor asked. He turned in his seat, and Christine nodded cautiously.

"Chacha say this Afridi have so many guns. You be so happy, Lady Shepherd. You see."

"I don't need so many. Just —"

Janoor shook his head. "He do us favor, you know? He owns many gun shops in bazaar, but it is no good there. All closed, and lots of shooting over there. Some crazy with drink stay in their shop and like their own drugs too much, I think. You understand? Too much bang-bang? So, Mister Maroof do Chacha big favor."

Which meant to Christine that she'd better be serious about buying guns. If that was their goal, and she prayed it was, she'd buy an arsenal.

"I can't pay much," Christine countered.

The grin widened on Janoor's face in anticipation of some good haggling. "No worry, Lady Shepherd. Chacha take good care of you. Then if Afridi happy, he help find your husband. You trust Janoor, yes?"

"Yes."

Janoor looked happy, just the way she wanted to keep him. Perhaps this was all about money. Janoor had told her earlier that the Afridi clan was one of the most powerful families in the area and that she was fortunate to be meeting Mr. Maroof. She hoped so.

Two guards, wearing red berets, emerged from the brown haze with handguns pointed at the van. Shouting instructions in a language Christine didn't recognize, they flung open the doors of the van, small AKs with folding metal stocks secured against their shoulders. Janoor's arms shot up. He glanced back at Christine once more.

"We go."

The courtyard was a macabre setting of ornate fountains and sculptures. Bright pink and green onyx, marble and bronze, and even figures clothed entirely in gold leaf were positioned around them as they approached the entrance to the three-story coral-colored mansion. There were so many pieces of sculpture that it took several moments before Christine noticed the bronze doors leading into the arms dealer's house. By this time the guards had lowered their guns and Chacha, like a travel guide, led them through. Not only did Chacha speak English, but his speech was unnervingly clear as he pointed out three expensive Mercedes. He swore that they were identical to cars that James Bond had driven in his movies, adding that the Afridi who lived here spent a lot of time in that electric city in the west.

"Lotus Vegas?" he asked Christine.

Christine just nodded and watched as two new guards, turbaned this time, armed, and layered in cloth, stepped from the shadows and escorted them into the house.

A deep blue marble lined the floor and walls of the foyer, which held a few pieces of intricately carved mahogany furniture. A mosaic of tiny mirrors reflected small dots of light from the ceiling above them. Pictures of powerful looking men, draped in embroidered cloth and armed with swords, hung from the walls. They passed through one room after another, each filled with people, some clad in Western dress, others in traditional garb, all speaking in foreign dialects. The air reeked of tobacco, pot, and booze, and Christine reached up under her sheath, holding her nose as they walked. The burqa was hot and uncomfortable, but at least it gave her privacy.

Ahead of her she could hear the Afridi. There were other voices, but Wazir Azidi Maroof's voice dominated. A guard stopped them, frisking the men. Upon seeing Christine, the guard waved her on, and a woman appeared.

Christine followed the woman to a corner with a drawn curtain. Behind the curtain, the woman helped Christine take off her burqa. As was custom, Christine wore a *shalwar qamiz* underneath. The woman slipped off Christine's backpack and ran a metal detector over the long blouse and pants. When she finished, she tucked in the last pieces of exposed hair around Christine's *dupatta*, then gestured for her to go. Christine hardly missed the burqa, but she wanted her backpack.

"Mujbe meray paison ki zaroorat hai," Christine insisted, reaching for the backpack. The woman held the bag away from her, not understanding. "My money, rupees, paisa," Christine gestured. Finally the woman opened the bag, rifling through its contents. There was no reaction on the woman's face as she pulled out the brick-sized wad of cloth-wrapped rupees that

Christine had brought with her from the bank in Islamabad. She handed it to Christine, but kept the bag.

When Christine stepped out from behind the curtain, she found Nazeem straining to see past the guards. He wasn't going to lose her. Clutching her rupees with one hand, Christine secured her scarf with the other.

They entered a vaulted room, draped in brocades and tapestries. Christine's first thought was of a New York designer's showroom. Despite the thick hangings on the walls, Maroof's booming voice seemed to reverberate around them. The air was thick with dust and lint and smelled of gun oil. It reminded her of Cloid's kitchen at the range house, except it was not a friendly gathering, it was a smuggler's den.

There were other customers, and Christine would have to wait her turn. The room was cluttered with brass and copper and gold merchandise. There were flamboyant opium pipes and embroidered pillows piled high along the walls. Rugs, Kashmiri, more beautiful than she had ever seen before, were lying about, and she couldn't help but think of Liz. Past the bodies of the guards in front of her, she could see the bottoms of robes where two customers talked in Pashto to Wazir Maroof. He sounded overbearing and Christine imagined the Afridi to be obese and disgusting. She shifted her position and got a glimpse of three women seated on pillows next to Maroof's robes. One was young; the others looked older, a bit haggard. Their large scarflike *chadors* were pinned neatly beneath their chins.

One customer ahead of them wore a red-and-white headdress atop a startlingly white robe. Christine guessed that he was from Saudi Arabia. It was obvious that the man was rich and had come quite a distance to see Maroof. She looked over at Janoor. She still didn't trust him but she was glad that he had not lied about the importance of Chacha's contact. Maroof had to know of Farrukh.

Bowing and offering Allah's blessing to Maroof, the two customers who were ahead of the Saudi man rose from their pillows. Their business was concluded, and two guards followed them out of the room as the Saudi stepped forward. Christine followed with Nazeem, who seemed as tentative as she.

Maroof slipped easily into Arabic as the Saudi greeted him. Christine thought about trying to peek around the Saudi, but decided it was more prudent to wait. She tugged once more at her *dupatta*. She caught the eye of one of Maroof's women, but the woman quickly averted her eyes.

Then the Saudi bent over to inspect a gun, and Christine got her first good look at the dealer. She was surprised to see that the man was not huge, but slight. The cheekbones of his face were knobbed, his nose was hawklike, and his ears were large and flat. Tufted brows hooded two glimmers of black that peered out until the man from Saudi Arabia stood, blocking her view again.

When the Saudi finally left with his merchandise, Christine prepared to face her host. It seemed as if his bulk took up an entire corner of the room. There couldn't be much body in there, Christine decided, but there was no mistaking the powerful voice. The face in the folds greeted Christine in perfect English.

"Welcome to my home, Christine Shepherd."

It took Christine a moment to respond. She nodded.

Maroof looked young, under thirty, but his teeth were badly stained, and one in the front looked as if it had died at the root.

"You can drop your scarf. You are safe here."

When Christine started to lower her scarf, Nazeem grabbed at it. Janoor snapped at him, and Nazeem reluctantly withdrew his hand. Christine looked to the women for support, a signal, anything to let her know how to proceed. They stared ahead as if she didn't exist. Maroof was waiting, and she finally let go of her scarf. Still, she felt exposed, and was acutely aware of the feel of the stale air against her bare skin. Nazeem lowered his eyes.

"I hope I have enough to please you," Maroof smirked, eyeing her oversized block of rupees.

"I didn't want to leave it —"

"You don't trust Farhat?" he asked, gesturing toward the woman who had taken her backpack.

Christine started to speak, then shrugged, cocking her head in perfect Pakistani fashion.

The Afridi smiled. "A cautious woman, I think . . . You are a spy?"

"No."

"American?"

Christine didn't respond.

"You are ashamed?"

Christine took a breath. "No."

"Then you are an American, I believe?"

"Yes," Christine confirmed, bracing for the barrage of bullets. There was none, no signal from Maroof, no shuffling of feet. The guards were standing by . . . waiting . . . bored.

A boy, his head bowed, brought her a glass of juice while the Afridi picked through an impressive array of arms. There must've been forty pieces, including grenades and what looked like some kind of antiaircraft missile in a small suitcase.

"Before we start, may I ask the lady what she wants with guns. Muslims are a peaceful people."

"I'm a woman alone."

Maroof nodded, still studying the weapons. "Perhaps the counsel of a guide would be of more benefit?"

"I have a guide."

Christine was desperate to ask about Farrukh. "I'm looking for someone. And I thought you could help."

"Your husband?"

Christine was self-conscious. Nazeem was waiting for her to respond. After all, this was what he had risked his life for, and now the idea of disillusioning him overwhelmed her.

"Men do not like to be surprised by their

women here, Mrs. Shepherd. Maybe you should've waited at home, *hai?*"

The gun dealer's voice startled her and Christine swept her scarf back over her face. No one had held a gun to her head. Maroof had merely to raise his voice, and she had no more courage than the mannequins sitting next to him.

"Please, Madame," Maroof sighed.

"Farrukh Ahmed," she blurted out. "I'm looking for Farrukh Ahmed."

She couldn't look at Nazeem. She was not only a liar, but an American who was looking for a Muslim brother. She waited for the guards to pounce.

"What do you want with Ahmed?"

"I think he knows where my husband is."

The room had quieted, and the Afridi had fallen silent in his mountain of textiles. There was no movement, no sound, only the distant yapping of a dog.

"Do you have enough money to pay for that kind of information?"

Christine let the scarf fall from her face. Once again she felt dead air on her cheeks. But this time, she didn't react. She held out the block of rupees.

"I have this . . . and I can get more."

The merchant paused. More than paused. He was studying her. Probably still thought she was a spy. Christine dared to look at Nazeem. It was just a glimpse, but there was no anger, no look of betrayal. The young farmer still believed she was looking for her husband. She looked up at Maroof and hoped he believed the same.

"You are my guest," Maroof finally commented. "And I have offended you. You will need guns. Let me sell you something."

"And Farrukh?"

Maroof cocked his head.

Now she understood. The room was filled with people and Maroof couldn't talk freely about a man many considered a hero. First he would sell her guns, and if she pleased him, then maybe he would tell her of Farrukh. She had no idea what he would ask for, but she didn't care. For the first time in months she was hopeful.

So they began. Christine pointed to a number of handguns, several of which had been copied by the tribes. She praised their workmanship, and he, in turn, counseled her as to the best ones to buy. The locally made copies were good, and much cheaper, but Christine had no idea how they would perform compared to factory-made weapons. It didn't take long for her to settle on five Kalashnikovs — a sixth he threw in for good will — a Soviet Tokarev automatic pistol, and a couple of RPG launchers. He also gave her a fountain pen. At least, she thought it was a fountain pen until she saw that the hole in the bottom had been enlarged.

"A gift . . . a souvenir of your trip," Maroof offered. "Of course, the gun will take only a single nine-millimeter round. But if the lady insists on pursuing her husband, she might need all the firearms she can acquire."

Then the haggling began for real. Christine tried to hold her own, but Chacha eventually jumped in, and she was surprised how fervently the Pakistani driver fought to get her a better price. The Afridi didn't seem to mind. He clearly preferred the rough-and-tumble of negotiating with an expert. Soon a price was agreed upon, and Christine excused herself, stepping behind a pile of pillows so she could count out the money. Wazir Maroof sighed again, and grunted something to the serving boy. By the time Christine had returned with the correct amount, the boy had reappeared with another glass of juice.

Christine had just finished the last glass. The room was stuffy and hot. Christine felt full, but didn't dare insult her host's hospitality. She noticed that the men in the room had collected around them. She had become accustomed to gawkers, but she was beginning to feel claustrophobic.

"Mujhe pani chahiye?" she asked without thinking. "Water, please."

"Of course," said Maroof.

Christine looked down at her hand and there was a glass of water in it. She couldn't remember the boy handing it to her, but she drank it down.

"Maybe the counsel of a guide would be of more benefit?"

Christine lowered the glass and focused on Maroof. *Had she heard him right? Had he offered a guide again?*

Her mouth moved to respond. She started to say, "No, thank you," but Maroof was already nodding as if she had answered. By then the room was sweltering, and Christine suddenly noticed that her glass was full again. Who filled it? The suspicion that she had been drugged entered her mind, but she drank anyway, emptying the glass. Then she tried to remember her last thought. She had a feeling it was important, but the room began to shift. Christine looked down at her feet. She hadn't moved, yet the room moved around her. She raised her eyes and the ugly merchant's mouth was working. He was talking, calling, giving instructions to someone behind her . . . but she couldn't hear. And then the room stretched, and bulged and —

I've been drugged! Her mind cried out. The glass fell from her hand. She watched it break, without a sound, shattering . . . slowly. And all she could think of was that she was so thirsty.

Christine tried to face the Afridi once more, but her gaze caught Maroof for only an instant as the room tilted sideways. Then she was staring up into images, hundreds of them, all reflecting her smiling face. She felt hands on her arms, and something was supporting her head while she stared up at herself. A cackling of horns and tinny Indian music buffeted the insides of her mind. She smiled at her many faces while the horns drew out, became louder, until it sounded like someone was shrieking.

The images of the smiling woman frowned at the human cry, and Christine felt panic overtake her. The realization that she had been drugged came to her again, and she strained to hold it.

"Nazeem," she wailed. Her voice sounded like the peal of a horn. "I've been drugged . . . I've been drugged!"

She tried to turn toward Nazeem, but the canopy of mirrors and triangles and bits of colored glass caught her attention and she thought of a Mughal palace . . . a prince . . . her prince. The cry was blood-curdling, and Christine managed to turn her head. Nazeem was slumped over a chair in the blue hallway, his head at an awkward angle, a slash of red at his throat. Pakistanis bent over his form. They stared at him, some with their arms crossed, others at their sides, bystanders watching, curious, always curious . . .

Already there was a pool of blood be-neath Nazeem, and it seemed to be spreading over the shiny marble toward her.

Christine opened her mouth and screamed long and piercingly, and sud-denly their voices came rushing back to her. She threw herself forward, falling in front of Maroof. She watched his fin-gers, like tendrils, emerge from the fur-rows of gold and pick at a bowl of guavas. Christine thought of Zubeda and knew why she was crying in the dream. Nazeem was dead, had been murdered, and the river she was throwing flowers into had overflowed with his blood and was spreading toward her.

Christine tried to back away from the Afridi. Hands, leathery and goat-scented, came in from behind her and slid by her lips. She bit, her neck straining with the exertion, and a guard behind her cried out in pain.

Maroof looked up from his guavas and said something, one hand waving about while the other reached for another guava. His mouth was full of fruit. She watched, entranced, as juice and bits of pulp fell upon the gold threads on his chest.

Christine found herself standing upright. She spotted Setin in a doorway, exchanging something with a figure in rags.

Drugs, he's taking drugs, and with that thought she could feel her mind yawn and tear. She reached for her mouth, but couldn't feel her fingers, the fingers that were smudged with henna, that threw flowers into a river of blood. *They drugged me.* Her mind turned, and turned . . . and turned.

Christine felt the press of faces upon her, all watching, waiting, curious, and she tried to move through them and they let her. She stumbled, and one of the guards, a young one, reached for her, but quickly withdrew his hand. She had glowered at him and he was Muslim. His religion prohibited him from touching her, or maybe he was afraid she might bite him. She didn't know which.

Christine got back to her feet and caught another glimpse of Maroof in the golden room behind her. He was also Muslim, but he was grinning, enjoying her struggle. He waved her forward as he ate his guavas.

So Christine lurched ahead as best she could. She slogged through the hallway that twisted with the faces of Pakistanis who fell into laughter as she passed them. She tripped again, feeling the softness of fiber in her hands. She focused on the cloth she was gripping. It was the pantleg of a pair of trousers. *Made in Ameri-cain, made in Americain,* her mind taunted.

"Nowhere to go, Lady Shepherd. We have your money, *hai?* But I not hurt you."

She looked up from the man's pantleg into Janoor's smiling countenance. She held him for only an instant because her gaze was being pulled toward the ceiling, toward the glittering images.

Someone took her head and Janoor bent in close. She could smell the decay on his breath. *He's dead,* she thought, and Christine wondered when the toads would start to spill from his mouth.

"There's still more money for you, *hai?* Maybe the stupid husband, yes?"

Christine could hear herself breathe, "Yes."

"So you safe. Good. Who to call, lady? Tell me."

"Janoor," Christine uttered. "They . . . they killed Nazeem. Oh, God . . . they killed him."

Janoor sneered, rising up, letting her head go and it hit the floor. She looked up at Janoor, whose body seemed to stretch high above her. Beyond him were the tiny mirrors, but she couldn't see the faces because Janoor's face was large before her, changing, contorting like the room. His mouth moved, and now it was Nikhil who glared down at her. She saw him, and Christine reached out for that pantleg to help lift herself up. Instead, she felt metal against her palm. The face that resembled Nikhil reacted, and then she knew it was not a pantleg but someone's gun she had grasped. Before Janoor could stop her, she pulled the Kalashnikov to her.

There were hands, and startled voices, and the faces on the ceiling were grimacing, but she ignored them all and pushed herself back against a wall. The weight of the gun felt oddly familiar, and

264

she didn't hesitate to point it at the Pakistanis who crowded around her. Nikhil was gone, but there was Janoor and Setin, and she heard someone yell in the distance. It was Maroof's voice, the gun dealer, the one who had drugged her. She thumbed off the safety and pulled the trigger.

Three-shot bursts, just the way Cloid liked.

Her breath came in short, barking gasps, but it wasn't just her breath. It was the sound of the gun jerking in her hand. And then she was up, and the Pakistanis, who seconds before had been curious onlookers in an age-old bloodsport, were jumping out of her way as she headed down the hall. She didn't know where she was going, but no one stopped her as she gripped oversize handles and flung the doors wide.

She was looking for Arshad and Nazeem. They would be in their field, waving, trying to warn her, but she couldn't see them. It was dark out, fleeting shapes, darting in and about the moonlight. There were more shots . . .

Was that her? Or Nikhil?

Christine went to a wall, skirting along it, not feeling the roughness that scraped at her elbows. She glanced down past the rifle to her feet and they were . . . tiny and jeweled. Nazeem was dead and Zubeda was throwing flowers. She was crying, because her husband's brother was dead.

"No," Christine screamed into the night. "They're out there!"

Men were coming from different directions by then, but Christine was back in the minefield. She could hear Nikhil behind her, and she raised the gun again and shot into the darkness. In the back of her mind, she tried to remember that she only had thirty shots . . . thirty chances. The magazine was emptying, and she heard cries, thought she saw someone fall before her, a guard, the one who had backed away from her.

And then bits of the wall exploded in front of her, and she leaned back against it. She froze, waiting, her mind still whirling. She wanted the images to stop. She was desperate to get away from them, but she had to wait. And then the shots stopped, and she ran, coming to the end of the wall. Another shot caromed off the corner and concrete flew back in her face. She scrunched her eyes and turned away, her finger jerking impulsively at the trigger of the automatic. The dirt in front of her kicked up, and she yelled.

Beyond the wall was darkness. Scrambling over the uneven ground, she plunged into the brush and rocks. Things gashed her legs, but the sounds from behind kept her going.

More gunshots, but she remembered she had finished the magazine. She was so sure it was Nikhil behind her. *Ullas's gun was leveled at her. Nikhil was firing; he wanted to kill her, but it wouldn't work. He would step on a land mine any moment. He would be killed and she could already picture the mutilated face of the camel, Nikhil's torn khakis . . .*

Christine's foot turned, and down she went. Something cracked into her chin and she cried out. Heavy breath jerked at her chest, and she saw them, a group of them, one old with white hair. They were shooting, their bodies silhouetted, flashing in and out of the moonlight like dancers caught in a strobe. *It was dark . . . she was out . . . she wasn't suppose to be out after dark . . .*

"Arshad . . . Nazeem — help me! *Madad kijiye!*"

Christine rose, crawled, came upon them, and there were more dirty faces, strangers. Their guns pointed at her as she dragged herself to her feet. She searched their faces, and suddenly something snatched at the gun in her hands.

Not Arshad, her mind registered. *And where's Nazeem?*

"*Siddar, kither hai,*" she said, and thought she saw their faces react. She had asked for the head of their clan. "*Madad kijiye,*" she repeated, asking for help.

The white-haired man approached her. She smelled the alcohol on his breath as he peered at her. He wasn't Arshad, but he wasn't Maroof either.

There was a succession of shots behind her, and the white-haired man knocked her down. She cried out, or thought she did. Then she was breathing into the dirt. Dust flew into her eyes. She closed them, hearing the prattle of foreign voices around her. One was louder, harsh, while the others were yammering above her.

She was straining to stay conscious when the shots stopped. The acrid smell of gunpowder filled her nostrils, and she looked up. The old man was shouting at someone behind her. There was a belt of bullets around his grizzly chest, and he held up a big rifle. She couldn't see what kind, but he was aiming. Christine covered her ears as the gun fired, a flash of fire against the blackness, and empty cartridges, smoking and still hot, hopped about on the ground.

She looked back toward Maroof's estate and she caught glimpses of their faces, the ones who had stood over Nazeem while his blood spilled onto marble. They were hiding behind rocks and in the bushes. They were afraid, as Nazeem had been afraid. Someone was shooting at them.

Then the old man left her, and dark sandaled feet came down on each side of her head. The men around her had guns, many guns. More shouting, screaming; then the sandaled feet were gone and someone else was crouched next to her. Christine tried to rise up, but an elbow drove her back down.

The tribesman snapped at her. She couldn't understand him, but she knew he was angry. He leaned into her and she could feel his body vibrate with the movement of his automatic. He was so close; her ears were ringing. The stench of sweat and alcohol overwhelmed her. Gunpowder and dust choked her. There was a lot of gunfire, then silence . . . another outburst of automatic fire. And then it was over.

Chapter
13

She had asked the tribesmen for help, and now she was theirs.

Christine couldn't remember much after the shooting. She had been so doped up that she had lost days while her mind played with her. When she finally began to trust her perceptions, she found herself locked in a courtyard with a bizarre tribe of women and children. Their complexions and hair colors ran the gamut, from dark to light and even reds, a conqueror's legacy. But at night they slept together in rooms of concrete and wood furnished with only the barest essentials — a few blankets and a bucket. During the day they cooked in the center of a dirt courtyard, tended to a flock of goats and chickens, and took turns serving their men, who lived inside the big house that loomed over the courtyard.

The women were Pashtuns and they lived in purdah, kept hidden in a compound from the eyes of men not of their clan. She had spent little time with Maroof, who she understood was part of the Afridi clan, and now she had been rescued by a rival clan, the Maliks. The family who had saved her was less opulent than Maroof, but according to the Javids, the Maliks, the Afridis, and the Khan families (she had not yet met them) were the principal clans of the tribal areas. And like the men of their clan, the women here couldn't understand English or Urdu, so Christine signed frantically while trying to pick up words of Pashto, the predominant dialect in the North-West Frontier. Still, the Pashtun women showed little interest in her.

Except for Abdul, the ten-year-old boy whose duty it was to escort the women in and out of the barred courtyard, Christine felt isolated. She served herself and was expected to work alongside the women. But in the heat of the late afternoon when the women gathered in small groups to talk or sew or even paint each other with henna, Christine sat alone. Tribal law dictated that if the men fought for her life, she was theirs. She was *property,* and Christine missed the days of being the revered guest.

On the fifth morning, she heard a vehicle approaching the compound. The women scurried to the tall, tin doors that they had bent back along the sides so they could peek through.

Christine was surprised to see Arshad's van. A load of men climbed out of the vehicle, two of whom were guards she recognized from Maroof's estate. The others looked like local Pakistanis. Then Janoor jumped out last, and Christine stepped back from the tin doors. For the first time the women seemed to take notice of her. The matriarch of the tribe, a toothless old hag with a large droopy face, saw that Christine was upset and stepped up to the doors of her courtyard. She turned her gaze on the lank, dirty Pakistani in Western dress and shook her head. Snarling something under her breath, she spat. Her face was a mass of folds, but her tone was defiant. She didn't like the look of Janoor either. Christine thanked her in Pashto and in return received the slightest hint of a shrug. Then the old woman ambled back to her cot, which was covered with hand-embroidered cotton bedspreads and heaped with pillows. It was a place of prominence where the matriarch, the first wife, would remain for the rest of the day beneath the only tree in the courtyard.

Abdul entered, rattling instructions to the women as he slid a piece of wood across the opening to secure them from the inside. Christine suddenly felt like she was in a fort and wondered if they were going to be attacked.

"Don't worry, lady," Abdul confided. "Dadi will fix, A-okay?"

Abdul had a knack for languages. He told Christine when she had first arrived that he had picked up English from his imam, who had worked for three years in a souvenir store in New Delhi. It didn't take him long to learn, the boy had boasted, "The infidel's words too easy."

Abdul stood at the door with Christine, peering out at the strangers. He was so charged up for battle that she could hear him grinding his teeth. There was no sign of Maroof, only his guards, Janoor, and seven other men who, as Christine studied them, took on a family resemblance. They must've been from another clan.

And facing them were the formidable males of Abdul's clan, twelve in all. The women crowded in behind Christine to get a peek at "Dadi," the eldest son of the Malik clan.

Christine recognized the strong, lean features that had flashed above her as shots rang out around her that night. She looked for the white-haired man with the bandolier across his chest, but saw only men with potbellies and gentle faces. A few others, like Dadi, were dark and lined and bore permanent scowls. Christine thought Abdul's clan resembled an odd assortment of devout Muslims and hardened criminals. Still, they all wielded guns, and whether they were holy or merely ruthless, the visitors looked anxious.

Offering Allah's blessing, the two families greeted one another and then disappeared from view.

With the men gone, the women almost immediately dispersed. Christine tried to pull at the curled corners of tin to see more, but the boy reassured her that his grandfather, Qazi Ali, was the most powerful elder of the Malik clan, and he would protect her and that she should not worry. With that declaration, the young man unbolted the door, stepped out, closed the doors behind him, and grabbed at his own weapon, which stood just outside. He turned, grinning proudly at her through the narrow opening between the doors, hefting the rifle, a World War II–era

274

Garand M-1. Christine figured it would take years for him to grow into it.

It didn't take long for the visitors to reemerge from the house. Their faces were grim, and an exchange between Janoor and one of the Malik males was terse. The moment they were visible, the boy scampered back inside the woman's purdah, dragging his gun behind him. He peeked with her as Janoor and the family of the men climbed back into Arshad's van.

"Bastard," Christine hissed angrily.

"Bazzz . . . urdth," the boy mimicked. Christine looked down at Abdul, who was watching the men intently. Her nerves were still raw, but the anger felt good. When the van finally disappeared into clouds of dust, the boy looked up at her and beamed.

"See, Lady! Dadi tell them to go away. You very safe here, I think."

Bumps raised on her arms. Maroof had told her the same thing.

When she pulled back from the doors, the women were loitering around her like sheep, the clan's livestock. Abdul told her that four of the women were married to his grandfather. Christine thought about the white-haired leader and had a sick feeling she might end up the fifth.

"Do the women ever get out . . . if they want?" She hoped she didn't sound desperate.

"To the bazaar?" Abdul asked.

"No, not the bazaar, just —"

"At night they go to the house. When my uncles say A-okay."

"No, I mean. Can they just leave . . . get out . . . if they want?"

"How you mean . . . *get* out?"

"You know, get out of here, this courtyard — here." Christine pointed around her.

The boy was stumped by the question, but asked a pregnant woman whose skin was badly pockmarked. She still had a number of teeth, so she was probably in her late twenties. It took Abdul a few moments to translate, but finally the woman cocked her head in an annoyed shrug.

The boy turned back to Christine and likewise shrugged. They didn't understand the question, and Christine was beginning to wonder if perhaps she was the one who didn't get it.

Christine faintly remembered, when she had begun to grasp her situation, her bondage, that she had tried once to escape out the tin doors. But the boy and the women quickly dragged her back inside.

To the women she was an ungrateful newcomer. Beyond the walls were the men with their guns, and their alcohol, and a wildness that extended into two countries. Why would the women want to leave? Why would any woman want to leave?

Another day went by, and out of boredom Christine started embroidering her own scarf. It kept her from picturing Nazeem, his throat cut. Hallucinatory nightmares woke her at night and she struggled to stop herself from crying out.

Often she tried to figure out the number of days she had been with the clan. *Six days . . . seven, or was it eight?* She was having trouble holding a thought and wondered if she'd ever feel normal again.

Then the Aussie arrived.

Christine recognized his voice and his barbarous accent even as he drove up. She ran to the metal doors and saw Reggie's hairy profile with one of the blistering melanomas right in her line of sight. Dadi approached Reggie just as he had the first group of visitors. Christine had no doubt that the tribe of brothers, armed and deadpan, was not far behind him. Reggie managed a few awkward phrases of Pashto, and then he disappeared from sight.

As Christine waited, a woman with ropy

white eyebrows and runny eyes, a woman Christine had dubbed "Mrs. White," started yelling. Apparently, it was Christine's turn to do laundry. The last time Christine had washed clothes, she was barely coherent and could work for only an hour. The clan used a metal tub with a cylinder that had to be turned manually. Her hands had blistered, then bled into the tub of garments. She had a vague memory of the second wife hitting her with a cane. The one-legged old woman relied on two canes to walk. She hit Christine, scolding her while she hobbled past her.

And now the old woman was about to come at her again. Christine heard the woman's one swollen foot dragging along the dirt, and like Mrs. White, she was also screeching. Mrs. White was twenty years younger, but she immediately obeyed. There was no ignoring the hierarchy in that group. The one-legged woman was Qazi's second wife. The first, and grande dame, sat beneath her tree, sipping juice, while her second in command waved her cane, threatening to beat the lazy foreigner.

"Hey, Lady! Dadi want you," Abdul called out excitedly, pushing through the doors.

At that, the matriarch who had taken

little interest in Christine moved from her throne. The second wife retreated as the giant woman, her jowls swinging, muttered something to the boy. He responded and the woman flaunted a toothless grin. She seemed surprisingly eager to help, bellowing to a young girl to retrieve something. The old woman jerked at Christine's unfinished chador, grumbling angrily under her breath. In a moment, the girl returned with the queen's own finely embroidered chador. She swept it over Christine's unwieldy hair.

As the old woman fussed, Christine tried not to think of what the men would demand. Of course, having little more value than a goat could work to her advantage. She had already proved herself worthless in the courtyard. Maybe they'd let Reggie take her off their hands cheap and be grateful for a bargain.

Inside, the "men's house" wasn't nearly as flamboyant as Maroof's. There were only two kinds of pictures on the walls, of Jinnah and of a man in white with a long white beard. She guessed he was the clan's spiritual teacher. There was a small fountain inside the front door, and several pieces of intricate furniture, but there was little gold. And instead of marble, the flooring was cement inlaid with broken bits of tile.

Abdul led Christine to a sunny room near the back of the house. A large mirrored table sat at the room's center, and around it, the men sat like knights of Camelot. Unlike their English counterparts, however, these knights pledged no loyalty to any king or government; they ruled only themselves. Every male member of the family was sitting cross-legged on ornate rugs. The usual bottles of orange soda and bowls of syrupy *gulam jaman* had been brought out especially for guests, and a woman from purdah, covered in a burqa, stepped out of the kitchen with two more sodas. Christine thought she recognized the woman from the courtyard, but they had never spoken. Most of the women kept their distance, so it was no surprise when the woman passed her without comment.

Reggie was talking with the white-haired stranger who had rescued her. Thanks to Abdul, she knew the stranger's name was Qazi Ali Malik, that he was Abdul's grandfather, and that he was the clan's leader. It was surreal to see him again; she had seen him first the night she was still drugged.

Neither the Malik leader nor Reggie bothered to look up when Christine entered. The boy pointed to a chair and Christine sat. She knew better than to interrupt.

Finally, Reggie paused and Qazi Ali gave consent for Reggie to speak to Christine.

"G'day." He smiled at her.

"Are you here to . . . uh," Christine paused; the clansmen were staring.

"Save your hide?"

Christine glanced nervously at Qazi Ali. Reggie grinned.

"This old guy doesn't get a word of English. I don't know about the other blokes here, but I've already explained the fix you got yourself in, and they're willing to deal. Except it's a dead certainty that they gonna put the bite on us now that you've killed one of their own."

Christine's mouth gaped as the Aussie continued.

"Not really one of their own, but still a raghead. But they kept the family of the kid from taking you, so they're gonna want something for that."

Christine remembered the carload of men with Janoor. They *were* a family. "I killed someone?"

"You don't remember?"

Christine recalled Maroof, his fingers long and spidery, Janoor's face and how he reeked of . . . but it wasn't Janoor. It was Nazeem who smelled of death. That part, his murder, the men gawking at him as he bled to death, stuck in her mind.

"I can't remember," she groaned, on the brink of tears.

"You don't remember shooting a guard? Look, you were trying to get the hell outta there. These blokes get it. He wasn't one of their family. But by not giving you up, they set themselves up for a blood feud. You'll have to pay. Vendettas are serious business here."

"My God . . ."

"It's hit ya, huh?"

The memory *had* hit her. Her eyes welled with tears as she recalled the guard who had backed away when she was stumbling through Maroof's hall, a boy, really. At the time, her mind was reeling. She had a gun, felt the trigger, and kept pulling it. She didn't care who she shot; she just wanted out. And now she remembered the gun recoiling, and the guard falling.

"I suppose you don't have any cash on you," Reggie said.

"I had money, but Maroof —"

"You're broke?"

"I have a safe-deposit box in Islamabad."

"You got the key?"

Christine hesitated. She wanted to trust him, but . . .

"C'mon, Chris, use your head. Qazi here tells me his second son's ready for a third wife, and you're getting better looking every day. That's probably the only thing that kept them from selling you to the other tribe."

Christine could feel Qazi's son watching her. She tried not to look, but her eyes flicked past the rough-shaven, balding primitive who Abdul had told her was named Faiz. He caught her glance, and his lips puckered slightly. Before he could deliver the smack, her eyes were back on Reggie.

"If you don't pay, and pay good, this bloke's gonna have you. And if you fight the marriage, they'll just turn you over to that guard's family. Then you're dead."

"What if you don't come back?"

"I don't know how much you have in that box, but if it's not enough to get you out —"

"You'd steal it?"

Reggie sighed.

"What about Cloid? Or my embassy? Maybe the Pakistani government can —"

"They can't help you. You're sittin' on tribal land."

Faiz started smacking at the air behind her.

"This guy's got it bad. What the hell did you say to him?"

Before Christine could respond, the other brothers started throwing out their own kisses, taunting her.

"Shit." Reggie grinned at the primitive lot, trying to play it cool. "I don't like this," he said, keeping his eye on them. "Just gimme the bloody key, will ya?"

"I need to, ah . . . go somewhere private."

Reggie didn't waste any time. He turned and spoke to the leader in Pashto. She caught the word for toilet. Qazi Ali didn't look happy, but he signaled for the boy.

Abdul appeared and took her out back to a pile of timbers. There were gaps between the splintered poplar trunks, obviously a toilet for men's use only. Abdul spun around, facing away and cupping his ears. Straddling the littered hole inside, Christine glanced once more for anyone watching, then lifted her shiftlike blouse and untied her pants string. She reached inside and felt along the edge of the French-cut panties that had been torn at by Nikhil when he had raped her, had been stained during her period while she lived with the Javids, and now concealed the small bank envelope containing the key. This last pair of her favorite cotton underwear was the only garment she had left from the United States. Everything else had been destroyed in the land mine explosion.

At the bank in Islamabad, Christine had excused herself to go to the bathroom. It was clean and new with a Western toilet. She'd felt a little foolish shoving the small envelope into her underwear. But when she stood before Maroof with her block of rupees exposed, she was relieved that she still had the key and access to another ten thousand in cash.

In the room again, Christine tried her best to ignore the eyes of the men as she approached the Aussie. If he failed her, she would have nothing to fall back on. Reggie held out his hand. Qazi Ali said something, and the Aussie laughed, waiting for Christine to give him the key. Her hand shook as she handed it over. If Reggie noticed, he didn't show it. Seemingly engrossed in his conversation with the Malik leader, he casually slipped it into his vest pocket.

With the key gone, Christine felt trapped. Abdul appeared at her side. Her time on stage was up. Making no attempt to acknowledge her, the Aussie was jabbering away, his hands waving.

"Reggie?" Christine tried.

Qazi Ali scowled at the interruption, his face reddening, and Christine sensed the heat of his sons' glare around her. Looking very angry, Reggie muttered an apology to the elder, then turned to Christine.

"You're not in Kansas, Dorothy," he growled under his breath. "I wouldn't do that again if I were you."

The Aussie had no intention of returning. Christine was certain of it. He would take her money and disappear. She had heard it in his voice, and she desperately wanted to kill him, to kill them all for her humiliation and mistreatment.

Her voice broke, "I hope you don't have any trouble. I mean, have a safe trip. The roads —"

"You mind your own roads, if you know what I mean. And stay covered up, for christsake."

Reggie's voice was harsh but she tugged at her scarf, which had barely loosened.

It's over, Christine thought. No more key. No more hope. Even if she managed to escape, there was still the guard's family who wouldn't hesitate to cut her throat . . .

just like Maroof and Janoor had done to Nazeem.

She was close to crying and she needed to leave. The smacking sounds had stopped, but the men were glowering at her, and Dadi was shifting his hand to his belt. Abdul told her that Dadi was the one who had fired his rifle to save her, but clearly he would just as easily slay her to keep her from dishonoring his clan. She dropped her eyes as she pulled her scarf up to hide her face.

She wanted to place her hand on Abdul's shoulder for support, but she couldn't do that either. Reggie and Qazi Ali were once again engaged. She had gotten the message and obediently followed Abdul out of the room.

The Malik males laughed raucously and ate like animals, tearing at the lamb, then grabbing fistfuls of rice and beans.

In the kitchen, Christine, red-faced and sweating, attended to a spit of chicken and lamb while Mrs. White snapped instructions. Her mouth working, she pointed to a small rock-hewn tandoor, and Christine plunged her hand inside the burning mouth of the oven. Her arm brushed against the side of the oven, and she gasped. The rheumy-eyed woman just glared at her trainee, then demonstrated again how to bake bread. Sticking her own sooty hand inside the oven, she retrieved the bread and flipped it aside. Then she plucked up another ball of dough, flattening, slapping, and twirling, all the while explaining her actions in what sounded to Christine like a series of harried grunts.

It was hopeless. The Ameri-cain was tired; she was fighting loose bowels, her stomach ached, and she didn't know the language. Still, there were two other women who were exhausted from jumping to meet the appetites of the men in the next room, and Christine was desperate to keep her job in the kitchen and stay away from the men. But when a piece of uncooked chicken breast with bits of feathers still on it fell from the skewer onto the concrete floor, Mrs. White snatched the tongs from the inept Ameri-cain, gave it to one of the other women, and handed Christine two bowls of steaming rice. Christine tried to take back the tongs, but Mrs. White slapped her face hard. Christine had barely regained her wits before she found herself in the next room.

The brothers were so diverse in their coloring that she thought again of Alexander the Great and his armies sweeping through this land of dark-skinned natives over two thousand years ago. Qazi, with his striking white poll and fair skin, sat at the end of the rug, where a tall, gnarled pipe, its base bubbling with water, percolated. It gave off a sweet scent of tobacco . . . and pot. Not from the pipe, but from the nubs of reefers strewn among the chicken bones. The men were stoned, and Christine thought of her chador and hoped that she was properly covered. At least, the large scarf came down to her waist.

When she first entered the room, the laughter died. The men managed to keep their eyes on their food until Christine bent down between them. The room was tight with men's bodies, and Christine was determined not to brush against anyone. She had to crouch low to reach the carpet, her body close to two of the more hulking brothers. She teetered, their eyes on her, waiting, not chewing, not making a sound. Only the noise of Qazi sucking on his pipe could be heard. Christine had no doubt there would be plenty of hands to catch her if she toppled. She just wasn't sure that they would let her up. She managed to regain her balance without incident and set the second bowl down easily. Even so, there were whispers and smirks all around as she hurried back toward the kitchen.

Just as she was about to escape, someone barked a command at her back. Christine chose to ignore it, but the older of the two women, standing by the door, stopped her.

It was Faiz, the second son, balding and potbellied. Bits of lamb were stuck to the fringe of his beard, and his thick, brown lips glistened with animal fat.

"Sisser," he mouthed. *"Goo-rhiss."*

And then he asked her something in Pashto. His bite was so askew, his smile looked more like a grimace. Christine just nodded. She turned back to the kitchen.

"Li'l Sisser!" Faiz cried.

Abdul stopped her this time, whispering, "Mamu wants rice, *hai?*"

Christine thought about feigning ignorance, but one of the women, a teenager with a broad nose and dimpled chin, had retrieved another bowl from the kitchen, gave it to her and pointed to Faiz, who was staring at Christine with an idiotic grin. Christine circled the room as the brothers sucked their meat bones clean. When she came to Faiz, she crouched behind him and tried not to react when his head spun around at her like an owl's. His breath was gamy, and Christine fixed on her hands, using their motion almost like a meditation. She could hear herself breathing as she tried to relax. The last thing she needed was for him to read her rapid breathing as amorous.

Watching the two of them as if they were an act in a porn show, the brothers were still making noises with their mouths. Christine piled Faiz's plate high with rice, and he blurted out something that sounded like her name. Then he murmured something to her. The men were grinning, some licking at their lips, others nodding. There was a lot of lip smacking. Clearly, they approved.

At the door of the kitchen, the teenager was glaring at her enviously, but the other woman, a fair-skinned, green-eyed woman named Namja, clearly felt sorry for her. Neither tried to stop her as she passed them.

Inside the kitchen, Christine picked up the tongs and went to the meat, but Mrs. White handed her a plate of roti instead, and cocked her head back toward the men.

"Please . . ." Christine pleaded, Urdu phrases spilling from her mouth. She tried to explain that she was very nervous around the men, but the stark white eyebrows were almost crossed. When Christine tried a few words of Pashto, the woman sputtered something and raised her hand to hit her again. But this time Christine swept up the large knife she had used to cut the chicken, to break its bones, in fact, and passed it before the woman's throat with one hand while jerking her head back with the other. Mrs. White's one rheumy eye rolled around, panicked. Christine didn't care; she was tired of being hit. She repeated the words in Pashto, asking to be excused, this time with her teeth clenched. Mrs. White nodded. Christine slowly released her, then drew her hand across her own throat, a signal she had seen on one of her buying trips to a remote Indian village. A woman was having trouble with one of her older sons. The gesture had been effective and the son had bowed graciously, acquiescing. The mother and son were Hindu, but Christine was glad to find that the gesture's meaning crossed cultures. Mrs. White didn't bow, but she got it.

In the courtyard the next morning, Christine looked around at the women and children sitting on their haunches eating mangos from a basket. She was late for breakfast and knew that she might go hungry.

She hadn't slept much. Not because Mrs. White might pull a knife in the night, although she knew that was a possibility, but because of her stomach. She thought she had gotten used to the parasites by now, but maybe the change from the Javids to the tribals had brought on a whole new batch. Namja, the fair-skinned Pashtun who had tried to help her with the men, had given her some kind of bitter plant during the night, and it had helped.

As she approached the group, she tried to remember their protocol. Initially, there had been a few crude gestures to let her know what to eat, where to dispose of bones and seeds, and where to wash her feet before prayer. Christine knelt down, careful not to soil the fresh outfit that Namja had gotten her after she had thrown up on the other one. She took a mango and bit into it. The fruit tasted good. Again, she was aware that she was feeling no pain and wondered about the plant. Namja sat across from her, and Christine thought about asking about the plant, but Namja looked different in the sunlight and gnawed at the tough skin of her mango as though she had not eaten for days. The woman who seemed to have befriended her the night before hardly made eye contact, and so Christine waited.

That day she watched as the sun moved across the dry sky and knew that Reggie had taken off with the money. Islamabad was no more than a half-day's drive, and now she wondered if the Aussie had even bothered to tell Cloid, or her mother, or anyone, where she was. Why would he? There was ten thousand in her safe-deposit box, and that could last him for quite a while. She thought of Liz, and heard the muezzin calling afternoon prayer. As the women sat about on rugs of knotted cotton and camel hair, Christine decided today she would join them. Keeping her feet tucked in close to her, another body part considered dirty by the Muslims, she sat beside Namja. Like the others she faced Mecca, but kept her head down so that her scarf fell forward, covering her face. She did not rub at a string of beads, nor did she pray to Allah. She was a Methodist; she prayed to the Heavenly Father that her sister was still alive.

That night, Christine held up her chador by candlelight and inspected her work. Her stomach growled; she hadn't eaten much. But she didn't care. She had finally finished it, and the accomplishment satisfied her. The stitches were uneven and the colors she had combined were off, but she had done it. For days she had asked for help, but the tribal women had little patience for someone who was so unskilled. So, she worked alone. She didn't mind; she was thinking, scheming a way to escape.

Christine knew that the guard's family was waiting, probably just outside the walls of purdah, to take their revenge, and kill her. But she didn't care about that either. She could feel herself sinking into a depression. Then she might as well be dead. She had been so tired lately. If she didn't do something soon, she would remain the property of Qazi Ali, and the bald, greasy son would have his third wife . . . this one with teeth.

Christine had been spared kitchen duty the following morning, but at the midday meal Abdul came for her, Namja, and a woman whose hennaed hair was so red that it showed through the white of her chador.

During the walk to the men's house, Christine tried to whisper a greeting, but Namja ignored her, quickening her steps to stay ahead. Christine tried again to approach her, but the woman with the clownish red hair snarled a warning at her.

Christine had a feeling that Mrs. White had been talking.

When Christine entered the dining room with a platter of crisp lamb, the noises began. She tried to act as if it were the food that made the men salivate. She set the platter down among them, quickly turning toward the kitchen. Then Faiz called out to her.

Patting the rug by his left hip, where there was hardly any space between him and the next brother, Faiz gestured for Christine to sit. She'd have to squeeze between them. She remembered the way Janoor had pressed against her the first time she had met him. So, instead, Christine ignored his instruction, pulled at her scarf, and sat just behind him. To keep him from lashing out at her, she caught his eye and smiled beneath her chador as she knelt. Faiz leaned back, and Christine also leaned, casting her eyes downward. Minutes later, he tried again, and again. But, each time, Christine leaned farther, just avoiding his touch, all the time smiling and looking down as if in submission.

She could tell Faiz was pleased because he rattled on to his brothers at every seemingly shy reaction. Grunts of approval sounded, and even the smacking sounds eased.

When Abdul appeared, Christine stood, relieved that she had managed to avoid the tribesman. Then Faiz touched her backside, and she gasped. This time there were no sounds of approval. Dadi snapped at his younger brother, and a fierce debate ensued. Faiz had crossed the line, and only when the old Malik leader intervened did the argument end. Though desperate to get away, Christine waited. But Abdul wasn't moving. She dared a glance at Faiz and saw that he was wiping at his beard, preparing to address her.

"Li'l sisser?" he tried. His bite scissored back and forth as he spoke directly to her. She thought he might try to touch her again, but his hands remained in his lap. His words were foreign, but they also sounded adoring, something Christine didn't like. She let him finish, then cast her eyes down. There were more grunts of approval, and she thought she might bump Abdul if he didn't move, but finally he did.

When they got back behind the safety of the tin doors, Christine asked the boy what Faiz had said.

"Mamu says to take you as wife. He make a good husband, I think."

A painful breath caught in her chest, and Christine blurted out, "I can't marry. I'm already married. I have a husband, understand? And he's a Christian, like me, like my whole family, and Christians . . ."

Christine stopped the rant. Abdul had caught her by surprise; she couldn't help herself. Still, she had to do something, but now the boy was staring at her in stark horror.

"Abdul, please . . . I need your help."

The boy didn't let her finish. His mouth agape, he scooted out the doors. Christine called after him, but he was gone. Eyes were on her. The women had seen Abdul's reaction and stared warily at Christine. She wanted to explain and tried her Pashto, but they turned away. Even Namja wanted nothing to do with her. Mrs. White had been thorough.

Not more than an hour passed before the boy returned and without saying a word jerked her by the arm.

"Abdul, what's wrong? Why are you angry?"

He didn't answer, just pulled her toward the doors. He held onto her, kicking one of the doors wide. Qazi Ali, Dadi, Faiz, and two other brothers were waiting by a small truck outside. Suddenly, her prison

298

seemed a sanctuary, and Christine tried to twist her arm free of the boy and get back inside. Abdul screamed at her in Pashto, his voice deeper and shockingly cruel, then yanked at her arm with a strength that startled her.

"Stop! You're hurting me! *Na! Na!*" she shouted, but Abdul just glared at her. Finally, he managed to get her beyond the threshold, and then the men took hold of her. They didn't struggle with her long, and Faiz no longer ogled her. Instead, he seemed to be scolding her. When she tried to pull away, he forced her into the truck.

The last thing Christine saw were the faces peering from between the tin doors of purdah as Abdul locked the women back inside. Smaller children who were crowded in beneath the women were also trying to peek out. They were all there — Namja, Mrs. White, and the old woman with one leg, scarves drawn up to cover their faces, their eyes questioning, frightened. The old matriarch had left her cot, and even she stared, her mouth slack in puzzlement. Christine wanted to call out something, but she didn't have the words. The men drove off with her.

Chapter
14

The second son's feet, dusty and callused, were only inches from her head as flecks of dirt flew up into her face through the cleft floorboards of the truck. Christine grimaced, trying to burrow deeper into the folds of her long blouse. Her face was already stiff with dirt, and her back ached from bending. They had been driving overland for almost an hour, and Faiz had kept her head down at his feet, not letting her up once. Just when she began to wonder how much longer the torture would last, the jeep stopped rocking and began to travel more smoothly, but then it was tiny bits of tar that came through.

The road was paved. In northwest Pakistan there weren't many like that, and Christine was sure they had come to the main road, the Grand Trunk, the road that was patrolled by the government, and for a moment she forgot her discomfort. When the jeep settled down, Faiz's hand lifted. He seemed anxious not to touch her. The men would go back and forth over her. She managed to catch a few words; they were talking of bad women and honor and the evil eye. Clearly she had dishonored them somehow, and she felt that familiar wash of panic. There were horns and bicycle bells and children's voices. They were going through a village. If she could just get out, she might have a chance to lose them in the crowds.

Christine turned her face away from the sole of Faiz's sandal and focused on the bottom of the door handle. The seat started bouncing again. *More ruts.* She breathed, getting exasperated.

Faiz's hand returned to her back. Christine wanted to curse, but then his hand lifted once more, waving about, preoccupied with his own ill-tempered rant. Christine's heart raced in anticipation. She would have to twist and push, throwing the door back before Faiz could grab her. She didn't know how fast they were going, but it was more the jagged condition of the road that concerned her, and she tried not to think of what an impact with it would do to her.

A bitter taste of bile rose in her throat,

and Christine swallowed. She had to move while the men were still talking. They had called her *kari* which meant, "black" or "evil." Wives and daughters who had dishonored their families were murdered for less, and she was a stranger. She pictured them running over her body after she hit the pavement. She had to nerve herself to move. Already there were fewer horns, and she no longer heard bike bells. She took a breath and clenched her fist, but she hesitated. Her mind flooded with images of the road, her leaping in a cacophony of warbling horns, her body bloodied, broken . . . and then the truck swerved.

Go! Go! a voice in her head shouted, and Christine grabbed at the handle. But before she could even touch the metal, the heel of Faiz's meaty hand came down on her wrist and Christine recoiled.

Cursing, Faiz hammered her back with two more blows. She couldn't catch her breath, but she wouldn't cry. When Christine could turn, she smirked at Faiz even as he hit her. His face reddened, and he sputtered something at her, pushing her so hard that her forehead bounced off the thin flooring. One of the men up front turned in his seat and spat down at her as he scolded her. *"Kari,"* "evil one," "infidel," and "Zionist" were hurled at her as thoughts of escape vanished. There were no more horns, and even the sound of the road beneath her changed. The truck rocked and dust puffed up through the cracks, causing her to cough.

She sat up, and Faiz leaned away from her in disgust. He only let her catch her breath, then he pushed her back down. But Christine had gotten a chance to look around; the Grand Trunk was nowhere in sight.

When they finally stopped and pulled her out of the car, she expected to see a wide expanse of nothingness, a place to shoot a gun or make camp or set fire to a woman. Instead, they had stopped in front of a stall, one of many on a dirt road that was lined with stalls. A range of craggy cliffs loomed behind the isolated but teeming marketplace. It looked like a smuggler's bazaar, and the simple shops were overflowing with rifles, handguns, assault weapons, and machine guns. She saw American grenade launchers, Soviet .51-caliber antiaircraft machine guns, RPGs, AKs, Dragunovs; M-60s, M-14s, M-16s; even a couple of ancient M-1s, M-3s, and a BAR were on hand for show. And there were blades, plenty of blades. Tables sagged beneath stacks of stilettos, switchblades, machetes, sabers, bolo knives, broadswords, and she thought she even spotted some Bowie knives. And behind and between the stalls were the explosives: pipe bombs, blocks of Semtex, land mines, Soviet-era flamethrowers, toe-poppers, and artillery projectiles of all kinds. The stalls were brimming, and the merchants were fat.

Christine had never seen so many weapons. And with the munitions were the drugs, heroin that was raw, black, rolled, or powdered, hashish from the purest form to the lowest grade, and then, of course, the opium . . . lots of opium. Water pipes littered the walkways, and animal skins stuffed with marijuana, offered as novelty items, hung from broken rooflines.

Suddenly Dadi smacked at her head, shifting the chador so it completely covered her face. Blindly, she stumbled over dry ground after him.

Her ankle twisted as she stepped into an open ditch. She peeked down from underneath her chador and could see that her foot was covered with sewage. The brothers huffed and yelled at her, and Christine closed her eyes, bracing for a blow. Instead, someone poured a jug of water over her foot. She mumbled thanks

304

in Urdu as she was pulled forward again. Finally, they stopped, and her chador was snatched back, exposing her face. Faiz and Dadi stood with a merchant who was meticulously groomed, his salt-and-pepper mustache carefully shaped, his pale pink tunic and pants pressed. The merchant looked her over carefully, checking her teeth, touching her hair, asking questions of Dadi.

Christine caught a glimpse of an old Pakistani sitting cross-legged in a lean-to near them. There were baskets of copper bullet casings around him. He was filing and polishing, preparing them for reuse. The old man didn't look up. Christine was being purchased the same way his casings would be. She was a commodity, and she heard his boss haggling for her with Dadi.

The white-haired Qazi, the leader, didn't bother to participate. He was off somewhere having a cup of tea, or buying guns, or drugs, or maybe it was just that her presence repulsed him.

Christine glanced up at Faiz and Dadi. Their faces were stern, and she knew that whatever price the vendor was willing to pay, it wasn't much. And for some absurd reason, that mattered to her. She felt a sudden impulse to smile. She had always been praised for her toothy grin, and she raised her chin just a bit, and did smile — then caught herself.

It worked. The haggling intensified, and Christine was struck by what she had done. *A product.* They were selling her like product, and she had helped them. She *was* of value and she proved it. And now more rupees were visible, almost more rupees than Dadi could balance on one hand. She watched the Pakistanis dickering over her and wished she had tried to say that Christine Shepherd, an American, a woman, was a human being and not for sale.

Instead, she had smiled.

But she didn't have the words. Even if she had been able to speak their language, her actions had been enough to condemn her.

The negotiations didn't last long. Christine was soon given over to the merchant. When he paid Dadi, she closed her eyes; she didn't want to see how much she was worth.

As the merchant nudged her forward, she realized she hadn't thought about Farrukh for days. That dream of saving her sister now seemed long ago. Lost in her thoughts, Christine hardly noticed when the Maliks, without so much as a word, left her.

A back section of the merchant's stall was partitioned off from a showcase of arms. It was small, hardly the size of a closet, no place to sit, and Christine had to urinate. She looked around, nearly stepping on a small pile of animal bones apparently left from lunch. Cigarette butts, a half-full tin bottle of whiskey, and stained *chai* cups were also scattered about. Beneath the mess were three overlapping Persian carpets so filthy Christine could barely make out their designs.

Still, light seeped in through the loose weave of hand-blocked panels that hung between her and the store. She heard the merchant moving about his wares, picking up guns, pitching his merchandise in yet another unrecognized tongue, while in the shops beside them there were more voices, more sales. Demonstrations — gunshots — went off in the distance. The back wall was nothing but hanging tarpaulins. She parted the weighted coverings and stuck her head out into a walkway that backed against a sheer rock cliff. Men carrying boxes and boys balancing trays of *chai* and milk confections ducked in and out of stalls. She quickly popped her head back inside. It was still light outside, and she would have to wait until it was dark. Christine sat on an empty gunpowder keg and scoffed at how easy it had been to housebreak the "Ameri-cain." She rankled at the idea that she had become little more than a "good dog" and waited until the burning in her bladder receded to a small corner of her awareness.

Memories sustained her, and before long she found herself in darkness. There was a cool breeze and she shivered. She had been perspiring. At the moment, she felt hot and angry, remembering her last moments with Reggie. It was common knowledge that ransom for foreigners was generally thirty-five thousand. The ten thousand in her safe-deposit box in Islamabad would hardly be enough. Reggie had pocketed it; she was sure of it. He had betrayed her, and she was desperate for another chance to meet him.

Someone outside went through a magazine on full automatic and Christine jumped, and instantly felt the fool. *What she wouldn't do to have that automatic?* And yet she was shivering, but it wasn't from the cool breeze this time. The gunfire was close by, and men were yelling. There were more shots, and then she heard laughter. *They were drinking,* she realized, and Christine remembered what Janoor had said about the bazaars at night.

Then her bladder reawakened. It was night and time to relieve herself. She listened for the merchant, couldn't hear anything. The walkway behind the stall was clear, and she crouched in the dirt and peed, flinching and holding every few moments. It burned, and she thought she might never finish, but finally she did.

She looked down toward the end of the stalls to an open area where flashes of blue and white light lit the sky. It had to be a shooting range.

She stood, and went back into the stall. The shop was still; the merchant must have gone out. He probably believed she wouldn't have the nerve to leave. Nikhil had underestimated her as well. She was already contemplating escape.

Then she remembered the smile, the smile that got Dadi a better price and the shame of what she had done consumed her.

Christine closed her eyes, trying to forget what her life had been. Her arms felt weighted to her side and her body was suddenly heavy and cumbersome. There was no escape, she decided, and sleep overwhelmed her.

Fumes of alcohol burned the inside of her nose and Christine tried not to react when a hand attempted to grope her. Body odor and damp bodies were crowded around her in the backseat of a car. It was pitch black outside, and they were traveling. She could hear the engine and feel the motion, but she couldn't see. She could only feel their hands. There was laughter, and finally she struck out blindly into the darkness. Another hand, and again she swung, but this time she caught flesh.

Then everyone laughed, except someone hit her back. It shocked her, and Christine screamed, *"Saada sodar,"* calling him a pig. It was a curse in Pashto she remembered from the women in purdah. There was no more laughter, and she froze as their hands immobilized her.

A car light flashed on above her and Christine closed her eyes, not wanting to see what was beside her. They had taken her from the stall in darkness, and she dreaded what she would see in the stark reality of the light. Still, the voice of the merchant sitting up front was clear and all too real.

"You are a nasty girl, I think. Yes?"

One of the men shifted beside her, and Christine flinched, bringing her hands to her face. The men grunted at her, but at least they had stopped groping her. She peeked through her fingers and saw the merchant's white teeth glistening in front of her.

"You know about college . . . about engineers — electrical engineers? There are nine in my family. My father is a doctor. We are not stupid, and we are not animals."

The men conversed, switching from what sounded like Pashto to a language she had not heard before, and after several minutes they seemed to forget about her. Still, her hands stayed at her face. Later, when the jeep lurched to a stop and the men piled out ahead of her, she felt the merchant's hand on her arm.

"Let's go, nasty girl."

He hauled her out of the car, and she went easily; she knew she'd been lucky to escape a beating. The merchant shoved her toward what looked to be a tent. She stumbled, dodging a small cooking fire. Unfortunately, she couldn't clear it completely and the hem of her *qamiz,* a long blouselike tunic, flared up. The men jabbered among themselves, lighting cigarettes and ignoring her as she scrambled to put out the fire. When she finally managed to put out the flames, the men had left.

Beyond the light of the small campfire, she saw other men milling about other fires, other tents. She heard voices, all male.

An engine kicked into operation, a light flashed on, and she saw the merchant standing at the open door of his jeep. The interior light illuminated his face. He was waving a cigarette around, talking with a man who was layered in clothing, long scarves covering his head and trailing down his back. She had seen men dressed like that in Peshawar, Afghans. The driver of the jeep seemed impatient and signaled to the merchant. He never looked back at her, just climbed into the jeep and drove off.

Pocked with what seemed to be a thousand galaxies, the expanse of sky behind the tents reached up and over her, and she wondered what latitude she was at. She had a good idea. The men who moved around the camp were Afghans. It had to be some kind of refugee or training camp, which meant she was probably near the border of Afghanistan.

Someone bellowed, and Christine jumped. The Afghan who had been talking to the merchant was striding angrily toward her. He was waving his arms, his long beard wagging beneath his chin as his mouth moved. She desperately wanted to understand because the way he was moving she knew he would hit her if she didn't grasp his meaning before he reached her. Then she heard small voices from inside the tent and she understood. Christine started to peek inside, but there wasn't time. The Afghan was almost upon her, so she scampered into the tent.

There were three women inside. Two of the women threw on burqas the moment she entered. The other, an elderly woman with clouded, unseeing eyes, leaned into the ones who were covered, gripping her own burqa just in case Christine got any closer.

Christine tried to smile, but the women shrank from her, cowering like prey caught in her sight. Slowly, Christine removed her chador, and the two women, glancing past Christine to be sure that the flaps of the tent were closed, removed their burqas. Both were decorated in henna, and their lips were stained red. The makeup was haphazard and they looked almost clownish.

313

"*Salaam alekum,*" Christine whispered, greeting them as she eased to the ground.

Frozen, the women watched her. They were scared, and any movement — a smile, a gesture — made them tense. Gradually, their faces faded from her sight as the fire outside grew dim. During the day they would get out, but their burqas were their purdah, their prisons and their refuge. For now, however, there were no men to hide from, only the stranger, but in the safety of darkness, each began to relax, curling into herself like a cat, not touching the other, alone. And Christine did the same.

Dust swirled about her face, and it was hot and the specter of Nikhil still haunted her. Christine felt something touch her, and she jumped.

It was one of the hennaed women. Christine sat up before the women, and they stared at her, their eyes wide with fear. Her skin felt grainy and tight, and her hair was matted with dirt and ash. She realized she must look pretty scary and covered her head with her chador. Christine reached for the tent flaps to exit, but one of the painted women stopped her, handing Christine a bowl of water and a burqa.

"*Shukriya, behin,*" Christine thanked her. She had called her "sister" in Urdu, with no response. She tried Pashto, but the woman still misunderstood, shaking her head and pointing to herself. She voiced what sounded like *"Kish-war."*

Exasperated, Christine wondered if any two people west of Peshawar spoke the same language. She nodded, repeating her own name several times and settling for a noise from the Afghan woman that sounded like a sneeze. Kishwar helped her slip the burqa over her *shalwar qamiz,* then led her out into the sun.

It was a settlement of tents, and beyond the tents were fields of flowers. Early morning, the men had just finished prayer. They were still rolling up their prayer mats where they had bowed in submission to Allah as they faced the holy city of Mecca. Most of the Afghans were bearded and had large mounds of coiled cloth upon their heads. Small, nearly naked kids ran amok, their hair and skin already dried and cracked from the sun while old men laid out rows of *pan,* preparing to stuff beetle leaf with a spicy goat mixture. Skeletal stray dogs and the occasional cat lingered beside tents for scraps. There were burqas, and girls in chadors, cooking the morning

315

meal over open fires, and she could hear music playing. To her surprise, very few men carried guns.

Without a word, Kishwar took Christine to a fire where women attended to the dismembered carcass of a goat. Its head, freshly severed, lay beside a girl close to the fire. It was windy, so the girl kept a corner of her chador over a bowl of rice and a few pieces of bruised fruit. They ate in silence while the men of the camp took little notice of them, preferring the company of other men, squatting three at a time, or sitting in neat rows on string cots that were angled around the tents. Some men napped, others talked, their heads bobbing. They shrugged, passed cigarettes, kept their movements small; it was too hot for broad gestures.

There were tents larger than the one Christine occupied, and she figured that the men spent most of their time inside those. She saw other burqas leaving those tents and tried to imagine the beings underneath them.

"You're up, yes?" a voice boomed behind her. The women around the fire scooted away from her as Christine craned her neck around. Between the cloth of the mesh in the burqa and the glaring sun she couldn't see much, but she recognized the merchant's voice.

"Yes, I'm up," she said angrily, and was surprised at the strength of her voice. She immediately regretted her tone, and changed it.

"Can I ask where I am?"

"Yes, you can." He grinned at her.

Christine waited, then blurted out, "I'm an American citizen, and I'm protected by international law. I demand that you take me to my embassy."

The Afghan's grin disappeared. He bent down, bringing his face right into her grid. The bristles of his mustache stuck through the patchwork of holes and pricked at her face. Christine held her breath, but met his eyes. After seeing the women in the tent, she was determined not to end up like them.

"Only *sharia* protects you here, not your America. Not in Afghanistan."

Christine's breath caught, struggling to hold his gaze. She wasn't in a refugee camp inside Pakistan. She was in Afghanistan, where Muslim holy law — sharia — and the oppressive regime of the Taliban had virtually taken over the country. The merchant grunted coarsely. She was powerless. *Even worse,* her mind spun. *I might be a liability, a hostage . . . a political hostage.*

Liz had left the safety of her country to find rugs, and Christine to help Liz. Although her sister had always been the bleeding heart, neither of them would ever compromise their country. They were Shepherd women, and they knew more than most what it meant to travel beyond their nation's borders. Cloid had often talked of his suspicion of an international network of assassins, a growing alliance among fanatics, sects, countries, who used religion as an excuse to terrorize others. There was no sign of the darkly clad Taliban she had seen in Peshawar, but then she wondered about her captor. *What would keep him from using her to get someone out of prison, someone much worse than Farrukh Ahmed?*

Christine's mind raced for options, but there weren't any.

"The Malik said you had a husband. Is he prominent?" asked the merchant.

"No."

The merchant slapped Christine, and she barely felt it. Angry tears began rolling down her cheeks.

"Answer me or I'll kill you."

"What am I supposed to say?" she hissed under her breath, bracing herself for a knife, a perfect tribal replica of some classic serrated piece, to rip into her flesh.

The merchant bent down again. His eyes were blank and he spoke evenly. "Qazi Ali told me you are married to a dirty Christian. It is better for you if your husband is prominent. Understand?"

The merchant signaled to two Afghans waiting nearby. Christine glimpsed a gun on the merchant's belt. In that moment, she knew she didn't have a chance, but at least she'd end it before they could use her. She swiped at it. It came up out of the holster. She almost had it, but the merchant was faster, knocking it from her fingers. Christine watched it skip along the dirt as the men seized her from behind. The Afghan merchant hit her face, but she barely reacted.

"I don't want to hurt you," he said, picking up his gun.

"You did hurt me!" Christine screamed, bending and twisting in her burqa as the men pushed her through the rows of tents. The merchant snatched at the top of her burqa, snapping her head back, tearing at her hair, and she groaned.

"No, Christian woman, we did not hurt you," he said. "We are good Muslims, and you must cooperate now. Otherwise, you could get hurt and that would make me very sad."

Afghan villagers glanced up, but no one moved to intervene.

A slab-concrete shelter was located in the brush not two hundred yards from the Afghan camp. When the four of them entered, there were three heroin users, tangled together with their needles and paraphernalia. One was injecting himself in the groin. Another was waiting his turn, while the third was cooking his drugs on a flat piece of metal. All of them were startled, but could hardly react fast enough as the merchant's men chased them out of the building.

Christine was pushed into the vacated space. There was a broken table, three plastic chairs, and a ragged couch. The room looked like it had been used for meetings, and now it would be used to interrogate a hapless American woman.

The merchant grabbed a chair and seated himself opposite Christine. He pulled off her burqa. She still had her *shalwar qamiz* underneath, but her chador had come off with it, leaving her hair exposed. The merchant smiled. Christine tried not to be intimidated.

"My name is Usman. There is more, but

Usman is all you need to know. For me, I need more. So I will insist that you speak only the truth. Is your husband prominent?"

"I don't have a husband."

Christine's body was shaking so much that she thought her teeth might start to chatter. Usman said something to the men behind him, and they laughed. She closed her eyes and bit her lip, so as not to speak.

Usman asked her why she was so afraid. He was not a violent man, just a merchant trying to make a living. Christine didn't respond, but she was beginning to hope that maybe using her as a political hostage wasn't what the merchant had in mind. As humiliated as she felt, anything had to be better than that.

Christine finally admitted that she was touring Pakistan, looking for crafts to sell, had been kidnapped by a drug lord, then rescued by the Malik tribe. All was well, until the son of the clan's leader decided he wanted to marry her.

Usman couldn't help but smile at this. "So you lied."

"Yes."

"Too bad. The Malik son would be most prominent. You missed your chance." He smiled, "You sell things . . . you make good cash?"

His intent *was* ransom, not political gain. She was relieved, except now it was her mother, and not her country, she worried about. A quick payoff would be the only way. Her mother would try to follow her instructions, but the banks would question her. Cloid would have to help. As much as he would try, the Bureau, even the media might get wind of the abduction and then there would be phone calls or cryptic messages that might go on for weeks. Usman told her he wasn't a violent man, but the payoff couldn't be quick enough. Sending a freshly severed finger, or an ear, to her mother to hasten negotiation would hardly make him flinch . . . but certainly kill her mother.

"Yes, I sell things," she blurted out. "But I'm just getting started, you stupid lout! Someday I *will* be rich! You'll see. And then I won't have to come to this godforsaken place!"

The men went for her. Christine thought they just might kill her on the spot, but if they didn't, she might have a chance. They managed to knock her out of the chair, but before they struck her again, Usman called them off. She was still trembling, but now it seemed to be more from anger than fear, and she climbed back into the chair.

Usman was glaring at her when she faced him, and she glared back. The thought of putting her mother through that hell kept the anger real. Usman finally settled back in his chair. He was waiting for her to say something else, but she was finished.

"Not good in business," the merchant decided, "and too stupid to be a spy. Just a woman, I think. Yes?"

Even if Usman checked out her story and discovered she was lying, she had bought herself time. That was all she needed. Except the merchant made it clear that he, too, was a businessman. Because she had no "prominent husband," because he had paid a good price for her, she would have to work.

That night it didn't take long for the shadows to appear outside their tent. The women barely had a chance to throw on their burqas before two Afghans, dressed in traditional Islamic *hijab,* entered and took two of them.

As the men pulled Kishwar and Christine through the community of tents, groups of Afghan men hollered at one another and laughed, shouting praises to Allah and making rude gestures. A few men with their families turned away while their women spat at them as they passed by.

Christine didn't have to be told what was happening. The women in her tent were also expected to earn their keep. Kishwar and the other woman, for whatever reason, had been deemed unmarriageable and were the camp's prostitutes. And the old woman? Christine guessed that she had no husband, no family, and was just lucky to be alive.

The men were obviously drunk, a habit that was condemned by good Muslims. Rape, however, especially in that part of the world, was hardly an issue. The men led the women to a small truck that was parked inside a covered lean-to. The sides and roof of the truck were painted in greens, reds, and yellows depicting lush gardens, a vision of where the Muslims believed Allah resided and, one day, of where they hoped to be. But the truck was also littered with junk, and the women barely had a chance to clear a spot before the men were on them.

Christine stared up through the mesh of her burqa, but the tarp that covered the shelter was shredding and bits of it were falling into her face. The Afghan's hands were already underneath her burqa, and

Christine turned her head. Kishwar, who lay beside her, seemed nearly comatose as the other man groped her.

Christine wanted only to survive and was desperate to think that to survive was enough. But she couldn't. Something about Kishwar's stillness repulsed her, and when the drunken idiot tore at the *shalwar qamiz* beneath her own burqa, Christine reacted. She pushed at him. It didn't take much because he was so drunk. At first, the Afghan seemed perplexed. He swung at her, but his movements were sluggish and there were so many layers of clothing between them that Christine wriggled easily from his grasp.

The Afghan on top of Kishwar seemed oblivious to the commotion beside him. He was also drunk and having his own problems with getting to Kishwar through her clothing.

While Christine's Afghan stared at the deflated burqa in his hand, she slipped from the truck's flatbed onto the ground. He saw her start away from the truck and went after her. Kishwar cried out, loud enough to disturb the man on top of her. He looked up, but only smiled as he watched Christine and his friend brawl. Seemingly amused by his friend's clumsy efforts, the Afghan chortled drunkenly before returning his attention to Kishwar.

Christine had managed to break free. Angry and disoriented, the Afghan spun around, looking back into the truck, then beyond the camp into darkness. Christine had vanished. Grumbling under his breath, he tried to find her again, then lost his footing, stumbling down a low embankment. When his bulk finally skidded to a halt, Christine crept back along the embankment and saw that the man was asleep, snoring, in fact.

Christine looked out behind her, away from the camp. There were no lights, no other obstacles except the unknown. This was her chance. Then she heard Kishwar's Afghan grunting and moaning. The fear that usually gripped her vanished, and without thinking, Christine climbed back over the bank of rock and approached the truck. The Afghan seemed oblivious as he moved over Kishwar. But Kishwar's eyes were open and seemingly undisturbed until she saw Christine appear over her, a soda bottle in her hand. Before Kishwar could utter a sound, Christine struck the man. He crumpled easily.

At first, both women just stared at each other. As the enormity of Christine's deed registered, Kishwar drew her hand to her mouth. A gasp escaped her lips; such defiance terrified her. Slowly, Kishwar left the truck and crouched next to Christine. Together they watched the man breathe. He was alive, but he was out, completely out, like his drunken friend. Kishwar's hand came up to her mouth again. This time, however, Christine realized the woman was trying to stifle a smile. Christine was also struck by the absurdity of it, until they heard something. Kishwar grabbed for Christine's burqa, but Christine had other ideas. Taking Kishwar's hand they ran into the night.

Out of breath, the two women finally halted and looked back at the camp behind them. Kishwar seemed entranced by the sight. They couldn't be more than a quarter mile from the tents and Christine wondered if it was possible that Kishwar had never been that far from camp.

The Afghan woman whispered something under her breath. Christine couldn't understand, but Kishwar, who had been clutching at her own burqa, dared to lift it just over her head. Peeking from beneath the canopy of fabric, she turned, gazing at the shadows around her. When she faced Christine she grinned, her eyes crinkling.

Then, with an intake of breath, Kishwar threw back her hands and let go of the burqa behind her. Once exposed, she had a moment of panic and froze. The distant sounds of the camp settling and the wind whistling around them seemed very distinct.

"It's safe, Kishwar," Christine whispered. The Afghan woman looked at her and seemed to understand. She looked down at the yellow *shalwar qamiz* she wore beneath her burqa and marveled at the way the moonlight reflected off of its color. She said something, her voice lilting, then turned her face to the moon. As the rays of light moved over her skin, Kishwar closed her eyes.

The garish makeup she wore softened in the light, and the hair of Kishwar's brows seemed scant and lighter than the kohl that shadowed her eyes. Her cheekbones were unusually pronounced, but the nose that punctuated them was small and delicate. And there were dimples on each cheek, with another just underneath her left eye. Her eyes still closed, the woman lifted her face higher, enjoying the light, her dimples deepening as she smiled, almost as if she knew that Christine were seeing her for the first time.

Christine also turned to the sky, but it wasn't the light she was seeking, it was the stars, and she faced east toward Pakistan. Her eyes narrowed as she strained to see something. She had thought of escaping many times, but had been too afraid. She had no idea how far she was from the border, but she had heard stories of life in Afghanistan and knew that this time she would have to try.

As she contemplated escape, she felt a hand take hers. Kishwar had slipped back into her burqa, but her eyes gleamed through the face grid. She spoke, and even though the sound was foreign Christine understood; it was time to go back. Christine cocked her head away from the camp, ever so slightly. It didn't take much. Kishwar knew what she was proposing. The Afghan woman hesitated. For a moment Christine thought she might agree to go with her. Christine looked at the camp, and then again out into the void that could be their salvation, but Kishwar pulled at her hand. She wasn't ready and Christine thought about leaving her, letting her return to the camp alone. Then Christine remembered the men. She doubted that they would remember much, but she also wasn't ready to desert Kishwar. By now,

Kishwar was gripping her hand tightly, and Christine suddenly thought of Liz, missing her terribly. She decided she would go back, get water, some food, and try to get away the following night. Kishwar might be ready then. If not, Christine would go alone.

Even the hard ground was a comfort to Christine, so when shots rang through the camp before dawn, she woke with a start. The other women were already awake, had put on their burqas, and were peering out the flaps of the tent. Clearly something was wrong. Christine slipped on her burqa and sat up next to Kishwar.

Pickup trucks and a jeep were tearing through the camp as a mullah — by his black robes, a Taliban — called Muslims to prayer through a bullhorn in the back of one of the trucks. Two Taliban soldiers positioned behind the tall, bearded, man shouldered Soviet grenade launchers. Christine looked back at the women. They were rolled forward, their heads pressed against the ground. She had never heard the morning prayer sound so harsh. She looked out and watched as haggard Afghan men trudged toward a small mosque that lay just beyond the camp.

As the vehicles ripped through the lines, smashed transistor radios banged against the trucks' bodies like trophies. The jeep came to an abrupt halt beside a man she recognized as one of the rapists from the previous night. He dropped to the ground. She couldn't help but feel sorry for him as enraged men with long tails to their black turbans jumped out of the jeep and began thrashing him with steel cables. They took turns pulling at his short, closely cropped beard, scolding him. He had dared to trim his beard.

Christine had read about the men in the black turbans. They were the Taliban, the law, the sharia of Afghanistan. She had heard that most of them were orphaned when the Soviets invaded Afghanistan. For almost a decade, the Afghan people fought, beating back Russian tanks with sticks and rocks. But by the time the Russians retreated, Afghanistan had been destroyed. Warlords vied for domination, and young men, their families scattered or murdered, went to madrassas, religious schools that became their only refuge, where imans preached Islamic fanaticism and encouraged jihad. Now the oppressed had become the oppressors, victimizing their own. Christine wanted to feel sorry for them as well, but she couldn't. She watched as others were reprimanded, even bludgeoned, on their way to prayer. One woman whose head was covered with a chador, not a burqa, was also whipped, and Christine had to resist an urge to jump from the tent and intervene. An AK-47 was propped just outside the flap of the next tent, but Christine wasn't going anywhere. When one of the trucks, with turbaned Taliban hanging from each side, swung around, Kishwar pulled Christine back with her into the tent. Christine didn't resist. Like the others, she sat silently, her burqa covering her as she waited for the menace to pass.

Once the mullah's brigade had left, Christine was sent to gather brush for the evening fire. She didn't mind. It gave her more time to plan her escape. At the edge of the camp, small fields of poppies broke up the brown terrain. She saw the scarved heads of men and women bobbing above the orange carpet of flowers and realized the Afghans were harvesting opium. The men from the night before had smelled not of goat, but of ash and earth and alcohol. Under Muslim law alcohol was forbidden, but a few still managed to find their drink. Drugs were also strictly forbidden. However, aside from a young, rich Saudi named Osama bin Laden who had been financing the Taliban and their hard-line Islamic regime since 1996, opium was the Taliban's principal income.

Christine circled the perimeter of the camp, beyond which there was no sign of life, only mountains and rocks. A few outbuildings were carefully guarded by men who didn't wear the formidable garb of the Taliban, but wore ammunition belts and carried Kalashnikovs like soldiers, not farmers. She didn't remember seeing them before that morning and she guessed they worked for the Taliban. She doubted that there would be any music that night, or drinking, or anything that did not coincide with the mullahs' interpretation of Islam. The Taliban was taking over the country, and the farmers and their families had no choice but to comply.

In her momentary reverie, Christine's eyes had stayed on the guard too long, and he had noticed her. Even in a burqa she was conspicuous, and she hurriedly returned to collecting brush. As she stepped forward, a gust of sand enveloped her, blinding her briefly, and she stumbled onto what felt like a pile of sticks. As she wiped the grit from her eyes, she saw she was standing amid the bones of a woman, still clothed in pieces of a burqa. There were smooth, rounded rocks, perfect for pitching, lying in and around the skeleton.

The woman had been stoned to death.

A shriek left her lips before she could stop it, and Christine looked up. Too late; the guard was heading toward her. He said something to her, but Christine could only point at the remains. Carrion eaters had picked off most of the woman's flesh and the sun had dried her bones. Wisps of her sun-bleached burqa fluttered in the breeze, but there was no shock in the guard's eyes. He looked at Christine. She didn't dare speak; the guard was already suspicious. Christine lowered her head and went back to gathering. He watched her, then said something. Christine only nodded. It seemed to be enough, and the Taliban's guard returned to his post.

Only the old woman was in the tent when Christine returned. "Kishwar?" she asked.

The woman pulled back the tent flap and pointed. Christine saw her, one burqa among many, tying bags of the poppy pods that contained opium at the edge of the field. Christine hesitated, unsure of whether to approach Kishwar. The dead woman had been executed. Given the guard's expression, there was probably no mystery surrounding the body. Christine wondered if the small cluster of women she was watching could have had a hand in their sister's death.

The old woman pointed again, unsure if Christine had seen her. Christine hastily nodded, and the old Afghan ducked back into the tent. The other women binding sacks watched warily as Christine approached their group. But when Kishwar saw her, her eyes lit up. The two of them finished tying another bag, then Kishwar followed Christine back over to their tent. Instead of going inside with the old woman, Christine squatted in the shadows. Kishwar laughed at this, but sat with her. Christine knew she was smiling, but she didn't return the greeting. Instead she opened her fist, revealing a tattered piece of burqa. There was a pattern on it with the woman's dried blood staining its fringe. Even before Kishwar reacted, Christine was sorry she had showed her. She glared at Christine through her grid, her eyes filling with tears. She muttered something under her breath and snatched at the bloodstained fabric. Christine didn't resist, and she watched as Kishwar took it to the barely smoldering campfire. The Afghan stirred the fire until she was rewarded with a tongue of flame. She threw the cloth into it, her body heaving as she did, and slowly and methodically she worked at the fire until the cloth blackened. When it finally disappeared, Kishwar spat after it, then whipped her head around and spat at Christine.

There was a strange quiet in the tent that night. The women seemed to be waiting for something or someone. But when the men came they weren't drunk, and they weren't sloppy. They knew exactly who they wanted. They didn't take Christine to the truck. They took her to the fields. When Christine realized where they were going, she fought. A gun butt came down on her shoulder and Christine fell into a heap.

Her bladder let go as the men grabbed her feet and dragged her through a corner of the poppy field. Her shoulder throbbed, and she started to yell at them in a mixture of Pashto and the few words she had learned from Kishwar, pleading with them to stop.

One of the men dropped her feet while the other held her down. By the faint smell of rotten flesh and the buzz of flies, she knew the bones were close by. She struggled against him until the other man fell on top of her. His pants were down, but she could feel that he was flaccid. He shouted at her, his face in a grimace. Finally, he pulled off of her. When she tried to get up, the other kicked her back down. She got a whiff of poppies before the man, his pants also undone, fell to his knees beside her. He viciously clutched at her hair, jerking her head back. Christine cried at the strain in her neck as his fingers tore at her grid. There was air; she was exposed. She closed her eyes as the man thrust his pelvis in her face and forced himself into her mouth. She thought about biting down until a gun muzzle cut into her scalp.

Christine cried, was choking, while the other man ripped at her burqa, at her *qamiz*, at her pants. Then the man pulled himself from her, backhanded her, then let the other Afghan take her. This time he was ready for her. She was pushed flat, her mouth in dirt. She tried to pray, could feel her lips moving, but couldn't hear her own appeal to God . . . to Allah . . . to whoever would hear her. The man over her started yelling, and Christine, already in pain, thought she'd be struck again.

She tried to speak, but the man only ranted. Finally he started to come, and his words stopped while the other Afghan shouted at her, circling, kicking at her sides as his partner moved atop her. He saw Christine looking at him and he spat at her.

When the man on top of her finished, she tried to roll away, grabbing at the dirt, desperate to get away, but they both pulled at her, hitting her body, her head. For a moment their hands lifted, and she tried to get to her feet. Then she felt the wetness. It was the acrid smell of urine that finally made her scream, and she dropped to her knees into the bones of the woman.

The spray stopped. Christine saw that her palm was bleeding; she had cut it on a rib . . . on the dead woman. Her body convulsing with sobs, Christine started cursing. Something swung at her, but she managed to catch the hand, and bit down into its flesh. She inhaled the stench of blood, but hung on, until something knocked her over. Her eyes closed, her body throbbed at first from the blows. It didn't take long for the numbness to set in. Images streaked past her, her mind shutting down. And just as she felt the hands take her, flipping her body over, her lips moving, praying, caking with dirt, some merciful deity heard her, and she blacked out.

Traces of movement and blurred faces and the roar of the van, Arshad's van. Christine could see Setin rubbing the purple and yellow marks along the light under flesh of his arm, and she could hear the engine. And then there was Liz, by the river, clad in her neon green sari. She looked radiant as she threw large colored blooms into the water. Then her face became stricken with anguish and she started to cry. Christine saw that the lovely float of green around her sister became a burqa, and it was frayed and torn, its pattern baked by the sun.

The engine erupted again, and Liz vanished. There was a broken floorboard inches from her face, and now Faiz cursed over her. He was angry. She realized it was because she couldn't wait. She had peed on herself. It was all over her, and she was hurting. Faiz's face darkened, and the wind blew past him. His eyes glared, not with lust, but with hate . . . like

Kishwar's eyes, through the mesh, when she recognized the burqa of her murdered sister, and the engine roared.

Christine was suddenly jerked up and pulled out of the tent. The odor of stale flesh, body odor, and blood was overwhelming.

"Muf . . . jeyeh," she sputtered apologetically, and someone spoke. Christine tried to open her eyes. The lids felt swollen. They wouldn't open, then a sliver of light broke through and Christine heard herself moan.

"What the hell happened to her?"

"We believe she's a spy."

"She's mine."

Christine flinched at the sound of his voice. She squinted. There were turbans, large, black ones, with dark figures standing over her. And there was someone else.

"How do we know you're telling the truth?" one of the dark figures inquired.

"Christine?"

Someone took her by her arms and she cried. Her shoulder hurt. Everything hurt. When he sat her upright, she whimpered, but she was in his shadow and she felt cooler.

"Chris?" he said again, and then turned away. "Damn it, you almost killed her."

"She was disobedient."

The sun had left her face, but just the strain of trying to see was almost too much. Then her eyes cracked open. They were tearing, but she could see that wonderfully ugly face.

"You came back," she said. Her voice was slurred.

"Of course I did. I'm . . . your husband." And before she could react, Reggie's fingers pressed into her shoulders.

Christine grimaced from the pain, and her head fell back. Reggie took her into his arms and held her.

"It's all right, I'm back. We're together again. I found you . . . I found you."

She managed to say "Husband," and the Aussie eased his hold.

One of the turbans leaned toward her, and she tried not to react when she recognized that the man was a mullah. "Is this man your husband?"

It took effort to nod. She was so stiff. Christine looked back at Reggie, and he was looking at her with such compassion that she started to cry.

"They raped me," she barely muttered, and the compassion vanished.

The Taliban watched, waiting, and the click of Reggie's tongue was audible. Reggie looked up once at the turbaned men, then back down at her. His eyes unsettled her.

"You bitch!" he barked and struck her face. His hand was open, but still she couldn't believe he hit her.

"Reggie . . . what's . . . wrong?"

"Shut up!" and he jerked her to her feet. "I should kill you for what you've done to me."

Christine would remember later the expressions of approval on the mullahs' faces; Reggie's identity had been confirmed.

Chapter

15

The house was decorated in polished teak and silk-upholstered furniture with an MG and a new Mitsubishi Pajero SUV in the driveway. Two armed guards were posted outside the tall, white, iron gates. The property was hardly exceptional by Western standards, but guards were not an uncommon security precaution in Islamabad's more affluent neighborhoods.

Inside there was no latrine that one was expected to squat over, but a shiny Western toilet. Three, in fact, and when the rebel leader emerged from one of the bathrooms, his hands smelled of scented soap. Still, there was a week's growth on his face, and his eyes darted nervously as he scanned the faces of his followers. There were fewer, only eighteen, and Farrukh Ahmed looked less complacent than he had a month earlier, when he had killed the Shiite leader and his soldier. Since then, he had eliminated many and the burden of jihad had marred his skin with blemishes that wouldn't heal and tiny blood vessels had burst in his eyes, flecking the whites.

The rebels watched as Farrukh approached. In his dirty fatigues and frayed red turban, their leader looked out of place in an urban setting. But they too wore filthy uniforms and looked worn. Only Farrukh's lieutenant, Attaullah Hamid, his turban a remarkable, unstained, white, watched without expression.

They were in what had been the house of Hamid's father. With the old man's death the house had been passed on to him. His father had worked under both Bhuttos, and the time had come for Attaullah to consider taking a place within the new regime. Like most of those who had tried to navigate the Muslim state, the last prime minister had been unsuccessful, and now a rich businessman ran the country. But Attaullah wasn't sure that there was a place for him in the government. Yet. He decided he would pray for wisdom and patience. Pakistan was still so new and he was young. There was time.

While Ataullah was contemplating his

future, an argument broke out between Farrukh and two older Punjabis who had been with him from when he first gained prominence as a freedom fighter, battling in the peaks of the Himalayas.

As he had been doing for several weeks, the lieutenant managed to subdue the periodic outbursts of temper. But Farrukh had become unpredictable, and Attaullah kept an eye on his leader's hand. Attaullah had already decided that if Farrukh reached for his gun, he would intervene. He would have to; they were in an elite suburb of Islamabad, and gunshots might draw attention. Besides, Farrukh had killed a brother the previous week, and they couldn't afford to lose anyone else. They still had work to do.

There was a time when the lieutenant had felt a kinship with the infamous Farrukh Ahmed. Attaullah Hamid had trained as a chemical engineer and graduated at the top of his class. Farrukh was the son of a weaver. But they both hated India. When several of Attaullah's college friends claimed, mostly in jest, to know the fierce rebel, he agreed to meet Farrukh, and in him he found a brother. By that time, he had grown tired of the decadent parties and his peers had begun to bore him. He couldn't relate to his father's circle of cronies and the country was bankrupt. There were no jobs, and soon he felt himself starting to drift. Then he met Farrukh Ahmed, who was uneducated and coarse, but dynamic . . . and committed.

Attaullah watched Farrukh, his tirade forgotten, gather the motley group of leftovers around him. One Pakistani, his forearms still greasy from replacing the spark plugs on their truck, sat beside him. Attaullah tried not to cringe as he saw the man soil the arm of his couch. Farrukh didn't seem to notice. He was too busy berating the Westerners, especially the Americans. Attaullah thought they had enough to worry about with the Indians, and he wondered how long his leader would last if he decided to broaden his war.

Farrukh outlined the plan for their next violent action. They had support from a network rooted in Egypt that had many arms now. Funding was needed to support their brothers in the jihad against the West, so Farrukh reminded them that they must not be greedy. Their own mandate was still Kashmir, and they must always try to draw from their own, when they could.

One of the men added that he had an uncle in Abbottabad who could supply them with the materials they would need to do the job. Farrukh's eyes fell on the young man, a vendor's son who had never fought, but sold bolts of fabric to village women and stringed kites to children. He was eager to join Farrukh. His aunt and a nephew had been killed when an Indian mortar shell fell into their courtyard. His distraught father still lived in the hallowed wreckage of their home, and the young man was determined to get revenge.

His voice clearer than it had been for weeks, Farrukh gave the rookie instructions. The boy was new, and Farrukh was anxious to impress him.

Nodding, cocking their heads in the manner that made it clear they understood, the others listened. There was not much discussion. Their leader had ideas, ideas that scared them, but they would follow him. Without Farrukh, they had little purpose, no life. Besides, they were Muslims, and their brothers were dying in Kashmir. They had no choice.

Chapter
16

Christine had been more or less incoherent since they left the camp. Her body fell limp as Reggie loaded her into the Suzuki pickup. The gunslinging guards Reggie had brought with him to face the Taliban averted their eyes.

The day before, Reggie had told Cloid Dale that he thought he knew where Christine was being kept. The old man was going to book a flight for that night and meet him at the American embassy in Islamabad, but when he showed up at Los Angeles International Airport in a wheelchair, two IVs, and bags in tow, he was turned away, his money refunded.

With the bad roads and traffic it took Reggie the rest of the day just to get his entourage back across the border into Pakistan. The Shepherd woman didn't have any papers, and Reggie wanted to avoid going through Khyber Pass, the main government checkpoint. Fortunately, Reggie's Afghans had no trouble finding a place to cross over. The rocky, unmarked border extended for hundreds of miles, and was wide open, but going overland was rough, and Reggie was anxious to find a room for the night.

Once back in Pakistan, Reggie dropped his Afghans off at a tea stop on the Grand Trunk nearest the refugee camp, paid them well, then drove on into Peshawar with Christine. Except someone was following them. Reggie had seen the same jeep trailing them in Afghanistan, and he had little doubt that the swarthy faces pressed up against the dirty windshield behind them belonged to members of the dead guard's family.

Qazi had warned Reggie of the vendetta, and Reggie realized that he might've let his armed escorts off too soon. Nevertheless, he drove to the Pearl Continental Hotel, asked the bellman to park his truck in the back of the building, then checked in, with Christine dragging next to him. He had gotten a room on the second floor that looked out over the parking lot. He saw that there were two jeeps, not one, with about a dozen people. Christine had no trouble identifying the men who stood alongside their vehicles, waiting for her and Reggie to exit. And they did exit, but out the back and into Reggie's Suzuki, escaping to the far end of town.

Reggie found a room in what looked like a condemned building. There were a garment stall, a teahouse, and a fruit stand downstairs. By the time Reggie drove in, even the money changer who worked out of his motorized rickshaw on the corner was packing up. It was late, and dark, and the roads were nearly deserted. By morning they would be congested, and even a Westerner like himself could get lost.

In the room, there was a niche with a boxed-in hole as a toilet at one end, and a rusty showerhead with a scanty shower curtain at the other, one chair, and a single string cot. Reggie started to apologize for the accommodations, but Christine hardly seemed to care. She was only intent on getting to the cot.

While she slept Reggie took out his mobile phone and tried Cloid. He couldn't get much of a signal, so he pulled up a chair, propped his feet on the end of Christine's cot, and promptly fell asleep.

He slept until the woman groaned. By

the way she favored one side he suspected at least one, maybe two, of her ribs had been broken. Remnants of her burqa were stained and torn and she smelled. The pungent burqa had twisted around her like a mummy, probably pressing against the cracked ribs.

"Let's get that damn thing off," Reggie muttered.

The moment he touched her, she reacted, kicking out at him.

"Are you just pissed, or daft? I need to know."

"I need a shower," she cried. Now fully awake, Christine could smell herself. Her first thought was of the rank odor of liars and those who had been damned, and now she feared that God was taking his vengeance on her.

Reggie stared at Christine. She was hissing at him like something rabid and ready to fight. In the United States she'd be given a meaty dose of Prozac, but in Peshawar Reggie was at a disadvantage; they'd probably torch the bitch.

"I need a shower!" she cried louder.

Reggie reached over and turned on a lamp. The light was dim, but he could see that her eyes were brimming with tears. She was frightened. Christine had been raped. He got it. He pulled up his chair. Not too close. She had already kicked him once.

"It's all right," he tried. "It's just bugger nights, you know? I get them all the time."

"I don't want to smell like this. It's a curse . . . I'm afraid it's a curse."

"Look, I know what you've been through —"

"No, you don't!" she screamed, and tried to rise off the cot.

Reggie looked over at the shower slab in the corner and sighed. Above it hung the badly corroded plumbing fixture, with a remnant of plastic for a curtain. A crusted piece of soap lay by a filthy grate. Even so, the place was a bargain. He hadn't expected a shower for fifty rupees a night.

Christine was lucky. Not only was Reggie surprised to find her alive, but the mullah had taken eight thousand for her release, low for extortion in that part of the world. Nowadays the Taliban were trying to appear legitimate, a failed strategy if they were known to be holding an American woman. Still, Reggie was exhausted, and Christine couldn't even raise her arms.

"Hold on," he said, watching her struggle with the burqa. The hood had been torn off and it was time to lose the rest.

He went to help her and stopped. "I'm just going to rip the bloody thing off. All right with you?"

She barely nodded.

The material was threadbare, and tore easily. Only her *shalwar qamiz* remained, or what was left of it.

Christine looked down at her body. There were brown stains where she had been scraped and rubbed raw. She would have to strip. *Someone will have to strip me.* She stared at the stranger Cloid had sent to her. She wanted to trust him, but this rough-looking man was strong enough to hurt her. Still, he had come back for her. *If he hadn't, I'd still be there in the poppy field.*

"We going to do this or not?" he asked.

"I hate the way I smell."

"Yeah, you stink."

Christine stared at the Australian. He didn't understand. To him it was just "bugger nights." But Nazeem was dead, her sister was missing, and she had been raped and almost killed. Somehow she must be responsible. Christine had lived in a different world too long, and the thoughts and superstitions that came into her head scared her. She wasn't sure that a shower bath would be enough.

He started on her clothing.

"Wait."

"For what? You can barely stand."

"Can you wait until I'm behind the curtain?"

"Yeah, yeah. Go."

She had managed to stand, but felt impaled by her own ribs the first time she tried to move.

"Shit," she said.

"Right." He stepped forward.

It was slow and painful for both of them, but Reggie got her to the shower. She grabbed onto a long metal pipe that came down from the overhead fixture.

"I got it."

"You'll break your bloody neck."

"I got it," she insisted.

He let her go, and her face contorted. She leaned into the pipe, inching herself onto the slab and behind the curtain.

Once she was out of sight, Reggie reached in and tore blindly. The blouse and string pants fell to her feet.

Reggie waited for her to start the shower. There was a gasp, a heavy intake of breath. He imagined that she was trying to turn the knobs, and each time she did, there was pain.

Then he heard it. The request — plea really — was a whisper, but unmistakable.

"Right," he said again, reaching in to turn the knobs. They were frozen. He tried again, but was forced to open the curtain to get a better hold. He tried to ignore Christine who had grasped the pipe with one hand, her breasts with the other. The water gurgled, then gushed, and Reggie drew the curtain closed.

"How's that?" he called out, trying not to smile.

Christine grunted, loudly. "Cold."

She stifled another cry as his hand flew behind the curtain and twisted blindly at the knob.

"Wrong way —" she gasped.

The Aussie madly twisted the knob the other way. "All right?"

"Good," she breathed, still smarting.

"You okay?"

"Soap . . . I need soap. I'm so . . ."

The soap was still at her feet. She could barely move, much less bend over, and Reggie groaned even louder than she. This piecemeal approach was not working, and the Aussie had run out of patience.

"Christine . . . Chris. You know, I've already seen you naked. Right?"

"I . . . guess."

"So . . . maybe . . . we can make this quick."

No response.

"For chrissake, woman! You're skinny as hell, and you smell like somethin' from a barnyard. Gimme a break."

Reggie got his response. It was weak and shrill, but she asked for help.

He threw back the curtain, soaped her up, rinsed her off, and managed to keep Christine from breaking another rib as she stumbled from the shower back to the cot, squealing as she went. He threw a blanket over her, then grabbed his rucksack. He needed a smoke. Christine was so cold, her teeth were chattering.

"You're welcome," he blurted out and lit up a cigarette.

By the time the early-morning call to prayer sounded over the rooftops, Christine almost felt warm. Reggie mumbled something under his breath. He had stationed himself by the window to keep watch, but was on his last cigarette.

"Are they out there?" she asked.

"Who?"

"His family . . . the guard's family?"

"Nope, we left them at the Pearl. But they will be."

Groaning with the effort, Christine

rolled onto her back.

"You need a chemist," Reggie remarked, flicking his cigarette away.

"I need my sister," she said. She looked at him. It pained her to turn her head, but she was intent on seeing his expression in the light. She held his gaze until he dropped his eyes. He hated this. He wasn't paid to bathe the woman or tell her that her sister was dead. That was for the old man.

"I'm going to a chemist," he declared. "You need something, and I'm plumb outta cigarettes."

He snatched up his rucksack, avoiding her eyes, then stopped at the door. When he looked back at her, her gaze had shifted. She was somewhere else, as she should be, as he would be if he thought he had lost someone. She needed time. He couldn't give her much, but the trip to Islamabad wouldn't be easy. Whether she wanted it or not, she needed a painkiller for those ribs. And he needed a joint.

"I guess I don't have to tell you not to go anywhere," he said. "You know where you are, right? Right?"

"I know where I am," Christine responded flatly.

Reggie took a rickshaw to a stall under a

sun-bleached sign of coiled snakes and a cross. Inside he scanned the sparsely stocked shelves of generic, out-of-date, medicine tins while a burly Afghan sat at a counter counting out colorful stacks of currency that looked like play money. Third world infirmaries were all too familiar to Reggie, but he wondered how much he could say. He was no Yank, but sentiment for any Westerner ran chilly nowadays.

The man's wife stacked crates of orange soda in the back of the stall. The woman was scrawny, and Reggie guessed that she probably sported a fair number of bruises. The bit of arm that protruded from her burqa was briefly exposed, but telling as the woman reached for each crate. Even Reggie, who had never considered himself much of a gentleman, had to restrain himself from helping her. He studied the vendor who was picking at a box of milk sweets and reading the Koran while his wife toiled.

"G'day."

The tilt of the chemist's head was almost imperceptible.

"English?" Reggie tried.

No response.

Reggie sighed. He guessed that the

Afghan knew English but didn't want to give him any advantage. Reggie struggled through a mixture of Pashto and Urdu, telling the man that his wife had cracked a couple ribs and was generally pretty banged up.

The Afghan sucked at his syrupy fingers, seemingly uninterested in the foreigner's business. Then, slowly, his eyes rolled up. Reggie knew the drill. He had already pulled out a wad of rupees, and the haggling begun.

Shortly after, Reggie walked out of the dusty stall with bandages, denatured alcohol, a couple of dozen colored tablets, and even a few grunts of medical instruction. Reggie was told to bind Christine around the middle, feed her three tabs each day of some unnamed antibiotic for a week. Then he would ply her with hash. The latter was Reggie's idea; it had gotten him through a few scrapes of his own. He hated to waste much on her, but it was cheap locally, and he had to get her out of that headspace she was in. He knew Cloid Dale wanted her in the embassy infirmary, but the road to Islamabad wouldn't be much better than the one in Afghanistan, and he needed to take care of those ribs. When he went through those militia checkpoints, he needed her covered and quiet.

An hour and a half had lapsed and Reggie could tell by the way Christine looked at him that the possibility he might not come back had crossed her mind. There was no greeting as he came through the door, no smile, no soft words of acknowledgment, but when he sat on the bed next to her, he didn't have to fend off any blows either.

She barely gasped when he sat next to her, but he knew she had to be hurting.

"I'm trying to feel sorry for you," Reggie started as he bit at the dirty foil with his teeth, "but you kicked me." The foil tore and he slipped out a green tablet. He grabbed at a fresh bottle of water, one of six he had purchased.

"I got you good water, not that you're not already crawling with bugs."

"Men . . . men are bastards, aren't they?"

She grimaced, finally acknowledging the pain as he lifted her up into a sitting position.

"I'm no tribesman, but I'm no pussified Yank either. Don't push it."

He handed her the bottle and the pill. She took it, watching him as she did, trying to remember that he wasn't the one who had hurt her. After she swallowed the pill, he held up a roll of bandage. "Your ribs . . . We're gonna have to wrap them, otherwise you'll howl the whole way to Islamabad."

Christine mumbled something under her breath.

"You going to kick me?"

She thought about it. "It would hurt too much."

"Good," he breathed, unrolling the bandage. "Once you're wrapped, we'll get another couple hours sleep, then we'll head out."

He finished, holding the end of the bandage. "C'mon, Chris."

She dropped the blanket and turned away.

"This may not feel good," he said, wrapping it around her bare chest and middle, "but it has to be tight."

He babbled something about his own broken ribs in '72, and '94, and those damn Filipinos, keeping his eyes on the narrow strip of gauze the entire time, until she was covered. When he finally looked at her face, he saw that her expression had softened.

"Thank you," she said.

"We're not all bastards," Reggie reminded her, and started back to his chair.

"Then tell me the truth about Liz."

Reggie stopped. He turned back around. He couldn't believe it. After all this, the bloody female was still going to cry on him.

"That's *it!* That's fucking *it!*" he yelled. "No more mucking about now. I mean it! Fuck! I *mean* it! I need sleep — couple hours, that's all I'm asking. I'm not a shrink, I'm not a goddamn babysitter, and you're fuckin' with my *head.* Sorry 'bout your sister, but I need *sleep* . . . I'm not good at this. Sorry, sorry . . ."

Reggie had to turn away. His back to her, he waited for her to break into sobs. The silence was worse.

Muttering another apology under his breath, Reggie took his chair and stuck it behind her cot. He did it quickly, worried that she might turn to face him. Then he'd break down, tell her everything, and she'd cry, and he'd never sleep. But she didn't. Her back to him, she didn't move, not a sound. Reggie stuck his feet up on the other end of the cot and closed his eyes and tried to forget the way she had looked at him, forget how her breasts fell, how he yelled at her, how her body felt beneath his hands in the shower, forget, forget, forget . . .

At the sound Reggie bolted awake. Even in his sleep his first thought was of the guard's family.

But the room was quiet, and Christine was still sitting on the cot. Except now, she was facing him, dressed, ready to go, and holding a Colt Special — his Colt Special.

He moved toward her, and she raised the gun. If she fired, a .45-caliber bullet would hit him square in the chest. He stopped, reaching instead for a pack of cigarettes lying on the floor next to her.

"Mind?"

Christine's hand was unnervingly steady. Reggie decided she did mind. He sat back down. "By the looks of it, you know how to use that."

"Yes, I do."

"See you found the new outfit I bought for you. Like it?"

She didn't respond.

"Whatever you're pissed at, we can work it out."

"The DNA tests are in and she's dead, isn't she?"

"Maybe we should call Cloid," he suggested. He reached for his rucksack next to her. She raised the gun.

"You didn't answer my question," she said.

"Yes, the DNA tests are in." When Christine didn't reply he told her of the evidence, of what he knew. By the time he finished, he wasn't sure she was even listening.

"Chris?"

Christine had trouble catching a breath; she thought that maybe her bandage was too tight. Still, whatever it was they had found, it was Liz; it was her sister, and whether she liked it or not, tears started to come down her cheeks.

The Aussie sighed. "Fuck the bloody gun. I need a joint."

Reggie grabbed his rucksack. He pulled out a baggie of hashish and papers, rolled a joint, and lit up. He took a drag, watched her, took another, and then offered her a smoke. She shook her head.

"Maybe we should talk about it, huh?" Reggie asked.

The gun was still up. "About Farrukh?"

Actually, he was talking about her sister. There was a manic stare in Christine's eyes, and all he could think about was that gig in Africa he should've taken.

"Farrukh, your sister, the dickheads in Afghanistan, anything you want to talk about. We've got time. Cloid Dale's hung up in L.A. And as far as your friends out there, if you're not worried about someone wanting to cut your throat, I'm not. Anyway, those kind of blood feuds get a bit old after a while."

Christine unconsciously cocked her head in response, just like a Pakistani, and for a moment Reggie wondered if the woman *had* gone daft.

"When Farrukh Ahmed attacked the village, he killed Ullas . . . Ullas was my friend's husband. He didn't live there. He was just passing through . . . but still they found him, with the others . . . Children too, seven, I think."

Christine brought down the gun, staring at it as she turned it over in her hand. Reggie almost moved to take it from her, but thought better of it.

"Yeah . . . Ahmed . . . I've heard of him."

Christine shrugged again, the gesture smaller this time. "It's a shame, isn't it?"

"What?"

"That my country — both our countries, I guess, have all these rules, but no one else pays attention. So all these people, these kamikazes, these suicide bombers, win."

"If you think dying is winning."

"But they don't care, do they?"

"About rules?"

"About dying."

Reggie took another drag on the joint, and shrugged, Western style. "Sometimes they don't."

"Do you?"

"Most of the time."

"My dad used to say that it gave them an advantage. I mean, strategically."

Christine watched as Reggie leaned in, putting out his joint. He said something, but an image of Dabboo crumpled over her cigarette as Raghavan told her of Ullas's death distracted her. She remembered Dabboo, her face streaked with tears. The Indian woman had been crying because her husband had been murdered . . . and Liz had been murdered. *They had found her.*

Christine thought about the terrorist who had killed so many and squeezed the gun between her palms. There was a stillness in her body, not unlike the way she felt in the desert, baking, near death. And yet she was acutely aware of the gun's cool, metal grip, its fit in her hand.

For some time, she had been cognizant of a shift in her thinking. *I'm slipping into their mind-set.* Her breath quickened. She looked up at the mercenary whose lips were moving, but she couldn't hear his words. She was too preoccupied with fantasies of killing Farrukh. When she discovered that she had killed the guard, she understood how his family felt. They couldn't rest until they found her, and for some reason she realized she also couldn't rest until she found Farrukh.

Then Christine caught herself. She wasn't like them. The guard and his family, the Taliban, the men who had raped her, were tribal, and backward, some of them no better than animals themselves. She wasn't an animal. She was an American, a Westerner, who was only trying to stop a terrorist.

As a child she had heard all the talk, the fantasies, of what it would be like to get a shot at Carlos the Jackal, or Noriega, or the Cambodian butcher Pol Pot. They weren't discussions of morality; they were designs in warfare. The United States was a democracy, a system that everyone agreed was far superior to any other. Yet it was flawed.

And rebels, whose only agenda was to die for their cause, accomplished alone what all the agencies and heads of states combined couldn't. The men at the rifle range had argued. Her father and Cloid, too . . . But the conclusion was always the same. The zealots, the fanatics, the kamikazes, whatever you wanted to call them, were always the most formidable, the most unpredictable, and usually had the greatest chance of tactical success.

And Christine thought of Farrukh Ahmed. She believed her dad would've gone after Farrukh himself, but her father was dead, and Liz was dead, and she was in Peshawar. *There had to be a reason.*

The gun was gone. Reggie had taken it from her while she was daydreaming. Now the mercenary was watching her. He knew what she was thinking. Christine wanted to kill the terrorist, the criminal who had murdered her sister, who had murdered others, and would murder again.

"You weren't paid nearly enough," she began.

Reggie hardly reacted, but Christine knew she had his attention. "I'll pay you more, a lot more than Cloid, if you'll help me kill Farrukh Ahmed."

"Revenge?"

"No," Christine said, a little too emphatically. "I'm just trying to stop him. If you had had a chance to stop Hitler, knowing what you know, wouldn't you?"

"Is this bloke Hitler?"

"Does he have to be? Farrukh's already slaughtered over two hundred people."

"And your sister."

"And my sister."

Keeping an eye on her, the Aussie reached over and picked up a fresh pack of cigarettes. He tapped it on the floor.

"Could you do that?" she asked. "Could you help me kill him?"

"I could," Reggie Duke said a little too easily. "Could you?"

Christine realized that the notion of going after Farrukh should scare her, but with what she had been through, how she had lived the last six months, and now with Liz gone, her own life hardly concerned her.

"I'm a soldier," Reggie reminded her, "an ex-SAS squaddie. I know you've had your share of trouble, but I'm a professional."

Christine reached over and took the handgun from Reggie's rucksack. While he had slept, she had handled all his guns, his "traveling shit," as he called it. The Tokarev and the Smith & Wesson she had left, but she was partial to the Colt Special. She remembered that her dad had had one just like it. Christine held it up and looked at the autoloader and knew that it was used for combat. A .45-caliber single action with a skeletonized trigger and an elongated slot hammer, it also had an adjustable rear night sight. The handgun was relatively lightweight, with a five-inch barrel and an eight-shot magazine, and Christine fondly remembered doing some major damage to targets she had opened up on with one.

It had been so long since she had fired the gun, but it felt right in her hand. She moved easily over the hard chromed finish, loading, reloading, and ejecting a cartridge, another, and another, cleanly, without a pause, just as she did when she practiced with her dad and Cloid. Once the gun was empty, she remembered that the Australian was watching her. She laid the semiautomatic in her lap.

"You're not a soldier yet," he said.

"Not yet," she agreed, "but you can help me, and I know you understand."

Unfortunately, he did understand. Reggie had lost many friends — some to guys like Farrukh. And when he saw her handle the gun with such familiarity, he had already decided that he would have to do some research on the terrorist, and on the Shepherd woman. He had wives to support, and this gig made as much sense as the rest of them. He could buy a couple of weeks just by telling Cloid the girl needed time to recuperate. After that, well . . .

Chapter
17

Mir Hasan's eyes were gray. There were flecks of blue, but the color reminded her of days that were so foggy that you didn't want to venture out. It was that feeling that gripped Christine as Reggie introduced her to Mir, the Pakistani he had hired to take them north.

Mir's rail-thin driver, Sinkindar, was also Pakistani, originally from the province of Baluchistan, where even electricity was a luxury. He spoke no English, and Christine had a feeling that the neatly pressed cotton of his long-sleeved tunic hid the scars of a seasoned heroin user.

The men concerned her, and she pulled Reggie aside. Mir had fought with Reggie against the Soviets in the 1980s, was fluent in English, had studied in New York, and knew the northern areas. Of course, Mir had been a kid at the time. Now the kid had streaks of gray in his hair, and Reggie had bad teeth. But Reggie insisted that when you fought with a bloke, you knew him, no matter how many years had passed. As to their driver, Mir believed in Sinkindar, and that counted for more than worrying about another addict on the roads.

Besides, the Aussie confided as he lit up another cigarette, he had told Mir and Sinkindar that Christine was married to a freedom fighter, a Muslim separatist who fought to save their Muslim brothers from the evil Indian oppressors. Reggie grinned. He admitted that he hadn't mentioned Farrukh, as yet. The Pakistanis with their twenty-one political parties and their conflicts between Sunni and Shiite Muslims were a bit of an unpredictable bunch. But coming down on Pakistan's side of the Kashmir issue was usually a safe bet. He told her not to worry.

The plan was that Mir would escort Christine to the bank while the driver and Reggie dug up more arms. The fourteen hundred Reggie had left from the money Cloid had given him, and the two thousand remaining from money he had found in Christine's safe-deposit box should cover whatever guns they needed, but eventually they would need more cash.

The '84 Toyota hatchback Mir had rented was white and clean, and actually comfortable. Dressed in a pale blue tunic and pants, Mir was immaculately groomed, even attractive, and if he hadn't had an AK-47 strapped over his shoulder, she would've forgotten that she was in a town known for its lawlessness. Reggie had already warned Mir of the tribesmen who might want to hurt Christine, and to keep an eye out. Mir didn't ask questions. Didn't need to; the clans were notorious.

The Pakistani drove in silence through the streets of Peshawar while behind him Christine adjusted her chador. She was glad to be rid of the burqa, but kept the scarf drawn high on her face so only her eyes showed. It galled her to think she had become dependent on the scarf, but for some reason Mir made her nervous.

The bank was less than fifteen minutes from their hotel. They had moved that day to another hotel with twenty rooms, not as nice as the Pearl, but it was a change upward. Reggie figured that Christine's pursuers would have left the Pearl and would be looking for them. They had been in Peshawar for two days. That gave them one more day to get their guns, their money, and anything else they needed for the journey. Visitors to Peshawar, especially Westerners, who stayed longer, had to be careful. Not just because of vengeful tribesmen, but because it gave local merchants too much time to consider their value.

The bank had polished marbled floors, silk-upholstered chairs, imported mahogany desks, and impressive technology. Christine assumed that huge sums of drug money passed through it. She had called her bank in L.A. and with the false ID Reggie provided, the twenty-thousand-dollar withdrawal was a relatively easy transaction. Large amounts didn't seem to fluster Mir as they had Arshad. He was Americanized, she thought, or maybe he was a drug smuggler himself.

As they left the bank, a figure came at her from the side. Before Christine could react, Mir was in front of her, his gun in his hands.

"Whoa, whoa, Chris! It's me, Joe."

It was Joseph Riccardi, the political officer who had tried for weeks to find Liz. In the end, however, he proved to be as ineffective as she was in getting through the bureaucratic muddle. Joe smiled; he was glad to see her. He wasn't such a bad guy and she wished she felt glad to see him, except the man he was with looked familiar. Then Christine remembered. It was the man she had spotted at the Pearl Continental, an operative that she was sure had to be CIA. Joe smiled again. She couldn't help but wonder what a State Department political officer assigned to India was doing in Pakistan.

"What are you doing here?" she asked.

"I could ask you the same thing," Joe returned, his smile fading. He turned to the spook. "This is Russell Dobbs. He works with me at the State Department. Russell, Christine Shepherd."

Dobbs offered his hand. "Miss Shepherd."

Christine was too furious with Joe to shake anybody's hand. He had lied to her. It all made sense now. She had been with him for weeks in Delhi, and still she had missed it. She was wondering what he was doing in Peshawar, and now she knew. *Joe was also CIA.* It wasn't exactly a big secret that State POs were a frequent cover for the CIA. And now Joe, the spook, was in Peshawar.

She felt the chador slip, and quickly clutched it. Something stabbed at her beneath her bandages. For a moment, she couldn't breathe. Her knees buckled, and Joe reached for her, but Mir already had her around the waist.

She pushed Joe's hand away. "I'm fine." The moment she was stable the Muslim released her.

"You're hurt," Joe said.

"And you're a liar."

She kept from grimacing as she turned away. The car was a couple of hundred yards from the bank, and she was anxious to leave.

"I don't know what you're talking about," Joe said to her. He tried to keep up, but with Mir he could only get so close.

"You know exactly what I'm talking about."

Joe started to object, but she turned on him.

"Don't play with me. I know why you're here, and I also know you and this sp—"

Dobbs' eyes widened in horror. The street outside the bank was filled with all sorts of dangerous-looking individuals and Christine was getting ready to blow his cover. And she would have, except Joe looked miserable. Any other time she would've sympathized, but Liz was dead, and instead of tracking down her sister's murderer, the spooks were wasting her time. She moved on, but Joe stayed with her. At least, Dobbs was smart enough to hang back.

"Cloid's worried about you. You know that, don't you?"

Christine would've responded, but a whiff of sandalwood distracted her. When they reached the car, Mir, with his AK strapped across his chest, stepped in front of Joe, blocking him from Christine. As Mir unlocked the door, Joe was forced back onto the curb. He was livid, but Christine only noticed the width of Mir's shoulders. His neck was moist, and the scent of sandalwood had become more intense. Her side throbbed and she wanted to lean against him, but she knew better.

"Chris," Joe said, "this is not a place for a woman alone."

The American officer was easy to read. She had seen the same proprietary look on the faces of Muslim men, tribesmen.

"I'm not alone," she told him. "And I'm okay . . . Call Cloid for me, and tell him I'm okay."

Christine crawled into the car before Joe could respond. As the engine started, she kept her face turned away. She didn't want to see how helpless Joe was, or Dobbs . . . how helpless they all were. The CIA had no jurisdiction in Peshawar, and certainly no power to detain a U.S. citizen. There were rules, travel advisories, U.S. and Pakistani laws that she would ignore, that she had already ignored. What she wanted to do was illegal, evil to some, but all she knew was that she had to stop a madman. It wasn't revenge, it was a necessity, and as an American, as a sister — as a woman — she was tired of feeling helpless.

As Mir drove, Christine decided to stop thinking of Joe, or her dad, or even Liz. She had to concentrate on Farrukh, only Farrukh. She thought of where they were going. Farrukh and his men were traveling through the mountains of northern Pakistan. Three of the world's largest mountain ranges intersected out that way, and Reggie was already more concerned with finding the terrorist than killing him.

Up ahead, people packed together in the center of the road, some yelling, some raising their arms in protest, others just watching. Christine saw uniforms and other men, heavily armed, with trailing black turbans. Her stomach knotted at the sight of the Taliban, then Mir detoured onto a side road. There was unrest. The radicals spilled out on that road as well, forcing Mir to detour once more. Finally, their way was clear.

"What was that all about?" Christine asked, trying to sound casual.

Mir only shrugged, no cock of his head, just a gentle rise and drop in his shoulders, Western style. "That man," he asked, "does he know your husband's mujahideen?"

He was talking about Joe. "I, ah . . ."

"Forgive me, I misunderstood. Reggie told me you were married to a freedom fighter."

"You didn't misunderstand. I am married to a freedom fighter."

Mir Hasan glanced back at her in the rearview mirror and Christine saw that the flecks of blue in his gray eyes seemed even more prominent in the waning light.

"Why?"

"Because . . . I fell in love with him."

"No, I mean *why* is he a freedom fighter?"

Christine must've taken too long to answer, because Mir shot off another question.

"And he's Muslim?"

"Yes."

"Did you meet him in the States?"

Mir was beginning to sound annoyed, and Christine wondered if she had already said too much.

"Yes," she said reluctantly.

"And now he's returned to fight," Mir concluded.

He muttered something. It sounded like Arabic. She wasn't sure, but the Pakistani was making her nervous. Christine knew the AK was propped up against the seat next to him. She couldn't see it, and needed to, just in case he reached for it. But when she shifted in her seat, the pain pierced her and she cried out.

"Are you all right?" Mir asked.

In the mirror, his eyes looked even grayer than before, but the glare had softened.

"It's just my side. Are you . . . angry about something?"

Mir Hasan looked back at the road. Now it was the Pakistani who took too long to answer. "It's not my business. I just feel sorry for your husband. He's fighting to be free of the Indians. But even if he succeeds, he'll still lose. There's no freedom here in Pakistan either."

Chapter
18

The bottom of the jeep bounced up and slammed back against the road with a crash. Christine's first thought was of a land mine. Even after the boom dissipated, images of the camel, her own bloody leg, and Nikhil's shattered hip flashed through her mind. Sinkindar swerved off the road when the explosion rocked them, and after they finally came to a stop, just missing a roadside tea stall, they all looked behind them at the fiery gate and guardhouse. Several people ran toward the debris and the downed guard who had been at the gate.

Christine started for the door, but Reggie grabbed her hand.

"Think — no burqa. Not a time to be playing Florence Nightingale. You're a friggin' sore thumb as it is."

Reggie signaled to the driver and at once they were back on the road. Christine craned her neck around, trying to see.

"But he's hurt. We can't just leave."

"It's all right," Mir assured her. "His people will take care of him. The man's alive, see?"

The guard was alive, even sitting up on his own as two old Pakistanis, doubled up on the same bicycle, came to a stop by him. Christine couldn't believe how calm they all seemed to be. There was no big hurry, and, in fact, the guard was now standing, his shirt and pants bloodied, while children hopped about the ruins, picking up souvenirs.

Christine turned around in her seat. Only Mir seemed to be concerned, and more about her than the unfortunate guard. Sinkindar fiddled with the knobs on the radio, trying to find a good station while Reggie picked at a scab on his earlobe.

"Did terrorists blow up that gate?"

Disgusted, Mir shook his head. "It's the tribesmen. Government's doing another sweep, trying to keep them from selling on the Grand Trunk."

Christine didn't need to ask what they sold. Sinkindar said something to Mir. The driver had a strange lilt to his dialect, so she didn't catch all of it.

"Did he say that the Maliks did it?" she asked.

Reggie was still concentrating on his earlobe. "Yeah, this one, but next it'll be the Afridis. I swear those damn clans take turns stirring it up. It's gonna take a helluva lot more than a few foot soldiers to keep those buggers from pissin' on their road."

Sinkindar almost yelped in agreement, his head bobbing, but Christine was stunned by the reference. She closed her eyes, determined to get past the memory of what had happened to her in Afghanistan.

Reggie stopped picking at the scab. He saw Christine's reaction, and remembered how her clothing had reeked of urine when he had picked her up at the mullah's. He knew what those thugs had done to her, and his impulse was to apologize, but then he remembered that she wanted to be a soldier.

Reggie hated the ones who spoiled it for the rest of their people. They weren't all bad; some of his best friends were mujahideen, and damn fine fighters. But the ones who were bred for jihad were a different lot. He'd help her if he could, and get paid while doing it. Not a bad way to go. However, when, and if, they found Farrukh, Christine Shepherd would have to be a soldier. He'd need her to be.

From the other end of the seat Christine watched as Reggie started on his nails. His hair was dry, and yellow, and stuck out at odd angles. It made her smile.

"You *are* a scarecrow," she remarked.

Reggie, a sizable thumbnail still in his teeth, winked at her.

He had been calling her "Dot" all day, and at times she did feel like Dorothy in Oz. So when she started calling him Scarecrow, he didn't seem to mind. That morning, he had almost taken them up the wrong road, and later, when there had been some dispute with a Tajik shopkeeper over cigarettes, Mir had to keep the Australian from killing the guy. And now Reggie was grinning again, acting just like her favorite Oz character without a brain. Mir was telling jokes up front. Even the addict, Sinkindar was laughing.

"What's so funny?" Christine asked.

"A camel shagger and a rabbi. Wanna hear it?" Reggie croaked between slivers of nail.

"I'll pass."

Reggie was fine with that, and Mir continued with his joke, but kept his voice low and purposely spoke in a dialect that she didn't understand.

Something about Mir attracted her. Maybe it was his accent, or the lack of accent. His time in America had cleared out of his Urdu some of the guttural sounds that always confused her. And there was a depth to his voice that reminded her of his eyes. Reggie shifted next to her, interrupting her reverie. He was watching her watch Mir. She felt caught and pulled her scarf forward so he couldn't see her face flush. But when Reggie didn't comment, she looked back at him and saw that any semblance of a grin was gone. He was staring out his window and she thought he looked oddly somber.

They had just turned onto a smaller road that curled its way north, a mere ribbon of boulder-free surface that would take them through the Karakoram Range, then the Himalayas and, beyond that, the Hindu Kush.

The mountains rose rapidly on both sides as they drove, and in the distance their peaks were already blotting out most of the sky. They were vast and daunting. Her head swirled, and Chris-

tine had to close her eyes until the ver-
tigo passed.

It wasn't only the tumult of the Indus
River that bothered Christine, it was that
the stars were partially obscured by clouds.
She worried that at any time it could turn
overcast and rain. The idea of more water
terrified her. They were camped on a
narrow shelf of rocky beach that separated
the river from the road, but the Indus was
notorious for flooding. Trying to ignore
the deafening rush of water next to her was
bad enough, without also worrying that by
morning their small party would be
washed away.

She sat up. "Scarecrow?"

There was a grunt from Reggie, whose
swirl of cigarette smoke could be seen on
the other side of the campfire.

"Think it's safe to camp here? Looks like
rain."

Reggie's smoke didn't break, and from
the smell she knew he was smoking pot.

"It's safe, Mrs. Shepherd."

It was Mir who had answered. The three
men had stayed on the other side of the
fire to give her privacy.

"You can call me Christine," she called
out. There was no response. Mir had lived

some years in the United States, and he was educated. But he was still a Muslim male from Pakistan.

He and Reggie were engaged in conversation, but Christine couldn't hear much over the roar of the river. She did, however, pick out her nickname, "Dot." The Aussie hated it when she sounded scared or weak, and she *was* scared.

"It's safe, Christine," Mir repeated. "And we can hear you, don't worry."

Her throat was sore, and suddenly she realized she had been yelling. "The river's so loud. Was I yelling?"

Mir started to respond, but Reggie cut him off. "Hell, yes, you're yelling! And I'm trying to sleep."

Christine caught Mir's voice, then Reggie's. Mir was angry, and she had a feeling it was about her. She looked in the direction of the river, then around her at the mountains. They were south of Besham, where the Karakoram Highway sliced between miles of mountains. Earlier, Reggie had told her that Karakoram actually meant "crumbling mountain," and now she was listening for landslides.

"Hey, Dot," Reggie called out, his voice calmer.

Christine didn't answer.

"Why don't you come to this side? Saves the vocal cords."

Somewhere nearby a shelf of rock broke off and fell into the water. It sounded like a freight train and Christine nearly bolted around the fire. Mir lay next to Sindinkar while Reggie, wrapped in his bedding a few feet away, smoked his pot. Sinkindar was sitting cross-legged, lighting the bottom of a square of metal lined with powder. Christine had been in Pakistan long enough to know that the brown powder was heroin. "Hairy," Reggie called it. Christine tried not to stare.

More noise from the river and Christine gasped, hugging her shoulders. She fell to her knees by the fire and started to shiver. Her teeth were chattering, and when a blanket was placed around her shoulders, she jumped, startled by the contact.

"You're cold," Mir said.

"Cold? It's a bloomin' hothouse here," Reggie grumbled. Christine's eyes were fixed on the river. "Look at ya . . . sweatin' like a bushman."

Christine finally managed to pull her eyes from the waves.

"Hey, Dot, it's just a river."

She cocked her head and tried to smile. Reggie rose up and came over to her. He took the half-smoked joint from between his teeth and offered it to her.

That day, after hours of dangerous curves, reckless drivers, and a mountain road that hardly existed, she had smoked the hash. In high school, she had tried pot once. The taste had been bitter, and the burn in her throat was painful. It only annoyed her at the time, but today her nerves had been frayed and it had helped.

Now the drug had worn off, and a boulder the size of a small car bounded in and out of the rapids before her.

Christine didn't hesitate. She took the joint from Reggie and inhaled, held, inhaled again, coughed, and grimaced.

"You're pitifully new at this for such an old girl."

She glared, and the Scarecrow grinned mischievously. "C'mon, you're old enough to be bothered . . . Least it got your mind off the water."

Reggie was right. Even the roar of the Indus was becoming just a backdrop of white noise. She took another hit, nodding as she held the noxious narcotic in her lungs. She looked over at Mir. He was up on one elbow, and his eyes, his blue and gray eyes, were on her. She held his gaze just long enough to see that there was no contempt for what she was doing, but then she saw something else.

Christine handed Reggie his hashish cigarette and stood, a bit unsteadily at first.

"Wanna take it back with you?"

"No, I'm okay now. Thanks."

She started back, resisting an urge to look over at Mir. When she got back to her foam pad, she lay flat and stared up at the sky above her. Just when she felt herself tense, it seemed as if something slipped from beneath her, and her breath eased out of her. Patches of cloud still obscured the stars that most interested her, but a few peeked out. Christine was able to make out the hindquarters of Capricorn, the old goat, and she giggled. She realized how long it had been since she had laughed and searched for another constellation, an even funnier one. And soon she fell asleep.

"Chris . . . Chris, wake up —"

Still moaning, Christine opened her eyes and even before she could register their faces, she felt the wrenching burn inside her stomach.

"I think you're having a helluva dream," Reggie said.

"Yes, I . . ." Christine tried to sit up and felt the bandages tighten around her middle. But the pain wasn't her ribs and it wasn't a dream, and it took everything she had not to cry out. Mir bent beside her, and glanced at her stomach, and for one horrifying moment she thought he might try to touch her. Instead, he stood, talking to Reggie.

"She's in pain —"

"Of course, she's in pain. Those ragheads worked her over."

Mir was bareheaded, but Sinkindar wore a turban, and even Christine could sense that Sinkindar was insulted. But Reggie didn't seem to notice or care. He was more concerned with how Christine was feeling. He squatted next to her.

"What's this?" he asked, touching her fist.

She was rubbing her stomach; it ached, and she stopped. She was afraid that it wouldn't take much of a display of weakness on her part for Reggie to call it quits. He was still eyeing her. "Something I ate . . . I don't know, parasites maybe."

"Bullshit, you've been here long enough to feel at home with those wily little pricks."

Mir left and came back with the last bit of Reggie's joint. He barely had a chance to light it before Christine grabbed it. She sucked, coughed, sucked again, and blew out.

"Slow down, Chris. It won't work if you take it in like a drinker."

She inhaled as her face contorted. They waited. She tried to take another hit, but couldn't. Reggie took the joint and handed it to Mir.

"I'm okay. Just give me a minute," she said, grunting with the torment, trying to lie back down. Reggie stood next to Mir, who looked as miserable as she felt.

Mir moved to give her more of the joint, but Reggie stopped him. Christine listened to them, her eyes darting back and forth as they talked. Then Reggie bent beside her again, studying her as she tried to control the pain.

"It's a bad bug, Chris. I've had them, and you're going to need something more powerful. You understand?"

Reggie was talking about opium. She could feel the effect of the hashish, but it wasn't blocking the pain, and she tried not to hyperventilate just from the thought of the dangerous narcotic.

"It's light," she blurted out. "We have to go —" she tried to sit up. Mir started to help her, but Reggie grabbed his arm, stopping him. She fell back against the pad, and saw that Reggie was waiting.

"Yes," she said, finally, "something for the pain."

Reggie signaled to Sinkindar, who moved toward the jeep. Mir almost jumped him. The skinny addict showed surprising strength as he shook off Mir, yelling back at him in Pashto. They argued, their words unintelligible. But Christine was groaning, gripping her stomach, no longer aware of them, and Mir acquiesced.

Moments later, Sinkindar returned with his stash. Taking out a small tarry black ball and a square of foil, he took a lighter and heated the foil from underneath. Soon, the heroin began to liquefy and smoke. And while Sinkindar held the foil and Reggie helped her to sit close, Mir caught her eyes. He shook his head. The gesture was subtle, but it made her hesitate.

"C'mon, Chris," Reggie urged. "Get on with it. I can't take it for you."

The heroin smoking in front of her, she tried to hold off, until finally she buckled in pain. She almost knocked the burning opiate from Reggie's hand.

"Damn it, woman!" Reggie cursed.

The pain was so intense that Christine could barely stand to be touched. Then she was crying for help, and the two men managed to get her back over the opium. While she coughed and whimpered between inhalations, Reggie chastised her, prodding her, pacing her, so she got just enough to cut the pain, but not too much. It didn't take long for the opium to take hold, and her cries eased.

"You need a hospital, Dot."

Christine opened her eyes. Mir tried to smile, but Reggie didn't. They were on a quest for a terrorist, and his soldier was sick. He couldn't keep plying her with drugs. Christine forced herself to stand.

"It's just pain . . . bugs. They'll go away."

"Is your boy worth becoming a junkie?" Reggie asked.

He was talking about Farrukh, but Mir was next to him. She got it. "I'm not going to need enough to get hooked."

"That's what I thought, and I still crave the shit."

"You need a hospital, Christine," Mir insisted. "Your husband will understand."

She looked at him, and tried to ignore what was in his eyes. "Thank you, but this isn't your business."

Reggie waited for her to come to her senses. She didn't. Instead, she pulled away and started collecting her things. The

395

sun was half over the horizon, and she was ready to go.

"Start packing camp, will ya?" Reggie instructed.

Mir complied, but Reggie had seen the way the Pakistani looked at the woman. In other circumstances, Reggie might have been concerned, but he had already made his decision.

Christine left the camp and headed down the rocky beach. Reggie could tell by the way she walked that the drug was having an effect. He caught up with her, but she waved him away.

"I told you I'm okay."

She tried to ignore him, but the narcotic *was* working on her. She needed help, and Reggie extended his hand.

"Need to pee, m'lady?"

Christine sighed, rolling her head away from him. In fact, she did. The Indus was as loud and as obnoxious as ever, but it didn't bother her. Nothing seemed to bother her, so she took his hand.

She was feeling so good that she barely registered their jaunt to the boulders. Then, slightly disoriented, she looked around her. In the distance, Mir and Sinkindar were loading the jeep while Reggie stood on the other side of an elephant-sized boulder, his back to her, watching the noisy river. He was waiting. For her, she wondered? Then she felt the urge to pee, and remembered why she had come.

As she squatted, there was no pain in her stomach, no pain anywhere. Her ribs, her bladder, the parasites, every one had retreated, and she liked that. She lived in Southern California, worked in a mall in the Valley. Christine knew about drugs and had no intention of becoming a junkie. If she wanted Farrukh, she had to be lucid. So she would limit herself to maintenance doses, solely to overcome the fire in her belly, and no more. Still, she had to admit that the absence of pain was glorious.

"Done?" Reggie called out.

She called back. "Almost." And she was. The sun was on her back and the warmth felt good, but Reggie was impatient and hardly modest and had started back around the rock. She rose slowly, pulling at her pants and tying them. When he took her arm, she grinned at him.

"I'm okay now," she said and walked past him, on her own. When she had gotten just a few steps ahead of him, he called out to her.

"Hey, Dot."

Christine spun around to face him.

"You would've made a good soldier."

She smiled and started to thank him, but her Scarecrow wasn't smiling back. Christine tried to figure out why, but by the time they got back to camp, she had already forgotten the moment.

Chapter
19

"Is that where we can cross over into India?" she asked.

Reggie didn't answer.

"Hey, Scarecrow."

That got his attention. "You don't have to worry about me," she reassured him. "I'm okay, really."

"Sure," he said, and smiled, but it was a strained smile, and it bothered her.

She had just vomited, but was feeling better. At their last stop in Jaikot, a Kohistani village just south of Chilas, they had picked at bony fish and blackened roti. The food obviously didn't agree with her, but it had been worth the discomfort. Reggie heard from some of the locals that Farrukh might still be in the heart of the Karakoram Range in northern India. At least, they were going in the right direction. Soon they would be leaving the fertile land of Kashmir, skirting the gorges of the Indus in and around the towering granite monoliths of the Himalayas, to a high vertical desert. There amongst the glaciers of the Karakoram Range, beyond the reach of the annual monsoons, little vegetation existed. Yet pockets of people, descendents from ancient conquests, somehow survived in its remote, almost inaccessible valleys. Christine stared outside her window at the lushness of dwarf pine and wild flowers as they made their way over the Rakhiot Bridge. In the distance, she could see the infamous "Killer Mountain," Nanga Parbat. The contrast of its stark white against the green of the meadow and its fir forests made her glad she wasn't a mountain climber. She started to call the men's attention to the sight, but the men were quiet. Since they had left camp, there had been fewer jokes, less talking, and worse, she had a feeling that Reggie was keeping something from her.

Sinkindar switched on the radio and Indian rock music filled the car. She was growing accustomed to the sound and even found herself moving with it as they bumped over the cracked and seemingly diminishing asphalt shelf that the Pakistanis insisted was the eighth wonder of the world. She started counting the white concrete signs along the road that memorialized the workers who died while trying to build a road to China.

Christine was just drifting off to sleep when she felt Reggie lunge forward in his seat, next to her. He reached down to grab a rifle and said something she didn't catch, but his tone was terse and a bit frantic, and Sinkindar was braking.

An old Land Rover and a Suzuki truck with a taped and broken windshield were blocking the narrow mountain road. They looked abandoned.

"Is it the guard's family?" she asked.

Reggie took a moment, then shook his head. "Doubt it." He checked his ammo.

Mir pulled a Kalashnikov from underneath his seat. There was still no sign of anyone, so Mir, rifle in his arms, signaled for Sinkindar to drive. As their jeep inched forward, scraggly-looking creatures with lurid grins emerged from the vehicles. Their smiles were marked with flashes of gold, and there were dark gaps of missing teeth. They were armed with M-16s and AKs. By the way they stood in the open, their guns hanging loose from their shoulders, it was apparent that the bandits expected little resistance.

But now Sinkindar was pulling up his own gun — something modern-looking, with a folding stock — from beneath him and set it on his lap while he repositioned his hand on the wheel.

"Christine . . ." Reggie murmured, but Christine had already pulled a Glock from his belt. She held it up, worked the slide, and waited to react.

Reggie studied her. "You know your guns, right?"

Her heart was pumping, but she nodded.

When the bandits were close enough, Reggie waved his AK out the window and the robbers scattered. They hadn't planned on seeing guns, but they didn't seem terribly surprised either.

As they ran for cover, Sinkindar gunned the jeep, slewing it sideways. Rock crumbled beneath their tires. For a moment Christine thought they might just go over the cliffs. But Sinkindar had positioned the jeep so it was also across the road, a standoff, and even before it lodged itself in the mountainside, a billow of dust closed in around them.

"Go, mates!" Reggie yelled, and Christine threw open the door. She stifled a gasp as she felt a strain in her side. She ducked down alongside the tire. Mir was next to her, and Reggie and Sinkindar were behind the other tire.

Sinkindar clutched his weapon. Christine could see now that it was a paratrooper's folding-stock version of an AK. She was glad they had bought what they did.

Lead was kicking at the dirt around them and Christine heard bandits whoop and chatter as they took potshots at them.

There were a few more random shots. Then Reggie reached up, swung open the back hatch of the jeep, and while the three of them covered him, he pulled out two grenades and a small submachine gun.

"I thought you said we didn't need an arsenal," Christine said as he climbed back down.

"This? This is no goddamn arsenal —" And Reggie began firing the submachine gun. The chatter and laughter stopped instantly, but once Reggie hesitated, the bandits responded.

Christine stayed behind the tire until the incoming fire eased. Once there was a pause in the action, she bent down beneath the jeep. She couldn't see anything in the dust, but heard one of the bandits call out in yet another dialect.

"What'd he say?" she asked Reggie.

Reggie listened as the bandit shouted something, his speech garbled, almost unintelligible.

"It's not Dari, is it?" Reggie asked Mir.

"We'll see," Mir said, and tried the Afghan dialect. Christine felt strange hearing the unfamiliar language come out of his mouth. His face took on the harsh look of his words as he yelled and threatened. But Reggie must've been right, they were speaking Dari, because the bandit shouted back, his tone equally angry. A hail of fire following.

Reggie hugged the tire wall. "I hate wasting a grenade. They're only bandits. We gotta be more trouble than we're worth."

Still, the bandits returned fire. Mir signaled the Aussie, and Reggie understood, even predicted the outcome. He groaned as he pulled the pin on his precious grenade, throwing it in one fluid movement.

Christine flattened on the ground, watching from beneath the jeep's chassis. She didn't see the grenade come down, but there was a flurry of frantic voices and legs, people scattering. One of the bandits was charging straight for them and she aimed high, fired, and the bandit went down. She gasped. He had fallen not ten feet from her. She held the man in her sights as his head turned, his eyes on her, still alive. A dirty AK-47 with a cracked butt clanked to the dirt beside him. Like its shooter, the Russian automatic was in pitiful shape. He reached for it, even as she watched, startled.

Shoot! You have to shoot!

Her mind was spinning, then the grenade exploded and broke Christine from her stupor. She gripped the Glock in earnest. She had the man in her sights and tried to squeeze the trigger just as she had done all her life aiming at bull's-eyes, but he wasn't a paper target. He was flesh and blood, and his face was bleeding. He was already hurt, dying, and Christine knew that shooting him could hardly be self-defense.

And yet he was moving again.

The cries of his comrades were everywhere. He had to know it was over, but still he was intent on killing her.

Christine glanced around her. The men had left her, firing as they went. She tried to scoot away from the wounded bandit, but flying rounds immediately had her scurrying back. She looked at the bandit. She had never seen anyone in such distress. As he got closer, she realized that the man was moving mechanically, as if he had been programmed. And her finger eased on the trigger.

His eyes went fixed, unseeing, dull with death. And as he dragged his body toward her, his movement futile, her heart ached for him. He was dying, just feet from her. The Glock relaxed in her grip.

And just as it did, the man's face changed. He was close to death, but not close enough . . . *and he smiled,* the smile of the victor. And instantly the Kalashnikov was poised, and then it was Christine, and not the man, who was staring into the black hole of a muzzle.

Christine pulled the trigger first. Her body had reacted, and she fired again and again. Gore and tissue splattered her face, but the horror she felt was not only at this. He had fooled her, and the last shred of calm she had managed, vanished.

By the time Christine could move, all the gunfire had ceased, and so had the enemy's chatter. She stood, a bit unsteady at first, then walked away from the bandit who had nearly tricked her out of life. She saw the men, her men. They were laughing, with their arms flopped around one another, like teammates after a winning game. Reggie shouted something at her, grinning, enjoying the moment. Christine smiled, even waved. She was fine, not hurt, but why couldn't she make sense of their words?

They found only three bodies. To clear the road, the men pushed the bandits' cars over the cliff. Christine went to the edge and looked down at the Indus. They were high above it, and all she could see was a winding strip of blue. She watched as piece by piece of mangled metal went easily over the side. When they started with the bodies, she almost said something. There was no proper burial for these men, and she looked up at even higher cliffs behind the thin, miserable excuse for a road. The mountains seemed to fold into one another, and she knew that the other bandits had escaped. Reggie was right, they had been trouble, and the bandits should have known better than to continue their attack.

Within an hour she was back in the jeep. Christine was feeling nauseous as Reggie climbed in next to her.

"You feeling it?" Reggie asked.

"Not really," she lied.

Sinkindar and Mir crawled into the front seats and put their weapons on the floor. Mir looked back at her and said something to Reggie in Urdu. Christine reassured him in Urdu that she was okay and didn't need any drugs, any *charas*. He apologized and turned back around.

Reggie, his hair wilder than ever, just watched her. Only a deep rut in the road, or a near miss of a bus coming around a curve, its horn blasting, could make Christine react. Otherwise, she remained silent. When they lost the light, they stopped at an inn, run by Pakistan's tourist development council, the PTDC. They were the only guests, although they heard a team of German mountain climbers were suppose to arrive later in the week. They ate at tables with mismatched chairs, wired and taped, barely held together. She had no appetite, and Mir offered to look for bottled water, but Christine just shook her head. Instead, she took a drag off of Reggie's hashish cigarette. It didn't help, but she smiled as if it did, and Mir seemed to relax.

Reggie, however, knew better and didn't offer it again. When she went to her room for the night, he followed her.

"There's a clinic in Gilgit."

She tried to ignore him.

"I think you've got some bad bugs there, and they need taking care of."

"I'm fine," she insisted, keeping ahead of him.

"Bloody hell, woman! You won't be any good to me throwing up on the side of the road every kilometer."

Christine stopped. The hall was cold, and she had to keep from reacting as she turned to face him.

"Goddamn you! I threw up *once*."

"Twice — in an hour."

"The *charas* will take care of it until we get Farrukh."

"The drugs won't hold off anything. I had a mate who went off when something got in his head. Don't fool with it, Dot. The bastard isn't worth it."

"Not to you."

Reggie glared at her. She waited for him to yell again. Instead, he sighed, "You gonna need something to sleep?"

She shook her head and he nodded. They went to their rooms. When she heard his door open, she sensed there was something he wasn't telling her. She turned back around and called out to him. He stopped.

"We'll cross over tomorrow, right?"

"We'll sleep on it," he said. He must have sensed her trepidation, because he tried to smile. "Ya did good, Dot. Ya did good."

Moments later, after Reggie had disappeared into his room, Christine stood for a long while looking up the darkened corridor. She felt the chill of the higher altitude, and she was struck by a realization, an awareness that was almost overwhelming. Suddenly, she needed to talk to Reggie and started back up the hall.

When she got to his room, she went to knock, then heard his voice through the door. He was on the phone with his wife. One of them at least, she thought, and smiled. Bored with hours of travel, Reggie had talked of his two wives. Only she seemed to be bothered, but she was in a car with a former SAS soldier and two Pakistanis and doubted that her views on bigamy would have much impact.

Reggie was still talking and she decided to let him be. But tomorrow she would tell him that she was *meant* to find Farrukh and he had to help her. Her mind reeled with the revelation. Woman's hoodoo, he would call it. But it wasn't. It was more.

The nausea had passed. She knew the parasites were still there, but it didn't matter because she *was* meant to find him. Then she remembered the bandit. *If he hadn't smiled, I'd be dead.*

The crispness that had invigorated her a moment earlier, made her shudder and

Christine turned the knob to her door. The room was dark, and she didn't want to go inside, not alone. Christine looked back up the hall. Mir was only two doors away and she thought about waking him. She needed someone, someone who cared, someone who might hold her —

"Stop it," she muttered and squeezed her eyes so tight that she stopped the thoughts, stopped the foolishness. She took a breath and her ribs hurt. Her bandages had loosened, and she knew she would have to ask Reggie to wrap her again. The opiate was wearing off, and she needed her sleep, her strength, because even as she shivered in the draft of the empty hallway she was determined to hold onto the feeling that she was meant to find Farrukh. And she would. And Christine forgot about being held and stepped into darkness, shutting the door after her.

Chapter
20

They had gotten a late start out of the government inn; Reggie was making phone calls. He had said that the calls were personal, but when they pulled up to the dilapidated terminal at Gilgit, rather than the town, he couldn't hide the fact that he was sending her back home. She was sick. No further explanation was necessary, and Christine had the feeling that her pathetically brief mission to stop a madman was over.

Reggie handed her a plane ticket. "This'll get you to Islamabad, then, I trust, you can get yourself out of there. Book through Frankfurt. There's a chemist at the airport, just in case —"

"Just in case I don't make it?"

The Aussie sighed. "It's a long flight, Chris."

Christine just stared at him. She had

tried to convince him to go on with the plan, that she could tolerate the pain, but Reggie Duke had made up his mind. One of the phone calls was not personal, as it turned out. He had already lined up another assignment in Africa, and would be leaving not long after her.

"What if I go after Farrukh alone?"

"Then I guess I'd have to write you off, Dot, 'cause you'd have to be daft to pull that."

Her mind was reeling, and Reggie could see it. "Why is it so important to find this bloke? He's not the only one, you know."

"I'm not going back."

Like most women, Reggie decided, Christine was naïve and compulsive. Naïve and compulsive people kept him in business, but somehow Reggie just couldn't muster the brass to cash in on this one. Christine must have sensed that, because she turned away from him and headed toward Mir and Sinkindar.

Reggie stayed close as she approached the Pakistanis. He was being obvious and he knew it. Still, he held his tongue. He wanted to see how far she would push it.

"Mir," Christine started, trying to ignore the Aussie, "I need your help. I'm trying to find —"

"Please, Christine. Your husband will understand. Go home."

Christine glanced at Reggie. He shrugged, hoping that she was done. She wasn't.

"I don't want to go home. I . . ."

Mir was waiting for her to continue, but it was the way he looked at her. She was having trouble holding a thought. Reggie groaned audibly.

"C'mon on, Dot . . . Let's get you through security."

He took her arm, but she pulled away. "Mir, please. I'll pay you —"

The moment she mentioned money, she saw his disappointment. "I can explain," she said and touched his arm. He was hurt and angry, and he glared down at her hand. She'd forgotten herself and took back her hand.

"There's nothing to explain, Mrs. Shepherd," he said coldly, avoiding her eyes. "You're married and I'm a Muslim."

When he turned away, Christine went after him. "Mir, wait . . . please. I'm not married."

Mir stopped.

"Bloody hell," Reggie muttered.

"You're not married to a freedom fighter?"

414

"I don't have a husband."

Reggie tugged at her, but Christine was more concerned with her scarf. People were starting to notice them, and she lowered her voice.

"Can we go somewhere private?"

"It'll have to be here," Mir said, his voice suddenly terse.

Christine glanced at Sinkindar. She felt self-conscious enough.

Mir muttered something to him, and the driver wandered off.

"I'm looking for . . . for Farrukh Ahmed."

The moment she uttered the terrorist's name, she regretted it. At first, Mir just stared at her. Then he asked, "To do what?"

"To stop him."

"You mean *kill him*," Mir amended.

"If I have to," she admitted.

By then, Reggie was frantically checking to make sure no one could overhear them.

"Who are you?" Mir asked warily. "That man from the embassy, the one who wanted you to visit him at the hotel? Are you some kind of agent — a spy?"

The way he said it was so harsh that she raised her hand to stop him from speaking, inadvertently touching his mouth.

"No," she said, quickly withdrawing her hand. "He killed my sister. He's a murderer and a terrorist . . . I just want to stop him."

Her eyes flicked back up to his face. He was watching her. She could barely look at him; it was the way his lips had felt beneath her fingers. Two women in burqas passed by, and Christine stepped back.

"I'm . . . I'm sorry," she faltered. "I'm too close."

And suddenly Mir was almost upon her. She felt his breath and the cloth of his tunic brushing up against her. She didn't dare react, but when he leaned into her, she was forced to look up. His eyes were so blue she ached. She knew that there was no painkiller strong enough to help her. She wanted to lay her head against his chest, feel his arms and the warmth of his body against her face. She thought she could hear his heart beat, but it was her own heart pounding, and she wavered.

"You're lookin' wobbly, Dot," Reggie confided. Then the Aussie was beside her, trying to steady her. "Better cover yourself. People are watchin'."

People *were* staring, some glaring. She was drawing attention. Tossing her scarf easily over her head and face, she stepped back again. Mir let her, but his eyes didn't leave her. She glanced around her. Except for Reggie, they were alone.

"Farrukh Ahmed is a very dangerous man," Mir said.

"You're a Muslim and a Pakistani. You more than anyone should understand how I feel."

When she said that, his eyes went flat. "I don't," he insisted. "I can't help you. Please go. You don't belong here."

His words were so devoid of emotion that she believed him. Reggie pulled at her and she relented.

A security guard, dressed in fatigues, with a hand on his gun holster, waved her toward a booth. Christine looked back, but she couldn't see Mir or Sinkindar.

"What did you think he'd say?" Reggie asked as he steered her toward the booth.

"I thought —"

"You thought he'd care enough to forget who he is?"

"I don't know."

"I told you the man's a good Muslim. Best if you stick to your own, Chris."

Christine ignored him, glancing back, searching, until Reggie whispered in her ear.

"I sort of . . . kept your hardware. Didn't

think you'd get through X-ray."

Reggie's distraction worked. She looked at him. His yellow hair was sticking out in different directions, his sideburns were dirty and matted, and he had a chessy-cat smile that made her think that maybe she was in Oz. *And Dorothy only had to click her heels and she would be home.*

Then she noticed the melanomas. The loathsome growths looked even bigger than when she met Reggie in Peshawar.

"Those buggers will kill you, you know."

Reggie smiled, and she realized he knew what they were.

"They'll have to wait their turn, won't they?"

He put his arms around her and held her.

"It was fun," he said.

"When?" she asked, her eyes welling.

"In the shower." And he grinned like an idiot, the scarecrow before he got his brain.

She almost laughed, but then remembered her dad and Liz. It had taken years to adjust to a life without her dad, but now Liz, her sister, her best friend —

"Please Reggie," she pleaded under her breath, swiping at a tear on her face. "There's nothing back there for me. Liz is

418

gone. There'll be others. You know that. We could've stopped him."

His grin disappeared. "I'm sorry 'bout that, Dot, but timing ain't right on this one."

A woman at the booth motioned to her. She was waiting.

"I'll keep in touch with the old man," Reggie said. "Who knows?"

Christine turned away, but cocked her head in an exaggerated Pakistani shrug. The Aussie laughed behind her. She stepped into the box, turned, and smiled. Reggie smiled back, and then, like Mir, he vanished as the woman drew the curtain.

When the woman finished scanning her, she pulled back a second curtain and Christine emerged on the other side. There was a hint of activity in her stomach, but Christine tried to remember that she only had to make it to Frankfurt. An image of her ripping out her own entrails en route intervened and she slipped by it, thinking, instead, of what it would be like to be home again.

The waiting room was packed with dark-skinned individuals and a few trail-weary bohemians, who sounded and looked Swiss. They looked morbidly pale compared to the Pakistanis and stared at her as she passed by. She was still dressed in her *hijab,* her Islamic dress, and it had been a while since she had changed.

Christine found a seat across from a woman whose eyes seemed to smile above the hard line of her chador. Christine smiled back, greeting her. The woman's eyes crinkled, and she nodded, but she didn't speak.

"She not speak," said a girl who was leaning against a wall next to her. "I very sorry."

"Your mother?" Christine asked.

"My sisser."

The woman's eyes smiled again. Christine got the feeling that the woman wanted to communicate.

"Can she hear?"

The girl didn't understand.

Christine pointed to her own ear. "Can your sister hear?"

"Yes, can hear. Only no toong."

The girl stuck out her tongue to clarify with an ease that startled Christine. Unfortunately, it was too late to censor herself.

"No good to be sad," the girl reassured her. "My sisser's husband very nice, very good man to spare my sisser. Only a toong."

And the girl cocked her head and tried to smile.

This time Christine was prepared, and she quickly returned the smile. Then she faced the woman, making small talk in Urdu as best she could. The woman bobbed her head, apparently grateful to be even on the receiving end of a monologue.

Christine could tell by their garb that they were from a village. She was reminded of Ruhee, the smiling, young bride, eager like this woman to meet with a stranger. Then she remembered Nazeem.

Her chest started to ache with emotion and Christine stood. Confused by her abruptness, the girl and the woman looked at her. Christine tried to wish them Allah's blessing, but suddenly she was too upset. She wanted to express how sorry she was that she couldn't help the woman, that the woman's husband was a barbarian who had cut out his own wife's tongue, and that bastards like Maroof and Janoor and Farrukh could get away with murder.

Instead, Christine walked away. The way she felt she was walking away from Liz, and Ullas, and Nazeem, and all of those who were yet to be murdered, because animals like Farrukh were out there, and she had bugs, and her country had rules —

A stranger brushed past her. Christine stopped. She already sensed who the gangly Pakistani was, even before he took his place beside the woman. There wasn't even a moment's hesitation. Christine flew at him, her arms waving as she screamed at him in Urdu and English. Christine was almost in the Pakistani's face, glaring, but the man would not meet her eyes. There were frantic shouts behind them, and the girl stood, trying to reason with Christine. Even the man's wife held up her hand, wildly gesturing. But she couldn't defend her husband because she didn't have a tongue. She couldn't speak; she couldn't tell the stranger that her husband, even as she chastised him, wouldn't respond.

Then thick, hard arms, grabbed her from behind, almost choking her. Christine heard the Pakistani guard's harsh voice, and felt the ease with which he hurt her. He was not afraid to look at her or touch her. He was not like the man in front of her, crying as his wife stroked his head. The woman looked up at her. There was no animosity in her large, luminous eyes, only confusion. Christine started to say something to the man. But she couldn't, and the husband couldn't acknowledge her. He was married and didn't look at other women. He was a good Muslim.

Then the guard wrenched her arm and

she went with him. As he dragged her back through the security gate, into the terminal, he yelled and turned her arm once more. But this time she didn't go easily. She struggled and hollered at him in Urdu, so everyone could hear what was being done to her. She managed to break away, and she ran until someone caught her and held her. She twisted in the stranger's arms, fighting, her bandages pulling, her side aching, then she recognized the voice, and froze.

"Mir?"

Mir's arms were around her, but he barely acknowledged her, because now there were two guards approaching. Mir argued with them, still holding her, not letting her go, and she saw him reach into his pocket and pull out money. People were passing, but no one stopped to ask questions, and then the guards were gone.

Mir took her behind a stand of souvenirs in a quieter corner of the terminal. The vendor was gone, and he wiped at her face, telling her that he couldn't leave until he knew that Christine's plane had safely departed. Christine shook her head, and Mir handed her the soaked tissue. He tried to convince her that she needed to go home, but her eyes filled again and she told him about her sister, about Nazeem and Ullas, about the man in the village of Padamthala who had lost his wife, and this time Mir believed her, believed that she wasn't a spy, and soon they were moving through the terminal. Her side was throbbing, and she was nauseous, but Mir held her as they walked.

When they reached the outside, hawkers and taxi drivers descended upon them. But she didn't mind. Mir was beside her. He waved to Sinkindar, who sat on a bench with other Pakistanis. The driver had been waiting, not for her, but for Mir. And when the driver saw her, he scowled. All she could do was adjust her scarf so she wouldn't be too conspicuous.

It wasn't long before Sinkindar pulled up in the jeep, and Mir opened the door for her. She paused before climbing inside. He cocked his head and she slid into the back seat without comment. She moved all the way to the other side to give him room, but suddenly Mir was close to her, and the fragrance of sandalwood held her. When she turned to him, his eyes looked into hers, softly gray and resigned.

"Christine," he began. She touched his mouth again, without thinking. But this time when she tried to take her hand away, he held it there, breathing in her own scent.

In a few moments, they were on the road. She greeted Sinkindar, but he ignored her. Instead, he rattled off something in Pashto to Mir, so she couldn't understand. Mir's replies were short, and Sinkindar grunted, and moaned in a way she hadn't heard before. He started grumbling to himself, and Christine knew it wouldn't be long before they would need to make a stop. The addict was restless.

Through her window Christine watched as an old man whipped at the bony frame of a large ox pulling at a cart. Children darted in and out of the roadway, and dust already obscured their crusty windshield. Horns and bicycle bells and voices clamored around her. Then Sinkindar turned on the radio and the familiar sound filled her with an unexpected contentment.

She looked over at Mir. He was staring ahead, his forehead creased, and deep in thought. Christine tried not to let it concern her. Reggie was on his way to Africa and Cloid was in the United States. As Joe Riccardi had said, she was alone. But she wasn't. Mir was with her. *Inshallah,* she thought. God willing, she had done the right thing.

Chapter
21

Sinkindar leaned into the wheel, wincing each time the jeep fell into a rut. Sheer, raw rock cliffs rose on their right, and green valleys fell away to their left. They were driving through the mountains just east of Gilgit through the Hunza, said by many to be the most beautiful part of the world.

Yet Christine had never seen such scarred hillsides. They passed another sign warning of landslides, and Sinkindar, his knuckles white, took his foot off the accelerator and coasted around a rim of rock. No one seemed surprised to see a line of vehicles there. A bus, two jeeps, a truck, and three cars were waiting for a handful of beleaguered Pakistanis with two pieces of the most primitive equipment imaginable. Men stood outside their vehicles, whispering to one another, while their women and children remained inside. It was a slide area, where almost any sound or movement could trigger the crumbling rock. In this small slide, however, no one had been hurt. The Pakistanis moved slowly, and after four tense hours Sinkindar was able to drive on.

They drove along the Karakoram Highway, just south of the Karakoram Pass where the Old Silk Route, a caravan route traveled and traded on for centuries, continued on into China. Women's dress in the Hunza was less restrictive. They wore embroidered hats that left their faces and hair exposed, and some pulled up the sleeves of their garments so the sun could warm them. If Pakistan had any tourist industry, it was in those northern parts, and photographs of the Hunzakuts were common. People of the Hunza were accommodating, but foreigners as guests did not hold the same appeal, and Christine missed the almost frantic socializing she had experienced in the Javid family in Banalwala, where there were no tourists and any new face was a novelty.

As they drove, Christine told Mir what she knew of Farrukh. Mir said little at first, then asked about her contacts and her funding. He also wanted to know more about Liz. Christine tried to be forthcoming, but as she outlined her reasons for wanting to kill the terrorist, she noticed that Mir became solemn, almost grave.

At one stop for tea, Christine watched the Indus River crashing across the road. Its thunderous swells were as intimidating as ever, but her concerns were elsewhere. Like many Muslims, Mir Hasan felt conflicted. He had told her that as a young rebel Farrukh Ahmed was known as a fierce freedom fighter, "a hero," and it wasn't until later that he became the monster she was pursuing. Mir cocked his head and shrugged. He could only conclude that even good hearts were sometimes seduced by power and —

"Blood lust," Christine added tentatively.

"Yes," Mir conceded sadly. "A trait found in many of us, I'm afraid."

As he handed her a cup of steaming tea, Mir met her eyes and smiled. She was relieved to see that his eyes were, once again, as blue as the patch of sky above them. They sat beneath a tin overhang, and Mir leaned back in a cheap plastic chair, content to stare out at the mountains that nearly enveloped them. He had finally relaxed and Christine thought that it might be the proper time to confront him.

428

"He'll keep killing. He won't stop," she said and sipped at the sweet, milky, tea.

"Yes," the Pakistani agreed, his gaze unwavering.

"And he'll kill others, including Muslims."

"Yes, Muslims, too."

His lips were moist and dark and his black mustache seemed to caress the stained porcelain as he drank. Then his gaze left the mountains, and settled on her. Mir sipped at his tea and watched her. Christine wanted to take a breath, but couldn't.

"You think you can stop a man who has cheated death so often?" he asked simply.

"Inshallah."

That made him smile. "Yes . . . if God wills it."

He continued to study her. When he finished his tea, he asked, "How sick are you, Christine?"

She shrugged.

Now it was Mir who had to take a breath. It was the first time she realized she wasn't the only one struggling, and she leaned forward.

"I know how this sounds, but I think God wants me to find Farrukh."

"And kill him?"

Christine didn't answer. Her stomach was aching and it wasn't because of the parasites.

"Thou shalt not kill," Mir continued. "Isn't that one of your sacred decrees?"

Christine tried to drink her tea. She didn't want to think about the decrees of her own faith. "There are exceptions," she said.

"Yes," Mir agreed, "as in Islam. Interpretation is full of exceptions."

There was a slight tremor in her hand as she set down her cup. He reached over and touched her hand. "There are some who believe that they will end up in Paradise if they kill."

Christine tried to hold his gaze. At one time there had been no doubt in her mind that she would end up in the Lord's Kingdom, but Mir was scaring her, and she reminded herself that she knew little about the Pakistani and drew back her hand.

Moments passed and Christine glanced around her.

"Are you looking for a toilet?"

Mir's openness startled her.

"Won't be pretty, I'm afraid," he said and smiled. She smiled back, grateful for the break in their conversation. He asked the owner, who pointed to the back of his establishment. She eagerly left Mir behind.

When Christine returned, Sinkindar was just sitting down at the table. Mir ordered more tea, but Sinkindar hardly seemed interested in tea. His eyelids drooped over pupils that were large and fixed. Mir asked the driver where he had found a vendor. Sinkindar was slow to respond, but told him of an old Uzbek who lived above the road. Traffic had been slow over the Karakoram Highway, so Sinkindar had managed to dicker the drug dealer into the ground. The opium for the American woman had cost him virtually nothing, which meant he could purchase twice as many packets of the stronger brown powder that he needed. He wasn't injecting, yet, but heroin was cheap in Pakistan; one U.S. dollar bought a fix, and Christine knew Sinkindar was well on his way to becoming one of those walking body bags that she had seen so often on city streets.

Christine thought of the tarry balls, and tried not to think of the ache that she was forced to tolerate. She hadn't needed much of the opium, and fortunately the more serious bouts of pain weren't consistent. Still, her doses would have to be

431

exact. To avoid Sinkindar's fate, she'd have to depend on Mir to help her. She hoped that she could really trust him.

It was black on all sides as they crept along the treacherous, unfinished road. Sinkindar's night vision had deteriorated, inevitable with addiction, and Mir had to take over the driving. Hours earlier they had turned off the Karakoram Highway and driven through Skardu, an isolated haunt where mountain climbers met and yaks grazed. Mir said the mountainous area where checkpoints and militia were scarce would make the crossing into India easier. He also knew of a place where they could spend the night. His cousin, Gulfam, had married into a good family just inside Kashmir.

The jeep rocked, and a piece of road broke beneath them. Christine held her breath as Mir jerked at the wheel. She was already nervous enough about that part of Kashmir. Skirmishes and border disputes were frequent in the northern areas, but then Mir reminded her that if she was truly *meant* to meet and defeat a notorious killer, a few villagers lobbing shells back and forth should hardly stop her.

Just when it seemed they would tumble

into an abyss, where their destruction would never be seen or heard by anyone, the road opened up. The jeep's headlights swept a settlement of wood, mud, and stone buildings. Some of the homes were two-story with stands of blue pine and juniper between them. When their jeep came to a stop, their headlights off, there was enough moonlight to see the typically constructed Himalayan home. Its roof was already piled high with the sage and brush needed to get a family through the winter. Yak and draft animals slumbered in a pen on the side, while goats and sheep, their fur thickening with the cold, scoured the hard ground for anything left to gnaw on. Christine couldn't see beyond the house, but suspected that there had to be fields, probably wheat and barley, with kitchen crops of turnips and potatoes. In the summer months there would be pastures where children would watch over the village's herd, and irrigation lines, green and lush, would streak the rocky terrain. Mir's cousin was fortunate; she had married into a working village. Still, Christine couldn't imagine how anyone could survive in a region so remote.

After the men got out of the jeep, Christine reached into the back and rummaged through the guns Reggie had left behind. Mir had assured her that she would like his cousin, Gulfam, but memories of Janoor and the cousins in Rawalpindi were still fresh. She picked through the AKs, a sub-machine gun, several blocks of C-4, a box of detonators, and what looked like a tommy gun. She also found two boxes of grenades and was surprised at how much two thousand dollars could buy in that part of the world. Still, she only needed something small, and pulled up a tribal copy of a Luger, a 9-mm pistol, a compact and accurate weapon, and it had a full magazine.

Inside, Gulfam offered Christine a plate of her deep-fried *samosas,* explaining as best she could in English that it was a pop-ular Pakistani appetizer. Christine selected one and stuffed it into her mouth. As Muslim etiquette dictated, she had started off in the *baltac,* the room reserved only for men, but the women were anxious to visit, so Mir excused her early.

The women, however, were tireless. As Gulfam ducked in and out of the *baltac* to serve the men, the other women prepared dinner, all the while talking to Christine. They asked about her home, her family, Americans' strange marriage customs, and even divorce, the last of which spun into other topics that were almost impossible to follow. Christine tried to keep up, but the women were hardly shy, animated, in fact, gesturing, gossiping, with descriptions of scant headwear, or no headwear, and predictions of who would be betrothed to whom in their village.

As their inquiries eased, Christine tried to overhear what the men were saying in the next room. Mir had told her that his cousin's family might know of Farrukh, and she strained to hear Farrukh's name, something — anything.

"*Samosa, ji?*"

Gulfam was offering her another appetizer. Christine had a feeling that she had been caught eavesdropping.

"*Shukriya,*" she said, thanking her and taking the savory. Gulfam nodded and went back into the kitchen. Once Mir's cousin had left her, Christine glanced toward the open archway. She saw Mir talking, gesturing with the same hand that had touched her earlier, and her body reacted. Her scarf was down, and her auburn hair fell about her shoulders. She had washed it in Gilgit and knew it was soft and shiny. She tried not to think of what it would feel like to have Mir's hands in it.

Then Mir looked in her direction, as if he had read her mind, and she turned away. She thought again of Mir's interest in Farrukh and knew she wasn't thinking clearly. But she needed to trust him, and reasoned that if he was going to betray her, he would've done so already.

When she looked up, Mir's cousin was watching her. Gulfam smiled, and Christine smiled back.

Fresh lamb and *dzo,* a rice dish, beans, an unleavened bread soaked in broth, and salt butter made from the milk of a yak were set out on a huge room-size cloth on the floor. The evening meal was nearly ready, but Christine needed a moment alone. She asked Gulfam if she could clean up before she ate. It wasn't customary for a guest to leave before dinner, but Gulfam cocked her head as if she understood and took her upstairs.

It was a children's room with stringed kites and children's books stacked between the cots. Once Gulfam left her alone, Christine took out a comb and put it through her hair as she stepped over to the window. She looked out into the darkness. It was past the time of prayer, but Christine doubted that she would need to worry about Pakistani spirits that night. They were too far out in the middle of nowhere for the Jinn to bother with them. Even by the glass she could feel that the temperature had dropped. It was only a short walk up to the second floor, but they were high in the Himalayas and the air was thin. Outside, there were lights, other homes, built on different levels into the rocky slopes.

Christine glanced around the room. Like most of the homes she had visited, there were plaques of Koranic verse, and flowers, with the ubiquitous photograph of the family's spiritual teacher. Christine gazed at the holy figure. Like the others, the man was gray-haired and bearded, and his face was kind. This time, however, Christine turned away from the kind face and pulled the Luger from her backpack.

Christine stared at the pistol. She fell back on a cot, almost shrieking as something squeaked beneath her. It was only a child's toy, and Christine suddenly felt stupid and paranoid until someone knocked on the door. Before she knew it, her arm was up with the gun in her hand, cocked and ready to fire.

"Christine?"

Mir's voice was tentative. He'd probably heard her cock the gun.

"Christine, are you all right?"

The way he said her name made her feel worse. She unlocked the door and didn't even bother to hide the gun.

He smiled and Christine felt herself redden.

"Were you expecting someone else?"

"I just wanted to fix my hair . . . and put away my things."

"I can see that."

She looked up at him. He was smiling, but she needed to ask him.

"Did you ask about Farrukh?"

His smile faded. "You're going to have to give me time on that. There are some people who —"

"Who think he's a hero, I know." She went back into the room, leaving him at the door, and grabbed at her scarf.

"You won't need that here," he said.

She hesitated. The scarf had become a habit. Still, she threw it aside, blurting out, "Good," as she stepped back toward him.

"And you can leave the gun. Dinner's informal."

Her humiliation was complete; she was still holding the gun. Backing away, she picked up her backpack and put the pistol inside. She glanced around her, trying to find a place to store it, when Mir took it from her and stuck it underneath her cot.

"That way, it's within easy reach."

They looked at each other, and suddenly they were very aware of being alone in the room together.

"Are you allowed to be here?" she asked.

"We're not in Peshawar." Still, after a moment Mir moved back to the doorway. When he turned to her, he smiled. "Is that better?"

Christine followed him to the doorway and took a breath. She had to relax. "I'm sorry. I'm just . . . We're in Kashmir, I know, so I guess they must be Kashmiris, but is there anything I should do, or not do? I don't want to shame you —"

"Chris, you won't shame me . . . Probably'll have to eat a lot of food. You know how that goes."

"Yes," she smiled. "I know how that goes."

They stood there, neither moving. It was the way Mir looked at her that made her drop her eyes. Her hair fell forward off her shoulders, and just the scent of him made her lightheaded. Mir moved close, and she let her forehead rest against his chest. He was warm; it wouldn't take much. But she could hear them. They were all down there, waiting. So when she felt his hand on her hair, she breathed, *"Jaiye,"* telling him to go. It took a moment, but Mir finally stepped away.

The conversation between the men had already taken place, so now the men and women ate together. The women still served, but the protocol was quite relaxed. The women wore their scarves down off their head and around their shoulders, and they would interrupt the men, even chastise them about their manners. A neighbor woman quipped about the fickleness of men's needs, and her plump husband laughed the loudest. Gulfam also threw in a snipe, but her husband was too busy eating to care.

The gathering had enlarged since she had first arrived, but it was getting late and Christine wondered how long the party would last. Mir and a short, squat, man were intently playing a game with cigarettes and an empty pack. Apparently the game involved surrounding the pack with cigarettes, following complicated rules. Finally Christine asked about it, and Mir's opponent laughed, muttering something under his breath. Mir translated.

"It's an old Afghan game called 'Seizing the Castle.' He says I can't have played in a long time; I seem to have forgotten the rules."

There must've been something in the way she responded, or maybe it was the way he told her. Whatever it was, the woman who had commented on "men's needs" made a crack about the two of them, and Christine blushed. Their attraction must have been apparent, because the whole room broke into laughter. Even Sinkindar was smiling. When Christine finally mustered the nerve to look at Mir, she thought he would also be embarrassed. Instead, his eyes were on her, and his feelings for her were so obvious that she became apprehensive. Couldn't Mir see that there were other people in the room? Yet it was Christine whom the wisecracking woman embraced, chortling in her ear and patting her back as if she were naïve and young.

After another cup of tea, Christine excused herself. Their reaction, and his, jarred her, and she wouldn't look at Mir as she left the room. Once she got upstairs, and was alone, she went back over his words, his expressions. When he watched her, she felt as if she had been touched, caressed even. She had been in a room of devout Muslims, and she was surprised someone hadn't hurled a stone at the two of them.

Reggie was right. She wasn't in Kansas anymore. Even American men would cautiously test the waters, sometimes jockeying to find an advantage. Then she recalled Mir's face, so trusting, so open. Advantage didn't seem to be his concern. How different he was, but Christine was not Muslim, and she wasn't Pakistani, and Mir's undisguised feelings scared her.

Later, when she couldn't sleep, she sat up in the cot and sighed miserably. It had been three hours since Mir had touched her. Scenarios that she knew were impossible rolled over and over in her mind, torturing, teasing her. She had been so preoccupied that she hadn't even noticed the temperature. There was no green glow of insect repellent in the room; it was too cold for mosquitoes. Gooseflesh rose on her arms. She snatched at a blanket and threw it around her shoulders.

Christine heard voices and went to the door. The men were still downstairs. They were whispering, but there was no mistaking Mir's voice. He was arguing with the neighbor, the one whose wife liked to joke. Both men seemed fairly heated. At first, she was worried it had to do with her, but they were talking of Indians and Kashmir. She didn't hear anything about terrorists, and decided, this time, she would leave the men to their politics. Whatever they were saying, Mir could tell her in the morning. It was late and she needed sleep.

Christine opened her eyes. It took her a minute to orient herself. She could see her breath as she scooped her wristwatch up from the floor. It was just past four and long before dawn, and still there were sounds. Except the sounds were coming from outside. She reached underneath her cot into her backpack for the Luger and went to the window. With a halfmoon overhead, she could just make out people moving over the rocky hillsides.

The men's argument, their game with cigarettes, it all came together for her as she ran out of the room and down the stairwell.

In the main room, a fire was still burning in its stone hearth while a village, it seemed, of women sat before it. There was no more laughter or jokes. A dozen or so children were tucked among the women's bodies, the first Christine had seen. Their mothers had probably turned them in early so that they could be awake when their fathers and brothers and *mamus* and *chachas* went to fight the Indians.

That was what they were doing. The men and Mir. She knew that now. She had heard bits of their plan, but she was too distracted by her own concerns to put together what was happening.

Christine walked past the women to where there were thick homespun shawls and boots by the door. She took a lantern and grabbed at the boots when she heard Gulfam approach. Mir's cousin called her by name, but when she spotted the gun in Christine's fist, she quieted. Christine muttered something about helping the men as she slipped a shawl over her shoulders. The Pakistani woman seemed to consider this; her man was out there as well. Then a boy cried out, running to Gulfam's side. He grasped her leg, and Gulfam suddenly looked very tired. She bent down to him and Christine realized Gulfam couldn't go. So she pulled at the door handle.

Christine thought about Sinkindar and his bad night vision. Clouds had obscured the moon so that people seemed to appear, then disappear in the shadowy terrain. She could barely see, and she couldn't call out for Mir. It was too quiet, and at some point it came to mind that wandering in the dark with a glowing lantern might not be the smartest move. She blew it out and left it.

As she made her way over uneven ground, her hand scraped against a rock that was slick with ice. It was cold, and she glanced back at the house. She saw only a glimmer of firelight through the window, where the women and the children of the village were huddled together. She was struck by the thought that maybe she should have stayed with them, when something chuffed in the distance. She craned her neck, hearing the low whirring overhead. There were stars, thousands of them, but then a mortar round detonated, and the night briefly vanished in a brilliant flash.

Shouts and gunfire erupted, and Christine dropped to the ground. She dared to look up and saw crouched men advancing past her as bullets and mortar fire sailed above. There were Pakistanis carrying grenade launchers on their shoulders while red tracer rounds sought them out. There were shots, and sounds, and booms coming from the east. They couldn't be far from the border; it was a battle, and sud-

445

denly the Luger felt puny in her grasp. She moved, staying low, until she got to the jeep. The back had been emptied of weapons, as she knew it would be, and she couldn't help but wonder how long Mir had been planning the raid.

A rocket-propelled grenade rode a fiery trail and she bent low, covering her head. There was an explosion, a spray of rock and shrapnel, and men were shouting. Christine got to her feet, dodging villagers as she moved. Something was blazing near one of the houses, and two men were already headed toward it. There were obstacles, a hole, a bush, a bank of rock. It was all so unfamiliar to her, and down she went again.

Then something arced above the men who had reached the burning house. Another round exploded, and she felt the blast even as she saw the same men killed in front of her. She hit the ground. There was no sound, no voice, only the roar of the explosion as she pressed her face into the field while debris showered down upon her. She looked up into a cloud of ash, got a lungful, and coughed spasmodically into the turf. There was gunfire, and Christine crawled over to where the explosion had knocked the Luger from her hand. She raised the gun, but couldn't see anything to aim at. She heard scuffling and grunting where, nearby, men were fighting hand to hand. Suddenly the frenzied rapping of a Kalashnikov sounded, and something flashed green and a man went down beside her.

Christine moved over to him, and the man almost pulled her down on top of him. His chest was sticky with blood and his eyes bulged at her, cartoonlike. He was gulping for air, trying to talk, but she couldn't understand him.

She placed her hands on his chest, her palms sinking into a gaping wound as she did. She couldn't make out his face, it was too dark, but he had to be one of Mir's friends, or Gulfam's family. The man was sobbing and so was she. Her hands felt clumsy; she wasn't helping. Another mortar shell struck, lighting up the sky, and Christine looked up. There was a man in uniform, his assault rifle raised to fire. Whoever he was, he clearly had no love for the locals; he was firing at Pakistanis as he ran past. Christine grabbed her gun and got off two rounds, her wrist recoiling as she did. The first one missed, but the second shot landed and the Indian dropped from sight.

Beneath her, the man moaned. She bent to him, then a light blinded her. She raised the Luger, braced to shoot, and —

"Christine!"

Christine cried out and her hand hit the ground, jarring the Luger, and it fired a single round as she did.

There was no thump, no cry in the darkness; she had missed. When she saw Mir, she wanted to throw her arms around his neck. Instead, she cried out, "Mir, help me!"

She bent down to the injured man and tried again to stop the loss of blood. But the man barely responded.

"Christine."

"Help. Please!"

Mir had not moved.

"What's wrong with you? He's dying! He's your friend."

"He's not my friend . . . Let him go."

Mir angled the light and even through the gore she recognized the insignia. He was just a kid, but he was dressed just like the man she had shot.

Mir said they had to go, calling her *"Mara ashiq."* It was a term of endearment; a name used between lovers, but she could only think of the boy's blood on her hands. Mir had to pull her to her feet,

448

away from the Indian.

There was the sound of shelling, so they headed back toward the village and into a wall of smoke. Christine started coughing when she caught a glint of steel. She raised her gun, but the man had already lunged. Mir pulled at his AK strap with one hand while trying to push Christine out of the way with the other. She fell to the side as the Indian swiped at Mir with a long, wide blade. Mir dodged it, but his gun was jerked from his grasp. The two of them circled. Christine leveled the Luger, but Mir was too close. Again, the knife cut through the smoke, but Mir got hold of the man's wrist. They struggled. Christine aimed, desperate to shoot. In moments it was over.

Mir crouched briefly over the body, his hands on his knees, breathing hard. Christine saw that the attacker was older, his body thick. The Indian had been no match for the Pakistani, who managed to turn the knife in on him. Still, Mir was tired. The older man didn't have a chance, but he was acclimated to the higher altitude. Mir wasn't used to the thin air . . . or to the killing, it seemed. He wouldn't look at the man as he stepped over him to grab his AK. Then someone shouted his name. Mir looked for his friends. The smoke was clearing, but more rounds had fallen on the village, and another house went up in flames.

"I'll be back," Mir said.

"Let me go with you. I can help." Christine was shivering and had only the shawl to cover her.

"Stay here," he insisted, taking off his coat. He had her kneel, hunkering down beneath the chassis of the neighbor's car as he laid the coat over her.

There was more rapid fire from assault rifles, then a grenade exploded near them. Mir bent his body over her until debris stopped falling. When he pulled back from her, she saw that he had been injured. A thin line of blood snaked from his hairline down his face. It was minor, but Christine panicked. As he stood, she threw her arms around his neck. There was no scent of sandalwood; Mir smelled like earth and sweat, and around them voices were crying out.

"Chris —" Mir tried to pull away, but Christine was so paralyzed with fear that she held on to him.

"Please . . . Please don't go," she pleaded.

Then she heard them. It was the women

who were crying for help. "Go," she said, releasing him. "Go! They need you!"

Without looking back, Mir ran toward the burning buildings. An area of smoke cleared, and for an instant she could see it all. The village was burning. People were darting in and out of the flames, some carrying torches, others children. "Oh my God," she muttered to herself, and rose to her feet. Moments before, she had been freezing. But as she ran, her face flushed with heat. She stopped, the cries ringing in her ears, trying to remember which house she had stayed in.

Then, even amid the pandemonium, she could hear him. She ran ahead and found Mir standing alone between two walls of flame. He was shouting and screaming hysterically, and she didn't know what had happened to make him like this. Then he sprinted behind the fire and up a hillside. Christine saw two Indian soldiers, two kids really, unarmed, scrambling to keep ahead of him. She yelled after Mir to stop, but by the time she got to him, he had already shot both boys. Mir was crying by now. She wanted to go to him, but he was berating the Indians, kicking them, even as they lay dead beneath him.

The heat was overwhelming and Christine leaned into a shelf of rock, where it was still icy and cool, and where Mir couldn't see her. She needed to vomit, but when she saw another Indian running toward Mir, she emptied the Luger's magazine, still pulling the trigger long after the man had gone down.

Except for the crackle of flames and the occasional burst of gunfire, it was fairly quiet. Christine remembered the women screaming, but that had been before. Now there was just a single ghastly wail.

The sky lightened and the Indians had long gone, but the smell of burned wood and charred bodies hung in the air.

It took most of that day for the villagers to be buried; the Indians were dragged away and left for the vultures. After the Muslims had prayed, they buried their loved ones, then dispersed on foot to the homes of relatives in other villages.

Mir was almost inconsolable. Sinkindar had been killed. Night-blind and useless as a freedom fighter, he had gone to help the women and children, perishing with them when the Indians had barred and set the house on fire. Mir told her that Sinkindar was his brother, not only his Muslim brother, but his own blood, his family, raised like him in Baluchistan, Pakistan's poorest province. Rubbing his eyes and sobbing over Sinkindar's blackened corpse, Mir confessed that he was the eldest, the lucky one. While Sinkindar slaved away in their family's hay fields, Mir was given an education and a life that his brother would never know.

There was no white cloth to wrap Sinkindar's body in and the ground was hard and cold, and Mir didn't want to leave him. Only when Christine doubled over in pain at his feet did Mir respond. She had been feeling sick all day, and he lay on the ground with her. The sun was setting, but they held each other until it was dark. And only then, when Mir could no longer see Sinkindar's resting place, could Christine convince him to leave with her.

Chapter
22

Huddled against the smoking remains of the house they had rested in, Christine watched as Mir slung a Kalashnikov across his chest along with a bandolier of cartridges and a knife. The knife was taken from a dead freedom fighter, its blade still smeared with the dried blood of the enemy. Mir refused to clean it, sticking it into a tattered sheath.

The trek back to civilization would be long, and it was getting colder. Mir had managed to save his wallet from the fire, but not his clothing. What remained was thin and torn. Even if they stayed on the southern slopes where there would be better sun exposure during the day, Christine knew Mir would eventually freeze. Unlike the other village survivors, he wouldn't strip the bodies of his comrades, and the thicker coats of dead Indians were not a consideration. Christine, however, scavenged what she could. She took a coat for herself, and when Mir wasn't looking, found a *kambal* that had probably been woven by one of the women who had perished. The wool blanket was black with soot, but still intact. She followed Mir up the hill, but only when she was stumbling beneath her load was Mir willing to take the blanket to cover himself.

For the first two hours, they hardly spoke of what had happened. Christine had seen the bodies of the Indians and thought that the media would probably tally a victory for the Muslims. Mir's few utterances, however, gave no hint of a victory. He told Christine that most Kashmiris didn't want to be governed by Pakistan any more than they wanted to be ruled by Hindus. But the local Muslims had been fighting too long. He had tried to discourage them, but Gulfam's husband, and his brothers and their friends, had ignored him and crossed over the border into Indian Kashmir. The Indian police post they had targeted had been destroyed, as planned. But they hadn't anticipated that there would be some kind of counterguerrilla group on maneuvers in the area. Mir admitted that he had no stomach for killing, but when the Indians came back after the rebels and began slaughtering their women and children, he had had no choice but to fight.

"You had to. It was self-defense," Christine said.

"They're all blood feuds, *mara ashiq,* even for Farrukh."

"Farrukh's a murderer. He kills innocent people — not soldiers."

Mir didn't respond, stopping at a ledge of rock. He pulled at the strap of the Kalashnikov, and Christine saw that, once again, fresh blood was soaking through his stained tunic. It was just a flesh wound on his left side, but when she moved to touch it, he stopped her.

"You're bleeding again," she said.

Christine could find little blue in his eyes, and Mir turned away from her. It was late in the day, and soon it would be dark.

"It'll be warmer by the rock. We'll camp here," he said, laying down his rifle.

As Christine took refuge at the base of the rock ledge, Mir took off his blanket and put it over her.

"No," she said, pushing it away.

"I don't need it."

"No," she said again, standing. She went to give it back to him, but his eyes caught her. Mir's face was so drawn. She could no longer detect any scent of sandalwood, just

456

the odor of ash and gore on his clothing. His wound had stopped bleeding, but she had to touch it. She laid her hand over it and she ached for him.

"I've had worse, and so have you, my little sister," he told her and took her face in his hands. Their lips touched. When Mir gently lowered her onto the hillside, the dry sage cushioned her, but the breeze was cold. He must've felt her shudder, because he moved over her so completely that at first the weight of his body was unsettling. He didn't ask; he didn't hesitate. She was cold; therefore he needed to shelter her from the elements. She dared to look up at him as his body lay still over her. His religion and his maleness intimidated her, but Mir's cheek was wet, and he looked at her with such longing. Christine rose up to kiss him, and his mouth was over hers and he pressed hard against her. His movement was so intense that she gasped. He kissed her again, and when she kissed him back, he slid his hand beneath her clothing, and she let him. She wanted him, and no longer felt the cold, only his hands, and his body. She knew he was trying to hide — to forget . . . and so was she.

The same snowy peaks that she had seen

earlier were painted on the side of the Tajik's small truck. The yak herder was bundled up in skins, and he grinned a lot, his eyes almost squinting shut. Tajikistan was just north of Pakistan, bordering China, and the man appeared to be a mix of Tajik and Chinese. His eyes were distinctly oriental. Yet he spoke Urdu and told the couple that he was taking yak milk to market in Islamabad. Before offering them a ride, he asked if they were interested in his milk. They weren't, but the Tajik grinned anyway.

After Christine climbed in, she caught a glimpse of herself in the rearview mirror. Skin that had always been pale was a soft copper. Her face was smudged, and her hair lacked luster. She was thinner, more angular, but against the darkness of her skin her green eyes were vibrant. For a moment, she was taken by her strangeness.

She no longer looked American, but she didn't look Pakistani either. Her clothing was exotic and her hair unruly. Then Mir crawled in beside her and she saw that he also looked different. He was a mix like herself, like the Tajik. Since the Tajik had crossed borders, his experiences had changed, had changed him . . . and would change his children.

When Mir talked with the Tajik his words were metered and precise. He had been schooled in the United States, but Mir looked duskier and rougher now than he did when she first met him. His clothing was torn and streaked with dirt and sweat and dried blood. He had changed, like the Tajik . . . like her.

Two other women rode in the back of the painted truck. They were Tajik women, but the effect of living between two worlds was clearly evident in their clothing as well. Like their Muslim sisters in the south, they wore the *shalwar qamiz* with a number of brightly colored hand-blocked shawls, but their faces remained uncovered. Intricately embroidered caps with a long scarf framed a face that had prematurely aged. In these thin-air regions their shoes were sturdier and closed-toed, unlike the delicate sandals Christine had become accustomed to. But the people here were purported to live longer, and the younger one, her eyes already lined, smiled at Christine. The older woman just sat, bobbing with the bumps of the road, her eyes rolling shut.

As Mir settled in next to Christine, he caught her eye in the mirror. He smiled and touched her shoulder. He didn't seem to notice the disparity between what she had become and what she had been, or he didn't mind, and he kept his hand on her as he spoke with the yak herder.

They would notice and they *would* mind, she realized. The tribes, the Taliban, and Farrukh, even the people she had grown up with and loved. Her mother and Cloid would also see and be bothered, or fearful.

They wanted a lift from the Tajik, to where? Christine didn't know. It hardly mattered. Despite how others felt, she was where she wanted to be.

When the road from Skardu swung back into the Karakoram Highway, the jagged peak of Rakaposhi was just north of them. They left the Tajiks, who were going south, and hitched a ride with a SUV full of French mountain climbers.

Since they had made love, they had not spoken of Liz, of Sindinkar, or even of Farrukh. Instead, they took a room in the Karim Hotel in a small northern town called Karimabad, where the magnificent Rakaposhi seemed to be almost on top of them. They played with the idea of traversing the pass over the Old Silk Route into China. The altitude there would be almost 18,000 feet and there was always the chance of avalanche, but with what they had been through, that was hardly a concern.

The feelings she had for Mir were so intense that she had even begun to dismiss the idea that she was riddled with parasites. Christine decided the growing ache in her belly was just stress, and she hardly noticed the pain, until the next day. She woke up in a sweat, vomiting, her gut twisting. She needed a hospital, but the hospitals in Pakistan were ill equipped. And besides, Christine had no papers. There would be questions.

Mir hated the drugs, but he hated heroin more. So he gave her the hashish, and it helped. But when the pain and fog of hash finally subsided, Mir was already packing her bag. The French climbers had told them of the Punjab Medical Store in Gilgit, a place frequented by mountain climbers and travelers. Its walls were lined with hundreds of dusty packets of antibiotics. Mir agreed to try the antibiotics, but if she didn't heal, he was taking her to the American embassy in Islamabad. There was an infirmary there where she could be properly cared for until Mir could arrange her passage home. They argued. Christine didn't want to go near the embassy, or the police, or even a hospital. There would be questions. The border skirmishes with the Indians had become an international issue, and Mir might be arrested. But Mir wouldn't discuss it. When they got to Gilgit, he drove straight to a bank where he withdrew more money. She wanted to call in a wire of her own funds, but he insisted on taking care of her until he couldn't do so anymore. He booked them into a room in the Kashgar Inn, a hotel in the Cinema Bazaar in downtown Gilgit. It was a bit noisy and not a great location for privacy, but it was near the Medical Store. They registered as husband and wife. A tourist town, their association would not be as conspicuous. Still, Christine stayed covered. And Mir bought the antibiotics, bought more hash, and they waited.

The airport was socked in with clouds, not uncommon since the strategically placed market town sits in a low valley surrounded by soaring peaks. With only one airline flying to Islamabad, it didn't take long for the flights to back up. At least, the window to their room faced the back of market stalls, so Christine wouldn't be tortured by a view of the mountain ranges. The formidable Hindu Kush wasn't far away and she was desperate to drive to the spot where the three mountain ranges met, but it wouldn't happen. Mir was sending her home.

When the skies finally cleared, their flight had been delayed three days, and still the large, flat antibiotic tablets were hardly touching the pain. She smoked the hash and sometimes in the blur of her drug daze, she would cry, asking why he didn't care for her, why he was sending her away. At first, Mir would try to explain. She was sick, she had to go, and he couldn't go with her. In the end, Mir could only take Christine in his arms and hold her, frustrated and hurting with her, as she whimpered in pain.

The next day Mir bought more hash, but by that time Christine was pleading for opium. She was in so much pain, she barely remembered the argument. She didn't want to be left alone in the room, and besides she hated the room, how closed in it felt. So Mir took her with him, almost carrying her to the Toyota he had rented locally. It wasn't until she saw a Pashtun dealer passing two packets of sticky balls to him in a souvenir shop that she knew he had acquiesced. Mir was upset, and didn't speak as he drove back toward the hotel. The day was cold but clear. They were stuck in traffic, just off the main drag of Gilgit. People were passing by in the bazaar, tourists and Pakistanis of all colors, dark and light, red-haired, even freckled.

Then Christine heard a sound she thought she'd never hear in the summits of the Hunza, a southern drawl. And when she turned she saw them, a man in plaid and a woman with big hair that never moved. Christine smiled at the American tourists, but as she did, something ripped across her middle and she remembered that she was sick.

In the rearview mirror, her face was shiny with sweat. Her eyes looked tired, and the whites were yellowed and blood-shot. She was squinting with pain. It was time to get relief, but she wouldn't go back to the room. So Mir continued up the road, away from the crowds, and parked beneath an ancient Buddha cut into the face of a mountain wall.

The sun was going down and they were alone. She bent over the foil of heroin Mir had prepared, suddenly self-conscious. She wanted Mir to turn away, but he couldn't. She would need his help.

As Christine inhaled the narcotic smoke, she stared up at the Buddha. She heard

464

Mir's voice instructing her, and she tried to relax. The likeness of the religious figure was magnificent, and she marveled that such an ancient carving could have withstood so many centuries of harsh weather. Mir said something, but she didn't catch his words. The pain was finally leaving her, and she breathed deep, watching as the last rays of sunlight moved down the astonishing image. Then Mir's voice rose and he snatched at the foil. He said she had taken too much, but she was confused.

Ten minutes later, when Mir pulled into their hotel she felt the rush. She had been careless and the high crashed over her like a wave. She could barely recall Mir's words as he cautioned her to slow down, and she didn't notice when Mir picked her up and carried her up a stairwell. For a moment, she understood that he was truly frightened. Then her concerns moved on. But even as she soared, forgetting the pain, there was still a thread of awareness that she had gone too far.

With Christine all but immobilized by the opium, Mir was forced to turn in the airline tickets. He told her he would drive her back over the Karakoram Highway to Islamabad. It would be a long and hazardous journey compared to the relatively short flight over the mountain ranges, but Christine didn't mind. In her drugged state, she mustered the nerve to ask him to go back with her, to the United States, to marry her. But he didn't answer, or if he did, the reply wasn't what she wanted to hear. There was an instant when she panicked, thinking that he must already be married, and that she was just a dalliance for him. Or maybe one wife was not enough and she was just another prospect. But Mir wasn't married. There had been someone, arranged, but Mir had lived in the United States too long. He was also caught between cultures, and marrying a stranger was something he couldn't do.

Shortly after they left Gilgit, the pain returned. Mir plied her with antibiotics, but she cried out for the narcotic. The first night on the road she couldn't sleep. Her arms hurt and the muscles in her back throbbed. Mir gave her hash, and that helped, but she was painfully aware of the difference, and they continued to argue.

The next morning the pain in her stomach, for whatever reason, subsided, and for the first time in a while she became conscious of Mir's arms around her. His embrace was startling at first. Then she noticed that his eyes were swollen and his face felt gaunt beneath her fingertips. Time had passed, and she thought she heard him say that it had been three days since they had left Gilgit; Christine could barely remember a day. Mir told her that the hairy had almost taken hold of her, the way it had his brother, and he thought he might lose her, and she kissed him. She could taste the salt of dried tears on his face, and she promised him she wouldn't take it again.

It took two more days to drive over the Karakoram Highway. There had been two landslides, one that had almost caught the back of their car and the other that took nine hours to clear. Fortunately, there was a teahouse nearby where they could fill themselves on bread and beans.

By the third day on the road, the pain had almost left her. They had finished the antibiotics and Christine tried to have hope that she might be cured.

After they passed through the bandit area of Kohistan without incident, they stopped again in Besham. They drove to the C&W Resthouse and Christine and Mir stayed in the same room she had had before. The innkeeper had a reliable phone line, and she tried her mother. Christine was shocked by the rush of emotion that threatened to overwhelm her when she heard her mother's voice. At first, all her mother wanted to hear was that she was safe. Christine assured her that she was. Her mother hesitated. She talked about Cloid, and Joe Riccardi, and how they had searched for her everywhere. It wasn't until Cloid had tracked down Reggie Duke in Africa that they had some idea of what had happened to her.

Christine decided to trust that the Aussie wouldn't say much. She told her mother that she had stayed back to meet with some very important textile merchants in Gilgit, that she had scoured the bazaars, and had found some amazing craftwork for their import company. But before she could finish her tale, her mother cut her off. Christine had been caught in a lie, but it wasn't like her mother to call her on it. That had been her dad's job. Still, her mother was quiet and Christine braced herself.

They had talked for twenty minutes, and not a word of Liz. As her mother told her of Liz's memorial service, given just the week before, her voice was eerily restrained. There were the friends who had attended the memorial, the pastor's sermon, and the lovely eulogies. Her mother went on about the meal afterward, the number of flower arrangements, and other details that Christine knew her mother couldn't possibly care about. But Marsha Shepherd's voice was cracking. She was coping, but barely. Christine decided it was time for her to go home.

Since there were no other guests, the innkeeper of the resthouse joined them for a meal. Christine caught herself laughing at a story of a Swiss couple riding over the mountains in an Orange Crush truck and realized that she was feeling no pain. She spoke Urdu, without pause, surprising the innkeeper. The Swiss couple forgotten, he started a diatribe about his partner's lazy wife. Christine listened, and sympathized, even offered a bit of advice. Eager for conversation, he talked of his seven sons, two of whom also owned inns and bragged about the upcoming marriage of his daughter to a very successful money changer in Taxila.

Christine cocked her head and praised the father's wise choice for a son-in-law. The foreign words came easily, and the man seemed pleased. Mir could barely keep his eyes off her, and she smiled coyly.

Mir asked the innkeeper if he knew of a nice place to stay the night on their way to Islamabad. Hands waving, the owner went on about a beautiful inn that he and his wife had stayed in before the first of their eight children had been born. It was near Mansehra, where mango trees grew and the Indus ran quietly.

Christine had to laugh. Given her experience, it was the bizarre idea that the Indus River could run quietly anywhere. Mir glanced over at her, and their eyes locked. The man reddened. He mumbled something to Mir and left the room.

Christine noticed that the flustered innkeeper had left the table. "Where'd he go?"

"He's writing directions to the inn."

Mir took her hand. The way he looked at her made her drop her eyes. Then she realized that she was going home without him. She started to speak, but he squeezed her hand, almost as if he anticipated what she was about to ask him.

"You have to trust me, Christine."

"What if you're meant to be with me?"

Mir started to respond when the innkeeper came back through the door. Christine pulled back her hand and thought that maybe they had missed a moment, but Mir whispered to her in Pashto. His words were slow and deliberate. He told her that he loved her, and that once she was well, they would be together . . . *Inshallah.*

"*Inshallah,*" Christine repeated. And she believed with all her heart that God was willing. She just wasn't sure about Mir.

After dinner, they went back to their room, and despite the soreness in her body they made love. She dreamed that night of Zubeda and her baby. The baby was crying. At first it appeared the child was pained, but when Zubeda took the baby to her breast, the infant laughed and Christine awoke.

It was the next morning and Christine saw that the sun was just coming over the tops of the hills. There were no more towering mountains, and the air was warmer. It was late autumn, and she knew the Javids would be harvesting the last of their fields.

Christine felt Mir's eyes on her and turned to him. He had been awake for a while. She told him about her dream of Zubeda and the baby, and he was sure it was a good omen. She snuggled in close to him, closed her eyes, and prayed that it was.

When they reached Mansehra, an old

471

Pakistani selling stringed kites to kids pointed them in the direction of the inn. It would be another forty minutes, driving through the lush countryside of Kagan Valley, before they found the isolated dirt road that the innkeeper had described. According to the map the Indus was miles away, but soon there was the sound of water running beside them. Mir guessed that the stream flowed down into the Tarbela Reservoir where the Indus, running parallel and just west of them, also flowed. Soon they pulled into a driveway that was almost hidden, curling around a sharp bend to face a two-story block of concrete with lines of men's tunics and trousers and women's *shalwar qamiz*s zig-zagging across its front. The concrete had once been painted blue, but the paint was old and peeled. There were patches of pink underneath the blue, and Mir wondered if they had just missed the inn's peak, "pink" years when the innkeeper and his new wife had arrived some twenty years earlier. Christine wasn't sure. Then she spotted some green beneath the pink and wondered if it was really the "green years" that would be sorely missed.

The innkeeper, however, had not exaggerated. There was a grove of mango trees, no fruit, but mango trees nonetheless. And the sad river of water that the sentimental innkeeper swore was the mighty Indus did meander quietly, even serenely. There were goats tied to the trees, a small garden, and a large rusty cage that held someone's pigeons. Along the riverbank and in front of the inn there were several castoff plastic chairs where guests could lounge and drink sodas, but the old men preferred their string cots, chewing their savories wrapped in leaves, while scrawny dogs and too many children crisscrossed in front of them, kicking up dirt and clumps of sparse grass. And around the oversized front door there were two, not just one, strands of faded gold tinsel. And above the entrance, in the familiar graceful strokes of chipped black paint, was a greeting in Arabic to all those who entered.

Mir stared at the monstrosity, and Christine laughed.

"We're only a couple of hours from Islamabad," he said. "There's a Marriott with *real* toilets and Dove soap, and —"

"It's perfect," she said. "Really, it's perfect."

Before he could respond, a speaker buzzed overhead, and the village's muezzin called all Muslims to prayer.

Across the river and alongside a sparse forest of poplar and eucalyptus trees stood a mosque, a beautiful mosque. Mir stared at it, and Christine realized that he hadn't gone to the mosque to pray since he had been with her.

"*Jaiye,*" she said, telling him to go.

Mir turned to her as men, carrying their prayer mats, approached from the inn. Accustomed to touching her, he reached for her shoulder, but Christine stepped back. They weren't in the Hunza anymore, where such brazen behavior might be excused.

"We'll meet inside, after prayer," she said.

He nodded, and she watched him follow the other Muslims across the rope bridge over the river. Once he was out of sight, she adjusted her *dupatta* and went inside the inn.

The *baltac,* the room reserved for men, was empty. They had all gone to the mosque, and the clerk, a prayer mat rolled under his arm, was just leaving. Christine started toward him, but the clerk caught her up short with his eyes. She had forgotten her manners. She was unescorted and should not approach Muslim men.

The woman cleaning the floors behind her eyed her suspiciously as Christine promptly turned to her and asked, in her best Urdu, if she and her husband could have a room. The woman studied the stranger, shrugged, and motioned her forward. Christine thanked her in Urdu and followed her to a screen that separated the room from a small table with a cash box and a scattering of paperwork.

The woman told Christine that the room would be two hundred and fifty rupees. It was high for the area, but Christine wasn't in the mood to haggle. After she paid, she followed the woman toward the back of the inn. There was a strong scent of game and spice that came from the kitchen.

"*Rogan josh!*" Christine exclaimed. "*Bhook lagi hai,*" she continued, telling the woman that the mutton smelled delicious and it made her very hungry.

The woman beamed and launched into a heavily accented monologue as they passed a room where a group of men was preparing to leave for mosque. One of the men, dressed in a white tunic and trousers, with lots of dark hair and bad skin, called out to the proprietor's wife. Christine drew the scarf up to her face as the man approached. He called the woman *behin* and told her to retrieve his prayer mat from his room. The man's sister left with barely a word to Christine.

While waiting for the woman to return, Christine stepped over to the front window. Men filed past her and out the door. As was custom, she took no notice of them, but watched through the window as they started across the rope bridge.

Prayer had already started, and Christine could hear the woman's brother in the kitchen, seemingly in no rush to follow his Muslim brothers. There was something about him that seemed familiar, and Christine tried to recall where she might have seen him.

The front door opened and a drove of children in school uniforms swept past her. *"Mamu! Mamu!"* they called out. Christine turned with them to see the reunion. The children crowded around the brother as he emerged from the kitchen. They called him *mamu,* which meant uncle, or mother's brother, in Urdu, and the man in white *hijab* laughed, ruffling their hair, picking them up, kissing them, and feigning horror when he forgot a name.

The man's sister came huffing down the stairs with the prayer mat. He gently chastised her for taking so long, took the mat, and went back into the room.

Christine took a quick glimpse of the man inside the room as she passed by the open doorway. He was on his prayer mat, facing Mecca, but he was alone in the room, and she couldn't help but wonder why he hadn't gone to the mosque.

The children were loud, and the man's sister was trying to quiet them as they all squatted on the floor in different parts of the house. Christine also sat. She had become accustomed to the frequent prayer. After they had finished, the woman was once more sidetracked by the children. She apologized to Christine, promised she would only be a moment, and disappeared into the kitchen. Christine didn't mind waiting. She was remembering the way Mir had looked at her after they had made love the night before, watching her with loving eyes and . . .

The man's eyes skewed to one side.

There was something about the *mamu*'s face that stuck in Christine's mind. Even as she had prayed, there was something about him that distracted her. The muezzin's call droned on in the distance, and Christine approached the room. There was just a hint of his voice from the room, a low mumble as the *mamu* prayed to Allah.

His lips were thin . . .

Concentrating, Christine was hardly aware that she had pulled her scarf back up to her face.

The photograph was grainy, his beard, shorter and neatly trimmed. His eyebrows were dark, and his hair was parted in the middle, tucked behind his ears. He was smiling. He had been younger then, young and idealistic, "a hero, a fierce freedom fighter," Mir had claimed.

Someone smacked her shoulder, and Christine jumped. It was the sister, and she was furious. Christine had been caught watching her brother as he prayed, but he wasn't praying anymore. Farrukh Ahmed was looking up at her with as much interest as she had in him. There were no fatigues, no Kalashnikov slung over his shoulder, no blood splattered across his chest, but it was the terrorist, and his eyes were on her. Christine dropped her eyes, mumbling apologies in Urdu as she stepped away from the doorway. She could hear Farrukh's sister behind her, scolding her. She just kept going, moving out the door and onto the porch. Christine wanted to run, but kept her pace steady. She didn't dare appear the way she felt, completely terrified.

She had been staring at him. Of course, he had noticed. Or had he noticed her because she was pale and red-haired?

Christine frantically reached up, feeling for any errant hairs. She was covered, but she tried to recall whether she had accidentally uttered any English. She hadn't. It was only their protocol she had to worry about. She had been staring at a Muslim man who wasn't her husband. So naturally he had scowled at her, as had his sister.

Christine was walking, trying not to hurry. The river was just ahead of her, and beyond it, the minarets of the mosque. Prayer was over. Men began to emerge, so Christine bent by the water's edge, ostensibly to smell a patch of flowers. But as the men started across the rope bridge, she raised her eyes, scanning the blur of dark faces. She had to find Mir before the splintered blue door opened behind her, before Farrukh sorted out that she was an American.

A few Muslims headed toward the inn, while others turned up the dirt road towards Mansehra. Then hands gripped her shoulders and Christine spun around.

"I'm sorry, *mara ashiq*," Mir said, smiling.

It seemed as if there were men all

around them, and she recognized a few of them from the room. They had to be Farrukh's men.

"Christine —"

She pulled out of his grasp and walked away from the inn to the edge of the mango grove. It wasn't far enough, so she moved down through the rows of trees, trying not to run, not to seem frantic. Finally she stopped. She could barely see the men. Despite the early stirrings of winter, there were still leaves on the trees to shield her. Mir had followed her, but he was scowling. He was scowling like Farrukh, and a horrible thought seized her. When he reached her, Christine couldn't move.

"Are you sick?" he asked.

She sank to the ground out of sight of the inn. He turned to see what she was running from. There was no one. He bent down to her, and she forced herself to look up at him.

"Christine, what's wrong? Why are you so afraid?"

She was afraid, but it was too late. She would have to trust him.

"He's here," she breathed. "Farrukh's here."

Chapter
23

More than a shadow came over Mir's face when she uttered Farrukh's name. It was a look of resignation, and something in her gave way.

"I need to tell you," he began, but before the words were out of his mouth she knew.

"You're with him."

"No, no, *mara ashiq* —"

She tried to stand, to get away from him, but he stopped her.

"Let me go."

"I love you," he pleaded, and he pulled her to him. Christine was so hurt, she wanted to fight him, but Mir held her tight and told her that when he had gone to the mosque he had prayed for Allah's blessing, that she was his heart, and that they *were* meant to be together. Almost frantic in his appeal, he lapsed into Urdu as he said again that he did love her and

481

that she had to believe him.

Christine could feel his chest heaving against hers, and she wanted to tell him that she believed him, but before she could, Farrukh called out.

"Mir . . . Mir Hasan Majeed."

Mir's warm breath on her neck stopped, even as she held her own. They were on their knees, together in the woods, and Christine couldn't help but wonder why the terrorist had not already shot them.

Mir whispered something about "the one who sits in judgment," then stood and faced Farrukh.

Christine also stood, but kept her head down and her scarf drawn across her face. The two men embraced one another.

Liz and revenge pervaded her thoughts. But the guns were back in the Toyota, and there was Mir . . . She hadn't counted on loving Mir.

They were old friends and comrades. From the phrases Christine picked up, it had been years, many years. And then Farrukh shifted, and his eyes fell on her over Mir's shoulder.

"Bibi?" Farrukh asked.

"Ji," Mir replied, affirming that she was his wife.

Then Farrukh said something about

seeing her in the inn, that her skin and eyes were light, and asked if she was from the North-West Province.

Streams of perspiration rolled down Christine's back. Mir wasn't answering and Farrukh Ahmed was waiting.

Lie! Please just lie, the voice in her mind pleaded.

But Mir wouldn't. His tone was low, even challenging, as he told him that his wife was from the United States. He added the word "American," just to make sure that Farrukh understood.

Farrukh was staring at her. Christine dropped her eyes, but it was too late. She was sure he saw that she was afraid.

"It's been very long, my friend," Farrukh said, his English surprisingly clear.

"Too long," Mir returned.

"Yes . . . I'm afraid, too long."

With her head down, Christine could see the sandaled feet of the men. They stood close, facing each other, the skin of their feet dark and callused, their journeys probably all too similar. Farrukh turned and started back toward the inn. Mir went with him, and Christine had no choice but to follow.

In a moment, Mir was striding alongside the terrorist. Christine raised her eyes and saw that Farrukh's head was cocked at an odd angle. It appeared as if he had nerve damage in his neck; he moved stiffly as he talked. A large scar whited out half his right eyebrow, and his skin was pock-marked. She remembered the photos at the Central Bureau of Investigation in India and thought it had been a while since they had been taken.

As they left the cover of the mango trees, she saw Farrukh's men waiting on the porch. Christine wondered how long they would have waited before they would have gone into the grove after their leader.

As the three of them approached, a few of the men made their way down to the plastic chairs by the river and slumped into them. The rest of Farrukh's band, along with his sister and a white-turbaned man who looked like more of a dignitary then a rebel, waited on the porch. There was no sign of an AK or a bandolier of ammunition, just a few Pakistanis enjoying the day.

When Farrukh reached the inn, his sister mumbled something to him under her breath. He waved her off as the door opened and two more nieces sprinted out. The woman snapped at them, but they ignored her. Farrukh opened his arms, letting the youngsters run and wrap themselves around his legs. He laughed loudly, chastising the girls for not heeding their mother's words.

Introductions were swift. Only the man in the white turban, Attaullah Hamid, remembered Mir. The others had joined Farrukh after Mir had left. They seemed wary of the former comrade, and when a bony, drawn Pakistani snaked around the doorjamb with a Kalashnikov slung over his shoulder, Mir stopped short of the porch. His hand came up behind him ready to push Christine back, but Farrukh waved off his favorite nephew. He introduced the young man, who barely uttered a greeting. He had his uncle's bad skin, and he grinned, still holding the automatic in such a way that they wouldn't misinterpret Farrukh's good nature. Mir was still planted in front of Christine, and she glanced up at Farrukh. His eyes were on her, not Mir.

He hated her, she realized. She knew she hated him and dared to hold his gaze.

The men around Farrukh noticed her disrespect and grew angry. The nephew, his grin fading, turned toward her with his gun. Mir only had to look at her. But before she could drop her eyes, Farrukh laughed. The gesture was strained. Still, he signaled his nephew to back off, then jumped off the high porch. Farrukh patted Mir affectionately to reassure him, then announced that his old comrade and his wife were guests. In Urdu, Farrukh proclaimed that in the house of his sister all were one under Allah and that Allah was great and His blessing was upon them. With that said, he waved the two of them inside.

Mir stayed close to Christine as they entered the inn, but he wouldn't look at her. She knew she had shamed him. She thought of the Toyota parked just off the driveway.

Maybe they could make a run for it before . . .

They couldn't run, not because they would be shot, as she knew they probably would be, but because she wasn't sure that Mir would follow her.

"Mir's wife!" Farrukh bellowed and gestured her into the *baltac*. After all, she was a guest. Christine paused at the door and looked through to the next room. The women were scurrying to prepare the evening meal. Christine wanted to be with them . . . wanted to hide. But Farrukh was waiting. He took up one of the couches while the rest of his men filled in the few furnishings around him. Mir stayed beside her.

"What do I call you?" Farrukh asked the American.

A wife, a good Muslim wife, would always wait for her husband to give her permission to speak first. Christine looked up at Mir. He nodded, and she turned back to Farrukh, remembering to keep her eyes just off his.

"Christine," she said. "But some find it easier to say Kariz."

"Christine," Farrukh snapped impatiently as he flicked his hand, signaling for them to join him.

At first Farrukh's movements were labored and self-conscious, but gradually he fell into the usual prattle of politics and money. By the time they moved into the next room to feast, he had begun to relax. Even in the *baltac*, where guests were the focus, Christine had said little, and her reticence seemed to lift the mood of the men, including Mir.

It wasn't until dessert was served with cups of spicy tea and squares of sugary milk confection that Mir brought up the skirmish in Kashmir.

Farrukh seemed surprised. He had heard of the victory, but he thought Mir no longer fought for the jihad.

Mir assured him that he did, but he had hoped that there might be another way to defend their Muslim brothers. Then Farrukh rattled off something she didn't catch. There was mention of "commitment," "the brothers' objective," "honor," and "the jihad," but the rebel leader's tone was unmistakably contemptuous. Farrukh wasn't praising Mir; he was maligning him.

Mir could only shrug miserably, for he had become the hapless villager. She barely recognized him.

As Farrukh lashed out at his old comrade, he glanced over at Christine. He wanted to be sure she was watching. He was crushing the man she loved, and that was his intent.

She bit down into her lip, grateful that she had a scarf to hide her anger.

Finally the tirade ended, and Mir was urged to tell the story of that night in Kashmir. He did. Although the battle was considered a triumph for the Muslims, Mir's face hardly reflected joy in the telling. He *was* conflicted and couldn't hide it. At one point, Mir mentioned that Christine had shot two Hindus, and she realized that he was telling them of her participation in the mission. The men were taking more notice of her, and Farrukh held his eyes on her as if weighing her.

After Mir described the burying of their brothers, of the loss of Sinkindar, whom Farrukh remembered only as a lanky teenager with a fondness for ice milk, and finally, of the devastation of the village, the group was silent.

It was getting late and Christine's concentration was faltering, which made her nervous. Farrukh, his regal-looking lieutenant, Attaullah, and two others were deeply engaged in conversation, and she thought it might be a good time to leave. She turned to Mir, and when he looked at her, he smiled. Christine was relieved and asked permission to retire to their room. Mir nodded assent.

As she rose to leave, Farrukh motioned her to stay. He began questioning her about her family, and the Americans, the infidels whose only God was money and greed.

Mir didn't look at her. Only Attaullah Hamid seemed to react to the undercurrent of antagonism. Hamid glanced over at Mir, and Christine thought he might be trying to catch Mir's eye, but Mir ignored him. Mir was afraid, she realized.

The notion that Farrukh could so completely intimidate the man she loved infuriated her. She was trying to restrain her anger, but the women who served her wouldn't look at her. And Farrukh's men were eyeing her every movement, braced for the slightest signal to discipline her, even as Mir sat beside her. And Farrukh? Farrukh hardly seemed fazed.

"And they approve of your union with mujahideen?" he asked.

"My family approves of my choice to marry."

"And your choice to kill?"

Christine's gaze wavered. He was baiting her. She thought it was only human to regret taking someone's life, but the fanatic who sat in front of her didn't care that he had killed.

Farrukh was waiting for her answer. His mouth was turned up in a smirk, which only made her angrier. Then she remembered that Mir was beside her, suffering.

"You mean the soldiers?"

"There were others?" Farrukh inquired.

She thought of Nikhil. "There was another Indian," she admitted. "They're all dead because of me." She did not mention the guard or the bandit.

Her memories held her now, and she had to concentrate not to show her disquiet. After all, she had been responsible

490

for the death of five men.

The feeling was surreal. The man she had read about, she had talked of with people, with Cloid. They had all feared him, and now he was sitting in front of her, smiling, a glimmer of respect in his eyes as he waited to hear more.

"Maybe you *are* mujahideen," Farrukh finally conceded.

His patronizing tone had eased, but Christine didn't dare respond. If she did, her voice would break. He muttered something in Arabic. It sounded like holy verse and Christine bent her head in respect, but her heart wasn't in it. The thought that she could impress the man who had murdered her sister nearly made her sick. She swallowed, hoping to quell the queasiness in her stomach.

She looked up. He was studying her, and his expression hardened. For a moment she had been worthy of his notice, but then he saw through her bravado and once again she was merely a woman. To him, she was the property of his former comrade, property that he did not covet. He probably wanted to kill her, but she had spilled blood for them, and she was the wife of a brother. He would have to spare her, despite his hatred of her birthright.

But his gesture hardly left her comforted.

She asked Mir again if she might be excused, and this time no one stopped her. Later, when Mir finally came to her, he said little. That night, Christine's sleep was fitful, and they both found themselves awake before morning prayer.

Allah's praises were still being sung when Mir returned from the mosque. The women of the inn hardly noticed him as he entered. Their eyes closed, they rubbed at their beads, lips moving, their scarves nearly obscuring their faces while their men prayed just across the river.

Only Farrukh remained. He didn't go to the mosques, at least not the crowded ones in the light of day. When Mir walked back through the front door, he and Christine slipped past the room where Farrukh prayed, his forehead to the floor. Mir didn't need to say anything. She knew they were leaving, and together they went silently up the stairs to retrieve their things.

Moments later they were out the door. Mir had overheard Farrukh reciting verses from the Koran in Arabic, and he wanted to get Christine to the car before Farrukh's prayers were over.

By then Pakistanis were already returning from prayer. Christine saw a large, balding man ambling across the bridge who reminded her of Cloid, and wondered if her old friend believed in fate. She knew what the former federal agent would do about Farrukh if he were in her place. She knew what any of the men at the rifle range would do if they had a chance to — as Mir put it — "rid the world of Farrukh Ahmed."

She had found him, or had he found her? She wasn't sure, but either way she did believe in fate, and fantasies of concealing a weapon and killing the terrorist ran through her mind.

But she had no Glock, and she had lost the Luger in the fire. There was only the banged-up Kalashnikov in the back of the Toyota. The sizable rifle would be difficult to conceal — and there was Mir to think about. She'd be lucky to get off two rounds before being cut down, and Mir would die with her.

But if it is God's will, then Farrukh Ahmed will also die.

Mir opened the door to the car and Christine hesitated. Attaullah Hamid, his turban almost startlingly white, had spotted them from the bridge, and thoughts of killing the terrorist vanished.

"Get in," Mir said.

As she crawled into the Toyota, Farrukh's lieutenant started running toward them.

"What's going on?" she asked as Mir climbed in behind the wheel.

"I'll tell you once we're out of here."

Mir started the car, jammed it into reverse, and had moved no more than ten feet when Hamid appeared behind them, obscured by a haze of dust and exhaust.

Mir grumbled something under his breath and turned off the engine. Christine pulled Mir's Kalashnikov from between the seats.

"It's all right," he said. "I just need to talk to him."

Christine nodded, but kept the rifle level and firm in her grasp. Mir climbed out. In the rearview mirror, Christine saw Hamid cock his head at Mir, and they stepped into the bushes, out of sight of the others at the inn. Whatever it was Hamid wanted, the interchange was quick and intense. Christine cracked the door, just in case, and when she heard Mir raise his voice, she pushed it open.

She walked around just in time to see Hamid reach for something on his hip. Mir started to react, but Christine was faster, swinging the automatic up against her shoulder. She stared through the sight at Hamid's chest. Attaulah Hamid froze and Mir turned around. Christine had managed to keep her scarf in place, only her eyes visible, but her stance was set, and her finger was on the trigger. Farrukh's lieutenant drew back his hand, slowly. Mir reassured Christine that he and Hamid were done talking, and the white-turbaned man left.

After they got back into their car, Christine looked toward the mosque, her thoughts of self-sacrifice already dismissed. While holding the gun on Hamid she realized that her feelings for Mir's welfare were too strong, and ultimately, that intensity, in itself, would compromise her ability to kill Farrukh.

Prayer was over. As they curled around the driveway, Christine turned and glimpsed some of Farrukh's men, Hamid alongside them, standing on the porch. They watched them leave, and didn't move to stop them. Others were walking toward the inn, but the Toyota was already halfway up the drive, dust billowing behind it.

As Mir turned onto the dirt road, he accelerated. He glanced at the rearview mirror. There was an urgency to his movements, and Christine looked back toward the inn. Through the sparse bushes that lined the property she could see that the porch was bare. The men had gone inside.

"Mir —"

Visibly upset, he shook his head. Mir accelerated the vehicle and dirt kicked up around them, obscuring the inn and the road.

"Mir, slow down. You can't see."

The words were barely out of her mouth when the Toyota struck something, rocked back and forth, and then died.

"*Laariat hai,*" Mir cursed as he turned the ignition. The engine fired, but when he tried to back up, the car wouldn't move. Mir rolled down his window. They had snagged on a boulder. He cursed again and slammed his body back against the seat, his emotion fueled not by the accident but by the automatic gunfire coming from the inn. Suddenly, people were shouting and screaming.

Christine grabbed her rifle. "He's killing them."

"It's Farrukh. They're trying to take Farrukh."

Christine opened her mouth to respond, but Mir put up a hand. He was listening, his mind weighing the sounds as the gunfire became sporadic, the outcry dimin-

496

ishing. Finally, his face resigned, Mir pulled a second Kalashnikov from the backseat.

"I don't think they can take him alive, but maybe —"

Another rash of shots whirred from the inn. A man shouted and Mir froze. Bedlam broke out again.

Mir exhaled miserably. "It's not going to work."

"How many are there?

"Atta and two others. Farrukh wants to blow up the embassy — your embassy."

"In Islamabad?"

Mir nodded. "They're trying to stop him, but they're outnumbered. Atta hoped . . ."

Christine understood. "He hoped you would join him."

"Farrukh wasn't always like this."

There were more shouts from the inn. Mir closed his eyes and rubbed his forehead. "There was a dream," he breathed, "years ago. But even when I loved him I knew that someday . . ."

The gunfire was waning. Mir opened his eyes and breathed deeply, taking hold of his rifle. He checked the magazine; Christine did the same.

"No," Mir declared, and he took the rifle

from her, laying it in the back of the Toyota. He pulled out an ammo belt, strapped it around his waist, and swung the door open.

"Mir, I came here for this," she said.

He turned to her and cocked his head hard to the side. There was nothing vague in his gesture this time. It was a command, an order, to stay behind. Christine started to object, but he touched her lips with his fingers and after a moment his fingers lifted and he caressed the side of her cheek, gazing at her.

"You came here for me," he said, his voice choked with emotion. "I saw it in your face when you first talked of going after him. *This* is not you. *Farrukh* is not your destiny."

"How do . . ." her voice broke. "How do you know?"

"Please help me, Christine."

The last time she had kept him from leaving, women and children had perished.

She nodded. He promised her that he would come back to her, then bent over the weapon he held and kissed her.

After Mir disappeared down the road, Christine pulled her eyes from the rearview mirror and let her body settle into the seat. The shooting intensified, so she tried to concentrate on the sound of the river, its water moving, rippling, as it pushed its way over the rocks. With each shot, more birds took flight, and the dust particles that had enveloped their car earlier were finally returning to their place on the road. Her mind had slowed, but her senses were so raw, she thought she could almost feel the pull of the earth as it turned beneath her.

He had told her to stay, but she wasn't Muslim, she wasn't Pakistani — and Christine pushed the door wide.

As she headed back down the road, her brain was conjuring images of the moments ahead. She could almost picture the chaos, the opposing factions firing repeatedly at one another. The women and children would run for cover. But now, as the sounds from the inn seemed to be subsiding, she tried to believe that Attaullah Hamid had managed to take Farrukh. And Mir was with them, and he was safe.

But as Christine approached the inn, she hesitated. She could see that the front door and one of the windows of the inn had been destroyed. She slipped the sling of her Kalashnikov off her shoulder. Then she heard voices, and the hope that it was as she had imagined grew.

Mir's alive. Please, dear Lord, let him be alive.

Christine swallowed hard, barely able to hold back the tears. She stepped up to the porch when sharp raking blasts suddenly sounded from inside the inn. Fragments of blue, pink, and green blew out at her as she scrambled underneath the tall porch. She covered her ears, bringing her knees up while clutching the automatic rifle to her chest. The other window exploded, and glass showered the wood planks over her head. She flinched, expelling her breath in rapid gusts. Her ribs were hurting, but the salvos from inside were more dangerous. She recognized the sound, a submachine gun, easier to handle in confined spaces.

People were yelling, arguing, and then there was another burst from the machine pistol and someone laughed, not Mir. It was Farrukh, bantering, playing . . . not taken, still alive.

Christine moved toward the stairs of the porch, but a Kalashnikov spoke this time, its discharge familiar, and absurdly comforting.

She counted the shots. Two, seven . . . twelve . . . fifteen . . . nineteen —

She had to wait. Mir would come. He

had promised her. She had to be patient.

Then the clamor of gunfire ceased. The silence was so sudden that Christine barely registered the change.

It had happened so fast. The shots had almost blurred into one sonic eruption. There were three, but the last one, the last one in particular, she could feel.

And Christine was up on the porch. The splintered door to the inn almost came off in her hand. Then she was in the *baltac*. Two dead men barred her way. She stepped over them, her eyes taking in the jagged holes in the concrete walls. Still, there was only silence, and she moved cautiously into next room.

Christine thought she recognized most of those lying about the room. Some were older, Farrukh's age. They had probably been with him the longest, but there was also the seventeen-year-old, the newest recruit. He looked as if he had dropped early, caught in between, his body riddled with shots meant for others. She saw them all, the nephew, Attaullah, and Farrukh's own sister. And in her arms she held a child, one of Farrukh's nieces. Christine bent down and touched the girl's neck. There was no pulse.

"Mir?" she breathed. Somewhere there

was water running, a leak. She tried again.

"Mir?"

There was a noise, not the house, and Christine let the gun down into her hands, ready to fire. The door to the room where Farrukh prayed was half open, and Christine edged around the doorjamb. Mir was on his knees facing toward Mecca, his body doubled over, his forehead on the floor in supplication.

Christine entered the room and looked down at his body. As she bent down by him the Kalashnikov slipped from her hands to the floor beside her. Her lover came back easily into her arms, his body still warm. His eyes and mouth were open, as if he were trying to speak, trying to explain.

"Please, God," she begged, holding back a sob. "Don't take him —"

"Your prayer cannot be heard."

Christine reached for the rifle, but her movement was sluggish and halfhearted, and Farrukh kicked it away easily. He caught her under the chin with his arm. She dug her fingernails into his skin, but his forearms were hard and sinewy. Farrukh chuckled.

"He was praying," she yelled. "You murdered him while he was praying!"

502

He squeezed her throat.

"I'll let you go if you help me," he said, breathing hard.

"Go to hell," she screeched, struggling against him. Farrukh only smiled at her attempts to stop him. He jerked his arm back once more. Her air was cut off, and slowly her face darkened. She was desperate to hold on, to fight him as long as she could, but she was losing consciousness. Then the pressure eased and she gasped for air.

Farrukh cursed at her and shoved her forward. Choking, she fell over, trying to catch a breath.

"Mir Hasan shot me, and I need you to tie it off. I can't do it with one hand."

Christine felt Mir's body beneath her and she clutched him to her. "He was praying," she whimpered.

"He was praying for forgiveness because he was weak."

Farrukh crouched in front of her. Blood soaked his tunic between his neck and shoulder, just above his heart. *Mir came so close,* she thought. Still, the terrorist managed to grin at her.

"You fix it and I'll let you live. It's a deal . . . a good American deal, I think."

In one hand he held a length of white

cotton, the other the submachine pistol he had used to murder all those who had tried to stop him. She recognized the starched white of Attaullah Hamid's turban. Farrukh was smirking at her, holding the gun close, daring her to take it. She took the strip of cotton, instead.

"Your husband couldn't finish me off," Farrukh needled. "He robbed me of Paradise, but because he's my brother I sent him there in my place."

He leaned in so she could wrap him. At first, Christine couldn't focus. But she could smell him. He was close and she slipped the strip around him. Suddenly, she felt hot, and her body went rigid. She was concentrating so hard on pulling at the length of cotton that she was barely aware that Farrukh had been caught by surprise. She had not put the white cotton strip of his Muslim brother's turban over his wound, but around his neck. And Christine pulled with every bit of strength she had left.

It was the blood feud . . .

She jerked at the fabric, her knuckles white, then bluish. The pistol he held, fired. But she held fast to the cloth strip as the vision of her fate came into her mind. *She would die, but not before she had killed Farrukh Ahmed.*

Farrukh had missed her, and now his wound was bleeding anew. Farrukh struck her, and she fell against him. His gun fell between their bodies, and he frantically reached for something inside his clothing.

Even with her head throbbing from the hit, she managed to grab his hand before he could withdraw the knife. She pressed down against him. He struggled, but Mir's shot had weakened him. It didn't take much. The blade finally turned and sank easily into his body. Then when the knife had gone in as far as it could go, she pushed again. She could feel his hand go limp beneath her own hands, covering the hilt of the dagger. Farrukh seemed to pause beneath her, but she was too afraid to move. When a warm, sticky ooze came over her hand, she gained the nerve to raise her head. Farrukh was watching her. His life's blood was leaving him, and still he watched her.

"Liz," she murmured. "You killed Liz."

She wanted to say more, but just as she said her sister's name she thought she saw the terrorist cock his head.

The gesture was subtle, but the shrug was clear enough. He didn't care. Farrukh Ahmed was dying and he didn't care, because he was so sure he was going to Paradise. Christine went berserk. She raised up and hit him. He spat at her, the infidel, the woman! Then she hit him again and again. She didn't blink. Her sight fixed on his reddening face, her tears flowing. She flew into a frenzy. Her jaw was set with exertion; she bit her tongue. But she couldn't feel, couldn't taste; her senses had been suspended.

Her dad and Cloid were wrong. There was no higher cause. There was only rage and a hint of awareness that she wanted — no, she needed revenge. It was an eye for an eye. The realization that she might be no better than the man she meant to kill came to her, and her stomach turned.

But she couldn't stop.

He reached up only once to block her. His mouth was moving, but she couldn't hear because there was the sound of someone shrieking. She was hardly aware of her own cries. Christine could not taste her own blood, nor could she feel the bones in her hands breaking as she came down in a bloody sweep time and time again.

Finally, the rage eased. The being beneath her was motionless. She turned to vomit. There wasn't much, but it depleted her, and her arms fell to her sides. Christine felt dizzy for a moment with the abruptness of her body halting. Her eyes hurt; she couldn't see. She went to wipe them, and flinched at the pain in her hands.

Then she saw Farrukh, and for a moment she was startled. Deep gouges ran the length of his face. One eye was swollen shut while the other was exposed, its orb skewed and macabre. There was tissue and torn cartilage across his face.

Farrukh was gone.

She remembered that Mir had once loved this man, this mask of horror, this semblance of a monster who now stared benignly at her.

And what kind of monster was staring back at him?

Christine tried to stand, but without the use of her hands she could only roll off the body. At last she managed to sit up, her heart pounding in her chest, her side aching.

Mir's body lay close by, and Christine slid over to him, cradling her hands. Tears filled her eyes. The salt stung. She tried futilely to wipe at her eyes then saw Mir's face and forgot about the pain. She moved next to him and saw where Farrukh's bullets had exited through his chest.

Christine laid her head against his chest. Oblivious to the blood, she spoke to him. His right arm lay beside him. It was unsoiled and Christine closed her eyes, willing it to lift. She could almost feel his hand come down upon her head. Her hair would be rich and dense, and Mir would stretch his fingers into it. Christine moaned, but her cry was of pain, not desire, and she opened her eyes and saw that the arm was as it was before . . . lifeless. She barely had the strength to take a breath. The man she loved was dead.

Later, she didn't know how much later, when she had first heard the cry, she was afraid that it might also be imaginary. Still, she left Mir's body and moved toward the sound. The sun was setting and the shadows were long and deep as she traipsed through the inn to the back, where there was grass, a tree, and a shed. Kittens, listless from lack of milk, mewed, then scattered on uncertain legs as she approached.

From inside the shed came the sound of a baby crying. When Christine opened the warped doors, the women and children sat before her, huddled together but facing outward, their eyes wide and frightened.

One woman was holding a baby. She had bunched up her blousy *qamiz* and was trying to get the infant on her breast. Fretting, the baby finally found the nipple and eagerly took it. Its sounds were soothing, except as the baby nursed, the woman looked up and Christine realized that her own *shalwar qamiz* was almost completely saturated with blood.

Christine stared at the women and children, their faces dimming in the twilight. They were waiting, she thought, waiting for her to kill them. So she moved in among them, and sat, wincing at the pain in her hands as she did. It wouldn't take them long to realize that she wouldn't resist. Someone, an aunt, a sister, even a child, would find something sharp, something with which to kill her, to avenge Farrukh's life, and then she could be with Mir.

"Chris."

The voice was soft and distant, the way it had sounded when Lizzie had called to her from her dream. Her eyes welled at the thought that maybe God did have mercy. Her sister was calling again, and this time she would go.

Then something touched her. Christine looked down. A hand, a stump really, rested on her knee. She looked up from the deformity to a woman's face, partially veiled. One eye was clouded and unseeing. But the other was clear and alert, an almost unnatural green. Christine's throat closed. She wanted to reach up, but her arms felt weighted.

"Chris —" Liz gasped.

Christine hurt too much to respond, and her chest heaved with sobs as words grew muddled in her mouth. Liz was also crying, reaching for her, but Christine's body shook violently. It had to be another fantasy, not real . . . Then Liz's arms were around her, and Christine could feel her sister's heart beat fast against her own. The trembling eased, and suddenly *their* voices, *their* cries became audible, and she could hear the women and the children. They were crying, because they knew Farrukh was dead, because she had killed him. But Lizzie was alive . . . her sister was alive.

Chapter

24

The glare was so bright that Christine thought she was back in the Thar Desert. At any moment, she expected to see Shweta's uncle, topped by his oversized, saffron-yellow turban, step over her and shield her from the heat of the sun. But there was no heat, no warmth to this light. There was only white, a stark white, artificial and harsh, and Christine strained to look up into it.

"She's awake," a voice muttered, its American accent sounding foreign.

Christine tried to open her eyes. "Light hurts. It hurts —"

"Can you turn down the goddamn lights?"

The familiarity of the voice startled her. "Cloid?"

The light dimmed, and she felt her old friend's breath on her face as she looked up into eyes that were boring into her. Cloid's thin lips were drawn into a hard line, and he studied her with a concentration that would've scared her when she was a child.

"Is that better?" he asked.

Christine heard him, but she was distracted by the sight of two IVs that hung from a stand above her. She followed their long clear tubes to a needle taped to a bulging vein on the soft underside of her forearm. The skin around it was bruised a deep purple.

"Hairy! No needles. *Maf kijaye. Na. Na!*" Christine cried, clawing at the needle.

A nurse stepped in and assured her that the IVs contained a painkiller and antibiotics, nothing more. Christine saw that the nurse wore no chador, no covering. Her hair was short and dry and there was no henna on her hands. Instead, she wore latex gloves. A laminated ID was pinned to her uniform. Christine saw that both her own hands were wrapped, resembling two small white turbans, and then she remembered where she was.

"I'm sorry," Christine whispered as Cloid took his place back beside her. He patted her affectionately.

The walls of the room were not concrete, but drywall, painted in soft pastels. And the windows had matching blinds, the floor, a golden parquet.

"We had to bring you into the infirmary. The hospital here didn't cut it," Cloid told her.

Christine was slowly recalling the past two days. Her body had been broken and bloodied. There were women crying — and there was Liz. Then the men came, Pakistani militia, and carried them out of the shadows, from the inn, to Islamabad.

Christine was about to say something when a particularly well-groomed Joe Riccardi passed by the room. He was in a suit and looked stiff and uncomfortable. Behind him was another man dressed for business, probably a Pakistani. Riccardi barely acknowledged her as he and the other man called to a doctor who approached them from outside her room. Christine remembered that Liz had been cleared early by the Pakistan government. It had something to do with her eye, but Christine's mind was still fuzzy from the sedative.

"Is Liz really —"

Cloid smiled. "Elizabeth's in India with your mother. She needs a little eye surgery, but she's okay."

Christine glanced nervously at Joe and the Pakistani.

"And so are you," Cloid reassured her, squeezing her shoulder.

Prints of the Grand Canyon and the Golden Gate Bridge were tacked to the wall. A Norman Rockwell illustration of a country doctor and his patient, an all-American youngster with freckles, hung over the bed, and Cloid was beside her. There was a nurse, a doctor, Riccardi, and the man she assumed was some rep from the Pakistan government. Including herself, there were five Americans and one Pakistani. And they were all alive. Christine thought of Farrukh, his last moments, but her embassy was still standing.

"He didn't blow it up," she uttered, amazed. "He wanted to blow up the embassy, but he didn't."

She smiled at the thought, but the doctor who had entered with Riccardi and the stranger trailing behind him paused. The nurse's face went gray, but Joe and the Pakistani hardly missed a step.

"Who are you talking about, Chris?" Riccardi asked.

"Farrukh."

Riccardi glanced back at the doctor, but he and his nurse needed little prodding. They left the room. Riccardi turned back to Christine and smiled. She smiled back. Cloid, however, didn't. When the CIA operative tried to slide past him to get closer to Christine the old Fed wouldn't budge. He and Cloid eyeballed one another for what seemed like a long time. Finally, Riccardi grabbed a stool while the Pakistani, a somber man with jet-black hair, elected to stay at the foot of her bed.

"This is Colonel Sultana from ISI," Joe said. "The doctor says you might be up to a few questions. Okay with you?"

Christine looked at Sultana and he cocked his head in acknowledgement. And with no further greeting, he began.

"Miss Shepherd, were you aware that there was a travel advisory in Pakistan?"

"Yes."

"Were you aware that the North-West Frontier Province is restricted, off-limits to foreigners?"

"Yes."

"There's a suspicion that you might be mixed up in the death of a Pakistani citizen. Is that true?"

He was alluding to Farrukh Ahmed, but she only thought of Mir. She could feel the emotion building, but with these men, like the men she had known all her life, she didn't dare cry. Instead she muttered,

"Lrai pasand bakra, haula-haula." It was a disparaging quip, a quote from Reggie, comparing bureaucrats and agents with camels and goats. The absurdity of it made the urge to cry pass.

Cloid and Riccardi didn't catch what she said, but the Pakistani official eyed her warily.

"Your Urdu is commendable, Miss Shepherd. But I think you will have a great deal of trouble finding the phrase 'civil rights' in our lexicon."

"Are you a lawyer?" she asked.

"I'm a lawyer as well. Yes."

"And you're here to keep me from rotting in a Pakistan jail."

"That's up to you."

Riccardi intervened. "No one's going to jail. We just need to know what you were doing in Mansehra?"

Mir was in her head again. "I was passing through."

Sultana stared down at his notebook. "How long have you been in Pakistan?"

"Since May."

"Is Elizabeth Shepherd your sister?"

"Yes."

"And your father's name was Glen Shepherd?"

"Yes."

"Marsha Shepherd is your mother?"

"Yes."

"You're twenty-nine years of age?"

"Yes."

The Pakistani hadn't looked up from his notes once.

"And your occupation?"

"I'm a buyer."

"An import buyer?"

Christine sighed, tired of their protocol. "Yes, and so what?"

"Chris, it's all right," Joe started.

"No. It's not!" she snapped. "I know what this is. All you really want to know is if I killed Farrukh Ahmed."

"All right, Miss Shepherd. Did you shoot Farrrukh Ahmed?"

Sultana hadn't even flinched at her outburst. His voice was even and robotic, as if he hadn't heard her. But he had. "Civil rights," may not be in his lexicon but she had a feeling that "equivocator" was. She hadn't shot Farrukh, but she had killed him. She had more than killed him. It was revenge, not self-defense — *tribal,* and she could barely face the Pakistani.

She looked up at Cloid, but there was no sign, no words of encouragement. Like the others, he was waiting for her to answer the question. She knew what was going on,

517

and Cloid knew she did. So she answered him literally. "No. I didn't shoot him."

Colonel Santana looked up at her. "Then I can assume that you had nothing to do with the man's death. Thank you for your time, Miss Shepherd."

His face deadpan, the bureaucrat closed his book and stood with Riccardi. Christine saw a look pass between them. They were finished with her.

"I just wanted to ask . . . about Mir, where he's buried, and his family. Did you find any —"

Christine stopped short. The men were staring at her. For one awful moment, she thought they might not even know who Mir was.

"Are you referring to the driver?" Sultana asked. His tone was incredulous, and she saw that he couldn't imagine what significance "the driver" could have on his investigation. Joe Riccardi, and even Cloid, had no idea who she was talking about.

Without Mir, she'd be dead . . . Liz would be forgotten, and the American embassy would be nothing but rubble. How could they not know who he was?

Christine felt the tears coming, and this time nothing could stop them. Then a notion struck her.

"Was Attaullah Hamid involved in some kind of government operation?"

The CIA operative froze, but the colonel knew better than to react.

Christine didn't need to check her old mentor. Cloid was probably annoyed that it had taken her so long to figure it out. *How could she be so naïve? She and Mir had obviously stumbled into some kind of covert action.* And now, when she thought back, she wondered if Farrukh had already suspected that his first lieutenant was a traitor when Farrukh had approached them in the mango grove. He had probably hoped that Mir would help him, that his old friend's sudden reappearance had been fate's finger on the balance.

And Attaullah Hamid had probably believed the same. Why else would Mir be there? It had to be fate.

It was fate. Mir's . . . and hers.

"Miss Shepherd?"

Christine looked up.

"Are you feeling all right?" Sultana asked. "Would you like us to call a nurse?"

"No," she mumbled, waving her hand at him. The gesture was so abrupt that the IV needle with its tubing snapped free from her arm.

Riccardi started to buzz for the nurse,

but Cloid glared at the spook to back off, and so they waited.

A rivulet of blood streaked her forearm from the dislodged needle, but Christine didn't notice. She had heard enough talk through the years of government plots and cooperative assassinations. As Cloid once admitted, "the files in the Bureau were full of them." Some of the talk was conjecture, the rest was of cases, long past, fodder for bureau recruits and a few friends hanging out in an old man's kitchen. Christine figured that Hamid had probably contacted someone in the government, it didn't matter which government. They would all want credit, or no credit. What did matter was that a safe house for a known terrorist had been discovered. And so a plan was devised. Except she and Mir were not part of the plan, and Mir had died, had been killed, and maybe it wasn't his destiny.

The spot where the IV had pulled free from her arm throbbed and Christine felt weak.

"I think, Miss Shepherd," Sultana remarked calmly, "it would be difficult for my government to believe that a man like Farrukh Ahmed could be taken by a single woman."

By *any* woman, is what he meant to say.

"I know how difficult this must be for you," he continued. "To witness such a slaughter would affect anyone's judgment.

"My judgment is fine, Colonel."

And suddenly their agenda became pain-fully clear.

Christine looked up at the men. Their desperation to get her out of the country was palpable. The removal of Farrukh Ahmed *had* been the result of a coopera-tive action between their governments. Mir, "the driver," was hardly a concern — he was dead. But the presence of a witness, particularly an American female, could complicate matters. She could've re-sponded, made their jobs difficult. Instead, she cocked her head in that foreign and sometimes ambiguous shrug.

It was enough.

Riccardi looked back at Sultana. There was a swift and professional visual cue, just a glance between a camel and a goat, and Christine knew it was almost over.

It was all very strange to her. For months her life had been dictated by a very simple, if not brutal, paradigm. Now it was gratu-itously complex. Politics. She had for-gotten.

Chapter
25

Christine and her mother sat by the hospital bed and watched Liz as she slept, her eyes heavily gauzed. Liz had always complained of being overweight. Now her cheeks were sunken, and Christine barely recognized the thin limbs that protruded from her sister's gown.

Because she had no passport, it had taken eight days to process Christine's departure. Liz and her mother had flown to India a week earlier. Liz's eye was badly infected and needed surgery, but when the Indian specialist in New Delhi tried to examine her, she became hysterical. Christine had called from Pakistan, Cloid had called, and her mother had pleaded, but Liz remained frantic. Dark faces that had once charmed her now terrified her, and Liz refused treatment.

Christine's eyes fell on the stub that had

once been a hand, but she tried not to fix on it. She wanted to remember her sister the way she had been before Padamthala, before she hated anyone with dark skin who was Muslim or Hindu. She had loved traveling, and people, all kinds of people, but that had changed.

Cloid had told Christine of the massacre at Padamthala. It had all sounded painfully familiar, the explosions, the screams, and the mind-numbing shock of being hit. Apparently, Liz didn't know she had been injured until she had reached for a child who was cowering beside an overturned bullock cart. She saw her left hand was gone, the limb blackened and nearly cauterized. Then Farrukh's men grabbed her. She fought them with a ferocity that impressed Farrukh, and he spared her. But Liz never accepted her captivity, and twice she had tried to kill herself.

Christine reached across her mother and grasped the small knobbed end of her sister's arm. When she arrived at the hospital that morning, Liz was already in surgery. Her sister's change of heart had been sudden, and the surgeon didn't want to waste any time. Christine remembered her mother had been perplexed and giddy at the same time. Something had happened, she said. When Liz awoke that morning, she announced to her mother that she had had a dream about a dark-skinned stranger who had taken her to the stars. He held her in his arms, lifting her high above the earth. And as the stars loomed above, the man told her not to worry, that she would be safe, that she wouldn't hurt, and that he would protect her. And Liz believed him.

Christine watched her sister's slumbering form and muttered something under her breath.

"What?" her mother whispered.

"Did Liz say what color his eyes were?" Christine's voice was barely audible. She looked distraught, and Marsha Shepherd wrapped her arm around her.

"I don't know, honey. I don't remember. Does it matter?"

Christine shook her head, but it did matter. It took every bit of restraint not to ask her about *his* voice, *his* face, or the feel of *his* arms around her.

Liz had been suffering, and in her heart Christine was sure it was Mir who had taken her to the stars, Mir who had soothed her fears. He had eased her sister's pain, but Christine was also hurting, and it wasn't enough.

Christine got back to the hotel that afternoon and needed sleep. She had gone right from the airport to the hospital, and she was exhausted. Liz was still under sedation, but her mother promised to call if she woke. Christine flopped onto one of the beds in their room, acutely aware of its bulkiness, its vastness. It was so unlike the string cots in Pakistan. Still, she dropped off.

A tray of Indian hospital food was by the bed, untouched, while Liz picked at a bag of french fries from a McDonald's in downtown Delhi. When Christine stepped into the room, Liz almost gasped. Christine's nose had been broken twice, her hands were bandaged, and her skin was still dark from exposure to the sun. Christine went to hug her, but Liz's frail body stiffened against her.

"You okay?" Christine asked.

"You look like hell," Liz said.

"And you're eating McDonald's."

It was a joke, an old joke, but Liz didn't respond.

Christine sat on the bed next to her, but Liz looked away. Marsha Shepherd caught Christine's eye. Something was wrong.

"Did you get some sleep?" her mother asked.

Christine cocked her head unconsciously. "I got a call from the Indian Bureau. General Raghavan wants to meet."

Marsha groaned. "You girls have been drilled enough."

"I'm not staying," Liz blurted out, her one eye tearing.

"No one's staying," Marsha assured her.

"Where's Cloid?" Liz asked.

Christine looked at her watch. "Probably over Greenland by now."

"He didn't come with you to India?"

"I didn't need him to. It was Pakistan he was worried about. Here it's all protocol and paperwork."

"But you're out of there," Liz prompted. "Out of Pakistan. You don't have to ever go back, right?"

"Right," but even as Christine said it, she felt a pang. "I'll just be glad when Cloid finally lands in L.A. He must've been crazy to fly so soon after heart surgery."

"He is crazy," Marsha said.

A nurse opened the door of their room. "Mrs. Shepherd? There's a call for you at the desk."

"The airline." Marsha started to follow the nurse out, when Liz called to her.

"I'll be right back," Marsha responded,

then started to say something to Christine. She didn't need to. Christine smiled at her, and that seemed to reassure her. The door shut, and for the first time in over a year, the girls were alone. Except, suddenly, Liz seemed more interested in picking at her half-eaten hamburger than talking with her sister. Christine waited. Finally Liz spoke.

"What are you looking at?"

"My sister," Christine said, and went to touch her. Liz tensed, slipping her short limb under the blanket.

"I didn't mean —"

"They told me what you did to find me. But it wasn't all of it, was it?"

"It's over now."

Liz was quiet again. The hamburger forgotten, she stared at the opposite wall, avoiding Christine's eyes.

"What you did for me scares me," Liz said, her voice barely audible. "Can you understand?"

Christine wanted to tell her that she was also scared, that there were nights when she would wake with her throat constricted and her fists sore from clenching. But Liz was trembling. Christine knew they had told her of Farrukh, maybe even of the Taliban. But Liz was right, there was so much more. There was Shweta, who lived in an isolated mud dwelling in India, and there was her uncle, and the hopeless pursuit of two boys on a donkey. There was the kindness of Namja, a woman in purdah, and the sadness of an Afghan whore named Kishwar, and there was Mir. She was ready to talk of her love for Mir, but as she looked helplessly into the tortured face of her sister, she knew she couldn't.

"We'll be okay," Christine said.

"Why'd you come after me?"

"I had to. They said you were dead."

"I was."

"Please don't say that. You're my sister. I love you. And I know you would've come after me."

Even with the bandages covering her face, Christine could see Liz's jaw clench and her face redden. She reached over, but Liz was already shifting in the bed, trying to rise up. Christine finally understood and bent down, so Liz could throw one arm around her neck while she braced herself with the other.

"You're wrong about me, Chrissy," she whispered, her voice rasping as she drew her in close. "You're so wrong. I couldn't have helped you. I'm sorry. I love you. I love you so much, but if it would've been you . . . if Farrukh —"

Christine felt Liz's body break from a sob. "It's all right, Lizzie. It's all right."

Liz pulled back from her. "Can you go?" she cried. "Please, go."

That night Christine prayed that Mir would come to her, but he didn't. She awoke, her stomach churning, her breath shallow, and her palms hurting. Still sweating from a nightmare, she was barely aware of a light emanating from the bathroom, or even the sound of running water. It wasn't until her mother wiped the cool washcloth over her face that Christine remembered where she was. They had taken a hotel room close to the Aashlok Hospital where Liz had received her eye surgery. After her mother had turned off the light, she stood at the end of Christine's bed, a mere silhouette. When Marsha Shepherd sat on her daughter's bed she crossed her legs in front of her like a teenager. But she wasn't a teenager. In fact her hair was almost completely gray, and to Christine her mother never looked so old. Still she pulled Christine to her and stroked her hair, and Christine cried like a child and apologized again and again, her chest heaving with sobs. She told her mother that Mir was dead, and Nazeem, and others . . . all because of her. And now her sister was afraid of her, of everything. Her mother tried to soothe her, but Christine's head was spinning, not hearing.

That day she had met with General Raghavan. He promised her again that his department was doing everything it could to expedite her clearance. For the next hour and a half Christine answered the general's questions, most of which focused on Pakistan. Surprisingly the time went quickly, but Raghavan admitted that he would need to meet with her again, maybe a couple of times. Christine had no choice but to agree.

As she rose to leave, she told her mother that Raghavan had asked her if she would be willing to help identify a couple of Pakistanis who had recently been apprehended in Bombay. He believed that the men were somehow connected to Wazir Maroof, the infamous arm's dealer. He had pulled the photos from a stack of yellowed Polaroids. Christine didn't recognize the first one, but the second man stopped her breath. He had thick, black hair, was clean-shaven, and dark like the others. His features were hardly remarkable, but Christine did remember him. She had been drugged at the time, but she could still recall how his brow barely furrowed at the sight of the body next to him. The Pakistani in gabardines had watched Nazeem die with almost amused disinterest while the young farmer, his throat cut, bled into an expanding pool of his own blood. Christine identified the murderer, and naturally the Raghavan felt vindicated.

As Christine lay in her mother's arms she recalled that the general's comment to her as she left had been offhanded. Raghavan had thanked her again for her help, telling her that he had been after the arms dealer for some time, and that Wazir Maroof was nearly as notorious as her Farrukh, *her* terrorist. Raghavan could hardly know that his reference to Farrukh would cause her so much pain.

And now, in the middle of the night, the words taunted her. Christine remembered the fortune-teller who, on the day of Liz's disappearance, had predicted that her karma would follow her. She tried not to shudder at the thought of toads, and maggots, and the Jinn. She didn't want to think anymore of predictions or superstitions, but she had to know. Her mother kept trying to reassure her, but when Christine asked if what she had done was right, if ridding the world of Farrukh Ahmed had made a difference, her mother fell silent. She even stopped stroking her hair, and it was then that Christine thought she must be damned.

Marsha Shepherd leaned back and gazed at her. "Do you remember all the fights you used to get into as a girl?"

Christine had forgotten, but, yes, a comment, a gesture, it hadn't taken much in those days before she would start punching.

"If someone starting picking on you, or a friend . . . or anyone — you'd go after him. At first, your dad didn't pay much attention, but when we started getting calls from school . . . If there was a class discussion about the Holocaust, or the Kent State massacre, or even news of some local killing, you'd suffer . . . And you know what? Going to that damn range didn't help either. God forbid that Cloid's old cronies should censor themselves around a child. But maybe your dad was right, maybe you were just that way from the start . . . so protective, so hot-tempered.

"When I heard of what happened in Pakistan, I thought of your dad. He felt things like you . . . but you killed a man, Chris. I can't tell you that that was right —

532

to kill is a sin against God. You know that. But I can tell you if your dad had been alive, he would have gone after Liz. Right or wrong, he would've gone."

Christine wanted to respond. There wasn't much of a moon that night, but there was enough to see that Marsha Shepherd was preoccupied with thoughts other than her daughter.

Her dad had been dead for twelve years, Mir, for less than a month. She thought about her dreams of Zubeda and the baby, and Liz. She remembered Nazeem and Ruhee in the room above her, and she remembered the gunfire, the three shots, the last of which, she was sure, had killed Mir.

Had her mother sensed her father's deadly car collision as clearly as she had sensed the passing of Mir? Had she felt the metal twist and contort as the steering column drove itself into her husband's body?

Glen Shepherd was killed instantly . . . probably like Mir.

Could you hear it, mom? she wanted to ask. *His last gasp . . . or feel the breath as it left his body? Tell me, I need to know.*

Her mother was silent, and Christine was silent.

Then her mother bent in close to her, so close that Christine could feel the warmth of her breath. "I prayed," she whispered. "I always prayed for you, but in my heart I knew you'd find Lizzie. I knew."

The questions *were* in her head, but Christine didn't ask. She didn't need to. The feeling, the intuition, the gift they shared had always been there, and her mother touched her face, then stood, a silhouette once more as she returned to bed.

Chapter
26

After a third meeting with General Raghavan, Christine decided to walk back to the hotel through one of the markets. As she wove through the crowd, hawkers from their stalls and lean-tos packed with cheap merchandise called out to her. But she ignored them until an old Indian woman with two children crouched beside her and nodded in her direction.

The pleasantries were brief as the woman and Christine fell easily into barter over a pair of leather sandals. Christine remembered buying a similar pair that had been lost in a minefield. She had paid nearly six times their worth. But now she knew better, and after the vendor took her money she waved her children away and pulled out another stool from her stall. One of the children came back with a cup of *chai*. Christine took it, thanking the old woman, and sat beside her, sipping the spicy tea as she slipped off her tennis shoes.

In Los Angeles it would be chilly, and probably rainy, a typical winter day. But in Delhi it was seasonably mild. Christine felt strangely at ease in the ambience of a culture that to some seemed barely civilized.

She thought about her mother, and her father, who felt things like her, and still she wondered about her own morality. She felt so comfortable with the woman whose teeth were nearly gone, with the scent of garbage no longer discernible. And the scantily clad children that ran about, some of them maimed, no longer unsettled her. Raghavan had referred to "her terrorist, her Farrukh," as if she and Farrukh Ahmed had something in common. *Had she gone tribal, gone mad, like a dog that had killed, and only bloodlust would satisfy now?* Maybe she belonged on the street, beneath the tarp, selling camel-skin sandals with the woman. But India wasn't her home, and the mind-set that had killed Nazeem, that had killed Mir, sickened her. Yet she could no longer rationalize Farrukh's death.

She stood up from the woman, a bit abruptly, rattling off a mix of Urdu and

Hindi, then blurted out a good-bye. The woman looked confused. Christine was confused. She turned away, her eyes filling with tears, and stumbled. A man squatting on the road, screeched up at her. He had been eating his midday meal, and she had almost knocked him over. He was dirty and dark, and he yelled something at her as she pushed her way back into the crowd. *"Ameri-cain,"* he yelled. *"Ameri-cain!"*

The headmaster of the school in Banalwala had been one of the first Pakistanis she had met after the Javids had pulled her from the minefield. He had a phone, but it was barely functional. After three phone calls, his battery charge spent, the old man promised to gather up the Javids, borrow a car from his brother, and call her back from Aga Khan, a charity facility that was reputed to have the most reliable phone service in the area.

When Christine hung up, she realized there was no anger in the headmaster's voice, and she wondered if he knew that she was the one responsible for Nazeem's death. Joe Riccardi had already warned her not to contact the Javids, that the culture was primitive, that they might seek revenge. But she had to call.

By the time the operator rang back to take her credit card number and reverse the charges, Christine was already panicking. It had been a month since she had spoken their language, but when Zubeda greeted her in broken English over the receiver, the Urdu came easily. They talked for nearly a half hour. Then Arshad got on, with barely a greeting. He wanted her address. He was intent on paying her back for Zubeda's hospital care. Christine reminded him that he had saved her life. He only grunted, but she could tell he was pleased.

When Ruhee came onto the line, Christine did forget her words. But there was no hesitancy in the girl's voice. She talked of Amagee's care for a sick elder, Abagee's stomach problems, and young Samina's betrothal to a merchant in Faizalabad.

Then Christine asked about Zubeda's baby, and Ruhee grew quiet.

Ruhee didn't have to tell her; Christine guessed. The baby looked like its uncle, like Nazeem. Christine almost blurted out an apology, but Ruhee must've sensed how she felt and told her that she wished her "sister" well, and that she prayed that someday they would see one another again. There was no mention of the pain, of the nights alone, or of the dreams of her husband. Ruhee would live with her in-laws, caring for them, and if Allah willed, she would marry again. There were no bad feelings, no apology expected, no forgiveness necessary, only that Christine was missed. Still, Ruhee's voice was breaking, and Christine was relieved when Ruhee finally handed the phone off to her sister-in-law.

"So many weeks, not enough, *behin*," Zubeda said, switching to English.

Her friend's robust voice sobered her. "No, not enough," Christine agreed.

"Next time you will come longer, okay? My sister in Bahawalpur did not see you, and my cousin in Multan. She make so many children — too many, I think. But they want to see you. You will come?"

"I'll try."

"*Inshallah, behinji. Inshallah.*"

After Christine got off the phone, she went to the hospital. When she entered her sister's room, Liz was alone. They had removed the bandages from around her head. A slightly raised eye patch was all that remained. Liz asked where their mother had gone. Christine told her she was arranging her release from the hospital. Liz didn't hesitate this time. She left her bed and hugged Christine.

They sat at the end of the bed and Christine decided it was a good time to tell her about the family who had risked their lives to save hers, and if she could muster the courage she needed to talk of Mir.

Liz didn't comment; she listened. But by the time Christine told her of the man she loved, of Mir Hasan, his eyes, and the stillness of his body at the end, Liz began to tremble. Christine wondered if Liz was thinking about the man in her dream, but Liz stayed quiet. Her face was dry and chafed from the bandages that had covered her. Without sun for so long, she looked especially pale. Christine tried not to be distracted by the darkness of her own hands, now barely taped. Her skin had held the brown pigment, and Christine almost apologized, blaming the walks from the hotel.

Liz wasn't looking at her sister's hands. Her trembling subsided and finally she smiled. It was a pained smile. "I'm not coming back," she said.

"I know."

"But you are."

"Someone has to. We have a company to run, remember?"

"But you *want* to come back."

Christine nodded and watched as tears streamed down her sister's cheek. Then Liz reached up and took Christine's hand. She held it, until the tears stopped.

"We do have a company to run."

Christine smiled. "We do."

It wasn't difficult to spot the large purple hat with the pink sash in the crowded hotel lobby, and for the first time Christine had to appreciate Dabboo's style. After kissing Christine on both cheeks, Dabboo was momentarily distracted by her taped hands. Christine quickly spun a lie; she had burned herself on an overheated car radiator. Dabboo cocked her head. She hadn't asked.

At the bar, Dabboo ordered a drink, and the two of them sat and talked of politics, Indian men, and of Shores, Inc. It didn't take long to segue into the proposal she and Liz had worked out before she and her mother had boarded the plane back to Los Angeles. Christine told Dabboo that their company had expanded, that Liz would no longer be a buyer, but instead stay in Los Angeles and run the main office. She asked if Dabboo would be interested in helping her cover Asia and —

"The world?" Dabboo asked, flashing her freshly manicured nails.

Christine was thinking more of Europe, but "the world" would do. Dabboo reached into a purse that closely resembled the tail feather of a peacock, and pulled out one of her brown cigarettes. She lit up, sighed, hesitated, sighed again, and then as she puffed away, she told Christine she *might* be interested.

Christine sighed herself, took a drink, cocked her head, and then once Dabboo got to the end of her cigarette, she broke into Hindi. The women haggled for twenty minutes. Afterward, Dabboo told Christine that she had gotten her services "for very cheap," probably because she was so thrown by Christine's fluency in the language. Then the bird woman laughed. She didn't mind; the tactic was effective, and "*Ji hai*," she believed that the Ameri-cain would make a worthy partner.

Doug, the rifle range's line manager, was possibly even older than Cloid. So, Christine wasn't surprised when she had to shout her name twice into the phone before he understood her.

Cloid had called earlier, at two o'clock in the morning to be exact. The old man had

had a little target shooting, a sizable lunch, and felt like, as he put it, "jawing a bit." Except in the middle of the night in India Christine didn't feel like jawing with anyone. She'd call him back. Five hours later, she couldn't believe Cloid was still on the Big Bore line. In Los Angeles, in December, it was dark by four-thirty. Kept up long after hours, poor Doug was grateful to hear from her. He needed to lock up.

"Guess what I picked up in Peshawar?" Cloid said.

Christine hadn't talked to him in weeks, and those were his first words.

"Peshawar?"

"An M-14."

Somehow Cloid had managed to smuggle a gun out of Pakistan.

"Cloid," she sighed. "Was that smart? Smuggling? An automatic weapon? Do you even have a Cat-3 license?"

He babbled on, not listening.

"You should see it, Chris. Mint . . . I mean mint. I also picked up another Luger — a copy, but not bad. Let me see . . ."

She could almost picture him turning the handgun over in his large, leathery palm as he muttered to himself.

"How's Mom and Liz?"

"Better. Marsha told me what you're doing for Lizzie. You're a good kid. That company's everything to her. But you'll still have time to come to the range, right?"

"I love the range. You know that."

Then from out of nowhere, or at least to her it seemed like nowhere, Cloid asked if she felt like talking about the Pashtun tribesmen, or maybe the Indians. Cloid tried to joke, admitting that that part of the world still eluded him, but before he died . . .

Christine listened to the old Fed ramble on. Cloid didn't mention Farrukh, but she knew eliminating a terrorist was the dream of every law enforcement officer. She had listened to their banter as a child, their fantasies, but what she had done, how she felt, was real. She was hoping to forget, or, at least, to understand. But maybe the fortune-teller in orange had been right. Maybe her karma did follow her, and she would never understand.

"If you don't feel like talking . . ."

Cloid's voice was almost quavering with expectation, and she tried not to be bothered.

So, she talked. She talked for an hour and forty minutes, the phone cutting her off periodically, as phones in India do.

What had happened in the inn outside of Mansehra she left for last. After she finished telling of Farrukh Ahmed's final moments, Cloid was quiet. Her old friend's silence actually brought her solace. The terrorist had been eliminated, but her participation could hardly be thought noble, only human.

Cleared of all charges in both Pakistan and India, Christine could finally book a ticket home. She was scheduled to leave in three days, but she finished packing a day early. Liz had called and told her that their stores were decorated and ready for holiday business. She anticipated a good season and was anxious for Christine to come home. Christine was anxious as well.

With the majority of India being Hindu, there was little sign of Christmas. Still, Christine found a Christian church near Old Delhi and spent long hours sitting in the calm of the sanctuary. Her body had ached earlier, and she thought wearily she might need another round of antibiotics to finally put the bugs to rest, but when she settled into the worn seat of a teak pew, the aches seemed to leave her body.

She felt good and decided to forego the

ten-minute taxi ride back to her hotel. Instead she meandered lazily through the droves of people in Old Delhi, arriving back at her hotel just as the sun dipped into a layer of haze.

That night Christine sat in the darkness of her hotel room and listened to the clamor outside. She could hear the dinging of a bell that alerted the Hindu gods that a person was entering their temple. At the same time, a muezzin called out the evening prayer, and together the sounds were pleasing. Christine stood up and pushed the window open. She gazed out at the lights of traffic, of bicycles and carts and shops that were still open. The tumult of the city soothed her.

A pigeon lit on the sill in front of her, its beady red eyes peering at her while it cocked its head first to one side, then to the other. There was a mosque just across from the hotel, and the bird was white, like an apparition . . . like a Jinn. Christine felt her breath quicken, and her chest grew tight. Her impulse was to slam the window shut, but the fortune-teller had had a dream. And now she had a dream.

Zubeda and Arshad's baby had survived. Nazeem had been killed. Nikhil had died in the desert. The tribesmen had saved the life of a foreigner. Reggie had gone to Africa. Mir's life had ended in a romantic inn beside a river. Farrukh Ahmed would kill no more, and his nieces would never again see their *mamu.*

There had to be a meaning; Christine just didn't know what the meaning was. Nonetheless, and of this she was sure, her life would not play out so simply, so predictably.

Still, she had to force herself to take a breath as she bent down to the creature. No longer moving, its form fixed and seemingly unreal, the bird watched her settle before it. The street noises had recessed, and slowly, ever so slowly, Christine crossed her arms and set her chin down on her wrists. She peered back at the pigeon. Her heart beating, daring the Pakistani superstitions of possession and death, she finally opened her mouth to call out its name, and that was all it took. The pigeon took flight, and Christine watched as its whiteness faded into the night.

About the Author

Cheryl Howard Crew is married to director Ron Howard. They have raised their four children in Los Angeles and Connecticut, and currently reside in Armonk, New York. *In the Face of Jinn* is Crew's first novel.